THE PRINCE OF MARS

JAMES THOMPSON

Cover art by Sarah Bianchi.
Original cover photo: Gusev Spirit 01,
taken by NASA Mars Exploration Rover Spirit, Public Domain.

ISBN: 099785121X
ISBN-13: 978-0-9978512-1-2

for all those who would go

Liberty is to faction what air is to fire, an aliment without which it instantly expires. But it could not be less folly to abolish liberty, which is essential to political life, because it nourishes faction, than it would be to wish the annihilation of air, which is essential to animal life, because it imparts to fire its destructive agency.

James Madison
Federalist Papers, No. 10

PART I

HIM

I

All the executions took place in 2017.

Five men. Five lethal injections. Five different prisons.

Calvin Hamilton was executed on February 28th, Troy Beecham on March 9th, Byron Carruthers on May 3rd, Justin Jones on July 10th, and Tristan Martin on October 5th.

They had committed murder, each of them. None of them were wrongly convicted. Quite the opposite – the facts of their guilt couldn't have been clearer. After all, if there'd been any ambiguity in that regard then these men wouldn't have been selected for this mission. Which isn't to say that they knew they'd been selected. They had no idea.

The only thing that each of them thought they knew for certain was the date on which they would die. There was, as such, a sense of the inevitable in their strides as they were led off to the execution chambers. None of them put up a fight as they were strapped down and prepped for an injection. None of them asked for forgiveness in their final moments. And none of them glanced at the two-way mirrors, on the other side of which sat the witnesses to the execution.

Death, however, when it came for them, came in the strangest of ways. Which is to say that it didn't come at all. At least not on those fateful days, inside those clinically grim chambers, delivered at the tip of an I.V. needle. Because as it turned out, what they were given via their injections wasn't some lethal concoction; it was, instead, a particular sort of serum which rendered them unconscious while making them look legitimately deceased. Thus they each drifted off into a deep dark sleep, and when all of them woke up again, quite a bit later, they were in a very different place altogether....

II

Justin was the first one to revive.

And the first thing that he did was gasp. Not because of anything he saw; his vision was blurred for the initial moments of consciousness so he couldn't make out his surroundings. No, he gasped because the last thing that he'd experienced prior to drifting off to sleep had been his own death. Or so he'd thought. Which meant that all the emotions relevant to horror had followed him into unconsciousness, then lingered there inside him, down below the water's edge of his waking mind, and now, when he resurfaced, they came up with him. And he gasped.

Initially he wasn't even aware that he was incarnate; that he was still within a body. His body. The one he'd always had. But as the seconds ticked by, and as this awareness registered with him, a feeling of relative elation pushed his horror aside. So this was death, and he got to keep his body? Then death wasn't all that bad! It was the same him, same form, same mind, same sense of self. Ha!

Naturally, he assumed he was in hell. Where else was a guy like him going to go? Not that he was a genuinely bad guy. The only person he'd ever killed was the man he'd run over in the parking lot of that bar. But still, he *had* intentionally run him over. And, having been raised by a devoutly religious mother and having absorbed his fair share of fire-and-brimstone preaching, he knew the things he needed to know about eternal damnation and what's required to receive it.

And so he thought to himself, 'This is hell....'

It definitely wasn't anything like the hell he'd been expecting. The temperature was moderate and the setting wasn't exactly menacing, at least not in the traditional sense. As his vision de-blurred, his eyes began focusing on specific objects: two illuminated buttons which were built into the wall that was located a few feet in front of his bed; a white door next to those buttons; a large mirror set into the wall directly to his right.

Next he began examining the bed itself, turning his head slowly from side to side, groggily shifting his heavy limbs a little to give himself

4

a better view. This bed was strange. It was more like a large metallic crib or a…coffin. And he was lying not simply on it but inside of it, with the bed's metallic rim running about two inches higher up than his nose or the tips of his toes. Apparently the bottom part of the bed – the part that he was lying on – was padded, but there wasn't a pillow nor were there any blankets. Another curiosity: he was evidently wearing some white, light-weight night-clothes – a shirt with long sleeves and a pair of pants – but these weren't the white clothes he'd been wearing when they marched him to the execution chamber.

And now pure cold fear – that fundamental fear of the unknown, which the fear of death is merely one example of – gripped him again. The thoughts 'Where am I?' and 'What is this?' began racing through his mind like recurring reports on a newswire set to fast-forward. At the same time a burst of adrenaline shot through his veins and revitalized his limbs, causing him to bolt up to a sitting position. This, in turn, made him dizzy, so he gripped the metallic sides of the bed, or whatever it was.

Eventually the dizziness passed and when it did he was able to discern a sheet of metal which was rolled around a tube at the end of the bed. He instantly understood that the metal sheet was the bed's covering.

His heart began pounding even harder. 'Where am I? What is this?'

His instinct was to call out for help but he pushed that impulse down. All the time that he'd spent in the prison system had trained him to suppress his fears. The last thing to do when you're feeling vulnerable, he'd learned, was to let others know it. So he gripped the metallic edges of the bed even harder, took several deep breaths and waited for the panic to pass.

As he returned to relative calm, he began examining the room in more detail. Off to the right, below the mirror, was a countertop with a sink which had cabinets underneath it. Behind the bed was a metallic chest of drawers, and next to that were the metallic doors of a built-in closet. The wall directly to the left of the bed – just a few inches from the bed's rim – was blank, without any art, and painted white like everything else in the room that wasn't metallic and gray.

Although the room was minimally decorated, Justin was able to tell – to sense, more fundamentally – that this place wasn't done on the cheap. Everything in there looked like it was high quality, expensive-ish, understated though it was. Evidently hell had a budget. And if this was still prison – if he'd somehow survived the lethal injection and was still incarcerated – then he'd obviously been transferred to a nicer institution than the prisons he'd been locked up in prior to his execution.

He nodded as this idea formed in his mind. 'Yeah,' he thought, 'that's gotta be it.' The lethal injection hadn't killed him, they weren't sure why, and now they were probably going to run tests. This scenario didn't disturb him all that much; actually he found it reassuring to have a handle on his situation. And truth be told, as often occurs with convicts, he'd grown accustomed to prison, so he took comfort in the idea of being in a familiar situation.

All he needed to do to confirm this theory was to climb out of bed, walk over to the door, and try to open it. When the door didn't open then he'd know for certain that he was still locked up.

So that's what he did: he lifted himself out of the bed, swung his legs over the side, landed gingerly on the floor – his legs were so weak that they nearly buckled under him but he grabbed the side of the bed to steady himself – and then, like a drunken man trying to gain his balance, he took the necessary steps to cross the small room, tried to push the door open, and, when it didn't give way, he pressed one of the illuminated buttons next to it. The door slid open.

He gasped. 'What is this? Where am I?'

What he saw there in front of him, beyond the limits of his room, didn't make things any clearer. It was another room, similarly white, only much larger. This new room was circular, with a round countertop in the middle, around which were placed five metal chairs which were bolted to the floor. The wall of this room was taken up with screens, buttons, lights, built-in gadgets, two of what looked to be ovens, two of what looked to be refrigerators, a kitchen-style countertop, and multiple built-in closets. There were also four other doors in the rounded wall, just like the one leading into his bedroom.

Justin was completely terrified. For at least a minute he remained frozen, standing there in the doorway, eyes wide. 'Maybe this *is* hell....' He thought. What else could it be? Why would he be able to open doors like this unless he was dead?

Eventually he found his feet and forced them to take him into the circular room. When he reached the countertop he slumped into one of the chairs. Another minute passed as he sat there, clinging to the counter's edge and further inspecting the scene.

At a forty-five degree angle from his bedroom's door there was a short hallway, which led – about ten feet in – to yet another door which appeared much more robust than the door to his bedroom; it looked like a securable hatch on a submarine. It even had a circular window at the top of it, thanks to which Justin could just barely – from where he was sitting – get a sense of the door's thickness. Obviously that would be his next step: to see if that door was so easily opened as well.

He was about to rise to go inspect it when one of the other four "bedroom" doors – the one located on the opposite side of the round room from his own door – slid open and he saw another man standing there, staring back at him, wide-eyed and frightened. Like himself, this man was dressed in white night-clothes. And like himself this man was evidently of mixed background: a combination of "black" and "white" and other things. This other guy was, however, quite a bit bigger than Justin. It was Byron.

"…Where am I?" Byron asked, hesitantly.

Justin shook his head. "I…I dunno."

"What is this place?"

"I'm not sure."

The fear in Byron's eyes glistened all the brighter. "Who are you?"

Justin's prison-bred instinct for self-preservation prevented him from answering that question. "Who are *you*?"

Byron stared at him blankly, then he took a deep breath. When he finished it, he asked, "Am I dead? Is that what this is?"

Relief and dread instantly pulsed through Justin's body. If this guy was asking *that* question then evidently he was going through the same thing that Justin was going through, which was deeply comforting. But if this guy was asking *that* question then maybe they both *were* dead.

"You…just woke up?" Justin asked.

"Yeah….You?"

"Same."

"Where are we?"

"Like I said, I don't know."

"How long you been awake?"

"A couple minutes. I came out a that room there." Justin nodded towards his bedroom door.

Byron stepped – nearly stumbled – across the room and sat down in one of the metallic chairs. "Where were you, right 'fore you woke up just now?" He asked after he was seated.

Justin wasn't inclined to answer that question in any detail. "In a room. Another room. Not in this place. At least I don't think so."

"Did that room…have a two-way mirror?"

Now Justin knew that the two of them were in fact going through exactly the same experience, so there wasn't any point hedging about it. "Yeah. And a man wearin' a badge."

Byron exhaled slowly. "Well then I guess we're dead. This must be hell or somethin'."

"Not what I was expectin' it to look like…."

"Me neither. Not one little bit. And so…they put you down, and you woke up here?"

"Yeah."

"And you ain't seen nobody else?"

"You're the first."

"It looks like there're other doors here. Three besides yours and mine."

"Yeah, so I'm guessin' three other guys."

"What makes you think they're all guys?"

"'Cause if this is hell then there ain't gonna be any women in this place. If there are then I'm missin' the point."

Byron thought this over, nodding. "I hear ya."

"There's that hallway there, and that door. It looks pretty thick. I'm thinkin' that's the first thing to check. See if it opens."

"I couldn't believe it when my door there just opened, just now."

"Me neither. Same with mine."

As Justin was saying this a third bedroom door slid open and the two men turned to see Tristan standing in the doorway, wearing the same outfit as themselves, staring at them with a stone-faced expression and with his fists tightly clenched.

"Where am I?" He demanded.

Justin and Byron looked at each other and smiled morosely.

"You laughin' at me?" Tristan scowled. "Do that again and see what happens."

"And what?" Byron asked. "You gonna kill us? That would be,

what is known as, ironic."

"What're you talkin' 'bout? What's goin' on?"

"We look like we know?"

"We just woke up, just like you," Justin told him. "We don't know what's happenin'."

Tristan considered this. "How long you been out here?"

"Couple minutes?"

"Just the two a you?"

Justin nodded. "There're two other doors, and we're waitin' to see who comes out a them."

"I sure hope you ain't right 'bout who's comin' out," Byron said. "'Bout them bein' all guys."

Justin nodded again and raised his eyebrows.

Tristan decided to walk out into the circular room and take a seat at the counter. "What were you two doin' 'fore you woke up in this place?"

Byron frowned. "Same as you, I'd guess."

"You're messin' with me. You too?"

"Did it involve a particularly unpleasant injection?"

"Most definitely."

"Then there ya go. Welcome to the party."

Tristan shook his head and scowled. "So, what? You're tellin' me this is it? We're dead? This is hell?"

"That's the theory."

"This don't look like hell," Tristan said, glancing around the room.

"No kiddin'."

"What's all this stuff, on the walls here?"

Justin and Byron both shrugged.

Tristan continued swiveling his head around, examining his new surroundings, and while he did so a fourth door opened, revealing Troy, clothed like the others and looking absolutely petrified.

"Hey there," Byron greeted him on behalf of the group. "Come on over, take a seat."

Troy stared at them, frozen in place.

"We're here just like you," Justin said. "Come on over."

"…Where…am I?"

"Hell, far as we can tell, unless a lady walks out a door number five," Byron told him.

"…What?"

"Come out here, sit down, we'll explain it to you."

Troy remained where he was. "Who…are y'all?"

"Fun lovin' felons – just like you, I'm guessin'. Last thing any of us remembers is gettin' put down."

Troy began breathing hard, like he was about to pass out, but he grabbed hold of the door's rim, steadied himself, then hobbled weakly across the room to the countertop and pulled up a chair.

"You're a couple minutes 'hind the rest of us," Byron explained. "And there's still one more to go. One more door."

Troy nodded, trying to absorb this information. Then he leaned forward, placed his elbows on the table and sank his face into his hands.

Tristan grimaced a smile at him before turning to the other two. "Where's that hall lead there? You checked that out yet?"

"We were just 'bout to, when you showed up."

Tristan slid off his chair and walked around the countertop, over to the hallway, then pushed on a large metal latch which was attached to the thick door. The latch gave way against his weight and the door began to open.

"Ho ho!" Byron exclaimed, rising to his feet and walking over to Tristan.

Justin stood up as well but walked over to the one bedroom door which hadn't yet opened. As he knocked on it, Troy raised his face out of his hands to see whatever happened next, Byron turned around, and Tristan stopped pushing on the thick door and returned to the circular room.

"Who's out there?" Someone yelled from behind the door. It was a man's voice.

Justin turned to the others and raised his hands in the air, as if to say, "Told ya so."

Byron frowned.

Again, a yell from behind the door: "Who are you?"

"We're four brown dudes," Byron yelled back, "How 'bout you?"

There was an extended pause. Eventually the man behind the door asked, "Where am I?"

"Hell!" Tristan yelled, approaching the door.

"…Seriously?"

"Apparently," Byron confirmed. "So let me guess, the last thing you remember was, you went down for the count, under the needle, you know what I mean?"

"…Yeah…."

"So come on out a there. We're all just like you, tryin' to figure this thing out."

"Is the door unlocked?"

"Yeah it is. Come on out, fool!" Tristan demanded.

The door slid open, revealing Calvin to the rest of the group. He was short, intense, and in a karate pose, his hands held up in front of him like knives, ready to defend himself. The other four laughed.

"Come out here. We ain't gonna hurt you," Byron assured him. "We're already in hell – what're we gonna do to you?"

Calvin's eyes darted from one man to the next, then circled the large room, taking in the scene. As the shock registered on his face, he asked, "What…is this place?"

"Ain't you listenin'?" Tristan asked. "It's hell. That's what we're thinkin'."

"I…." Calvin said, his brow creasing with confusion as he kept glancing around. Then he eased up on his karate stance, steadied himself and quasi-staggered out into the circular room. He slid into a chair when he reached the countertop.

The others each took a seat as well, and now the five men stared at one another, sizing each other up. Calvin was the smallest, Byron was the biggest – both tall and wide – while Justin, Tristan and Troy were all of middling build. Tristan definitely looked the meanest, although there was also something vicious about Troy, which seemed connected to his general agitation.

"So…" Calvin asked, "you were all executed too? You were all on death row?"

The others nodded.

Calvin pondered this for a moment. "So then…that means…."

"Yeah, that's right," Byron confirmed, guessing what Calvin was thinking. "It means we're all killers."

Troy shook his head and laughed quietly, tragically.

"How long you all been out here?" Calvin asked.

"A couple minutes," Justin told him. "I was the first one out."

"But I don't get it," Calvin said. "You're sayin' this is hell? That doesn't make any sense. This can't be hell."

"Why not? Ain't good enough for ya?" Tristan smiled ironically.

"Is that a…refrigerator there?" Calvin asked, pointing at two thin black doors in the round wall; one of the doors appeared to have a built-in ice-dispenser.

Justin stood up and walked over to the doors and opened them. Sure enough, it was a refrigerator, but without any food. "It's empty."

"Why do we need food if this is hell?" Tristan asked.

Byron shrugged. "You still got a body ain't cha?"

Tristan scowled at him.

"Yeah, no, this can't be hell," Troy concluded.

"So then where are we?" Byron demanded, exasperated. "We all died, didn't we?"

"Did we?"

"Didn't we?"

"We didn't make it to heaven, that's for sure," Troy said matter-of-factly.

"Could be purgatory," Justin noted.

"No point in sendin' me to purgatory," Tristan said. "I only need a one-way ticket to where I'm goin'. And I'm guessin' this is it."

"This can't be it!" Calvin insisted. "That doesn't make sense!"

"Fool – think 'bout it! We were on death row, all of us. We got executed. And now we're here. This is it! It's it!"

Justin stood up. "I think we should look 'round a little more 'fore drawin' any final conclusions."

"Agreed," Byron said, likewise rising to his feet.

"Yeah," Calvin concurred.

Tristan and Troy nodded as well, so then everyone walked over to the hallway and to the big, thick, white, metal, partially ajar door.

III

"What the…?" Calvin exclaimed quietly, as Justin pushed open the door, which gave way easily despite its size, revealing a long white hallway. The hallway walls consisted of a series of wide doors, about the size of garage doors, with handles at the bottom of each. At the other end of the hallway – roughly a hundred feet ahead – was another doorway which looked like the one they'd just passed through.

"Never knew hell would be so white," Troy said.

"I always knew it'd be white," Byron replied.

"I wonder what's behind these doors here, on these walls?" As Calvin spoke he reached down and pulled on one of the door handles. The door retracted up and inward, rising easily. Inside its container space were numerous black plastic boxes, stacked on top of each other floor-to ceiling.

"What's all that?"

"Hell's rations, I guess."

"Why don't you open one of them boxes and see what's in 'em," Byron urged Calvin.

"Why don't we see what's on the other side a that door there at the end a the hall, 'fore we start openin' up anythin' here," Justin suggested.

"Yeah, alright."

So the five of them stepped gingerly down the hallway, as if they were walking down a dark alley, even though the area was brightly lit by overhead lighting. When they reached the far door, Justin pushed down on its large metallic latch, and, just like the other one, this door opened easily.

"Ain't had so many doors open like this for me in a long time," Byron noted.

"I hear that, yeah."

"Last time I…." Byron began to say, but then he stopped short as the door swung wide.

"What the…?"

The five of them now found themselves staring into what looked like a double-sized version of a cockpit on a commercial plane. It was chock-full of built-in, extremely hi-tech instruments, and there were large windows which wrapped around the room's front and sides. Outside the windows was a butterscotch colored sky which turned pinkish and red as it blended into the distance.

Stunned by the sky's bizarre color, the men crowded up closer to the windows and looked out and down at the terrain. What they saw was an endless expanse of rocks, sand and dust. Like the sky the terrain was butterscotch up close but appeared in the distance to be pinkish-red.

"Yep, it's hell," Tristan confirmed.

"What the...?"

"What is this place?"

"Where are we?"

"Where's everybody else? Don't tell me we're the only ones who ever got sent to hell!"

"So is this a cockpit? Are we on a plane?" Troy wanted to know.

Byron shook his head. "Why would there be planes in hell?"

"Maybe this is the plane that takes us there, or here, or wherever we are," Calvin hypothesized.

Justin stepped onto one of the cockpit chairs and craned his neck to look backwards out the window. What he saw was the exterior of a large aircraft, painted the same color as the ground. The view stunned him, and at first he could barely speak.

"Yeah," he said, haltingly, "...there's a...I see a wing. But it's strange lookin'. It's all the way in the back, not in the middle a the thing, like it'd be on a normal plane."

Troy jumped up onto the other chair and looked backwards out the other window. "Yep, it's a plane. There's a wing on this side too!"

"Yeah, but...." Justin said, shaking his head as he stepped back down, allowing Byron to take his place on the chair.

Tristan turned to Troy and ordered him, "Come down off a there. I wanna see."

Troy duly obeyed, and Tristan took his place.

"You're right," Byron said to Justin, taking in the view. "That wing is in a weird place. Why's it all the way in the back there? And why's this plane painted that color? Is it supposed to be camouflaged?" Then he stepped down to give Calvin a chance to look.

Calvin's face froze in shock as soon as he stood up on the chair and looked out the window and saw the strangely-placed wing. Several moments passed, then he said, "...Yeah, ya know...ya know what this thing actually kind a looks like...?"

Justin glanced up at him, raising his eyebrows and nodding slowly as the two men shared the same impossible thought.

"What?" Tristan demanded. "What's it look like?"

"I mean...this is crazy, but...." Calvin's voice trailed off.

"What? What're you sayin'?"

"Well, you just...you see the inside a this thing, and the outside a this thing, and it just kind a looks like a...." Calvin couldn't quite finish the sentence.

"Like a what?" Troy asked with an edge of fear in his voice.

"You uh...so you ever watched one a those big NASA take-offs, on TV?"

"NASA?"

"Yeah. I know this is completely impossible, but this thing kind a looks like...."

"...Like one a those big spaceship things," Justin completed the thought, speaking vacantly, stunned by his own words.

Byron wasn't sure he'd heard correctly. "Wait. What?"

"One a those big NASA shuttle things."

"A...shuttle?"

"We must be dead," Justin said, "'cause this could never actually be happenin'...."

"What're you talkin' 'bout?" Tristan snarled.

Justin shook his head, unable to believe what he heard himself saying. "Pretty much the only thing I know 'bout those space shuttle things is, they've got their wings in the back, right? And that's where the wings are on this thing. So...."

There was dead silence. Then Byron declared, "That is, without a doubt, the single most insane thing I ever heard!"

"I agree. But that don't change the fact."

"Fact?" Tristan half-yelled. "What fact? The fact is, we're all dead, we died, we were executed, so it don't matter where we are or what kind a plane this is! We're dead! Who cares!"

"I care," Byron said. "So if this is a..." – and he could barely bring himself to say the words – "space shuttle, then what's that out there? That weird lookin' sky, that weird lookin' ground? Where are we?"

"It sure ain't the moon," Calvin said as he stepped off the chair.

"So what is it then?"

"Some other planet, maybe."

Justin's eyes expanded to double their normal size and he raised his palms to his temples

"What?" Byron asked him. "What is it?"

"I…just remembered some pictures I once saw…in the news…."

"Pictures? Of what?"

"Of a…planet…."

"Which one?"

Justin didn't reply. He couldn't. He felt like he'd just had the wind knocked out of him at a deep, existential level.

"Which planet?"

"Yeah, say it."

But Justin didn't speak. Instead he looked out the windows again. And…he just stood there.

Eventually he turned back to face the other men. "I…I can't even believe I'm sayin' this, but that out there, that just looks a whole lot like some pictures I once saw a…Mars."

"…Wait. What?"

"…Mars?"

"That's impossible!" Byron nearly yelled.

"Yeah, well," Calvin replied, "it's also not possible any of us are still alive. So either we're dead, and like this guy said," and he pointed his thumb at Tristan, "who cares anyways, or…we're on a space shuttle, on Mars."

"Then so we're dead," Byron decided. "'Cause we sure ain't on no space shuttle on some other planet!"

Justin began looking around frantically for something.

"What're you lookin' for?" Byron asked.

"Somethin' sharp."

"What for?"

"To cut myself."

"What?"

"To see if you bleed?" Calvin asked.

"Yeah."

"Why you wanna bleed?" Troy asked. "You're already in hell."

"Right. If we bleed, we can die. If we can die, we're not in hell."

"I can just punch you in the face," Tristan offered. "That'll make you bleed real good."

Justin kept searching for something with a sharp edge, but there wasn't anything, so he took a deep breath and then bit down on his lower lip, hard.

"You bleedin'?" Byron asked.

Justin touched his bitten lip with his finger, then turned his finger so the others could see. There was blood on it.

"So...." Calvin said. "So we're not dead, and we're...."

Byron leaned against an instrument panel and pressed one of his hands against a window, trying to steady himself. He looked like he was about to pass out.

Tristan, meanwhile, stepped off the chair that he was standing on and announced, "Blood or no blood, there ain't no way, just no possible way, we're alive and on Mars! So again, I rest my case: we're dead. You all have yourselves a nice day. I'm gonna go find myself somethin' to eat."

He strolled back into the hallway and lifted up one of the garage-like doors. Inside its storage space were a collection of folded-up and hi-tech looking contraptions. He opened the next door; it contained plastic boxes, but larger than the ones they'd seen in the first space. Another door revealed more contraptions. Another door revealed more plastic boxes.

"What's all this garbage?" He yelled. "If we can bleed, we can eat, and I wanna eat! Where's the food?"

One by one the other men followed him back into the hallway, quasi-inspecting the items in the storage spaces, but really just in a daze, unable to process what was happening to them. Eventually they all wound up back in the round room and congregated again at the round counter.

"Hey," Byron said to Justin, "what's your name?"

"Justin. Yours?"

"Byron."

Then the two of them looked at Troy.

"Troy," he said. "I'm Troy."

Calvin was next, going clockwise around the table. "I'm Calvin."

"Tristan," Tristan declared, settling angrily into the remaining chair, having found nothing to eat.

"So," Byron repeated, "Justin, Troy...." Then he forgot the next name.

"Calvin," Calvin reminded him.

"Calvin, and Tristan."

Everybody nodded.

Byron repeated the names, pointing first at himself, then at each of the others in turn: "Byron, Justin, Troy, Calvin, and Tristan. Well then, nice to meet you."

Justin, Calvin and Troy all nodded. Tristan scowled.

"I'm from Tucson," Byron said. "How 'bout the rest a you?"

"L.A.," Calvin said.

"Atlanta," Troy said.

"Cleveland," Justin said.

They all looked at Tristan.

"What? Ya wanna know where I'm from? Alright. I'm from the bad part of the worst part of the craziest city in America. That's where I'm from."

"And what city's that, exactly?" Byron asked.

"Baltimore."

"Baltimore ain't the craziest city in America."

"Oh yeah? You ever been there?"

"Twice."

"Is that right? You ever been in a gang in Baltimore? You ever been in a gang fight in Baltimore?"

"That must make the difference."

"That's right, it does, 'specially if that other gang is hooked up to some big drug cartel. You try that on for size and then come back and tell me what you think a Baltimore, if you still alive."

"Still alive?" Byron threw his hands in the air. "Man, what're you talkin' 'bout? We already got executed!"

"But we didn't get executed!" Justin insisted. "We *are* alive. My lip bleeds when I bite it."

"I wonder what else we all got in common," Calvin mused, "other than maybe not bein' dead. If there are more things, that could give us clues 'bout what's goin' on here."

"Good point," Justin agreed. "Okay, so you, Byron, you were in for murder, right?"

Byron shrugged. "Yeah."

"Who'd you kill?"

"A security guard."

"Why?"

"He got in my way?"

"When? Where?"

"In a parkin' lot. I was headin' to my car."

"Why'd he get in your way?"

Byron shrugged again. "I'd just robbed a liquor store."

Justin raised his eyebrows. "Okay. And I ran over a guy in the parkin' lot of a bar after we got in a fight." Then he turned to Troy. "You?"

Troy frowned. "Knifed two people."

"Why?"

"I was feelin'…stressed."

"'Bout what?"

"The fact that one of 'em was sleepin' with my old lady."

"What 'bout the other one?"

"He was sleepin' with the guy who was sleepin' with my lady."

This caught the others by surprise.

"So then…why'd you knife that other guy?"

Troy shrugged. "I dunno. I sort a felt like, if the first dude was sleepin' with my girl, and the second dude was sleepin' with the first dude, it was almost like the second dude was also sleepin' with my girl. I know that don't make any sense now, but it seemed to at the time…."

The others exchanged glances. Then Justin asked Calvin, "And you?"

"Got in a fight in a laundromat. Couple a guys, they tried to pull my laundry out a the dryer 'fore it was done. Things got out a control. I shot 'em."

"And you?" Justin asked Tristan.

"I already told you, fool – I was in a gang, so there're 'bout fifty different things they could a executed me for. Turns out they did it 'cause I wasted some dude in a little turf war, and somebody recorded the whole thing on a cellphone."

"But none a that does us any good!" Byron declared. "Different places, different motivations, different ways a killin'! It's all different!"

"But the similarities are real," Justin said. "We're all brown, and we were all on death row for a reason. Whoever chose us for…whatever this is, it's gotta be 'cause a those things."

"So then, what," Troy asked, "you really think we're not dead? I remember goin' out after they gave me the injection."

"So do I," Byron confirmed.

"Yeah, but maybe we all just passed out. Maybe they just gave us somethin' to put us to sleep."

"But so, what – we've been asleep since then 'til now? How long does it take to fly to Mars?"

"It takes a couple years, right?" Byron conjectured.

"I think it takes like maybe five years," Justin said. "Like those machines, those robots they sent there – or, here, if that's where we are – to go lookin' for water or whatever. I think it took 'em like five years."

"So you're seriously tellin' me you think we were asleep for five years?" Tristan was incredulous, shaking his head.

"Anybody seen that movie *Alien*?" Byron asked.

"I was just thinkin' 'bout that," Calvin said, nodding. "You think maybe they did us that way?"

"Must've. If we're on some other planet then they must've done it like that."

"Like how? What're you two sayin'?"

"In the movie *Alien*, there's this crew on a spaceship, and they go to sleep in these special beds for like months at a time."

"The bed I woke up in was pretty strange, I'll tell ya that."

"Same."

"Ditto."

"So then maybe that's how they did it," Calvin agreed. "Maybe they put us to sleep 'stead a killin' us, and they stuck us in those beds, and now…here we are, on Mars or wherever.…"

Tristan shook his head some more, still not believing any of this.

"But why?" Byron demanded. "Why take five death row cons and stick us up on some other planet? If someone – the government, maybe – is runnin' some kind a experiment or somethin', then why choose us? That don't make any sense!"

Justin shrugged. "Actually…maybe it does.…"

"Whad' ya mean? How?"

"Think 'bout it. If you wanna experiment on people by sendin' 'em off somewhere – who's better to get than some guys everybody else thinks're already dead?"

At this point the large screen which was built into the circular wall – and which looked like a flat screen TV but without any buttons – flicked on and displayed the image of a white-haired, middle-aged "white" guy. This person stared blankly out from the screen for a few seconds, and then, as if he was looking right at the five of them, he smiled.

IV

"Congratulations, gentlemen," said the white-haired man. "That didn't take you very long at all."

Justin was the only one of the five facing away from the screen, and he swiveled sharply in his chair to see who was saying this.

"Allow me to confirm your budding suspicions," the TV image said. "First of all, it's true: you are, indeed, alive."

This instant revelation hit the men in the round room like a ton of bricks. They all just sat there, firmly frozen in place.

"And you are, indeed, on a space shuttle."

Tristan shook his head, not believing it. The others were stunned. Troy looked like he was about to start hyperventilating.

"And you are indeed…on Mars."

The five men were barely able to form any thoughts in response to what they'd just heard.

Tristan was the first one to verbalize a response. "So who're you supposed to be?" He demanded aggressively.

The white-haired guy's sharp blue eyes shifted directly to Tristan and stared at him – through him, it seemed – for a second or two. When the gaze returned to the group as a whole, the man explained, "I am the one who chose you. I'm the one who saved you. I'm the reason you didn't all meet your ends in inglorious fashion with I.V.'s stuck in your arms back in those charming institutions where you were previously incarcerated. If it wasn't for me, right now you'd all be rotting away in cheap coffins while the worms close in. That – is who I am."

He paused for effect, as the men onboard the shuttle exchanged uncomfortable glances.

"More specifically," he continued, "my name is William Baker. My friends call me Bill. Since we're not friends yet, I'd prefer that you call me Baker."

Another pause, then, "I'll be happy to tell you more about myself in due time. For the moment, what's most useful for you to know is that I don't work for the U.S. government, or any government. I am a private individual, who happens to have a lot of money. And by "a lot" I mean quite a lot. I've decided to use that money to create a human colony on Mars. And I'm happy to report that the five of you, gentlemen, are the first members of that colony."

Baker smiled widely, with his lips pressed together.

"A…colony…?" Tristan responded.

"That's right. Now, what that colony will look like, and why I've decided to invest all my resources in this endeavor, are topics I'll address in a minute. First, though, I can imagine that the question which is burning most brightly in your brains is, "Why did I choose *you*?" Yes?"

He paused for confirmation, and the five men – still completely stunned – nodded vaguely.

"So then, allow me to address that right away. The fact is that I've chosen you for four reasons, each of which will, upon reflection, I suspect, seem entirely logical.

"Reason number one: you're already dead. Or at least everybody else thinks so. Which means that if you do happen to die up there – and naturally I hope you don't – then I won't have to deal with the fallout from your families, or the government, etc. Besides, in general it's easier to keep things secret when there aren't any families involved."

The five men just sat there, staring at him.

"Reason number two: as you were just now surmising before I chimed in, you're all part of an experiment. It's an experiment because it's never been attempted before. We – me and the people who work for me – simply cannot know, a hundred percent for certain, that this is going to work. There are going to be not merely challenges but hardships up there, and getting the right sort of people to volunteer for this type of mission – particularly a mission which isn't going to be made public back here on Earth anytime soon – would have posed some difficulties. And of course if we're not going to be sending volunteers up there then we have to send people without offering them the option to choose. Now, under normal circumstances, if people were kidnapped, rendered unconscious and then woken up on a spacecraft on an entirely different planet, they might get a little upset. The five of you, however, provide us with an easy way to get around that problem, since you didn't need to be asked to volunteer, and, obviously, if you weren't part of this mission, you'd be dead. Now I can understand if it takes you a little time to see it in this light, but I suspect that before long you'll recognize that you've all been given the chance of a lifetime – namely, the chance to stay alive, and do something absolutely extraordinary with your lives; something that you never would've dreamed was possible in your previous lives. And thus I anticipate that, as things progress, you're going to embrace this mission with gusto!"

The men still sat there, stunned, speechless. Byron's mouth hung open.

"Reason number three: you're all used to living in very confined spaces for extended durations of time. Which means that your current, somewhat confined situation isn't going to feel nearly so jarring for you as it would for people who are accustomed to all the daily freedoms of modern life. As a result, I anticipate fewer cabin fever scenarios playing out up there than would otherwise be the case.

"And finally, reason number four: you've all killed people. Now, under normal circumstances, of course, that would hardly be a résumé builder. But you're no longer in normal circumstances, are you? You've slipped the bonds of human civilization. There's no police force up there. There's no military. There isn't a fire department or hospital. Which means that ultimately you've no choice but to take your lives – your brand new lives, which I've just given you – into your own hands and do whatever you need to do to survive up there. More than anything else, you need to survive. You need to do what it takes. Whatever it takes."

Baker paused again for effect, as the men traded glances.

"No society has even been established in an environment that's as harsh as that one up there. Humans die within three minutes without air, and outside that shuttle there isn't any breathable air. Humans die after a week or two without water, and there isn't much drinkable water outside that shuttle; at least none that's readily available. I'll explain that caveat to you later. The point is, you're going to have to be strong, and you're going to have to do what it takes. And, as it turns out, back here on Earth each of you already demonstrated that you are indeed ready to do just that.

"Of course there is an obvious potential downside to putting five convicted murderers on a space shuttle for an extended period of time. Naturally, you all might try to kill each other. But I'd recommend against that, for one very important reason: in order for you to complete this first phase of the work that's needed to set up our little colony, it's going to require all five of you working together in a diligent fashion."

"And…if we do that," Byron couldn't resist asking, "then what? What's in it for us?"

"Precisely," Baker replied. "What's in it for you? Good question. The answer to that question is both very simple and very powerful. If you complete the work that's required of you, then you will all be allowed to return to good old planet Earth."

He smiled a wide, pressed-lips smile, as he allowed that point to sink in.

The five men in the round room looked at one another, and even Tristan couldn't hold back an expression of hope as it crossed his stony-featured face.

"Yours is the first shuttle. There'll be a second. It'll be arriving there in four months. It's purely a cargo ship. There're no people in that one. Once it gets there we'll land it a short distance from your location, and you'll need to unload all its cargo, set up all the equipment and so forth, and then, if that goes well, we'll allow the five of you to transfer your special beds over to that ship, and we'll fly you home."

"Can't this shuttle fly us home?" Justin asked.

"A logical question, to which the answer is no. We designed it specifically for a one-way trip. One of the vessels which we send up there needs to remain there, as a home base and living quarters for subsequent colonists. And to be perfectly honest with you – and you'll find that I'm always going to be perfectly honest with you, even brutally honest if need be – there's another reason why we disabled that shuttle's return capacity. The simple fact of the matter is that we don't want any of you thinking that there's a way off that rock other than to complete the mission you've been given. So no, that shuttle can't fly you home."

"How long did it take us to get here and how long's it gonna take us to get back to Earth?" Calvin was eager to know, as were the others.

"A one-way trip between our two planets runs for approximately seven months and a bit, if you time it right."

"So," Troy asked, "you're tellin' us we've been asleep for over seven months?"

"Quite a bit longer, actually, since you were all sent up there after your execution dates. Your shuttle launched in November 2017, and it is currently July 2018. July 6th, to be exact."

The weight of this news hit the five of them hard. Somehow it was this fact, more than any of the other facts they'd just learned, that brought it home to them that this face on the screen was actually real, that this whole thing was real, that they were still connected – however tenuously – to reality back on Earth and thus that they might someday partake of that reality again.

"So how did you get our deaths faked?" Byron asked.

The shoulders which were attached to the neck that went with the face on the screen shrugged. "I have a variety of connections. And money. And there really isn't anything that can't be accomplished if you have those two things."

"So you had it staged?" Justin asked.

"That's right."

"So who knew it was fake? Whoever gave the injections must a known."

Baker nodded. "That's correct. They knew the injections you were given were just something to knock you out, drop your pulse and slow your breathing down to next to nothing for a few minutes. And only they knew that the heart-rate monitors had been rigged. Needless to say, none of them had any idea that what they were doing was for the purpose of sending you to Mars."

"But so then, how can we go back to Earth," Calvin asked, "if we're supposed to be dead? We'll all just get arrested again. Have to go through the same whole thing all over."

"Not at all. You'll be given new identities. Plus, a bit of plastic surgery can do wonders to fundamentally change a person's appearance. Naturally, you'll have to sign a contract, agreeing to never reveal to anyone what you've been through regarding this mission. But then of course no one would believe you even if you told them. Still, there is a contract."

"Okay," Tristan said, folding his arms across his chest, "so why you doin' this, then? Why you want to build a…colony?"

Baker took a deep breath before launching into what he clearly considered to be a very serious topic.

"Mr. Tristan," he replied, "allow me to respond to that question by asking you one. And my question is this: what do you believe in?"

"…What?"

"Tell me what you believe in? Do you believe in God or divine providence or science or love or the human spirit or what?"

"I don't believe in nothin'."

"I see. And Mr. Calvin, how about you? What do you believe in?"

"I believe in God," Calvin affirmed.

"I see. Well now let me tell you all what I believe in. I believe in securitization. If you're unfamiliar with the concept, it's a term in finance that refers to spreading out your risk so that if one asset decreases in value you'll still hold plenty of assets which can sustain their value. Does that make sense?"

He waited until at least one of them nodded. Calvin did so. Then Baker explained, "Basically, it's the old idea of not putting all your eggs in one basket. I believe in having multiple baskets. It's the reason I'm as rich as I am and it's also the reason I want to establish a human colony on Mars. Simply put, I want our species to have a backup option.

"Now I'm not claiming to be some great humanitarian. I'm not. But I am in favor of the survival of the species. After all, I'm a member of this species. So are my children. So is my young grandchild. And I want us all to be part of a species that has a future. And I'm sure you'll agree that the way things are going here on Earth is hardly encouraging. We've got global warming, vaccine-resistant viruses, nuclear proliferation, rampant terrorism, and of course there's always the chance of another large-scale conventional war.

"Given those facts, therefore, as an investor, I apply the logic of securitization and that logic leads me to an obvious conclusion: the need to establish a human colony that can eventually be self-sustaining, and to locate that colony on a planet other than Earth. Now, as it turns out, Mercury's temperature variances are too extreme for us to send any people there, and Venus is too hot. As for Jupiter, Saturn, Uranus and Neptune, they're all just a bunch of gas. Those planets do have some potentially colonizable moons but they're all located inconveniently far away. And Pluto, which used to be considered a planet, is out there even farther. So that leaves us with one, and only one, possible option: Mars."

He paused and smiled his wide, lips-pressed smile.

"And of course we can't wait around for the public at large to embrace the rationale of colonization. The debates – not just in the U.S. but globally – about who gets to colonize, how to colonize, how much to spend on colonizing, would be interminable. Which is why I, as a private individual, have decided to spend my fortune on this little undertaking.

"Now, allow me to give you a preliminary, general sense of what this undertaking is going to entail." Baker glanced down and evidently began typing something on a keyboard. As he did so, the image of his face was replaced on the screen by a computer-generated diagram of the space shuttle.

"This," Baker's voice said, "is your shuttle. It's your home for the next four months. As you've already discovered, it's full of supplies. In this first container space" – as he spoke, the picture of one of the container spaces that ran along the hallway momentarily turned red – "is food. In this next one here" – and an adjacent space turned red – "is also food. Now this next one contains tools for working on projects outside the shuttle. This space also contains the parts for a rover that you can drive around outside. This next space contains equipment and a variety of soil compounds and other ingredients for creating a hothouse outside the shuttle. This next space contains more scientific testing equipment which I'll explain later. It also contains exercise equipment which you'll be able to set up after some of the container spaces have been unloaded.

"As I said, you'll be up there for four months. Every day there will be work for you to do; we've already planned that out. And the tasks have been assigned. So there won't be any bargaining or anyone lording it over the others or anything like that. You'll have a daily routine, and if we stick to that schedule then everything should be done on time.

"Now, there's something else you need to know, right away, so that you don't inadvertently cause a catastrophe. And it's this. See this lower space here in the shuttle?"

As Baker spoke, the bottom portion of the shuttle diagram turned red. "That's where the engine is. And the energy source for that engine is a chunk of radioactive plutonium. It's like having a nuclear power plant right under your feet. Now whatever you do, under any circumstances, you do not want to go down into that area. The engine is extremely hi-tech, extremely complex, and has lots of parts and pieces. And it's all running on power that comes from the plutonium, which is in a specialized container located at the back of the compartment. It would be very easy for someone walking around down there to accidently hit the wrong lever, or lean on a switch, or push something, which would then mess with the engine, and that, in turn, could foul up the way the engine is receiving its power supply. And guess what happens then? You all get incinerated in Mars' first man-made nuclear explosion, and isn't that fun. So whatever you do, under any circumstances, do not go down into that area. We've sealed it off, so you'd really need to work at it to get in there in the first place. But there's never going to be a first place. So that's what you need to know about that."

Baker's face reappeared on the screen. "Any questions?"

"Yeah, I got a question," Byron said.

"What's that?"

"Why're all of us brown-skinned up here? What's with the racial thing that's goin' on? Why aren't there any straight up white guys on this shuttle?"

Baker smiled his pressed-lips smile and nodded. "That's a very important question. There are two reasons for that. Reason number one: as you're all well aware, it is simply a fact that, within the prison system, race plays a central role in how inmates socialize, how they form gangs, and so forth. And what we didn't want was some race-based gang dynamic playing out up there. A mini race riot on a space shuttle would be, to say the least, counterproductive. So we made sure to choose people who had relatively similar racial backgrounds.

"Reason number two: as you're all also, no doubt, very well aware, in America today there is a much higher likelihood for a non-white person who kills someone to be given the death penalty than there is for a white person to receive that sentence for the same crime. Which meant that there was a certain statistical likelihood that, when we went looking for our five candidates, they might turn out to be non-white. Now what happened in fact was that we selected two of you – Troy and Justin – and, since they're both brown-skinned, with mixed ancestry, we tried, for the reason I just mentioned, to find three more who had that same sort of background and who were being executed around the same time. As it turned out, we were able to locate Byron, Calvin, and Tristin, and that gave us our five-man team."

Another pause from Baker, this one longer than the others, as he allowed the men on the shuttle to further process all the information they'd just received. When no one had any more immediate questions, Baker said, "Good, then. Let's get you something to eat. It's been many months since your last solid meal."

V

The men only realized how hungry they were after they started eating. Their beds were designed to send them into a hibernated state, so they hadn't woken up starving, but a human body going without food for several months is inevitably going to register a sense of depletion. Thus, as the men ate and reactivated their normal appetites, they grew hungrier and hungrier with every bite.

It didn't hurt that their rations were surprisingly tasty. "This isn't your grandfather's space cuisine," Baker explained to them. "I've always thought it absurd that we could figure out how to send humans into space and yet we couldn't provide them with high-class eating options. So chow down, enjoy yourselves, and I'll check back in with you in a couple hours. Oh, and by the way, the bathroom is through the two narrow doors to the left – my left – of this screen. The ones that look like closet doors." Then he smiled and the screen went black.

All the food onboard the shuttle was sealed in small plastic boxes which were packaged, in turn, inside the bigger plastic boxes which were stacked in the container spaces that lined the long hallway's walls. The food was of all types and the men sampled widely. To their chagrin they found that there wasn't any alcohol – just water and a variety of juices – but other than that they could hardly complain.

As they feasted their mood became festive. The nutritional rush played a role in that, but so too did the reality of their present condition, which they all progressively absorbed while they simultaneously absorbed their meals. The most fundamental fact – that they were alive – had an invigorating effect; made all the more so by the fact that they had all, in a sense, cheated death, and cheated the system back home. Better still, they were going to be given a second chance to make a fresh start once they returned to Earth. Even Tristan had to smile a little and shake his head in bemused, partially-believing disbelief.

"Dude's gotta be crazy rich," he said while he swallowed the last piece of his pizza and washed it down with grape juice. "To pay for all this? He's gotta have some serious cash to do this."

"What'd he say his name was?" Troy asked, still very much on edge, even as his mood improved. He was eating a steak sandwich.

"Baker. William Baker," Byron said as he nibbled an energy bar, which was the closest thing to candy that he could find.

Calvin finished the two hot dogs he'd been eating and now began inspecting the appliances and gadgets that lined the round room's wall. "Look at this," he said, to no one in particular, "a coffee maker! There's a coffee maker built into the wall here. I haven't used a coffee maker in, like, years."

Justin, meanwhile, had grown quiet. He'd warmed up a burger in one of the ovens, then proceeded to enjoy the first really delicious food he'd eaten in a long, long time, but the pleasure of the experience couldn't outweigh the significance of another thought which had taken center stage in his mind. It was simply too implausible, he concluded, that he and these other inmates had been selected for a mission to Mars, of all places. Yes, Baker's explanation technically made sense. And yes, his – Justin's – lip had bled when he bit it, but still, to think that they were all on a spaceship on Mars, was simply...crazy. A more likely explanation was that he was having some sort of death dream; that he was passing through a state of consciousness post-mortem. And because it was a dream, anything was possible, including being on Mars and bleeding and eating a space burger. And yet, precisely because he was dead, nothing real was possible, and this was all just some transitory experience. At any moment, he concluded, this whole scenario – these other guys, this ship, the face of Baker on the screen – could dissolve into a vast black nothing.

"So you said you're from Cleveland?" Byron asked him.

Justin forced himself to engage in conversation. "Yeah. And you said you're from...?"

"Tucson."

Justin nodded. "I've never been there."

"It's not bad." Byron bit off another piece of the energy bar and barely chewed it before swallowing.

"You been to Cleveland?"

"Once. I liked it. Met a girl there named Cherice. Real nice girl."

"I met a girl in Cleveland. Her name was Cherice too," Tristan said mischievously.

"I'll bet you did."

"I did," Tristan insisted. "What'd your Cherice look like? I'll tell you if she was the same one."

"Why don't you start, and we can play it that way."

Tristan shrugged. "I think you just worried I was with your girl."

"I'm not worried at all."

"Sure y'ain't." Then Tristan looked at Troy. "You've met Cherice up in Cleveland too, ain't cha?"

"What?"

Tristan leaned forward, over the countertop, and stared at Troy menacingly. "Cherice, up in Cleveland? Remember her?"

As if it wasn't unnerving enough to get sent to the death chamber and then woken up on a space shuttle on Mars, now Troy found himself obliged to choose sides between the biggest guy and the meanest guy on the ship.

"Uh, sure, yeah, whatever," he said.

"There," Tristan grinned at Byron, "ya happy? Everybody knows Cherice. Cherice up in Cleveland."

Calvin pushed against the double-doors that led into the bathroom. "Bathroom looks pretty normal," he announced.

"As opposed to what?" Tristan asked.

"As opposed to we're-in-space-so-things-are-all-different, that's what," Byron told him.

"There's no water in the toilet, though," Calvin informed them.

"So how's it flush?" Troy asked.

Calvin pushed on a lever near the toilet and a loud vacuum sound shot out from the bathroom.

"That's how," Byron said.

Calvin pushed open another pair of thin doors, next to the first pair. "Here's the shower," he announced. Then he walked back to the counter and sat down.

"So what'd you do, 'fore you got put away?" Justin asked Byron.

"What, you mean like work?"

"Yeah."

Byron shrugged. "Different stuff. I worked in one a those big home repair places for a while. I worked on a road crew. Worked in a kitchen at a greasy spoon kind a restaurant. You know – jobs. How 'bout you?"

"I worked for the Post Office. Then I went back to school, took a few business courses, got a job at a welding factory, doin' payroll stuff."

"And what'd you say landed you in the pen?"

"Ran over a guy after we got in a fight."

"What was the fight over?"

"A girl."

"What happened to her?"

"No idea."

Byron smiled. "When I got sent away, I wasn't all that surprised. Somehow I'd known it was comin' for a while. When I was a teenager, and early twenties, I was into a lot of bad stuff. Then I got a little older and I put all that behind me, but somehow I just sensed it was all gonna come back some day. And it did."

"You said you robbed a liquor store?"

"Uh-huh. Third one I'd robbed that week. I'd robbed some when I was younger too. Then I didn't do it for years. But I wound up havin' a real bad week – money dried up, my lady walked out on me, I got fired, my landlord stopped cuttin' me any slack – and I snapped. That was it. Robbed a store. Then another one. And like I said, at the third one there was a security guard standin' there and…you know…end a story."

"Mine wasn't like that," Justin said. "I'd done some things when I was younger, but nothin' real bad. But this dude in the bar, the way he was behavin', he just set me off. And that was that."

"You boys ain't got nothin' to write home 'bout," Tristan told them. "The stuff I done, it'd send a shiver down your spine."

"Well that's beautiful, man," Byron said. "Thanks for sharin'." He smiled sarcastically at Tristan, who scowled in response.

"And so how 'bout you then?" Justin asked Calvin. "What'd you do 'fore gettin' sent away?"

"Karate instructor."

"No kiddin'? So that's why you were standin' with your hands up like that when we found you?"

Calvin nodded. "I've been picked on a lot in my life. Look at me – I'm a little dude. I grew up in a bad place. I had to learn to stick up for myself. When I was a teenager I did that with a gun. When I got older I learned karate. And I ended up teachin' it. But that doesn't mean I got rid a the gun. So when I got into it in a laundromat, and the other guys were bigger, and there were a couple of 'em, I knew what I could and couldn't get done with just my karate. So I pulled the gun, and then they started to pull theirs, and that was pretty much that."

"And you?" Byron asked Troy. "What's your story?"

"What – work? I was a furniture salesman."

"Sounds fun," Byron replied dryly.

Troy shrugged. "I did it to meet women."

"Really? How'd that work out for ya?"

"Pretty good. It's how I met my girl. I mean, it was good 'til she started cheatin' on me with that other dude."

"She must a had mixed emotions," Calvin observed, "when you took out her boyfriend and her boyfriend's boyfriend. Like, she must a been sad 'bout the first dude, but kind a like, I don't know, like she got vengeance on the dude's dude."

Troy shrugged. "She never spoke to me afterwards. I was kind a surprised by that. I mean, she knew I'm kind a crazy, and then to go do what she did, and expect me to not react….I dunno. I was always hopin' we'd get back together. But then my day in the chamber came, and that was it. But now, here I am, and who knows, maybe I can go back and pretend I'm someone else and try to get her to be my girl again…."

The others exchanged glances, but said nothing in reply.

"So you all don't wanna know what I did, 'fore I got sent away?" Tristan asked.

"You told us," Byron said. "You were in a gang, you were a real bad dude."

"Naw, I mean like, my work."

"Oh, look at this – he was in a gang *and* he worked. What an inspiration!"

Tristan scowled. "I'm gonna have to spend four months up here with this fool?"

"Oh, I see, I'm the fool."

"You the biggest one, clearly." Then Tristan turned to Troy, as he had before, to confirm his position. "Clearly, he's the biggest fool on this ship. Am I right?"

Troy shrugged. "He's a big guy."

"See, there ya go."

"I wonder if we're gonna start out workin' tomorrow like, right away?" Calvin said. "It'll be good to get goin'. Just sittin' 'round here is gonna get old fast."

"Tell me 'bout it," Byron concurred.

"Yeah, but, I'm not real eager to get out there," Troy said.

"I guess we'll have to have spacesuits," Justin presumed.

"And who's gonna be lookin' the best in that?" Tristan paused, to see if anyone would answer. "Uh, that'd be me. That's right."

Byron shook his head, clearly thinking Tristan was ridiculous.

Then the TV screen turned on and Baker's face appeared.

"So, gentlemen," he said, "enjoy your meals?"

"Better than anything else I've eaten in a real long while," Byron confirmed.

"I can imagine. After all, prison riots so often start because of the food, isn't that true? In any case, you'll have lots to choose from, food-wise, over the next couple months. But for the moment, if I may interrupt your conversation, I want to give you a quick briefing on what comes next.

"Over to my left, which is to your right, you can see the digital clock built into the wall. It goes by international time, which means that, after 12:00, then it goes to 13:00 instead of 1:00, and 14:00 instead of 2:00, etc. Conveniently, a Martian day takes up almost the same amount of time as an Earth day. It's only longer by a few minutes. So it'll be easy for you to stick to regular time schedules in terms of sleep patterns and other routines.

"Now, tomorrow, right at 10:00," and the screen switched from Baker's face to the diagram of the shuttle, "we'll get to work. In this first compartment," and one of the container spaces along the hallway lit-up red in the diagram, "are your spacesuits. They've been tailored for each of you, to fit you perfectly, and they've got your names on them. You've each got two of them. They're very durable and are made to be worked in. They'll be very hard to rip or break. But, all the same, be careful in them. You only have two, and we'll need you all working each day to complete this mission, so we don't want anyone without a suit.

"Tomorrow morning, the first thing we'll have you do is unpack the container space that those suits are in, so that you can get to them, and then I'll walk you through how to put them on. Each suit can hold two hour's supply of oxygen, then you'll need to come back onboard and refill the tanks. So in general you'll work for slightly less than two-hour shifts, but tomorrow you'll only go out for about an hour, to get used to walking around outside.

"A key point to note on that topic: the gravitational pull on Mars is thirty-eight percent of what it is on Earth. What that means is, if you weighed a hundred pounds on Earth, you'll weigh thirty-eight pounds on Mars. And so forth."

"Alright!" Byron exclaimed. "I'm beginnin' to like this planet!"

"Yes, well, there are plusses and minuses. The plusses all have to do with mobility. The minuses have to do with the fact that our bodies are accustomed to responding to a certain gravitational pull. Our entire muscle structure is premised upon it. If you change that particular pull quotient, you impact the human body in terms of muscle mass and a lot of other things. And we don't want that. Besides, none of you are trained to work in zero-gravity, like the astronauts on the International Space Station; you're not trained for the motion sickness, or any of the rest of it.

"Now, onboard ship there, you're fine. We paid a lot of money to some brilliant people to devise a system that recreates the equivalent of Earth's gravitational pull there inside the shuttle. I won't bore you with the details of how that works unless you want me to. Once you go outside, however, the suits you wear will have metal weights in the shoes, so the gravitational pull you'll feel will be more akin to what you'd experience back on Earth. Any quick questions about that?"

None of the five men said anything, so Baker continued.

"Okay then, tomorrow, in addition to trying out your spacesuits, the first things you'll get ready to unload are the plastic boxes that are in the same container space as the suits and which are marked with the designation "AB1." All the things in those boxes are part of what we're calling "the garden." We're going to have you conduct experiments in that garden with plant seeds that we've got frozen there on the ship. We'll be testing to see if we can create a micro-environment there on Mars that allows us to generate a self-sustaining food supply."

Baker smiled. "Isn't that exciting? If we manage to make that work, then the colony will truly be viable, and ultimately it will be able to exist independent of any connection to the home planet. The majority of the work that you'll be doing, until the second spacecraft arrives, will pertain to that garden."

"How much'll we be workin' each day?" Tristan asked. "How

many hours?"

"That'll depend on the tasks at hand. Setting up the garden will typically require having two or three of you outside the ship working together. Other tasks will only require one of you. And while some of you are outside, there'll be other things to do inside – not only unloading and unpacking things but also running tests, experiments, and so forth."

"I've never conducted a real scientific experiment," Calvin said, excitedly.

Baker smiled. "We'll walk you through every step. By the time your little stint up there is over, you'll be genuine scientists."

"So we gettin' paid for all this work?" Tristan asked, uncouthly.

Byron shook his head and sighed bemusedly.

Baker stared at – and through – Tristan for a few seconds before replying. "Yes, you are, in fact. You're getting paid with something far more valuable than money. You're getting paid with life – this new one, which I've given to you by sparing you from getting executed. You're also getting paid with the future life you'll have when I return you safely back here to Earth. Indeed, if anything, you should all be paying me for giving you these benefits, but I'm doing this free of charge and I don't want you to feel obligated to thank me either."

"I'm happy to thank you," Calvin said. "Nobody's ever done this much for me, never. So thank you."

"You're welcome, Calvin."

"Yeah, thanks," Justin added. "This is all pretty incredible."

"Ditto that," Byron agreed.

"Yeah, same," said Troy.

Tristan shrugged and frowned, but then he nodded and said, "Yeah, you're right. This is a good thing you've given us. So, yeah."

Baker smiled. "I'm pleased you all feel that way. And I can only imagine that that feeling is going to increase over time as you take part in the founding of the colony and begin to fully realize its significance. There is, quite simply, nothing that could possibly be more important than the work we're doing together."

Then Baker added, with a smile, "And on that note, I'll see you all tomorrow at 10:00." The screen switched off.

The five men continued chatting amongst themselves.

Tristan grew less aggressive as the conversation wound along.

Byron was downright enthusiastic; between not being dead, weighing less, having a free food supply, and getting to return to Earth as a new man, he'd concluded that he'd hit the jackpot. Calvin was similarly enthused, and intrigued – more than any of the others – by the prospect of scientific experimentation. Troy appeared somewhat less afraid, less on edge than before. And Justin, meanwhile, had concluded that if he was in fact wrapped up in some sort of post-death dream, then at least it didn't appear to be fading away anytime soon, so he might as well try to relax and enjoy the situation as much as possible.

It was shortly after 17:00 when they finally finished eating. The shock of food entering their systems – after they'd gone so long without – made all of them exceedingly sleepy, and they climbed back into their beds in their respective rooms and rapidly dozed off.

VI

Justin's second awakening on the shuttle was much less dramatic than his first. Not only did he know where he was this time but he'd now fallen asleep and woken up in the same place twice, which made it seem more likely that this whole situation was legitimately real, especially since he'd had dreams – just a bunch of gibberish – while he was asleep, and how plausible was it that he'd have nonsense dreams while being in the midst of a lucid dream?

'Huh,' he thought to himself. 'This might be real....'

And he smiled, thinking that he had to be one of the luckiest people on Earth and/or Mars. But then, as he thought this point through, a wave of guilt washed over him. This happened periodically, ever since he'd run over that guy in the parking lot of that bar. Even back then, as he was doing it, as he'd gunned the gas and screeched across the thirty feet that separated his fender from that guy's shins, he'd known how wrong it was. But he'd been humiliated and all he could think about at the time, all he cared about at that moment, was revenge.

Things had gone badly in the bar. He'd met this seriously good looking lady, she was having a drink, he sat down next to her – the cliché scenario. And they hit it off. Her name was Leticia. She worked in a bank. Seemed sharp. Had beautiful cheekbones, gorgeous eyes. And then this jerk – Tobey Williams was his name, as Justin subsequently learned during the legal proceedings – walks up and ruins everything. He leans in between the two of them, tells Leticia he wants to dance with her. Justin tells him to get lost. Williams takes Justin's drink and tosses it in Justin's face. Justin grabs Williams, then Williams grabs Justin. They go flailing, rolling, kicking, elbowing onto the middle of the dance floor. Williams gets the best of it and pins Justin down, wails on him. By the time the bartender pulls Williams off, Justin's face is bleeding in multiple places. Leticia has disappeared. A group of men toss Williams and then Justin out the front door. Williams tries to pick a fight with one of the guys in the group, but he gets clocked in his temple by another guy and goes down, out cold for several seconds. Justin contemplates attacking him there, while he's vulnerable, but the bartender warns Justin off, yelling at him to "Get out a here!" So Justin stumbles towards his car. The group of men go back inside. Williams revives, climbs onto his knees, stands, and begins walking awkwardly across the parking lot, right in front of Justin's car, and….

"Stupid," Justin said, lying there in the metallic bed, shaking his head. It was what he always said to himself, out loud, whenever he relived the event in his mind. "So stupid." To let something like that determine the whole course of his life. To kill another human being, and in the process to ruin himself for this life and the next. The worst part was that Williams had a couple kids, and now they'd be growing up without their father, back down on Earth.

As he lay in the bed, thinking about all this for the millionth time, Justin decided, then and there, that after he got back to Earth and was given plastic surgery and a new identity, he'd devote himself to making sure that those kids were taken care of.

As soon as he made this resolution, he felt the weight of his guilt lift a little, in a way that it never had before. And it occurred to him that perhaps there was some sort of cosmic justice in play. Perhaps he'd been spared death so that he could make things right. Maybe this was kind of like purgatory, but a purgatory not predicated upon actually dying but only on proto-dying. And as Justin considered this point, he felt profoundly grateful to the forces at work, and to Baker in particular, for giving him this second chance.

Eventually he climbed out of bed, pushed the button to open the door, and looked out into the round room. It was empty. The clock on the wall said 4:04. Apparently the others were still asleep.

As he stood there, halfway through the doorway, he pushed the second of the two illuminated buttons which were next to the door, and heard a locking sound. Then he stepped back into the room, pushed the first button, and nothing happened. He pushed the second button, heard a de-clasping sound, then pushed the first button, which caused the door to slide closed, and he nodded. It was good to know that this door could be locked from the inside if need be, considering the other people who were onboard the shuttle with him.

After wandering out into the round room, he strolled down to the end of hallway and then sat in one of the chairs in the cockpit, looking up at the Martian sky. He sat there in silence for a minute or so, until one of the screens on the control panel switched on and Baker's face appeared.

"Hello Justin," he said, smiling.

"Hey. Uh, hi there."

"You're up early."

"Yeah, I guess so," Justin said, a little startled. "I got some good sleep though."

"Normal sleep this time."

"Yeah, right."

"And now you're just enjoying the view?"

"Right."

"Part of me wishes I could be up there with you."

"So…why didn't you come along?"

"Maybe someday I will. For the time being I need to oversee all the operations down here."

Justin nodded. Then something occurred to him. "Can I ask you somethin'?"

"Yes."

"If we were all asleep on the ride here, and if this shuttle can't fly back to Earth, then why is there a cockpit, and why are there chairs in here, like for pilots?"

"A logical question. When I purchased that shuttle from NASA, it came with everything in the cockpit there as you find it. So that's the first answer. But there's a more fundamental answer, which is that, as noted, my team and I have never been a hundred percent certain that everything would go according to plan on this trip. So, if for some reason we lost remote control of the ship while you were all flying towards Mars, the plan was to wake you up and instruct you on how to handle the craft manually."

Justin nodded. "Makes sense."

Baker smiled. "Now, can I ask you something?"

"Uh, yeah, okay."

"Before all of this happened to you, what did you want to do?"

"…Whad' ya mean?"

"With your life."

"With my life?"

"Yes. Back when you were on Earth, before you ran over that

person in the parking lot, before you got that job at the factory, back even before you were working at the Post Office – what did you want to do? What was your dream of what you wanted to do?"

"You mean like…what'd I wanna be when I grew up? That sort a thing?"

"Something like that, yes."

Justin shrugged. "To be honest," and he blushed a little, "I wanted to be a race car driver."

Baker contemplated this answer. "Why'd you want to do that, if I may ask?"

Justin shrugged again. "Sure. I just…I wanted to go fast."

Baker smiled. "What's the fastest you've ever driven a car?"

"I guess 'bout…110 miles per hour."

Baker nodded. "On the flight to Mars, your typical speed was over 12,000 miles per hour. And to put that in perspective: commercial flights here on Earth typically go less than 600 miles per hour."

Justin smiled. "12,000 miles per hour? That's fast."

"Allow me to offer you yet another perspective. Do you know how fast the Earth spins on its axis?"

"…No."

"About 1000 miles per hour."

"No kiddin'."

"Which means that when you drove 110 miles per hour you were actually going 1110 miles per hour, presuming you were driving west."

"…Huh."

"Which is to say that speed, like time, like just about everything, is relative. It's contextual. What we want depends on where we perceive ourselves to be."

"Yeah…sure."

"So, then, when you get back to Earth, are you still going to want to drive fast?"

"I guess I don't know. I mean, I don't know if there'd be much of a point, after flyin' to Mars."

Baker nodded. "Can I ask you another question? Just one more?"

"Sure."

"You say you wanted to go fast. Why?"

"Why'd I wanna go fast?" Justin asked, as if he'd never actually considered the question. "I guess 'cause it's excitin', and…'cause, when you go fast, it feels like you're actually goin' somewhere."

Baker smiled. "I see. Alright. Well, I'll let you get back to your morning in peace. I'll check in with you and the rest of the crew around 10:00."

"Yeah, okay, sure."

And then the screen went black.

VII

Prison is a good place to learn how to do nothing. Which meant that Justin wasn't annoyed that he had to wait another few hours before anything else happened on the shuttle.

He went back to his room, lay down inside the bed, and just…lay there. Periodically thoughts would filter through his mind. Back down on Earth, as he'd worked his way through the penal system, he'd developed the habit of contemplating the likely near-term behavior of the people around him. In part this was a survival technique, although a somewhat ironic one, considering that much of his incarceration experience had been spent in solitary confinement, and likewise considering his death sentence. But mainly it was just a mildly amusing way to pass the time. And he'd gotten good at it. Human beings, after all, are predictable. Certain types of external stimuli almost always produce certain types of responses. Patterns repeat over and over. People might be innately free but that doesn't make them innately interesting.

For instance, he could already see what was shaping up with the five-man crew onboard the shuttle. Tristan was clearly scoping out the competition, probing around for weaknesses, figuring out who his major challenger was for the position of top dog. He'd evidently decided it was Byron. So he'd begun prodding the bigger man, trying to figure out how much it took to provoke him. He'd also evidently decided that Troy was the most vulnerable member of the group and therefore the most easily manipulated, and thus he was already forcing Troy to take sides with him against Byron. The next step would be to try to corral either Justin or Calvin, or both. Typical wolf pack politics.

Eventually Justin heard someone stirring out in the round room, so he climbed back out of bed and opened his door.

"Hey there, man," Byron said. He was sitting on one of the chairs at the round counter, rotating his head, trying to work out a kink that he'd acquired while sleeping.

"Hey there." Justin took a seat on the opposite side of the counter.

"You been asleep 'till now?"

"Yeah. You?"

"Naw, I woke up a couple hours ago."

Byron rotated his head around a few more times. Then he said, "It's nice to wake up and know you're not dead."

"Sure is."

"You know what I was thinkin'?"

"What's that?"

"That we're like zombies. The five of us. We're like the undead up here."

Justin smiled. "Space zombies?"

"That's right – space zombies. I like that! We can form a band when we get back to Earth, call ourselves The Space Zombies."

Both men smiled.

"Although," Byron continued, lowering his voice, "I'm not sure I'll wanna hang out with everyone on this ship, after we get back home."

"I hear that."

"So you play any instruments?"

"No. Does that mean I can't be in the band?"

"Can you sing?"

"No."

Byron shrugged. "That's okay. You can still be in the band." Then he grew thoughtful. "Hey, you got family back down there, that you left behind?"

"Yeah. A mother, a brother, a sister, an ex-wife. You?"

Byron nodded. "I've got both parents, a five-year-old daughter, a girlfriend. I can't wait to seem 'em all again."

One of the other bedroom doors slid open and Calvin walked out. "Hey," he said, groggily, walking towards the counter.

"Hey," the other two replied.

"Sleep good?" Byron asked.

"Yeah, I guess. I dreamed I was on a spaceship and it had landed on Mars." Calvin smiled ironically and took a seat at the counter.

"So we were just talkin' 'bout our families back on Earth. How 'bout you? You leave people behind back there?"

Calvin nodded. "Yeah. My wife."

"You still married to her?"

"Yep. She stuck with me, through the whole thing."

"That's serious."

"Sure is. Now I just need to get back down there 'fore she hooks up with another guy. Been thinkin' 'bout that ever since I realized we're not really dead."

"You gonna tell her it's you when you see her?"

"Sure am. No way to avoid it. She's gonna know anyway. She'll figure it out in 'bout three seconds, no matter what they do to my face."

The other two nodded. As they were doing so, another door slid open and Troy walked out.

"Hey y'all," he said.

"Hey."

"You guys eaten breakfast yet?"

"Nope."

Troy looked over at the clock. It read 8:26.

"So what're y'all discussin'?" He pulled up a seat.

"The folks we left behind on Earth."

"Fun topic."

"What 'bout you? You leave anyone down there, other than your girl?"

Troy shrugged. "Not really."

"So Byron and me decided, we should form a band when we get back down there," Justin told Calvin and Troy. "We're callin' ourselves The Space Zombies."

"Ha!" Calvin laughed. "I like it."

"Can you sing?" Byron asked Calvin.

"No, but I can play guitar."

"You?" Byron asked Troy.

"Sure, I can sing."

"Alright!" Byron said. "And I can play the drums. So we've got a band."

"What 'bout you?" Troy asked Justin.

"I'm the manager."

Tristan's bedroom door slid open and Tristan strolled out. "Hey killers," he said, pulling up a chair.

"Hey," the others replied.

"What's the word?" Tristan asked.

"We're formin' a band," Troy told him.

"Oh yeah?"

"Yeah. Can you sing?"

"I can rap."

"You make stuff up?"

"Yeah, sure. I got some tracks."

"No kiddin'?

"Nope," Tristan shrugged. "So has everybody eaten already?"

"Not yet. We were just here talkin' bout the band, and 'bout our people back on Earth."

Tristan nodded. "I got two kids back down there. Someday I'll be tellin' 'em this story."

"Ain't we supposed to keep this a secret?" Troy asked.

"Forget that. Nobody gets to send me into space without askin' and then tell me what to do after I get back."

Troy glanced over at the flat screen TV, then leaned in towards the counter. "Don't you think that that rich dude might be listenin'?"

Tristan shrugged. "He's gotta be in his sixties, right. He can't be listenin' all the time."

"But he's gotta have hundreds a people workin' with him," Justin surmised. "Why can't he get someone else to listen to us when he's doin' somethin' else?"

Tristan shrugged again and rolled his eyes.

Eventually they all got up and began foraging through the plastic boxes for breakfast. Byron found some eggs and onions and announced that he was going to make omelets and would make one for anyone who was interested.

Calvin raised his hand. "Count me in, definitely."

"Yeah, thanks man," Justin said. "Me too."

"Real men don't eat omelets," Tristan opined, looking at Calvin, who ignored him.

"Oh yeah," Byron retorted, playfully, not angrily, not yet rising to the bait, "how would you know?"

Troy's eyes flicked towards Byron and then towards Tristan. He clearly wanted an omelet, but now Tristan was staring at him, waiting to see what he'd do. After a moment's hesitation, Troy said, "I'm gonna make me some sausages."

"Suit yourself." Byron pulled open one of the round wall's built-in cabinets; this one held utensils, as they'd discovered the night before. "Hey, Calvin, Justin, there're two chef's knives in here – one a you wanna help me chop the onions?"

"I'm game," Calvin answered, before Justin had a chance to.

"Thanks," Byron said, and he handed Calvin one of the knives.

Tristan studied the two men for a few seconds, noting the fact of them holding the knives, then he went back to making himself whatever sort of breakfast it was that real men eat. Once this was done, he pulled up a seat at the counter, next to Troy, and the two of them began talking between themselves. In the meantime Byron had launched into some story that he was telling Calvin, about one of his experiences working at some terrible sounding restaurant, and Calvin was laughing and enjoying Byron's company.

'So it begins,' Justin thought, looking at the two pairs.

Already it was clear that Tristan wasn't going to corral Calvin. Thus the teams had formed even quicker than anticipated. Now Justin was left to choose sides. He knew how this worked. For a little while his independence would give him power, as each team tried to persuade him to join them. But if he didn't choose quickly then he'd get sidelined in the evolving dynamic. And sidelined didn't mean "left alone." It meant "ally-less pawn." That was the worst position to be in, because pawns get sacrificed. So he'd have to choose sides. Such was the nature of anarchy.

It'd been the same way in prison. Of course in prison there are guards, and everyone else is locked up, so to an outside observer it looks like a controlled environment. But control isn't determined by bars and walls and guards. It's determined by whether or not, most of the time, people are willing to abide by the rules. When you've got a community in which nearly everybody – the inmates – are certified rule-breakers, then you've got anarchy. And when you're in anarchy you need allies. Allies mean gangs. And gangs mean fights. So the question now was, would these characters on the shuttle – these five guys who'd all broken THE rule: thou shalt not kill – would they abide by Baker's rules in order to get back to Earth, or would the logic of anarchy override even that?

'Yeah,' Justin thought, while he sat there waiting for his omelet. 'Probably.'

VIII

"Greetings, gentlemen," Baker said, as the screen in the round room switched on at exactly 10:00. "Everyone sleep well, eat well?"

The men nodded.

"Glad to hear it. I can imagine that before long your surroundings are going to start to seem almost normal to you. Although that probably isn't going to happen today, because today we're going to get you into your spacesuits and let you do something that no human being has ever done: walk around on the surface of Mars!"

Justin and Byron nodded, Calvin smiled eagerly, Troy looked anxious, and Tristan didn't do anything.

"So, are you ready to get going?"

They all nodded.

"Great. Now please walk over to the first right-hand container space in the hallway – the same one where you've been getting your food."

They did as directed, opening the container space's door.

"Now then," Baker explained, as his voice transmitted through the onboard intercom system, "we're going to need you to unload all those boxes in that area and place them out in the hallway. At the back of that container space are your spacesuits, as well as the airlock, which is how you're going to access the outside. So if you could please move those boxes out into the hall, then we can proceed."

The men did as directed; the moving process took about half an hour. And sure enough, as they hauled out the final stack of black plastic boxes, they saw the five spacesuits hanging on pegs against the far wall. A thick door – evidently leading to the airlock – was set into the back right-hand corner of the container space, and a control panel with lights and screens and buttons was built into the wall immediately to the left of that door.

The suits were what one would expect – with buttons and gauges built into the torso area; a built-in backpack of sorts; weighted boots – although these suits were butterscotch-reddish rather than the traditional white. Each suit had the last name of one of the five men sewn into it over the left breast. Glass-domed helmets were set on the ground beside the suits, and next to each helmet were a pair of space gloves. Light weight pieces of full-body clothing with tubes running through them hung beside the suits on pegs.

Byron was pleased to see the suit that had been specially tailored for his large frame "Look at this! Look at my spacesuit!"

"Nice. Very nice," Tristan concurred, examining his own.

"Cool," Justin agreed.

"Can we put them on now?" Calvin asked.

"Three of you can," Baker replied. "I'd like two of you to stay inside. Allow me to explain why. I want someone to stand next to the airlock, in case anything happens while the others are outside. And I also want one of you to sit in the cockpit. Some of the instruments in that cockpit will provide feedback on the spacesuits and the people who are in them, having to do with your vital signs and so forth. If anything goes wrong with you or with the suit, we'll know it instantly. There're also backup controls in the cockpit in case the airlock door jams or if you need to keep it shut. So I'm going to train each of you on how to man each station as you rotate through the different roles."

Baker paused for effect, then he told them, "Now, the moment has arrived to make a big decision: who gets to be the first man to walk on Mars?"

"Doesn't have to be me," Troy announced.

"I'll do it," Tristan said.

"I can do it," Calvin added, eagerly.

"I said I got this."

"I vote for Calvin," Byron said.

Tristan scowled at Byron and Calvin. Then everyone turned to Justin to see what he would say.

"Calvin," he voted.

Tristan scowled all the more, and Calvin beamed.

"Alright then," Baker nodded. "Who's going with him?"

"I'm definitely doin' that," Tristan insisted.

"Alright. And we need a third."

Byron and Justin looked at each other and both shrugged.

"You can go," Justin offered.

"No, man, I mean, if you really wanna...."

"Why don't you rock-paper-scissors it," Troy suggested.

Which they did, and Justin won.

"Fine. So now," Baker announced, "it's time to suit up. You'll find that the suits are fairly easy to slip in and out of. They're designed to be comfortable, at least once you're outside. The first thing you'll need to do is take that lighter garment that's next to each of your suits, unbutton that down the middle and step into it. That undergarment has a heating and cooling system built into it, and it'll keep the temperature inside the suit at a comfortable level while you're working outside."

The three men did as instructed.

"Great. Now you can put on the spacesuit itself."

Baker walked them through that process. Once all three of them were suited up, he told them, "Now, underneath each of your helmets there's a cloth headset piece that you'll need to put on. And after you've got those on, please put on the helmets."

After the headsets and helmets were on, Baker said, "You'll note the two buttons on the left sides of your helmets. One links you up to the general intercom system. The other activates a video camera that's built into your helmet, so that I can see what you're seeing. If you'd now please push both of those buttons."

They did so.

"Great. And now please put on the gloves."

This was quickly done.

"And there we have it!" Baker announced. "Our astronauts! Our Martian pilgrims!"

"Gotta admit," Tristan said, from inside his helmet, "I feel like a bad dude."

"We look like bad dudes," Calvin concurred.

Justin nodded. "Yeah we do."

"How much do each a these suits cost to make? Tristan asked.

"You don't want to know," Baker assured him. "It would only get in the way of your work."

"I'm bettin' it costs more than my first car," Calvin assumed.

"I'll bet it costs more than your last car," Tristan opined.

"What's the temperature outside right now? Justin asked.

"Our instruments show that it's about twenty degrees Fahrenheit.

Should get up to about the mid-thirties later today. But you won't feel that inside the suits. They'll keep you close to sixty-five degrees at all times."

The three suited men walked around awkwardly in their suits for about a minute, the weights in their boots pulling down on their legs, the helmets restricting their peripheral vision, and their thick gloves making it more difficult to clasp objects.

"You'll get the hang of it," Baker assured them. "And there's no better way to do that than to do it. So," and the excitement in his voice was palpable, "shall we send you out there?"

"Roger that, Houston!" Calvin said.

"Hey, that reminds me, speakin' a Houston," Byron said. "I've been meanin' to ask you, Baker – where are you, exactly?"

"Nevada."

"Like near Vegas?"

"Let's just say, somewhere in Nevada."

"Is that where this shuttle launched from? Nevada?"

"Perhaps."

"Oh, what, it's top secret?"

"Very much so."

"Why's that?"

"A variety of reasons. One of which has to do with what's about to happen next."

"What? You mean these three headin' outside?"

"Heading outside, and surviving. Let's just say that I have about a seventy-three to seventy-five percent certainty that everything is going to go right as we proceed here. But that does leave a little room for error. And if these three fellows suddenly can't breathe out there, for instance, then I don't want that image broadcast to every video screen on Earth. As you can imagine, that would put a little crimp in our ability to enlist more volunteers for the colony once we go public about our activities."

"So they could like die now?" Troy asked.

"Most likely no. If they can't breathe, they can just step back inside the shuttle and close the airlock. But if they get down on the surface and their suits give out, and all they're breathing-in is carbon dioxide – which is what's out there – and they start to panic, or get dizzy, or suffocate quicker than expected, then obviously that would be problematic."

The three suited men exchanged glances.

"Like I said," Baker reminded them, "this is an experiment. As a result of which there will be moments of relative danger. This is one of them. So let's get to it before we start thinking about it too much."

"Aren't these the same sort a suits astronauts wore on the moon, and on that International Space Station thing, and all that?" Justin asked, seeking reassurance.

"Actually yours are more advanced than those. They're the latest model and then some. But Mars isn't the Moon, much less the International Space Station. Mars' atmosphere, for instance, is thinner than Earth's, which means that it doesn't dilute the rays of the sun as much as Earth's atmosphere does, so there are radiation issues to consider. Of course that's the case on the Moon as well, but Mars also has other characteristics, such as wind, and therefore blowing sand and so forth, which makes everything a little trickier."

"Wait, so it's radioactive out there?" Calvin was now a little less enthusiastic about being the first man to set foot on Mars.

"Not radioactive, no. Just imagine if you were to lie outside in the sun all day without sunscreen. It's like that, only more so. But you don't need to worry about that since the suits are designed to protect you from exposure to any of that."

"Unless the suits don't work," Justin added.

"Right. But I think they will. So let's get to it, shall we. Now, I'm going to need Byron to man the airlock, which means that he'll need to handle that control panel that you can see there next to the interior airlock door."

"Mannin' the airlock," Byron said, walking up to the panel.

"Now Troy, I want you positioned in the cockpit, watching the feedback data, and handling the backup system, just in case."

"Okay...." So Troy walked down the hallway and took up position in the cockpit.

"Great. Now Byron, please push the big yellow button at the top of that control panel there in front of you."

Byron did as instructed, and the airlock's interior door slid open. The airlock was about ten feet by ten feet, with a second door set into the exterior wall. On the airlock's floor, to the left side of the door, was what appeared to be a collapsed, retractable metal ladder, and next to that was a large metal box.

"Great. Now Calvin, Tristan and Justin, in you go."

The three astronauts stepped cautiously into the airlock.

"Now Byron, please push that black button that's just below the yellow button."

Byron did so and the airlock's interior door slid closed.

"Great. Now Byron, please push the red button, at the bottom of that panel, just below the black button."

Byron pushed the red button, and the airlock's exterior door slid open, revealing, there in front of the three suited men, the vast, endless, empty expanse of brownish-pinkish-reddish Martian landscape.

Calvin gasped. Justin's eyebrows rose up his forehead. Tristan didn't display any reaction, but certainly he was feeling the same thing as his companions. They'd been incarcerated for so long, kept inside such constricted environments, that the impact of suddenly being faced with absolute openness, without any physical barrier between themselves and the horizon, was overwhelming.

"Gentlemen?" Baker asked. "Your first impressions?"

There was a long pause, then Calvin answered, "It's nice to be able to go outside. That's all I can say."

"Real nice," Justin concurred.

Tristan nodded.

"How's the flow of oxygen inside your helmets?"

"Fine."

"It's good."

"Yeah."

"Excellent," Baker said. "Now, here's what comes next...."

He explained to them how to hook the retractable ladder onto the edges of the exterior door, and then push the ladder out of the shuttle so that it mechanically unfolded, one step after another, until it reached the Martian ground approximately twenty feet below. Once the final step extended, a railing automatically rose up on the left side of the stairs.

"Great," Baker said. "Now down you go."

The three men looked at each other.

"You first, remember," Tristan said to Calvin.

"Okay...." Calvin acknowledged, taking a deep breath.

"You already died once," Tristan reminded him. "What're you afraid of?"

"That's the thing. After doin' that once, I don't ever wanna do it again."

"You'll be fine," Baker reassured him. "Just go slow and don't lose hold of the railing. And remember, once you're outside the shuttle, you'll be directly subjected to the planet's natural gravitational pull. Don't let that throw you. The best way to deal with it is to hold onto the rail at all times, sliding your hand down it, rather than re-clasping it with each step."

"…Right."

Calvin grabbed hold of the rail and took his first step.

"There you go," Baker encouraged him.

Calvin took a second step, and then a third, at which point the gravitational shift really hit him. "Whoah!" He said, twisting his torso so that he could grab the rail with his right hand as well as his left.

"Got it?" Baker asked.

"Yeah, I'm cool. No joke 'bout that gravity change."

"Gravity is not a joke."

Steadying himself, Calvin made his way slowly down the rest of the stairs, letting go of the rail with his right hand just before reaching the ground.

"Alright now…." Baker announced, as Calvin arrived at the final step.

And thus, and there, and then, it happened. Over one hundred and forty million miles from Earth, amidst the near-perfect silence of the empty desert landscape, Calvin's space boot touched down softly upon the sandy surface of Mars.

"That's one small step for an ex-con," Baker declared, "and one giant, top-secret leap for mankind!"

"Wooo!" Calvin shouted, his voice echoing across the intercom system. "Made it! I'm walkin' on Mars!" He staggered a bit as he adjusted to the gravitational pull.

"Alright now," Baker said, "who's next?"

"I'm up," Tristan said. He grabbed the railing aggressively, then stepped down the stairs in a determined fashion, first one step then another. Around the third step, however, as with Calvin, the gravitational change hit him and he wobbled, but he didn't call out, and he was clearly too macho to use both hands to grip the rail. After a few seconds of steadying himself, he stepped the rest of the way down, very deliberately, and took the last step onto the ground like he was stomping on a bug he wanted to kill. "That's me!" He announced, loudly. "I'm on Mars! Tristan Martin is on Mars!" He raised his hands in the air like he was being cheered by a live audience. "Thank you! Thank you all!"

"And now Justin," Baker said.

Justin stepped onto the ledge of the shuttle and looked out at the endless sea of sand and rocks. For the first time in a very long time, he felt an emotion which he'd assumed – without even realizing that he'd made this assumption – he'd never feel again: namely, joy. Exhilaration. A feeling that there was a reason to be alive, to be a human being. And so he smiled.

Then he grabbed the railing and took a step. Once this first step was completed, he paused. Then he took the next step, waiting for the gravitational change to hit him. As his foot lifted for the third step he felt the change begin, so he kept his foot suspended for a few seconds, then slowly set it down, allowing the new quotient of pull to take his foot down for him at its own rate. As a result, unlike the first two men, he arrived at the third step steadily, and was then able to proceed slowly but easily from there down to the ground.

"Very nice form," Baker complimented him.

Justin's boot touched the Martian surface and he exhaled with an "Ahhh." After a few wobbling paces, he began turning around slowly in a circle. The sheer room for maneuver made him giddy. He was also struck by the huge size of the shuttle, which he could now appreciate in full. Calvin and Tristan, meanwhile, were likewise turning this way and that, taking in the view, exhilarated.

"Someone should write a book," Byron suggested, as his voice was carried through the all-encompassing intercom system via a speaker on the airlock's control panel, "and call it *Cons on Mars*."

"No one's going to be writing anything about any of this," Baker told him. "We'll just have to enjoy it for ourselves."

"I'm enjoyin' it just fine," Calvin confirmed.

"Baker," Justin said, "you know that feelin' you get, when you go to the ocean, and you look at it, and it just feels like everythin's open?"

"I know exactly what you mean."

"That's how it feels up here. Right now that's how I'm feelin'. I wanna thank you for this. I can't even remember the last time I felt this."

"My pleasure, Justin."

Then the minutes drifted off into the distance, as the three men danced and pranced and strutted and laughed. Eventually Baker asked them, "How's the breathing out there? No issues, I gather?"

"No, it's fine."

"Great. Now Troy, I want to explain what all those instrument readings are showing there in front of you in the cockpit...."

And Baker walked Troy through the details. This done, he said, "Now Troy, see that switch to your left, the large black one, above the pressure-gauge screen?"

"Uh...yeah."

"Don't touch it for the moment, but if you flip that switch, then the button just below it turns yellow, and once it turns yellow, it'll allow you to open or shut the exterior and interior airlock doors. If for any reason the airlock panel buttons aren't working, you'll have that cockpit button as the backup. Got it?"

"Uh...yeah. Sure."

"Good."

IX

Baker asked Byron and Troy to switch places after about thirty minutes so that they could each get used to the other station. When the full hour had passed, the other three men returned to the shuttle so that Byron and Troy could then take their turns walking on Mars.

Troy looked nearly nauseous as he stepped out onto the ladder, he almost lost control on the way down, and for the first several minutes he barely stepped more than a few paces in any one direction on the planet's surface. Byron, in contrast, was having a great time, laughing and singing and dancing and providing continuous commentary over the intercom system. He and Troy were, like the first three, given an hour outside, while the others were instructed on the intricacies of the two stations.

After that second hour was up the two men were asked to return to the shuttle and then the five-man crew was given two hours to eat lunch and relax. They were all excited – even Troy – after walking around amidst so much open space, so they chatted happily, and even Tristan was relatively non-hostile. At the end of this two-hour stretch Baker's face reappeared on the round room's screen.

"Now that you're all fed and rested," he announced, "it's time to begin prepping for tomorrow's work load. Tomorrow we begin building the garden. And this garden – this first garden – is the key to everything we're doing up there."

"Like the Garden of Eden of Mars," Calvin said.

"Yeah, but without no Eve," Tristan noted.

"What makes you think we won't be sending women up there?" Baker asked.

Tristan shrugged. "Are you?"

"Of course."

The men all considered this.

"Then maybe I'll stay here," Tristan replied, "if you're sendin' up a steady supply a ladies."

Baker looked at and through Tristan. "That's not going to be possible. We've already decided who's going to get to stay up there and who – like yourselves – will have to leave."

Tristan frowned.

"Now then, gentlemen," Baker said, "I have an academic question for you. Who was Mars?"

"What?"

"Mars? Who was he? Who is that planet named after?"

"He was a god, right?" Calvin answered.

"Correct. And from which mythology? Was he Greek, Roman, Hindu, what?"

"Greek?"

"No, he was Roman. And do any of you know – or can you guess – what he was the god of? The gods in Roman mythology had specific roles; certain gods were in charge of fertility, or the weather, etc. Anyone know what Mars' role was?"

The men all shrugged, shaking their heads.

"He was the god of war," Baker informed them.

"No kiddin'?"

"Indeed. And the planet Mars got its name because its red color evidently reminded people of blood and hence war, and because, when Mars was observed by the Romans, they saw that it behaved differently than the stars. It appeared to be unpredictable and erratic in its movements, and the Romans equated that with being menacing, and menacing equated with war. Of course Mars' seemingly peculiar movement is due to the fact that it's a planet, not a star. Apparently the Romans didn't fully grasp that point. So that planet you're on is named after the war god."

"That's kind a cool," Tristan said.

"Yeah it is," Byron concurred.

Baker nodded. "Yes, but Mars also had another role; one for which he's given less credit. He was also a protector of agriculture. Now, think about this: we – and more specifically, you – are about to construct the first garden – the first agricultural space – on a planet named after a god who was the protector of agriculture. This is going to be the first of many gardens, the mother of all the agriculture that will ever transpire on that planet, and if all goes according to plan, and if terraforming is possible, then tomorrow will truly be the beginning of something magnificent."

Baker paused to gauge their reactions, and could instantly see that none of them were quite as excited about this as he was.

"In any case, what we'll need you to do now is arrange certain boxes in certain places. As previously mentioned, the boxes to focus on for the moment are marked "AB1." Most of the boxes that you moved out of your way to get to your spacesuits have those markings. And then there are some others in other container spaces. We're going to want you to stack all of those near the airlock, three high and three wide. That's what our external lift system can accommodate. But arrange them so that you can still access the airlock door. Alright? So why don't we get on with that, and while you're moving and stacking I'll explain some more details about our Mars garden."

Thus their work began. For the next two hours the men stacked boxes while Baker told them first about how a garden had already been established on the International Space Station, so setting up a garden away from Earth was nothing new. Their Martian garden, however, would be the first garden on the surface of another planet.

Baker then explained that experiments had already been run by scientists, back on Earth, in which soil conditions roughly equivalent to Martian soil had been tested to see if those conditions could sustain the growth of various vegetables. These experiments had produced some encouraging results, although nothing could be considered conclusive until the soil on Mars itself was tested. So soil testing was a primary task.

Radiation was another issue. Since Mars' atmosphere is far less dense than Earth's, and hence lacks the same filter for solar radiation, the level of radiation hitting plants on Mars would differ substantially from what plants back on Earth are subjected to.

And then of course there was the water issue. Although scientific instruments had indicated that significant quantities of water might exist in particular areas of Mars, there wasn't immediately accessible ground water anywhere near to where the shuttle had landed.

Finally, there was the issue of gravity: would plant roots dig deep enough, and would plant stalks stretch tall enough, in an environment with only thirty-eight percent as much gravitational pull as plants are used to?

These were all delicious challenges to overcome, as far as Baker was concerned, and he relished the telling of them even if he knew that the men onboard the ship were less viscerally enthusiastic. So as the five astronauts stacked and arranged boxes, paying only partial attention to him, he explained how the water issue would be addressed thanks to a nearly closed-loop hydration system, via which all the water onboard – gray water, brown water, etc. – was continually recycled to provide a steady supply for both men and plants. But that system would still lose water over time, especially since it would be necessary at some point to activate the electrolysis system onboard the shuttle, whereby the oxygen and hydrogen molecules in a portion of the water supply would be broken apart and the oxygen made available for breathing. Which meant that it was imperative to eventually locate a Martian source of water.

As for the radiation issue, that would be dealt with via specially-designed solar panels which ensured that the level and type of radiation reaching certain plants would approximate what they were used to back on Earth.

As for the soil issue, large quantities of enriched Earth soil were already stored on the shuttle, and there were mechanisms onboard for composting, but the men would also be running experiments to try to grow plants in Martian soil samples.

Finally, the gravity issue would be addressed by using vegetable seeds which had been genetically mixed with the genes from shrubs which grow in extraordinarily adverse, desert conditions on Earth, so that the new hybrid roots would shoot aggressively through the soil, even without an Earth-level gravitational pull.

What all of this entailed, therefore, was that the garden would have three main compartments: one for testing whether the hybridized plants could grow in Earth soil when placed under energy lamps; one for running soil experiments, in which hybridized seeds would be placed in planter boxes containing Martian soil, situated under energy lamps; and one for running radiation experiments, in which hybridized plants in Earth soil would be placed under two translucent panels, one of which filtered the Martian light and one of which did not. There would also be a smaller, fourth compartment where air and water for the garden would be temporarily stored after being sent from the shuttle to the garden.

"Any questions so far?" Baker asked.

None of the men had any.

"Good. So then, after you finish the stacking and arranging for today, you can relax, and I'll see you all again tomorrow at 10:00."

There was about an hour and a half's worth of work left to do, and after it was done the men spent the rest of the afternoon and evening at their leisure. There wasn't any TV programming in space, evidently, or internet, so they were obliged to amuse themselves. Eventually it was decided that Tristan should perform one of his raps, and he accordingly obliged. It was awful and awesome at the same time, and the other men laughed and applauded and hooted, slapping the counter top in rhythm to form a background beat. When he finished, Tristan took a bow, and the others rose to their feet and clapped some more. At which point – and for the first time since he'd woken up on Mars – Tristan smiled a natural, non-menacing smile.

"Drinks on me!" He announced.

"Now *that* is a generous offer," Byron replied, and the men filed into the container space and helped themselves to various fizzy waters and juices.

"Man, the lack of alcohol on this ship is a cyrin' shame!" Byron declared, as he flipped open the lid to a bottle of sparkling grape juice.

"I haven't had a beer in over five years," Troy noted. "I can't even remember what one tastes like."

"I can," Justin said, his thoughts immediately reverting to the last time he'd been a free man – to that bar, where he'd gotten in a fight, and then....

"So can I," Calvin added. "I was sittin' out in my backyard, with my lady, on the deck. It was summertime...." His voice trailed off.

"When you get back to Earth you can sit out there again and have another beer," Troy said. "You got somethin' to look forward to."

"I'm lookin' forward to a lot more than drinkin' beer."

"I hear that!" Tristan declared, smiling easily again, as if it was a normal thing to do.

'Hmm,' Justin thought, as he contemplated Tristan's increasingly relaxed demeanor. 'Maybe this isn't gonna be so bad after all. Maybe we'll be able to get through this trip without things gettin' out a hand.'

X

A serious confrontation transpired at the end of the second week.

The first week went relatively smoothly. Baker showed them how to operate the lift – it was that large metal box inside the airlock, next to the retractable ladder, which, like the ladder, hooked onto the side of the airlock's exterior door frame. After it was hooked onto the door and then pushed overboard it unfolded automatically and revealed a mechanized pallet which rested on top of a motor. The pallet rose or descended the distance between the airlock's door and the planet's surface, depending on whether a yellow or red button was pushed on a small control panel which was built into the mechanical arm that connected the lift to the airlock's door.

After this was explained, the men were able to start the process of loading black plastic boxes onto the pallet, sending them down to the Martian surface, carrying those boxes over to predetermined locations, then beginning the process all over again. And again. And again....

It took nearly the entire first week to get the ship unloaded and to remove the contents from some of the boxes, with the five-man team putting in six-hour days, working in shifts, and with none of them staying outside the shuttle for more than an hour and forty-five minutes at a time.

The work absorbed their attention and energy; as a result, in the evenings their conversations were fairly relaxed. But Justin could tell that the glow was slowly wearing off of Tristan's mood. He didn't have enough raps to maintain himself permanently in the spotlight, and once that method of controlling the situation ceased to be an option, it was only a matter of time before he started digging at Byron again to try to spark a showdown.

"Dude, how much you weigh?"

Tristan asked Byron this question during dinner on the seventh evening. The way he asked it wasn't casual, wasn't friendly.

"Whad'a you care?" Byron shrugged him off, although there was an edge to his voice. His patience was clearly beginning to wear.

"Curious. Whad're ya – 300 pounds?"

"Shut up, man."

Tristan grinned. "350?"

"Man," Byron replied, shaking his head, "you're so ghetto, you probably don't even know how to weigh yourself, so what difference does it make?"

Tristan grinned wider, pleased to have hit a nerve. "375?"

Calvin leaned back in his chair, folded his arms across his chest and nodded at Tristan. "You never have used a scale, have you?" He was making his stand, showing that he was strongly in Byron's camp and was ready to face down Tristan if need be.

Tristan turned to Calvin and his grin melted off his face. "Was I talkin' to you?"

"I don't care what you were doin'."

Troy's eyes flicked from Tristan, to Calvin, to Byron, then back to Tristan.

Meanwhile Justin polished off a space burger, then he turned to Byron and asked him, just to change the subject, "You said you're from Tucson, right?"

"Yeah, why?"

"That's down near the border, right?"

"Sure is."

"You got good Mexican food down there?"

Byron shrugged. "Yeah, I guess. Why?"

"I was just thinkin' I could really go for a good tortilla right now. I am missin' Mexican food."

"I love Mexican food," Troy piped up.

"See, I don't like that stuff at all," Calvin said.

And the conversation headed off in a new direction....

But the storm was coming. Seven days later it began to break.

They spent that second week removing the final contents from the boxes they'd stacked outside the ship – most of which consisted of the component pieces of the garden – and then constructing the garden itself. This task was accomplished by fitting together hundreds of panels – each one was rectangular-shaped, butterscotch-reddish, a foot-long, and one-inch thick – which were made, as Baker explained, from a specially designed synthetic material which was able to withstand extreme levels of radiation and was also ideal for holding in oxygen and moisture. The panels simply snapped together, and after they were thus joined the rubber lining along their sides sealed the join-line so that the connection point became air tight.

Each of the garden's three main compartments – the soil testing room, the radiation testing room, and the gravity testing room – were ten feet by eight feet. The room housing the air and water storage equipment was six feet by four feet.

In order to lay down the snap-together floor, the men first needed to prepare the ground, which meant removing the rocks and smoothing out the sand, after which the floor was set in place.

Next came the walls. The compartments were all separated by walls, but with a three foot by five foot opening in each one, leading to the next compartment. The entrance to the garden was through the small air-and-water storage room, which in turn had an exterior door which was also made from the snap together panels. However, in the area where the door was, the panels were fitted together so that designated sides – marked S1 – lined up with each other and in so doing created a hinge effect along that side. The rest of the door's rim was made by joining the panel sides marked S2, which allowed the connections between the panels along those sides to separate easily. The same sort of door was also set into the opening between this small room and the next room so that the small room could function as an airlock for the garden.

Finally the roof was built. In the radiation-testing compartment they left two open spaces in the roof and into one of these spaces was fitted a specialized solar panel which filtered the external radiation, while into the second space they fit a translucent panel which allowed radiation to enter unfiltered.

Thus the garden's external structure was completed by the end of the second week.

The men felt proud of what they'd accomplished; it was the first meaningful work they'd been allowed to do in years. And as a result the conversation started out on an agreeable note that evening. But it didn't stay that way for long.

Byron and Calvin were chopping vegetables for a stew that Byron wanted to make; it was from a recipe he'd learned from a Cajun chef. They were sitting at the round counter, using the two chef's knives, and when Tristan decided he wanted to slice up something – although what it was wasn't clear, since all he ever ate was beef stew and chicken stew, both of which came out of a can – he said to Calvin,

"Hey, give me that knife you got there."

"I'll give it to you when I'm done with it."

"I think you ought'a give it to me now."

"You know what I'd like to give you right now?" Byron said.

"Oh now that's real cute," Tristan replied. "Standin' up for your girlfriend. That touches my heart. How sweet."

"Actually, see a girlfriend," Calvin explained, "implies a female. I guess no one ever explained that to you."

"Man, I was gettin' ladies and killin' the competition 'fore you even knew your own name."

"Yeah, you're such a tough guy, we know," Byron replied, rolling his eyes.

"Man you got no idea. You got no idea what I seen."

"How's that possible? All you been doin' since you woke up on Mars is tryin' to convince the rest of us what a gangster you are."

"Convince? What you talkin', convince? I am that! That's all I am, all the time. I don't need a convince nobody a that!"

"Then why you tryin' so hard?"

"I'm not tryin' nothin', fool! I could kill you in my sleep, that's how bad I am."

"Man, the only thing that dies when you go to sleep is the sound a your big mouth."

Calvin and Justin both laughed, which triggered a deeper level of aggression in Tristan.

"Alright, c'mon," he told Byron, gesturing that he wanted to fight. "Let's do this, right now. You and me."

Troy stood up from the round counter and took a few steps away. Both Justin and Calvin frowned, and Byron took a deep breath, shook his head, and looked Tristan in the eye.

"You really wanna do this? Seriously?"

"What, you scared? I'll take you down even if you keep holdin' that knife."

"Man, you're crazy."

"Yeah, maybe. But I been fightin' all my life, so why stop now?"

"Uhh, because you're on a spaceship on Mars, maybe."

"Yeah, that's right. We're on a planet named after the war god. Perfect for me. And you – you just a short order cook who's too scared to put down that knife."

Byron frowned, took another deep breath, then handed the knife to Calvin and rose to his feet. "Alright, fine. You wanna do this, tough guy. Let's do this."

As the two men hunkered into crouched positions, fists raised like boxers, Calvin and Troy backed away to opposite sides of the round room like coaches in a boxing match.

At which point Justin jumped to his feet and inserted his frame between the impending combatants.

"We are definitely *not* doin' this!" He insisted.

"Get out a my way, fool!" Tristan ordered him.

"Yeah, Justin," Byron added, "might as well take care a this here and now. I'm not puttin' up with this guy's attitude for another three and a half months. He needs to understand the ways things are gonna be."

"Wait a second!" Justin shot back at both of them. "Think 'bout this! Think 'bout what Baker told us. Remember? He said if we're gonna finish the work he's got for us, we're gonna have to do it together. If we don't, if we don't finish this job, whad' ya think's gonna happen?"

"Whad' ya mean?" Troy asked, suddenly unsettled.

"Think 'bout it!" Justin demanded again. "We're a bunch a ex-cons. Actually we're still cons, and if anybody finds out who we are when we get back to Earth they'll throw us back in prison and finish us off right this time. We got nothin', no hope, no nothin', other than what Baker gives us. If he decides we're too much trouble, whad' ya think he's gonna do?"

"Whad' ya sayin'?" Byron asked.

Justin shrugged. "What if he decides not to send a second ship? What if he decides not to let us return? To get home?"

"Fool!" Tristan spat out the word. "Baker's gotta bring us back. What choice he got?"

"Choice?" Justin replied. "He's got all the choices! He sent us up here. If he doesn't like what we do, he can pull the plug, and no one'll be the wiser. We'll just die up here. Run out a food, or water, or air."

"He can't do that," Tristan disagreed. "He needs us."

"Now who's bein' a fool? Man, think 'bout it – what'd he say is the one thing he believes in? Remember?"

"Securitization," Calvin answered, on everyone's behalf.

"Right," Justin said. "Not puttin' all his eggs in one basket. You think he hasn't thought this through, planned for this contingency? You think that guy got that rich by bein' that stupid? If we don't work out for him, he's gonna cut us off!"

Justin paused for effect and allowed this point to sink in. In truth, he'd been planning this speech – at least the broad strokes of it – for the last few days, ever since he'd realized that a Tristan-Byron confrontation was inevitable.

"I wanna get back to Earth," he continued, driving home the point. "I wanna do all the things I never thought I was gonna do again, soon as I got that death sentence. I wanna do all those things. We all do. So let's not mess this up! All we gotta do is get through the next couple months, finish whatever work we gotta do, then get on that second ship. So let's focus on that! Let's stay focused on that second ship! We do that, we get out a here."

Byron nodded. "I don't wanna die up here. But Tristan, man, you gotta dial it back. I'm not kiddin'."

"I don't gotta do nothin'."

Calvin stepped forward and, handle first, offered Tristan one of the chef's knives. "You said you gotta cut somethin' with this, right?"

The tension in the room dissolved. Calvin's timing was perfect. Tristan had no choice but to frown a smile, then he took the knife, and that was the end of it.

The following week was spent installing equipment in the garden. It took three full days to set up the water and oxygen storage tanks in the small compartment; two more days to set up the hi-tech planter boxes – essentially glass-like aquariums with energy lamps on top – in the gravity-testing compartment; another day to set up similar planter boxes for testing how well plants grew in different samplings of Martian soil; and another day to set up planter boxes without energy lamps, which were connected via enclosed shafts to either the translucent or filtered ceiling panels in the radiation testing room.

Tristan managed to keep his aggressive tendencies under control throughout that week, but everyone could feel the tension returning.

In the evenings Tristan and Troy would settle in the corner of one of the partially-emptied container spaces, to talk between themselves. The other men would either linger in the round room, talking about whatever, or they'd go and lounge in their respective bedrooms until they fell asleep. Other routines arose as well. For instance, there was a treadmill that they'd unpacked during the first week, which Tristan, Justin and Calvin all used, and the three of them established a de-facto schedule so that there weren't any disputes over who got to use it when.

The next week – the fourth week – felt surreal for all of them, since that was the week they began using all the testing equipment they'd installed in the garden's three main compartments. Neither Tristan nor Troy had ever finished high school, and Byron had just barely finished. Justin did somewhat better; after high school he took extended education courses at a university. As for Calvin, his highest academic attainment was an associate degree from a community college. Yet now here they were, the five of them, carrying out experiments which the most highly educated, hard-core careerist scientists would have killed to be able to perform.

They collected Martian soil samples and placed those samples in various planter boxes, then seeded the soil for carrots and potatoes. They placed tomato seeds in the Earth-based soil boxes that were located in the gravity testing compartment. And they placed Earth soil in the boxes in the radiation testing room, then seeded the soil with mustard plant. As Baker instructed them to do, they conducted daily analyses of any plant growth in the boxes, made charts reflecting any observable changes, then entered all that data into onboard computers.

They used a device which looked like a hi-tech barcode scanner to scan the soil, inspecting each planter box for signs of microorganisms. If any such signs occurred, they were to take a small bottle labeled XYZ and drip – very carefully – a drop of its contents into the relevant soil. As Baker explained, the liquid inside the XYZ bottle had been designed by his scientists to kill living organisms other than plants.

"So then we're gonna eat plants that've sucked up that poison?" Troy asked, horrified.

"The chemical compound breaks down in the soil after two days. You don't have anything to worry about."

The men tried not to worry, and focused instead on their work.

At one point, while Byron was entering some data into the onboard computer, he turned to Justin and said, "Man, you know what song I got goin' through my head, over and over, while we're doin' all this?"

"What's that?"

""Harder Than You Think," by Public Enemy."

"Ahhh yeah."

And thus they conducted science. By the end of that fourth week they were all feeling pleased with themselves. And who knows, perhaps things could have gone on like that for a little while longer. But then it came time to assemble the rover and begin near-area reconnaissance….

XI

"Now then," Baker announced enthusiastically, "it's time to go for a drive!"

It was the first morning of the fifth week, 10:00 sharp, and the men were sitting around the circular counter as usual.

"As you may be aware, NASA has already sent a series of rovers to Mars. Three of them: *Spirit*, *Opportunity*, and *Curiosity*. Of course those aren't manned rovers, but the technology is essentially the same as what we used for our rover, which is convenient. The main thing we had to do was add a steering wheel and a seat to a close cousin of the *Curiosity* model."

As Baker spoke his face on the screen was replaced by a three-dimensional graphic of the *Curiosity*, with its rectangular, box-shaped body, its six treaded wheels and its multiple extension arms and mounted cameras. Images of a seat and a steering wheel were then superimposed onto it.

"And there you have it. That's your vehicle. We need to unload its parts, assemble it, and then we'll start taking it out for some test drives."

"I'm definitely goin' first on that one. This time it's me," Tristan announced.

"I appreciate your enthusiasm, Tristan," Baker replied, "but once again, Calvin will go first."

"What? Why?"

"Clearly, he's the most scientifically inclined."

"What's that got to do with anythin'? We're just takin' that rover out for a drive."

"That's precisely what we're not simply doing. We will need to proceed cautiously, analytically. Even though we have spare parts onboard, we can't risk too many accidents. So the first few rides will be taken by Calvin, since I know this sort of work will appeal to him the most. Once he's made a few runs then we'll start rotating the rest of you out there to do reconnaissance missions."

Tristan frowned, Calvin beamed, and then the work began. They unloaded the boxes containing the tan and red rover parts and then spent three days putting it all together. Once this was done, Baker told them to enter a code into a computer in the cockpit; when that code was entered a small door slid open on the shuttle's exterior, revealing a hi-tech electrical outlet. An electrical cord was then connected to that outlet and to an outlet on the rover.

It only took a few minutes to get the rover fully charged, and as soon as the charge was complete Calvin took the rover out for a spin.

"Now, what I want you to do," Baker explained, once Calvin had settled into the driver's seat, "is to turn that nob that's located just to the right of the steering wheel – turn it clockwise."

Calvin did so, and the rover's engine revved to life.

"Excellent. Now, very gently, I'd like you to step on the gas. As you can see there, the gas and break are situated just where they'd be in a normal car."

Calvin stepped gently on the gas pedal, and the rover rolled ever-so-slightly forward.

"Great. Now, see those two buttons in the middle of the steering wheel?"

"See 'em."

"One is yellow, the other is black."

"Got it."

"If you push the yellow one, that will put you into reverse. The black one will bring you back to forward. So now push on the yellow button, please, and then gently, again, step on the gas."

Calvin pushed the button and gently pressed down on the gas. The rover rolled ever-so-slightly backwards.

"Excellent. Now please push the black button."

Calvin pushed it.

"Great. Now, going very, very slowly, I want you to drive that rover around the front of the shuttle. Please do your best to avoid rocks and ditches as much as possible. The rover is designed to be able to deal with those things to a certain degree, but just take it as given that the best option is always to avoid them if possible."

"Okay, here I go," Calvin announced, as he stepped on the gas and began easing the rover around the front of the shuttle's nose.

"Great," Baker encouraged him. "Just like that. Just keep going, around to the shuttle's other side."

The "other side" had thus far been given much less attention by the astronauts. All their activities had been focused on the "work side," where the garden was. On the work side, the horizon was an uninterrupted sea of sand and rocks, punctuated only by the gentle slopes of sand dunes and by some small rocky ridges. On the other side, however, the horizon was broken by a vast, not-too-far-off rise in the terrain which ultimately culminated in a mountain.

"You see that mountain, in the distance?" Baker asked.

"Yeah."

"That's our destination."

"Seriously? You want me to go there now?"

"Not right now. Not today. But that's the ultimate goal."

"How far away is that?"

"It's a ways. For today, the goal is just to get a sense of how much distance you're able to cover by going at a very gentle pace."

"How fast is a gentle pace?"

"Let's start out here very slowly. Let's do that for about half an hour and see where that gets us."

"Okay."

So Calvin pointed the rover towards the mountain, stepped on the gas, and rolled very slowly into the distance.

The other four astronauts were huddled in the cockpit, watching screens which were relaying live video feeds from cameras which were mounted on Calvin's helmet and on the rover. After about five minutes of this, however, Tristan got bored and headed back into the round room to find a snack.

"One of the differences between this model and the *Curiosity*," Baker explained as Calvin steered the rover cautiously between rocks and ditches, "is that this model has a lot more variability with regard to speed. The NASA rovers rely on solar power as their sole source of energy. And of course they're driven by scientists who're still back on Earth and who don't have direct contact with the surrounding environment. All of which means that those rovers are obliged to move slowly. But we don't have those limitations. Although we have a solar option, we don't need it right now because of the fuel cells which are built into the rover, and which can be refilled by drawing on the shuttle's power supply. And, since you're up there, seeing everything clearly and directly in front of you, we have the option of maneuvering in a more proactive fashion than the folks do at NASA. All of which is to say that, in about another twenty minutes, I'm going to have you increase the speed a little, if you feel comfortable with that."

"Sure," Calvin said.

Twenty minutes later Baker asked Calvin to increase the speed just a touch, and Calvin complied.

"That's about enough for now," Baker told him, after another five minutes had passed. "Let's turn it around and head back to base."

"Roger that." Calvin decelerated the rover, turned it around slowly and then began driving back the way he'd come, following the tracks which the rover had made. By the time he reached the shuttle he'd been outside for an hour and fifteen minutes.

"I'm very pleased with how that went," Baker told the crew after Calvin stepped through the airlock's interior doorway and pulled off his spacesuit. "The rover covered a fair amount of ground with no incidents, so tomorrow I want Calvin to start out by going as fast as his fastest speed today."

"I'm ready," Calvin said.

And he was. At 10:00 the following morning he climbed down the stairs of the retractable ladder, mounted the rover, drove it around the front of the shuttle to the other side and then "sped" off at a steady clip, following the tracks which had now been ground twice into the Martian dirt. This time only Justin and Byron watched his progress via video feed. Troy had joined Tristan at their usual spot in one of the container spaces.

"Now Calvin," Baker said, "if you're comfortable with this, I'd like you to increase your speed by a couple of ticks."

"Roger," Calvin replied, and did as requested.

"How's that feeling?"

"No problems. It's comfortable."

"Good. Then keep that speed until you reach the point where you turned around yesterday."

"Roger."

Twenty minutes later Calvin told Baker that he was reaching the turn-around point.

"Good. Now decelerate just a touch as you go into new territory. If all seems well, we'll have you accelerate again in a couple minutes."

"Roger that."

A few minutes later Baker checked back in to see if Calvin was ready to accelerate.

"Sure am."

"Good, then you can take the speed back up to where you were before you reached the turn-around point."

Calvin stepped a little harder on the gas and then kept going at that speed for another ten minutes.

"Still good?" Baker checked back in.

"Roger."

"Ready to go faster?"

"Roger."

"Take it away."

Calvin pressed the gas pedal about halfway to the floor and now really began covering distance, as the base of the mountain loomed ever closer. For someone who'd spent the last many years in a jail cell, the experience of racing across an open landscape was beyond exhilarating.

"Now we're going to need you to turn the rover around and head home," Baker announced, after ten more minutes had passed.

"Shame."

"You've been outside for fifty minutes. We need to get you back within the two-hour limit."

"Yeah, I know. Am I still up tomorrow?"

"Oh yes. Tomorrow we're going to see if you can reach the base of that mountain."

Calvin grinned widely. "I love it." And then he repeated himself, hollering into the inside of his helmet, "I love it!"

XII

"We want you to start out," Baker noted, as Calvin settled into the rover's driver's seat at 10:04 the following morning, "going at the fastest speed you've reached thus far."

"Roger."

"Then we'll have you accelerate more after a couple minutes."

"I'm ready."

"I know."

So Calvin drove the rover around the front of the shuttle and then sped away, racing towards the mountain. The other four astronauts were all huddled in the cockpit, watching the screen, with even Tristan and Troy intrigued to see if Calvin could in fact reach his destination.

After five minutes, at Baker's request, Calvin pressed the gas down hard, nearly to the floor, as dust and little rocks shot out to the sides of the six wheels.

"Yeee-hawww!" Calvin yelled.

The men in the cockpit smiled. All of them – even Troy – were eager to be the next ones to ride the rover.

"I'm definitely goin' next," Tristan insisted.

"How's it feeling, Calvin?" Baker asked.

"Like I'm flyin'!"

"How's your control?"

"No problems. Control is fine."

"Any feeling of the traction slipping in the sand?"

"Nope. Traction is tight."

"Excellent."

Ten minutes sped by. Twenty. Thirty.

The men in the cockpit decided to place bets. Since there wasn't any money – or even property, other than their clothes – to gamble with, they made bets about who'd have to carry out which science experiments later in the day. The radiation testing was considered the most tedious, so whoever won the bet was to be relieved of that duty for the afternoon.

Tristan and Troy both bet that Calvin wouldn't make it to the mountain. Byron and Justin bet that he would.

At forty minutes out, Calvin realized that he wasn't going to reach the mountain if he didn't put the pedal all the way to the floor.

"Baker, I gotta go a little faster or this isn't gonna happen."

"Yes, alright."

So Calvin pressed it, all the way down.

Fifty minutes. Fifty-five. The beginning of the terrain's rise was just minutes away.

But he still wasn't going to make it within the hour.

"Calvin...you need to turn it around now," Baker instructed him.

"I need three more minutes. If I go at this speed the whole way back, I'll make it in under an hour."

It was now fifty-eight minutes out.

There was a long pause, and then Baker replied, "It's your call."

"I'm callin' it. I'll be fine."

The one hour mark sped past, and less than a minute later the rover began climbing the incline.

"I'm there! Rover's climbin'!" Calvin announced, ecstatic.

"Very nice. Now swing yourself around and head on home fast," Baker said.

"Roger that!"

Inside the cockpit Justin and Byron high-fived, delighted to have won the bet and to have proven Tristan and Troy wrong. The latter two, meanwhile, frowned and shook their heads and sulked back to the round room, no longer interested in watching the screen.

"Good work, Calvin," Byron said. "You just got Justin and me out a radiation room duty."

"Oh yeah? And so whad'a I get out of it?" Calvin asked, good-naturedly.

"Man, you get to be the hero."

"Yeah, okay."

"Now get on back here."

"I'm racin'."

And racing he was. Out on the desolate Martian plain, surrounded by a sea of lifelessness, by a total dearth of organic matter of any kind, the single human on a mechanized vehicle sped across the reddish tundra, spraying dust clouds behind him on either side....

And then twenty minutes into the return trip, the rover broke down. The wheels suddenly locked up, causing an instant deceleration which sent Calvin flying head-first over the steering wheel. His hands smacked the ground, followed by his forearms, which protected his helmet as he flipped onto his back and landed, splayed out, with a THUD.

The camera which was mounted on the front of the rover caught all this in its video feed, but everything happened so fast that no one who was watching the video was able to tell what had happened until a few seconds afterward. Meanwhile Calvin lay on his back, in full view of the rover's camera, while the video feed from his helmet's camera transmitted images of the sky.

"Calvin!" Baker said, his voice serious but not frantic. "Calvin!"

"Calvin! Calvin!" Justin and Byron both yelled.

"Let me talk to him," Baker told them. "We don't want to all do this at once."

Byron and Justin stopped yelling. Tristan and Troy walked back into the cockpit to see what was afoot.

"Calvin, can you hear me?" Baker asked, his decibel level rising.

"Uhhh...." Calvin's voice registered over the intercom.

"Calvin, can you hear me? Say yes or no!"

"...Yeah. Yeah I hear you."

"Are you hurt?"

"...Yeah. I just flipped over the wheel and landed on my back, so...yeah."

"Where are you hurt?"

"Like...my back. I guess."

"Can you move?"

"Maybe."

"Calvin – you need to act fast. You only have forty minutes of oxygen left, and if something is wrong with the rover then you need to get up, fix it, and drive it back to base immediately!"

"Yeah, okay. Roger."

Calvin rolled first to one side, then to the other, testing whether there was any serious pain generated by doing so. There wasn't, so he rolled all the way onto his stomach, planted his hands in the sand and pushed himself up onto his knees. After a few seconds he unsteadily rose back to his feet.

"How's your breathing? Does the air in your helmet seem normal? Has the helmet been broken or punctured anywhere?"

"It doesn't seem like it."

"That's what our all readings are picking up as well. That's good. That's the first thing. Now the second thing is to figure out what happened to the rover."

"It felt like the wheels just locked up, all a sudden."

"Our instruments aren't picking up anything. Which means it might not be a problem with anything inside the rover. That's good news if it's true. It may just be that a rock got lodged somewhere, or something like that."

Calvin circled the rover, bending down and pushing against each of the wheels. None of them budged. "None of 'em's movin'!"

"Try the ignition switch."

Calvin tried it. Nothing happened.

"Did the engine do anything? Make any sound?"

"No! So whad'a I do?" Calvin's voice began to sound frantic.

"Try it again!"

He did so. "Nothin'!"

There was a pause, and then Baker's voice returned, conveying a resolute steadiness. "Okay Calvin, there's only one thing to do now. If it's systemic failure – if all six wheels are stuck – and if the engine won't start, then something's happened inside the rover. And you can't fix that. Not even with me guiding you. At least not in the amount of time you need to get back to base. So the situation is very simple, I'm afraid. You're going to have to run."

"…What?"

"You're going to have to run, now!"

"Run?"

"Back to the shuttle!"

"Can I make it 'fore the air runs out?"

"No. Which is why one of the other men is going to have to run to you at the same time, carrying you more oxygen."

"…I…."

"So go, Calvin! Now!"

Without even entirely realizing what he was doing, Calvin began running, following the tread tracks towards the shuttle; a shuttle which was far enough in the distance, beyond little dunes and ditches, that he couldn't see it.

"Now," Baker said, addressing the other men, "who's going after him?"

This decision took about two seconds for the four of them to reach by consensus, without exchanging a word. The expression of fear on Troy's face immediately ruled him out. Byron was too big to move quickly for any length of time. And Tristan was a gangster who'd likely let Calvin die out there as a punishment for getting chosen as the first one to drive the rover. So of course it had to be Justin.

"I'll go!" He announced.

"Good, suit up!"

Justin spent the next three minutes putting on his spacesuit, while Baker explained to Byron where to locate a device which allowed Justin's oxygen tank to be hooked up to Calvin's; basically it was an extendable rubber tube with specialized plug-ins at either end. As soon as Justin was suited, Byron handed the tube to him, then Justin was through the airlock – Tristan operated the doors – and down the retractable stairs.

"You've got thirty-five minutes," Baker told him.

Justin raced around the front of the shuttle and began running as fast as he could, following the rover tracks.

"Can I get the weights out a these boots?" He asked as he ran.

"No. They're built in."

"Just hurry, man!" Calvin said.

"I'm comin'!"

Calvin was breathing hard now. Even though he'd been running daily on the treadmill, it was a completely different experience to run on solid ground, in a spacesuit, in weighted boots, even if the weights were offset by the reduced gravitational pull. Another part of the problem was that the spacesuit was designed to process carbon dioxide generated by a person whose heart rate was below a certain threshold; above that point, the process of carbon dioxide outtake versus oxygen intake became less efficient. And Calvin was already feeling it.

"This breathin' ain't easy!" He yelled as he ran.

"That spacesuit isn't designed to be run in," Baker explained. "You're building up carbon dioxide too quickly. That's also causing the oxygen supply to burn much faster than the original two hours that were calculated for. What that means is, in about ten minutes, you're going to need to slow to a walk to conserve more oxygen, while we let Justin burn up some of his extra supply by running to you."

"Wait…Seriously? You're gonna have me stop runnin'?"

"Yes. I've already had my people do the math. It'll give you the best chance of survival."

"Wonderful!"

"Go Justin!" Byron yelled, having returned with the others to the shuttle's cockpit. One of the screens was showing the view from Justin's helmet while another screen was showing the view from Calvin's.

Justin didn't reply. He was already experiencing the same thing that Calvin felt, and breathing was hard. The synthetic plastic-glass of his helmet was partially fogging up. Twice already he'd fallen: once from sliding in loose sand and once from tripping over a rock.

Ten minutes later Baker announced, "Okay now, Calvin, time to stop running. Stop running now."

"Okay...okay," Calvin gasped. Despite the fact that he was running for his life, his pace had already slacked off considerably over the last few minutes, as the carbon dioxide continued to build. He'd also strained his hip bone when he flipped over the rover's steering wheel and landed on his back. As he'd impacted the ground the spacesuit's backpack dug into the muscles around his hip, and it was only after he'd been running for a few minutes that he began to feel the repercussions of that injury.

All of which meant that by the time Baker told him to slow to a walk he was practically walking already. Now he slowed even more, and had to fight the urge to stop for a few seconds so that he could bend over and rest his hands on his knees.

"Justin, you have about twenty minutes left before you reach him," Baker said. "Don't say anything. Conserve your breath. Just keep going as best you can."

"Hang in there, man!" Byron said, not specifying whether he was speaking to Justin or Calvin.

And time raced by like a high-speed train in slow motion….

Ten minutes on, and Justin was staggering, just like Calvin had been. He forced himself forward, but the men in the cockpit, as well as Baker, could see by the way his helmet camera was bobbing up and down that he was struggling to maintain his balance as he ran, while the rasping sound of his breathing echoed over the intercom system, drowning out the softer wheezing that was coming from Calvin's mic.

Eventually Calvin's wheezing faded altogether, and Baker and the men in the cockpit watched as the video angle from Calvin's camera dropped and became level with the ground. Evidently Calvin had collapsed.

"Calvin!" Baker spoke loudly, but without yelling. "Calvin, can you hear me? Acknowledge that you can hear me!"

Nothing.

"Calvin! Answer me!"

Nothing.

"Calvin! Wake up! Calvin!"

He didn't wake up.

After a few seconds, Baker decided, "He must've passed out from the carbon dioxide."

"His vital signs are all still readin', right?" Byron asked, staring at the screen in the cockpit which was relaying Calvin's information.

"They are, but they're weak."

"He's got eight more minutes a air, doesn't he?" Byron asked, looking at the clock.

"No. Some of that got eaten up when he was running. His oxygen supply is down to almost zero."

"Awww, man!"

"Justin," Baker said, "just keep going. A few more minutes. If you can."

So Justin ran, and he stumbled, but then he caught himself before falling, and then he stumbled again, and caught himself, and ran, and....

Eventually Baker told them, "Gentlemen, it's over. Calvin is dead. His vitals have all gone flat."

Justin kept running.

Baker waited for a few moments, to allow the information to sink in, but Justin kept on running.

"Justin, he's dead. Now you need to stop running."

A few more yards of Martian ground passed by outside Justin's fogged-in helmet; his feet seemed unable to obey Baker's instructions. Then his legs buckled beneath him and he fell onto the butterscotch sand, landing on his hands and knees.

He remained in that position for a few seconds, gasping for air, then he rose back up onto his knees, trying – despite his fogged helmet – to scan the horizon to see if Calvin was in view. The rocks here weren't high, and the ditches weren't deep, so from that height he could vaguely see ahead of him for a distance which would've taken him at least ten more minutes to traverse. And there was no sign of Calvin, anywhere.

Recognizing this, he allowed himself to fall backwards, until his built-in backpack settled gently into the sand.

XIII

Baker instructed Justin to return to the ship.

Although he'd been outside the shuttle for about thirty minutes, Justin had burned up fifty minutes' worth of oxygen. And since he'd been running for nearly all of those thirty minutes, it would likely take at least an hour to get back to base. So, with his lungs aching, and with his heart sore from failing to save someone whom he'd come to consider a friend, he arrived back at the shuttle with about seven minutes to spare.

"Hey there, man," Byron greeted him, as Justin stepped out of the airlock, pulling off his helmet. "You did the best you could. The best any of us could."

Justin dropped his helmet on the floor and ran his fingers through his sweat-soaked hair, taking a long, deep breath.

"Yeah man," Troy added. "None of us could a done better."

Justin shook his head. "Calvin was the nicest one out a any of us. Shame it had to be him."

The four remaining astronauts stood in a circle, sharing a moment of silence.

"So whad'a we do now then, Baker?" Byron asked, breaking the silence, clearly shaken up by Calvin's demise. "Should we go get him so we can bury him?"

"Yes. That's the obvious next step. The body won't decompose as fast as it would back here on earth, given the lack of native microscopic organisms up there, but it'll decay nonetheless. So the sooner we get him buried, the better. You can do that now or if you want you can wait and do it tomorrow."

The four men looked at each other.

"The thought a him lyin' out there just don't seem right," Byron said.

Justin nodded. "Agreed."

"So I'll go now," Byron decided.

"Count me in," Tristan added, evidently feeling like some exercise, or simply vying with Byron for the role of "guy in charge."

Of course if Byron and Tristan were heading out then Justin had to go with them, since, if he didn't go, Tristan might take the opportunity to pick a fight with Byron. Besides, Justin felt compelled to complete the task of getting to Calvin and rendering him whatever service he could.

"Yeah, me too," Justin said.

"You're sure you want to head right back out there?" Baker asked.

"I'm sure."

"Alright then. The first thing to do is to get your suits fitted out with extra oxygen tanks."

Baker explained where more tanks could be found, and how to hook them up to the spacesuits. Having those extra tanks would make for harder walking, but obviously the added oxygen supply was necessary.

"You'll have four hours to get to him, bury him, and then return to the shuttle," Baker informed them, as the three men stepped into the airlock. "Bury him where you find him. It'll take too much time, energy and oxygen to bring him back to the shuttle area. So each of you should bring a shovel."

The shovels were lying near the garden and each man grabbed one before they headed on their way. Neither Justin nor Byron felt like talking, and Tristan – in a rare display of sensitivity – appeared to pick up on this disposition, so he didn't say much either.

It took over an hour to reach Calvin's body. This was the longest walk any of them had taken in years, and despite the depressing reason for taking it all three men experienced the raw, pleasurable sense of freedom which the walk provided.

While he'd been running, all Justin could think about was covering as much distance as fast as possible, but now, with more time to take in the scenery, he couldn't help feeling like he was walking through New Mexico or Arizona. He decided that after he got back to Earth he was going to treat himself to a camping trip out in the desert and just enjoy breathing fresh air.

Upon reaching Calvin's body they found him lying chest down in the rocks and sand, with his head turned so that the front of the helmet was facing away from the tracks, off into the distance, as if Calvin had wanted to take one final look at the horizon.

"I guess we should bury him off to the side here, away from the tracks," Byron suggested, "if we're gonna be usin' these tracks for our regular rode to get to that mountain."

"That's right," Baker confirmed. "I'd bury him at least ten feet away."

The men did as directed, finding a patch of sandy ground without too many rocks, then they dug up the area and pitched the sand behind them. It took half an hour to make a hole big enough to serve as a grave, then they rolled Calvin's body inside, covered him up with sand and dirt and stacked some rocks on top of each other to mark the spot. During this process none of them took an opportunity to look into the helmet and examine Calvin's lifeless face.

"We should probably say somethin'," Byron noted, once the body was buried.

"Go for it," Tristan told him.

Byron shrugged. "What can I say? He was a nice guy, and he was smart. And he didn't let people push him 'round, even though he was small. Which is why I guess he wasted those dudes in that laundromat. What I'm sayin' is he wasn't a killer, not like Tristan here."

Tristan didn't appear at all offended by this comment.

Then Byron turned to Justin. "You got anythin'?"

Justin thought for several seconds before speaking. "Well, he died twice. First back in California and now here on Mars. So I guess I'm hopin' that's enough to make up for whatever he did. That now he can go straight from here to a good place."

Byron nodded.

"It'd be kind a funny," Tristan opined, "if he wakes up on some spaceship on another planet."

"Man, shut up," Byron said.

Then the three of them walked back to the shuttle.

XIV

Baker told the four remaining men that, if they wanted to, they could take the rest of the day off – that they could forego gardening for the afternoon – but they decided to work anyway, in order to keep from dwelling on the concept of death on Mars.

At dinner, however, there was an unavoidable sense of emptiness in the round room, with one chair unoccupied at the circular counter.

"Man," Byron said, "I do not wanna die on this planet."

"I hear that," Troy affirmed.

"I always thought gettin' buried in the ground back on Earth was lonely," Byron continued, "but then today, when I was shovelin' all that sand over Calvin, and thinkin' 'bout him bein' out there all alone, with nobody else around, not even other dead people…."

"Someday there'll be more people up here," Justin noted.

"Yeah, but still…."

"Death is death," Tristan said. "Here, on Earth, on Saturn, it's all the same. It don't matter where."

The conversation traipsed along for a little while longer, until the men drifted off somberly to their bedrooms.

Justin lay down inside his bed, but he didn't fall asleep, so after a few hours he got up, walked out into the round room and made his way down the long hallway to the cockpit, where he settled into a chair and stared out at the endless Martian landscape and the endless Martian sky.

Eventually a screen clicked on and Baker's face appeared. Justin inhaled and exhaled.

"Hello Justin."

"Hey there, Baker."

"Are you alright?"

"Yeah, I guess."

"I suppose you're thinking about Calvin."

Justin shrugged. "…Yeah, sure…."

Baker studied him. "If I may say so, I think perhaps you're also thinking about something else as well. I suspect there's something else on your mind."

Justin nodded. "You're pretty good at readin' people."

Baker shrugged. "Remember how I told you that the reason I'm rich is because I believe in securitization?"

"Yeah."

"Well that's only half the story. The other half is that I have a talent for reading people."

"I believe it."

"So shall I tell you what I'm reading right now, or do you want to tell me yourself?"

Justin shrugged. "Go for it."

"Alright. I'll venture to guess that it has something to do with the distance you covered today; the distance between the shuttle and where you found Calvin's body."

Justin nodded. "You *are* good."

"Then since I'm right about that, I'll take it a step further and say that you're probably wondering how you or anybody else could have possibly covered that distance in time to save him."

"Right on target."

"Alright then, if that's the case, presumably you have a question for me…."

Justin nodded and took a deep breath. "Yeah, I guess I do."

Baker smiled pleasantly, waiting to be queried.

"…Did you know?" Justin asked him. "Did you know how far Calvin was from the shuttle? I mean, before we went and buried him?"

"There's a tracking device built into the rover, so we can pinpoint its position exactly. We don't have tracking devices on those spacesuits, but we could make a rough calculation of where Calvin was based upon how fast he appeared to be running."

"So then…you knew I wasn't gonna be able to reach him in time to save him."

"I knew Calvin was dead as soon as he tried to turn the rover's engine back on and nothing happened."

So…why'd you send me out there?"

"Would you have preferred that I told Calvin he was going to die, and that he should sit out there for forty minutes waiting for it to happen? And would the other four of you have enjoyed listening to him on the intercom as he sat out there waiting for the end to come?"

Justin considered this, and, he had to admit, Baker had a point. Nonetheless, something was still bothering him.

"You're seeing the logic of my answer, but there's still something on your mind," Baker observed.

Justin nodded, then smiled a little, submitting to Baker's almost telepathic powers. "Yeah," he admitted. "There is."

Baker waited.

After a few seconds Justin said, "You told us you'd always be honest with us. You said you'd be brutally honest if necessary."

"And I am being brutally honest. But back in the moment, in the middle of the drama, I did what was necessary to preserve the group, to preserve your collective sanity up there. Now that the drama has passed the truth can be appropriately delivered."

Justin nodded. "…Yeah, I guess." There was another pause, then he asked, "What 'bout the rover? Any idea what went wrong with it?"

"My people are running remote diagnostics. We should have an idea about that soon."

"Then what?"

"We might be able to repair it from here. If not, we'll need one or two of you to go fix it for us."

Justin nodded. Then something else occurred to him. "So what's so important 'bout gettin' to that mountain anyways?"

Baker shrugged. "The mountain is just a landmark. We're more interested in seeing how much ground can be covered in a certain amount of time."

"Why?"

"Various reasons."

Justin smiled. Evidently there were certain things Baker wasn't going to tell him about. At least not yet.

Silence filled up the space between the two men – between the face on the screen and the person sitting in the cockpit chair – as the vastness of the Martian sky loomed overhead.

"Now then," Baker said, breaking the silence, "I'll leave you to your thoughts. Goodnight."

"Night."

The screen went black, and Justin took another deep breath.

He sat there for a while, looking out at the sky, contemplating the fact that Calvin would never be making it back to Earth, to be part of The Space Zombies band. As this thought registered with him, certain musical riffs began filtering through his mind, and he nodded up and down to the rhythms in his head.

XV

Balance is not necessarily synonymous with harmony, nor does it automatically equate with stability. Which is to say that now that there were only four people onboard the shuttle, divided into two groups of two – Tristan and Troy, Byron and Justin – all the bubbling tensions on Mars were poised to boil.

Justin had always associated more easily with Byron and Calvin than with the other two; he had, as such, made his choice about which gang to join. But Calvin and Byron had always had a more natural friendship with each other than Justin had with either of them. Somehow the two of them – so different in size and temperament – had hit it off. But now Calvin was gone, and with Tristan and Troy off in their corner, talking between themselves, Byron and Justin grew closer by necessity.

"Can't help thinkin' they're over there plottin' somethin'," Byron said, on the second night after Calvin's demise, when, following dinner, Tristan and Troy went and took up their usual positions, leaving Justin and Byron alone at the counter in the round room.

Justin shrugged. "They wanna get off this rock, same as us, so they know they can't just get rid of us." Yet even as he spoke he wasn't sure that he was entirely convinced by his own words.

"But Tristan's crazy, man. You know it. Like, deep down in his bones crazy. And now that Calvin's gone, and it's just two against two, I don't know what he'll do."

And sure enough, the very next day Tristan's tone grew more aggressive, first during the work hours, then during dinner, and then after dinner, when he walked back into the round room to get a spoon so that he could eat some ice cream.

"Byron, I'm gonna eat the last a the ice cream now. If you wanna fight me for it, go right ahead."

"Man, first of all, there's plenty a ice cream, and second of all, don't be an idiot. You know we can't start fightin', with there only bein' four of us left. If we don't work together, who knows what Baker'll do."

Tristan shook his head. "You so chicken it hurts."

Justin could literally feel the fight coming, but it didn't happen that night.

His nerves were further set on edge the following morning when Baker didn't appear for his 10:00 briefing. Every morning since they'd first woken up on Mars, Baker had greeted them at 10:00 and talked with them about the day's work. In addition to which, he often checked in with them – via video or audio – at other times during the day, but there were no Baker check-ups that day. And naturally this led to some dinnertime discussion.

"Baker's given up on us," Tristan declared flatly.

Troy looked spooked. "How do you know? Just 'cause he ain't showed up for one day."

"He showed up every other day."

"I told you," Byron said to Tristan, "to be cool, or he'd get fed up with us. Justin said the same thing, remember?"

"Man, I'm cucumber cool. No one's cooler on this shuttle than yours truly. Fact is, since Calvin died we've been down a man. If anythin's makin' Baker lose interest in us, it's that, 'cause now we ain't workin' as fast. Doesn't got nothin' to do with anythin' I said."

"Yeah, well you're not helpin'," Justin shot back.

Tristan scowled at him.

The following morning Baker appeared on the screen promptly at 10:00 and everyone onboard – even Tristan – was relieved.

"Good morning, gentlemen."

"We were thinkin' maybe you'd left us," Tristan told him, with characteristic bluntness.

"Oh, no. No, no. I'm simply assuming you now have enough of an idea about how to handle things up there without me bothering you every single day."

"It's just nice to talk to somebody who's still on Earth," Byron said.

Baker nodded. "That's understandable."

Then he reviewed the work that needed to be done in the garden that day.

At 14:30 the organic matter detector picked up something in the garden's gravity research compartment while Troy was doing his rounds.

"Hey, I think I got somethin'," Troy announced.

Baker was right back on the intercom. "Yes? What've you got there?"

"...Somethin'...."

"Yes?"

"It's pickin' up somethin'."

"Alright. Stay with it for a few minutes. Then please go back to the shuttle and enter all those numbers on the scanner's screen into the cockpit computer."

"Okay...."

Troy did as instructed. After he finished entering all the data into the shuttle computer, Baker's face appeared on one of the cockpit screens and he read the numbers back to Troy.

"Is that correct?"

"Those are them," Troy confirmed. "Is it a plant? Or is it like a bacteria thing?"

"Most likely a plant," Baker replied, with a lips-pressed smile.

All four of the men – the other three having now crowded into the cockpit behind Troy – shouted with joy. They never would've imagined, back in their previous lives, that they could get this excited about a plant.

"Excellent work, gentlemen," Baker said. "Keep at it."

And so they did.

Later that evening, at dinnertime, a new sense of confidence had returned to the group.

"See, ya'll worryin' for nothin'," Tristan told the others. "Baker loves us. We keep gettin' those plants to grow, and we ain't got nothin' to worry 'bout."

But Baker didn't appear the next day at 10:00. Nor did he do so for the remainder of that day. Or the following day. Or the day after that, despite the fact that a tiny green shoot of tomato stalk – the one whose subsoil presence Troy had previously detected – stuck up just barely through the dirt. By the third consecutive evening of no appearances, nerves onboard the shuttle again began to fray, badly.

"Where's the dude?" Troy demanded, with an edge of panic in his voice.

"Gone fishin,'" Tristan said, with a shrug.

Byron frowned. "Maybe all he ever wanted to know was if plants up here can grow. Maybe that was the whole point. End of experiment."

"And what, you think he'll just leave us up here?" Justin asked, trying to sound incredulous, although he was in fact pondering precisely that possibility, and wanted to hear Byron talk about it some more so that his – Justin's – own fears could be more fully aired.

"Think 'bout it," Byron replied, trying to persuade them all of his theory's plausibility. "Why else would he send a bunch a death row cons up here – people everybody else thinks're already dead?"

The other men nodded, recognizing the simple logic of Byron's suggestion.

"What if there's no second ship comin'?" Byron continued. "At least no ship for us? There might be another ship at another time maybe. Probably with a bunch a white people on it."

Troy nodded, eyes growing wide. "So then that little plant I found – it's done us in?"

"Maybe, maybe not." Justin was attempting to sound reassuring. And truth be told, notwithstanding the logic of Byron's fears, he couldn't quite believe that Baker simply planned to let them all die up there; not after the conversations he'd had with Baker – just the two of them – in the cockpit. Yet Baker *had* admitted that he didn't initially tell them that Calvin was going to die because he didn't want to panic them. So maybe he would just leave them to their fates now, rather than telling them up front what was happening. But then, wouldn't it be more consistent with his previous lie if he kept talking to them each day, not giving them any clues that something was amiss until the very end?

"Maybe, maybe yes!" Byron retorted, as the full weight of his theory's plausibility settled in his mind.

"Look at you," Tristan laughed, mockingly. "Freakin' out like a little girl. Who knows what's really goin' on. Baker could come back on that screen any second."

"Man, I've had it with you!" Byron jumped up, pointing at Tristan, his deep concern now finding an outlet in anger; an anger which had been building towards Tristan in any case.

"Finally!" Tristan jumped to his feet as well and raised his fists.

"Uh, guys, now of all times is not really a good time to do this," Justin interjected, without bothering to stand up. He felt compelled to head off the fight if that was possible, but he was skeptical that it was. "If

Baker doesn't start showin' up again soon, then the only people we're gonna be able to count on to get through this thing are the four of us here in this room."

"Nice speech, coach," Tristan shot back, "but I just wanna deck this dude."

"You wanna deck everybody!" Byron yelled.

"Why you yellin', man? I'm right here. We're all right here. You know, I think maybe you're crackin' up."

Silence settled in the air, as if all the noise in the room had been sucked out by a giant vacuum. The men felt the violence coming.

But then something unexpected occurred. Troy, of all people, rose to his feet and, assuming the role Justin had previously played, stepped in between the two antagonists and raised his hands.

"Justin's right! Now ain't the time for this! Let's give it another day. Maybe we'll get some more plant readings. Maybe that'll get Baker back on the line."

Troy's behavior surprised everyone, even himself. And it disarmed both Tristan and Byron, who then shrugged and sat back down.

Baker, however, was absent again the next morning.

No further plant readings appeared that afternoon, and by early evening everybody could sense that something was about to happen.

Byron decided to chop some vegetables, since cooking helped him relax, but when he opened the drawer that contained the cooking utensils he immediately noticed that something was missing.

"Hey, where's the other chef's knife?" He hollered out to the rest of the crew.

"What?" Justin walked out of his bedroom.

"One of the chef's knives is gone!"

Troy and Tristan walked into the round room as well.

"What're ya talkin'?" Tristan asked, nonchalantly, sucking on a lollypop.

Byron glared at him. Then he grabbed the remaining chef's knife, pointed it at Tristan and hissed, "You took it, didn't you?"

"Byron, dude, you need to calm yourself down there."

"Where is it?"

"Man, you know all I ever eat is beef stew and chicken stew, and that stuff comes out of a can. I don't need no chef's knife for that."

"My point exactly!" Byron yelled.

"B-man, you're yellin' again. Seriously, I think you're losin' it."

"I'm not losin' nothin', and not no chef's knife, that's for sure! So where is it? Who took it? I'm serious!"

"You're seriously freakin' out, is all."

Byron stuck the knife out further at Tristan, angrily curling his lips.

"Alright, who last used one a those knives?" Justin asked. "I used one yesterday. I'm pretty sure I put it back in that drawer."

"I used one yesterday too," Troy confirmed. "I think I put it back there after I was done."

"You think or you know?" Byron demanded an answer.

"I…I honestly can't remember a hundred percent. I think I did…."

"There, ya see," Tristan said, shrugging. "Let's figure out where Troy the boy left it and then we can all get on with our lives."

So they spent the next hour searching the ship for the knife, but they turned up nothing. Then Tristan and Troy went and sat in their usual location in the container space, while Byron angrily resumed his vegetable chopping and Justin lay back down in his bed for a while.

Very little was said during dinner. A knife had either been lost or taken, and the natural target of suspicion was Tristan, which Tristan himself recognized, but he didn't seem to mind the negative attention. Eventually he and Troy returned to their lounging spot, leaving Byron and Justin at the round counter to discuss things under their breath.

"Tristan took it!" Byron insisted, in a whisper. His eyes were tight with fear and anger.

"Then now what?" Justin asked.

Byron shook his head, uncertain what to do. "I'll be honest with you – after I killed that guy, back on Earth, it hurt me. I mean it worked me over, day after day, night after night. It tore me apart inside. When I talked 'bout it before, like I was casual 'bout it, that was just somethin' I used to do for prison talk, you know what I'm sayin'. The truth is I always thought that I don't ever wanna kill anybody ever again. But now, with Tristan the way he is, and we're stuck up here with him, and now he's gone and taken that big ol' knife…I'm thinkin…."

Byron didn't want to complete the sentence, but Justin made him. He wanted to see if and how Byron would say what he was thinking, so that he – Justin – could gauge how serious Byron might be. "Thinkin' what?"

"You know what I'm thinkin'."

"If you're thinkin' it, then say it."

"I'm thinkin' maybe we gotta do this dude."

"*We?*"

"What, you're gonna make me do this alone? You're in as much danger as I am?"

Justin thought this over. "And what 'bout Troy?"

"Once Tristan's gone, Troy'll be harmless. But if it comes to a fight, and we don't handle Tristan real quick like, I think Troy'll go in on Tristan's side."

Justin shook his head, exhaling through his nostrils. "So what, we gotta take out Tristan, in secret or somethin', and then announce it to Troy that we killed his friend and now we'd like him to be our friend so that we can all be happy ever after on Mars?"

"Man, I do not wanna kill Troy."

"I don't wanna kill anybody."

"Then whad'a we do? Dude took that knife!"

"We don't know that for sure."

"Well I didn't take it. And I'm guessin' you didn't neither. Troy, maybe. Tristan, almost definitely."

"Well I'm not killin' somebody just 'cause they "might" a done somethin'."

"Then what're we gonna do? I don't wanna just let that psychopath take me out!"

Justin shook his head, pondering. Eventually he said, "I dunno."

XVI

To Justin's surprise, nobody died the next day before dinnertime.

As had now become usual, Baker didn't make any appearances that day. But the men kept working in the garden, in case Baker's face ever reappeared on screen. Besides, it gave them something to do. And of course they were intrigued to find out whether any more plants would begin to grow, especially since, if Baker never reappeared and the second shuttle never arrived, they'd need to grow their own food. In that regard there was some further good news: plant sprouts had shown up now in both of the planter boxes in the gravity-testing room, and a sprout had also shown up in one of the planter boxes in the radiation-testing room – it was in the planter box which was set under the radiation-filtering panel. But none of this news was enough to stem the rising tension.

"Justin, Justin, Justin," Tristan muttered, walking up from behind while Justin sat in the cockpit watching instruments which were monitoring the conditions of Byron and Troy, who were working in the garden.

Justin swiveled the chair around quickly. "Whad' ya want?"

"I wanna talk."

"'Bout what?"

"Our mutual friend."

"…Troy?"

"No man – Byron."

"Whad' ya mean you wanna talk?"

"Dude's goin' crazy, man."

Justin said nothing.

"You can see it. We all can."

Again, Justin said nothing.

"He must be the one who took that knife. He uses those knives more than anybody. And you saw how quick he was to blame me. That tells you right there he's guilty."

Justin shrugged. "You *are* the most likely suspect."

Tristan frowned and smiled simultaneously, shaking his head.

"Man, you know I don't need no knife if I wanna fight somebody. I told him before – you saw it – I told him I'd fight him without one even if he's got one. Whad'a I need a knife for?"

Justin stared at Tristan skeptically. "So what then? Whad're ya sayin'?"

"I'm sayin'," Tristan said, leaning in closer and whispering, even though he and Justin were facing away from the intercom speaker on the cockpit's control panel, thus there wasn't any chance that the other two could hear them, "that we need to handle this situation."

"I think you need to go back to your station, at the airlock."

"Listen to me, man – Byron's goin' crazy. And I know he took that knife. So we gotta stop him 'fore he does us all damage."

Justin pursed his lips, shook his head, and folded his arms across his chest.

"Besides," Tristan continued, "the way Byron eats, he's gonna eat through the food supply faster than any of us. Who knows if Baker's ever comin' back. And who knows if that second ship is really comin'. So we gotta start conservin' food 'round here. And we both know big Byron ain't gonna be contributin' to that particular effort."

"So…what? Say what you're sayin.'"

"Let's take him down."

"No."

"Dude, man, be reasonable."

"Maybe Byron ain't the one who's goin' insane 'round here. I'm thinkin' maybe it's you."

"Man, I was insane 'fore I got here. But that don't mean I'm the one goin' crazy."

"You're not makin' any sense."

"I'm sayin' I'm the one who sees what's goin' on 'round here. I'm payin' attention. I've been survivin' all my life and I'm gonna be survivin' now. So you gonna help me with this or ain't ya?"

"I think you need to settle down. And I think what we need to do is wait for Baker to show up again and tell us he's spent the last couple days doin' scientific experiments and that everythin's good and that that second ship'll be here in less than three months. That's what I think."

Tristan shook his head and puffed out some air. "Fool," he said. Then he walked back down the hallway and sat on the floor next to the airlock's interior control panel, folding his arms across his chest.

Of course Tristan's behavior now left Justin with the question of whether to inform Byron about what Tristan had said. Justin knew that if he did tell Byron, Byron would insist upon killing Tristan immediately. And if Byron – or Byron and Justin – killed Tristan, then they'd probably need to kill Troy as well. But if Justin didn't tell Byron, and nothing happened for another day or so, then Tristan would know that Justin hadn't told Byron about what had been discussed, in which case Tristan would assume that Justin was willing to allow Tristan to go after Byron if Tristan wanted. Yet if Tristan killed Byron, then Justin would probably have to kill Tristan, out of fear that Tristan – with Troy in-tow – would likely come after him next. And if Justin did somehow manage to kill Tristan, he might still need to kill Troy, just to be on the safe side.

Or in other words, the four men were caught in a Mexican standoff, but without any guns, and on a space shuttle, on Mars.

Ultimately Justin decided not to tell Byron anything until at least the morning, just to give himself more time to think. But as he lay inside his bed that night, rolling things around in his mind, he concluded that, one way or another, someone was probably going to die the next day.

XVII

"Troy!"

This was Byron's voice.

"Troy! Troy!"

Justin jumped out of bed and rushed into the round room. Tristan did likewise, and they both arrived at the hallway's entrance at the same moment. What they saw was Byron standing at the other end of the hall, a few feet from the cockpit entrance, and there, on the floor in front of him, lay Troy.

"Whad' ja do!" Tristan yelled at Byron as he ran towards Troy.

"I didn't do nothin'! I came out here to get a snack just now and I found him like this!"

Tristan knelt down and felt for Troy's pulse. Then he rose back to his feet and yelled at Byron, "You killed him! You killed Troy!"

"I didn't kill nobody! That's your thing, remember!"

"Byron," Justin said, in a shaken tone, inserting himself between the two of them, "what happened? Tell us exactly what happened!"

"It's…like I said. I came out here…just a couple seconds ago, to get somethin' to eat, and the lights came on, and…there he was, just lyin' there, just like that. I ain't even touched him."

"So then how'd ya know there was somethin' wrong with him?" Tristan snapped.

"Dude's not breathin', his chest's not goin' up and down, and he's lyin' out here in the hall! That's how!"

"You killed him!" Tristan repeated, his eyes sizzling.

"Justin, man," Byron said, in a pleading voice, "you know I didn't do this. You know I wouldn't wanna kill Troy!"

Justin nodded, trying – without much success – to take a deep breath. "What time is it?"

"It's…two minutes after midnight," Byron said, turning towards the cockpit to see the digital clock on the control panel.

Justin looked at Tristan. "You and Troy were both out here after

Byron and me went to our rooms. How long did you two stay out here?"

"'Til 'bout 22:00, I guess. At least that's when I went to bed."

"Troy stayed out here after that?"

"Yeah. I went to my room 'fore he got up from where we were hangin' out, over there in the corner, like we always do."

Justin turned to Byron. "Was this the first time tonight you came out a your room, after you went to bed?"

Byron nodded. "First time."

"So why was Troy even out here in the first place?" Justin asked. "Gettin' a snack too?"

"Maybe he fell asleep over there first," Byron said, pointing at the hang-out spot.

This made Tristan even angrier. "So, what? You tellin' me he fell asleep, woke up, walked out here in the hall, and figured, "I might as well just die.""

"Man, how do I know? I just walked out here like five seconds 'fore the two a you!"

Tristan and Byron stared at each other, hard, and then Byron, in a moment of magnanimity, said, "Look, man, I'm sorry, okay. I know he was your friend. Best friend you had up here. Alright. I'm sorry. Just 'cause I think you're a psycho doesn't mean I'd kill somebody just 'cause they was your friend. I'm tellin' you, I don't know what happened to Troy, but whatever it was, I didn't do it."

"Yeah well, if you didn't, who did? Justin and me, we was both in our rooms, fool!"

"Wait a minute!" Justin demanded, throwing up his hands like he'd just had a revelation. "Wait a minute, wait a minute…."

"What?"

"Yeah, what you got?"

"Think 'bout it – it's like you say," and Justin looked at Tristan, "we were both in our rooms. And then Byron walked out here only a few seconds 'fore we did."

"So you believe him?" Tristan was incredulous.

"And the knife," Justin continued, "who took that? We couldn't find it."

"So…?"

"And the rover – Calvin goes out on the rover, and then it dies on him."

"What're ya gettin' at?" Tristan demanded.

"Think 'bout it!" Justin repeated this phrase as his voice dropped to a whisper.

Byron's eyes spread out like full moons, and he asked, "Are you thinkin'…?"

Justin nodded.

"What?" Tristan demanded again.

"I need to spell it out for you?"

"Apparently."

"There's someone else on this shuttle."

"What're you talkin' 'bout?"

"Someone else," Byron added, "or some*thin'* else?"

Tristan shook his head, disgusted. "Now you're both goin' crazy! We're the only ones on this shuttle! We're the only livin' things on this whole planet!"

"Like in *Alien*!" Byron whispered, forcefully. "It might be like in *Alien*!"

"What?"

"The movie *Alien*! This freaky creature gets onboard a spaceship and starts killin' everybody!"

"There ain't no alien on this ship! And there ain't no*body* else on it, neither! That's impossible! We're it! I'm tellin' you two fools – we're it!"

"I never should a shot that security guard in that parkin' lot!" Byron declared, under his breath, shaking his head.

"It's probably not an alien," Justin concluded. "How would an alien know how to mess with the rover? And why would it steal a knife?" He paused to allow this point to sink in, then added, "If there's somethin' else on this shuttle, it's another person."

"Stop all this nonsense!" Tristan demanded. "It's impossible for anyone else to be on this ship! We been up here for weeks! Like five weeks! If there was someone else here, we'd a heard 'em or seen 'em by now! I'm tellin' you," and he looked at Justin while pointing at Byron, "this dude" – then he pointed down at Troy – "did that dude. End a story!"

"Did him how?" Justin asked. "I don't see any signs a struggle on him."

"What're you – Mr. TV-show homicide detective? You and me,

we was in our rooms. We come out. Byron's there. Troy's there. He's alive. He's dead. Where's the mystery?"

"I think there's someone else on this ship," Byron stated flatly, fatalistically.

"Man, you just tryin' to switch the blame from yourself, that's all there is to it! Couldn't be more obvious if you tried!"

"I wanna get the other chef's knife," Byron said. "I promise I'll put it back in the mornin'."

"Look at that – now he's admittin' he wants to take a knife! That proves he took the first one!"

"No it doesn't," Justin disagreed. "If anythin', it probably proves the opposite."

"How's that?"

"'Cause if I took the first one, dummy," Byron explained, "then I wouldn't need the one we still got."

Tristan scowled at him, then turned to Justin. "Look, I think this dude just killed Troy. I don't know how he did it, but he did it. So there's no way – no way – he gets to take that knife to bed with himself!"

"Okay, nobody take the knife," Justin decided. "Everybody just lock your doors and we'll all be fine 'till the mornin'."

"Well, whad'a we do 'bout Troy?" Byron asked. "We gotta bury him like we did Calvin, right?"

"Yeah, but…not tonight."

"So what – we're just gonna leave him out here?" Tristan asked.

Justin looked around, trying to figure out what to do with Troy's body. "Why don't we put him in the airlock? At least that way he's sort a out a the way."

The other two men considered this idea for a moment, then they nodded in agreement, so that's how the situation was handled.

XVIII

Byron didn't sleep at all that night. Justin only slept for a few minutes. Tristan, however, slept just fine, notwithstanding the sudden death of his friend. Evidently he'd been in uglier and more dangerous situations.

When the Martian morning finally arrived, the three men loaded Troy's body onto the external lift, lowered it to the ground, then carried it a few hundred feet to a point that was equidistant between the shuttle and the garden. There they dug a hole, rolled Troy into it, buried him, and marked the spot with a stack of rocks.

"Anybody wanna say anythin'?" Justin asked.

"Yeah," Tristan said. "Dear God, this person we just buried here, I want you to know he was killed by that big dude who's standin' right there, named Byron."

"Dear God," Byron countered, looking up at the Martian sky, "I didn't kill nobody! If anythin', it was this psychopath standin' right there accusin' me."

"Dear God," Justin said, wearily, "I'm goin' back inside."

So the three men trudged back to the shuttle and headed up the stairs, with Justin ascending the stairway in the middle so that the other two didn't try to attack each other on the way up.

"We gonna keep doin' the gardenin' thing?" Byron asked, as the three of them pulled up chairs at the round room's counter.

"All you ever think 'bout is food, ain't it?" Tristan snapped at him.

Byron, preoccupied by the thought that someone else was on the ship with them, didn't rise to Tristan's challenge.

As for Justin, he was fairly certain that there wasn't anyone else on Mars other than themselves. He'd only come up with that hypothesis the previous night to draw the focus of conversation away from Tristan's accusations of Byron.

Justin was also now relatively certain that Baker had, in fact, deserted them. After all, if he didn't show up on the screen after Troy died, then he probably wasn't going to show up for anything. In which case the three men truly were marooned.

Which meant, in turn, that it was only a matter of time – minutes, perhaps – before Byron and Tristan finally had it out. If Tristan won that match-up – which was likely – then he'd come after Justin next. And if Byron won, ultimately the end result might be the same, with just one man left standing. After all, the food supplies would eventually start running low. And besides, Byron already appeared to be buckling under the stress of the situation, so who knew what he would do. But Justin hated the thought of killing Byron. Not only did he think of Byron as a friend, but he didn't want to kill the last human being that he was ever going to see.

The whole situation was extremely depressing, and all Justin could do was wait and watch it unfold.

"Yeah," he said, in response to Byron's question. "I think we should keep gardenin'."

Eventually Tristan went and took a shower – out of respect, he claimed, following Troy's burial ceremony – and then after he came out the three of them got on with the business of determining the work rotation. Of course Tristan and Byron couldn't be left alone with each other, and neither of them wanted to be outside the shuttle with Justin while the third man was onboard, since the person in the shuttle might decide not to re-open the airlock door. So the only solution was for Justin to remain inside all day while the other two rotated on gardening duty.

Neither Byron nor Tristan were particularly enthusiastic about being the first one to leave the ship, so they did rock-paper-scissors, and Tristan lost.

"Ahh, man!" He huffed, and went and pulled on his spacesuit.

After Tristan left the ship, Byron walked down the hallway from the airlock station to the cockpit, and he asked Justin, who was sitting in one of the cockpit chairs, "So, you figured it out yet?"

Justin spun the chair around to face him. "Whad' ya mean?"

"What we're gonna do," Byron said, in a half-whisper.

Justin shrugged. "I'm guessin' at some point one a you is gonna kill the other one. That's what it's lookin' like?"

Byron frowned, his eyes full of anger and fear. "What 'bout the other person? Whoever else might be onboard?"

Justin shook his head. "There's no one else on this ship."

"What're ya talkin' 'bout? You said yourself, it's the only thing that makes sense!"

"Naw, man. I just came up with that to keep Tristan from killin' you right then and there last night."

"But…it explains everythin' – the knife, the rover, Troy."

"The rover just broke. And maybe Troy had a heart attack. And maybe it was Troy who took the knife and then he just left it somewhere. Seriously, where's someone else gonna hide on this ship? Tristan's right, if there was another person up here, we'd know it."

Byron shook his head, unconvinced. "I think there's someone down below. Where Baker said the engine is."

"The engine is down there where the engine is. That whole nuke thing – remember? Anyone down there'd just end up gettin' fried."

"How do we know for sure? Baker said a lot a things, and now look – he's left us up here to die! He could a been lyin' 'bout just 'bout everythin'!"

Justin shook his head. "You need to get hold a yourself, man."

Byron frowned expansively. Then he took a long, deep breath, straightened up, folded his arms across his chest, and asked, "So then what're we gonna do 'bout the man outside?"

"The question is, what're you gonna do?"

Byron scowled, then he walked back down the hallway with his fingers laced together and cupped against the back of his head, like he was being arrested. After meandering around in the hallway for about a minute, he began bending down and pressing his hands against various floor panels, seeing if they would budge, seeing if any of them were the entrance to a secret passageway which led to the lower level. At one point Justin turned around in his chair to see what Byron was doing, and when he saw it he just rolled his eyes.

The next hour and forty minutes ticked by slowly, at the end of which Tristan announced over the intercom that his turn in the garden was finished and he wanted to come back onboard. After a momentary pause, Byron opened the airlock doors, first the exterior one and then the interior. His chance to suffocate Tristan had passed.

It was nearly 13:00 and Tristan was hungry, as were the other two, so they sat down at the round counter for lunch. Byron had a hamburger followed by two power bars; Justin ate macaroni and cheese and a pork rib; Tristan consumed some of his usual chicken stew, adding in an extra-large helping of salt.

No one said much, other than when Byron told Tristan, "I've been tryin' to find out if any a the floor panels might be a secret hatch, like a way to get down to the lower level."

Tristan rolled his eyes. "Good luck." Then he asked, "Didn't Baker say if we went down below we'd end up settin' off some sort a nuclear meltdown?"

Byron shrugged. "At this point, I'm not believin' anythin' Baker told us."

Tristan rolled his eyes again.

When lunch was finished Tristan took up position in the cockpit and Justin took up position at the airlock.

As Justin helped Byron fasten on his helmet, Byron told him, "You gotta watch that dude!"

"I know."

"He's gonna try somethin'!"

"Just focus on the garden."

Byron frowned, then smiled ironically. Justin pushed the yellow button to open the interior airlock door, and, after Byron stepped inside, Justin pushed the black button to close it. Then he pushed the red button to open the exterior door. When Byron began descending the external stairway, Justin pressed the black button to close that door. He hardly had time to complete this process before Tristan walked up behind him.

"You know we gotta bite the bullet on Byron," he whispered.

"We don't gotta do nothin'!" Justin whispered in reply.

"Oh yeah we do."

"Go sit in the cockpit, man. Do your job!"

"My job? My job is to stay alive. That's my job."

They stared at each other, Tristan's eyes boring into Justin's, and Justin recognized, to a fuller degree than he'd previously appreciated, just how dangerous this other man actually was.

Tristan sensed Justin's emotional response, and Justin, in turn, could sense that Tristan sensed it, so, in order to make things perfectly clear, both to Tristan and to himself, Justin stated, very strongly, "No!"

Tristan frowned. "Fine." Then he walked back to the cockpit.

An hour into Byron's shift, Tristan got up and walked down the hallway again. As he passed Justin, he said, "Goin' to the bathroom."

Justin said nothing in reply, but his prison-bred survival instinct told him that something was up.

And it was. As soon as Tristan stepped into the round room and was out of Justin's line of sight, he silently slid open the drawer with the cooking utensils, pulled out the remaining chef's knife, tucked the knife up his sleeve so that its handle rested against his bent wrist, then he pushed the drawer closed, walked over to the bathroom and shut its two thin doors behind him. A minute later he re-emerged and walked casually past Justin, back down the hall, and resumed his position in the cockpit.

Twenty minutes ticked by. Thirty minutes. Forty minutes. Justin knew what was coming. There was simply no way Tristan was going to allow Byron back onboard the shuttle. The most likely scenario was that Tristan would hit the override button in the cockpit so that Justin couldn't open the airlock's doors. Then Tristan would probably come after him with a knife; Justin figured that was the real reason Tristan had "gone to the bathroom." The only questions that remained were whether Tristan had already hit the override controls, and whether he'd turn off the intercom system to block out Byron's screaming.

The answers to both those questions were revealed at the two hour and fifty minute mark, when Byron announced over the intercom, "Okay, I'm comin' back in."

"No y'ain't," Tristan replied.

"You – " Byron began to yell, but his voice was cut short when Tristan switched off the intercom.

Justin pushed the red button on the airlock control panel to open the exterior door, but the door didn't open. Tristan had locked it. Justin pushed the button again, just to be sure, and then again, but it didn't open. One more push, but with no result.

So Justin stood up, turned around, and slowly stepped out into the hallway.

Tristan was already standing at the other end of the hall, in front of the cockpit door, the chef's knife clenched in his right hand.

"You know we gotta do this," he stated, with an eerie calm.

"Yeah, I know," Justin said. As he spoke he reached down into his pants and grabbed the handle of the missing chef's knife – which was taped to his inner thigh – and brought it out.

Tristan nodded, then smiled. "So it was you. You took it."

"'Course I did. I could see what was comin' a mile off."

Tristan nodded some more, respecting Justin's survival instinct. "Still, it ain't gonna do you no good. I'm gonna gut you like a fish 'fore you even know I gotcha."

Justin shrugged. "Maybe."

"Oh yeah, I am. I been doin' this all my life." He took a few steps towards Justin. Justin remained where he was.

"First guy I ever killed with a knife," Tristan reminisced, "was my mama's boyfriend. I was thirteen. He'd come at me with a baseball bat."

"That's nice."

"'Fore that, my stepdaddy used to swat me around with a tennis racket. Did that to me when I was eight years old."

"Sounds like you had a happy childhood."

"I been fightin' and survivin' all my life, man. All my life! And you? You just a guy who got in a fight in some bar. You know I'm gonna finish you. And you know there ain't nothin' you can do to save Byron, neither."

Justin nodded, reflexively acknowledging that Tristan was likely to win a knife fight.

Tristan frowned with satisfaction. He'd just psychologically beaten his opponent. Now it was simply a matter of going in for the kill. He took a few steps forward.

"If this is it then," Justin said, "let me ask you a question?"

Tristan paused in his forward movement. "…What?"

"You kill Troy?"

"Sure did."

Justin nodded. "How?"

"Poisoned him with some a that nasty XYZ stuff. That stuff Baker told us to use to kill bacteria. He said it kills all livin' things other than plants. So I poured some a that in my beef stew and gave ol' Troy a taste." Tristan didn't appear bothered by his confession. If anything, he seemed proud of his ingenuity.

"Nice. You poisoned you're only friend up here. I wonder how long it took him to die."

Tristan shrugged. "Not sure. I had him eat some 'round 21:30 yesterday. Told him I'd had some earlier, thought it tasted a little funny, so I asked him to see what he thought 'bout it. Then I went to bed, and Byron found him 'round midnight, right? So I'm guessin' it couldn't a taken much more than 'bout two hours."

"So why kill Troy 'stead a Byron?"

"'Cause if I killed Byron, you'd know for sure I did it. You'd come after me. Troy might not know what to do. Might even side with you. But if I killed Troy, there was a good chance you'd think Byron did it. Then the two of us could take him down. Then I'd take you out. Simpler that way. Course you didn't exactly play along like I'd hoped."

Justin nodded, and began stepping backwards.

Tristan smile-frowned sardonically. "Might as well let me make this quick. Why drag it out? You only make it worse."

He walked forward as he spoke. While he did so, Justin stepped backward through the hall's doorway and then around the corner into the round room and from there towards his bedroom.

"Only one of us survives this thing," Tristan explained, following Justin through the doorway and around the corner into the round room. "Only one of us comes out on top. And I'm him. *I'm* him! I'm the king of the space shuttle." He pointed the knife towards his own chest. "*I'm* him!"

Justin took a couple more steps backward, into the doorway of his bedroom. Then he glanced down at the button that would close the door.

Tristan was now only about seven feet away. When he saw Justin's momentary glance, he instantly understood the spot to which Justin's eyes had flicked.

"You're a coward, man," Tristan said. "I mean, I get it. But still, you're a coward."

Justin shrugged. "Maybe. Or maybe I just like the irony."

"What irony?"

"The irony a lettin' you take yourself out."

"…What're ya talkin'?"

Justin shrugged again, then hunkered down into a fighting stance, which caused Tristan to momentarily pause in his forward advance.

"I figured you did Troy," Justin admitted. "Figured that out 'fore you told me. Byron's not a career killer and you are, so I figured it was you."

Tristan shrugged. "So?"

"Thing was, there weren't any signs a struggle on Troy. And he wasn't stabbed. So he must a been poisoned. And there's only one poison on this ship. So you must a done it with that XYZ stuff. Question was, how'd you get Troy to drink it? You must a put it in his food. But how could you know ahead a time what he'd be eatin'? You'd have to give the food to him to try. What'd be your excuse for doin' that? You'd say you wanted him to sample it. Why? Doesn't matter, you'd come up with a reason."

Tristan shrugged again. "Congratulations. So you're a smart guy. Doesn't mean I'm changin' my mind 'bout endin' you."

"Well now see here's the fun part – you only ever eat two things: beef stew and chicken stew. That means that if you asked him to sample somethin', there were only two options. So guess what – this mornin', while you were takin' a shower and Byron was in the bathroom, I put some a the broth from your beef stew leftovers into your chicken stew leftovers and I put some of the chicken broth into the beef stew. Get it?"

Tristan's eyes narrowed and his knuckles whitened around the gripped chef's knife. "...You lyin...."

"You added a lot a salt to that chicken stew today at lunch, didn't you? Somethin' 'bout that stew just didn't taste right, did it?"

Tristan's eyes narrowed even tighter, until he was squinting. His lips curled.

Justin glanced at the digital clock on the wall. "You said it couldn't a taken much more than 'bout two hours for Troy to die, right? And it's been just 'bout two hours since you ate that chicken stew, Tristan."

"You lie!" Tristan hissed.

"Yeah, well, guess I'll be seein' ya 'round, man. Maybe on some other spaceship."

Justin pushed the button to close the bedroom door. The door slid instantly shut. Less than a second later he pushed the button to lock it.

This done, his stance relaxed, he stood up straighter and then he took a long, slow, deep breath.

"You lie!" Tristan yelled again, from the other side of the door.

A few seconds elapsed and then Justin heard Tristan pressing against the bedroom door, trying to force it open. That didn't work.

Shortly thereafter something hard banged loudly against the door – apparently Tristan had thrown something at it. The door remained in place.

Next came a thudding sound, as if Tristan was taking a long object and repeatedly hitting the door with it, like with a battering ram. The door didn't give way. Various other objects impacted the door over the next few minutes, to no effect. Eventually the assaults stopped.

About ten minutes on, Justin heard Tristan yell out again, "I'm him! *I'm* him!"

And soon thereafter, everything fell silent.

Justin gave it another twenty minutes, just to be on the safe side. Then he gripped the knife tightly, hunkered down into a fighting stance and, preparing himself psychologically for the possibility that Tristan was still alive and standing right outside the bedroom, he pushed the button to unlock the door. Then he pushed the button to open it.

The door slid effortlessly open, notwithstanding all the abuse it had just been dealt.

All of Justin's muscles tensed, ready for a fight, but Tristan wasn't standing there. Of course he might be standing just to the side of the door, ready to attack as Justin stepped into the round room, so Justin did a momentary feint, jabbing the knife into the air first to the right of the doorway, then to the left. Nothing happened. So he stepped slowly into the round room.

No sign of Tristan.

As he walked towards the counter, however, he saw a foot at the end of a leg which was stretched out on the floor behind the countertop. He stepped cautiously around the counter and saw that the foot and the leg did in fact belong to Tristan, who was lying against the far wall of the round room, with both of his legs out in front of him, his arms limp at his sides, his hands lying on the floor with the palms turned upwards, and his chin lying on his chest.

His chest wasn't moving.

As for the chef's knife – it was there, on the floor, lying a few feet from the lifeless body.

Justin grabbed a cup off the countertop and, taking careful aim, he tossed it at Tristan. The cup bounced off Tristan's head without causing the slightest flinch.

So Justin sighed, dropped the knife and stepped backwards until his shoulder blades touched the rounded wall, then he slid weakly down the wall until he was sitting on the floor. He sat there for about a minute, as the full extent of his present circumstances registered in his mind.

Then he announced, out loud, to no one in particular, "Looks like *I'm* him."

PART II

HER

I

"Hello Justin."

Baker had waited for several moments after the screen flicked on, to see if Justin would notice and look up at him. When this didn't happen, he announced himself.

As soon as he saw Baker's face, Justin burst out laughing; it was an ironic, tragic, existentially bemused laugh. When he finally settled down, he said, "Hey there….Hey there, Baker. How ya doin'?"

Baker smiled. "I'm fine, Justin. How are you?"

"Fine." Justin laughed some more as he spoke. "Just fine. Can't complain."

"Glad to hear it."

"Where ya been?"

"Right here."

"The whole time?"

"The whole time."

"Watchin' the whole thing?"

"That's right."

"So then…you know everybody else is dead?"

"I do."

Justin considered this. Then he observed, "You don't look all that disappointed."

Baker shrugged. "I'm not. There was only ever going to be one of you who survived. That was the assumption all along."

Justin's eyebrows rose up his forehead and froze there. Then he nodded, as he tried to process Baker's statement. "Why's that? 'Cause a food supplies and stuff?"

"Food, oxygen, water – those are all important to conserve, of course. But that's not the main reason."

"Then…what *is* the main reason, exactly?" Justin's voice turned somewhat hostile.

Baker looked at – and through – him for a few moments, and then he answered, "There can only be one ruler of Mars, Justin."

"What?"

"There can only be one ruler of Mars."

"…Ruler of Mars?"

"Correct. And as it turns out, you've just successfully completed the interview process."

"…What're ya talkin' 'bout?"

"Well we couldn't exactly interview the five of you when you all were back in prison, now could we? And we couldn't run stress tests, or even give you a form to fill out. Besides, none of that would have been conclusive. The only way to know for certain who wouldn't crack up on that shuttle, who wouldn't get killed, who was truly capable of surviving, was to send the five of you up there and see what happened."

There was a long pause, as Justin pondered this idea. And then he nodded. "Securitization."

"That's right."

"But what're ya talkin' 'bout – "ruler of Mars"? You're sayin' I'm stayin up here? There ain't no second ship comin', is there?" An edge of panic entered his voice.

"There is in fact a second ship. And it'll be arriving there in three weeks, not three months. But it's not coming there to take you home. The simple fact, Justin, is that there is no returning from Mars. The energy required to lift a spaceship back up off that planet, the technology and the systems required, not to mention the resources for completing the return trip to Earth, all make it extremely prohibitive."

Baker allowed this point to sink in, then added, "Everyone who goes to Mars, stays on Mars."

Somehow Justin wasn't surprised that he was never getting off the planet, yet hearing it straight from Baker was still deeply unsettling.

"So you lied, when you told us we could all go home."

"That's correct."

"But…you said you'd always be brutally honest with us. I mean, I get not tellin' us right away when you knew Calvin was done. But this is…this is somethin' else. You.…" And he shook his head, winded by the impact of this new news. "You told us you'd always be brutally honest."

"That was a lie."

"How many other lies did you tell us?"

"Several."

Justin almost asked why, but then caught himself, assuming that Baker would simply say that such lies were necessary.

"So then..." Justin asked, trying to gather his composure as he rose to a straighter sitting position and folded in his legs, "how do I even know that you're tellin' me the truth right now?"

Baker smiled. "Let's try an experiment. Look at my face and tell me if what I tell you now is a lie."

Justin did as directed, staring intently at Baker's features on the screen.

"The second ship," Baker stated, "which will be arriving there in three weeks, will be empty, aside from supplies for you."

Baker waited for Justin to say whether he thought that was a lie. When Justin said nothing, Baker asked him, "What I just said – was that the truth or a lie? Based upon your reading of my expression, what's your conclusion?"

"I...think that was the truth."

"Actually it was a lie. Which means that you won't be able to tell when I'm lying and when I'm telling you the truth. The only way you'll know is when what I say is going to happen actually does indeed happen."

Justin shook his head in bemused exasperation. Then a thought occurred to him. "Wait, so you were lyin' just now when you said that the second ship is empty, except for supplies? Then what else is on it?"

"People."

"Seriously?"

"Yes."

"How many?"

"Ten."

"Ten people – and they'll be here in three weeks?"

"That's correct."

"Men? Women?"

"Both."

Justin's hopes slightly revived. "How many a each?"

"Five and five."

Justin considered this information, and Baker could tell what he was thinking.

"They're all over sixty," Baker explained.

"Over sixty years old?" Justin's hopes dimmed.

"Yes. We want you to get used to ruling people who don't present a major challenge. They're a warm-up, if you will, to the younger groups we'll be sending up there subsequently."

"When are those other groups comin'?"

"In a couple years."

"So…what? For the next couple years I'm gonna be the ruler of a retirement community on Mars?"

Baker smiled his pressed-lips smile. "Justin," he said, "I want to show you something."

"Show me somethin'? What? Where?"

"In the shuttle's lower level."

"The…lower level?"

"Yes."

"Where the nuke engine is?"

"There isn't any nuke engine down there. The main engines on a space shuttle are all on the outside, in the back. Of course the ones on that particular shuttle have been modified as per the requirements of an interplanetary journey, but they still look like typical shuttle engines. You may have noticed them – the three big, cone-like pieces. That being said, there *is* a small chunk of radioactive plutonium in a special compartment which is located in the bottom, third level of the ship. It's been supplying all the energy onboard the shuttle, particularly to the gravity-generation technology. But that's it."

"So then…what's down below if there ain't no engine?"

"That's what I want to show you."

II

"If you'll just walk out into the hall…." Baker instructed.

"Okay…."

Justin rose unsteadily to his feet. Awash in emotions – surprise, despair, confusion, resignation, sadness regarding Byron, relief but also sadness for Tristan – he stepped awkwardly into the hall. As he did so, one of the floor panels in the middle of the hallway slid open.

"What the…?" Justin said, instantly feeling like he was losing his balance; like his grip on his surroundings was slipping. But he steadied himself and walked forward in order to peer into the revealed space. As he did so, the top of a black, metal, spiral staircase came into view. It lead down into a brightly lit lower space.

"You gotta be kiddin' me."

"Please, feel free to follow the staircase down."

Justin took a deep breath. "Uh, yeah, okay…."

The metallic spiral led into a very large room which was the size of the upper floor's hallway and container spaces combined, and also had more distance between the floor and the ceiling than did the top level. This large room was decorated like the inside of a stylish New York City loft apartment, with abstract paintings on the walls, two metallic coffee tables hosting magazines and books, a stylish wood-and-metal dining table, an assortment of chairs in various places, a gray leather couch, and a small kitchen area built into the right-hand wall. Straight ahead, at the far end of the room – more or less below the spot where the hallway on the upper floor met the entrance to the round room – was a wall which had two doors.

"You…I…this…." Justin muttered, unable to form sentences.

"Yes?" Baker asked, over the intercom, which evidently was wired into this room as well. "Do you like it?"

"I…I mean…this…?"

"Hmm?"

"This…has been here the whole time…."

"Obviously."

"I can't believe this room was here and we didn't even know 'bout it."

"And not just that room."

"…Whad' ya mean?"

There was a pause, for dramatic effect, then Baker said, "Megan, if you please…."

"What?" Justin asked. But just as he spoke one of the two doors in the far wall – the door on the left – slid open and a woman stepped out. She appeared to be of Eurasian background – nice looking, though more attractive than beautiful – and she was wearing a long green dress with a silk flower-print running down the middle of it. The soft effect of her attire was balanced by her sharp cheekbones and by the sharpness of her expression, which was formed via the angle of her lips as she smiled – just a little bit hesitantly – and by the deep black shade of her eyes.

"Hello, Justin," she said.

Now Justin was truly, completely and utterly speechless. He just stood there.

"My name's Megan."

Justin remained frozen.

"I've been here on this ship the whole time," she said. "It's nice to finally be able to meet you."

"You…." Was all Justin managed to say, after several seconds. The pure implausibility of this woman's presence was made all the more bizarre by her hint of a New Jersey accent.

Megan smiled a little wider. It was an interesting smile; sharp, like a chef's knife.

"I was hoping you'd be the one who survived," she told him.

"As was I," Baker chimed in over the intercom.

Baker's voice snapped Justin out of his numbed state. "Baker, man," Justin replied, still staring – transfixed – at Megan, "you just told me that pretty much everythin' you've told me is a lie. So you can't really expect me to believe that."

"Then why do you think you were the first of the five to wake up? Hmm? It was because I woke you up first. And why did I do that? So that you'd be a step ahead of the others from the start. And I must say, you didn't disappoint. That business of stealing the knife, and then mixing the beef stew and the chicken stew, figuring out what Tristan was up to before he even told you – that was all very nicely done. Splendid, in fact."

"Who…are you?" Justin asked Megan, not seeming to pay any attention to Baker's statement.

"My name's Megan, like I said."

"What're you doin' here?"

"Same as you."

"Which is…?"

"Founding the colony. With you."

"With me?"

"Mmhm." She smiled still wider and took another step towards him.

"Did you…did you choose…to be up here?"

"Yes."

"You chose to come to this completely lifeless planet, knowing you'd never get back to Earth?"

Megan shrugged. "Lifeless for now. Not forever."

Justin shook his head, still trying to get his bearings, any bearings. "Where…where're you from?"

"New Brunswick, New Jersey."

"And…do you know where I'm from? Do you know all 'bout me?"

"Mmhm. You're from Cleveland. You used to work for the Post Office. Then you worked in the billing office of a welding factory." As she spoke she continued walking slowly towards him. "Then you got in a fight in a bar, the other person beat you up, and you ran over him with your car."

Justin nodded, embarrassed by the details of his past life. "And what 'bout you?" He asked, somewhat defensively. "Was comin' up here your ticket out a somethin'?"

She nodded. "Yes." Now she was standing close to him – hardly a foot away – and looking into his eyes, her gaze simultaneously sharp and soft.

"Megan was a nurse back on Earth," Baker explained. "Highly skilled. Well educated. But she wound up in the business of giving out – selling, I should say – painkillers to patients. And that one little step into criminal activity ultimately led her into a variety of unlawful enterprises. The result was that she was given a fifteen-year prison sentence. Early on in her incarceration, however, I managed to arrange things so that she could successfully abscond."

"You…?" Justin began to ask.

"Broke her out, yes. They're still looking for her back in Jersey. I suspect they're not going to find her. It'll be a real Sherlock Holmes who can track her down up there on Mars."

"You broke out a prison?" Justin asked Megan, as each of their pairs of eyes explored the others.

"Mmhm. Although Bill did most of the work. All I had to do was follow the plan he gave me."

"It was a medium security facility," Baker noted. "It really wasn't too complicated."

Justin nodded, struggling to absorb this information.

"So," Megan said, putting forward her right hand, "nice to meet you."

Justin smiled ironically, then shook her hand. "Yeah, you too."

"I'm glad to see you two are getting along so swimmingly," Baker observed. "Obviously, that's going to be useful if you're going to be the proud parents of the first Martian-born member of our colony."

"What?" Justin de-clasped Megan's hand, simultaneously jolting his head upwards towards the nearest intercom speaker, which was in the ceiling above his head. "Wait…what?"

"The first Martian-born child, Justin. If you're going to be the ruler of Mars, and Megan is to be your lady, then presumably you'll have the first child up there on the red planet. Why do you think we decided to have Megan join you up there in the first place?"

"But…I just…we just met."

"And clearly it's love at first sight. Or would you prefer to marry one of the sixty year old ladies we're currently sending your way?"

"…But…this is crazy…."

"Actually it's completely logical, which is probably the part that's throwing you."

"…I…."

"It's vitally important to the future of that colony, after all, that babies start getting born up there ASAP. Not only will that increase the size of the colony, but you obviously can't have a genuine society without children. And since we can't ship children up there – their rapid growth rates cause insurmountable problems when it comes to putting them in an incubation bed for seven months – you're going to have to make them up there yourselves.

"There's also another, fundamentally important point: we need to have people up there who have no direct experience of Earth; people who consider Mars to be their true home. If the colony is going to survive the coming decades, we'll need as many such people up there as possible."

Justin shook his head again, in continued disbelief.

"What?" Megan asked, with a smile, already knowing what the answer was going to be. "Don't you like me?"

"Yeah, no, it's not that. You're...you're great, it's just...."

"You'll notice," Baker said, "that Megan is a blend of Eurasian ethnicities. Her father – my college roommate, as it turns out – was from Uzbekistan. Her mother was from Turkey. Her lineage also includes some Arab, Chinese, and a hint of Indian. Now if you pair that with your lineage – African, German, Native American, and a trace of Mexican – we'll end up getting children with truly global genetic backgrounds.

"You remember, at the beginning of your stay up there, Byron asked me why all of you had brown skin, why we'd selected you all at least in part based on racial characteristics. And do you remember what I told him? I said that it was to prevent gang fights, and also because non-whites are given the death sentence at much higher rates than whites for the same crimes, so there was a certain statistical probability of finding five non-white inmates to fit the bill. Well, that was all true, but it was hardly the whole truth."

"Why am I not surprised?"

"It wasn't even the most important part of the truth. The primary reason the five of you were selected was because of the breadth of your genetic backgrounds and the fact that those backgrounds would nicely complement Megan's.

"We want the first children on Mars to draw from the widest possible genetic pool because that will minimize the risk of regressive traits becoming prominent in the group, and it will also mean that, should the human race on Earth end up getting obliterated, then the genetic history of our race will be preserved, as much as possible, in the DNA of our little Martians."

Even though Justin couldn't see Baker – there were no screens in that room for Baker to appear on – he could almost hear Baker smiling while providing this explanation.

"So, now then, Justin," Baker continued, "I know you've already had a big day, but we might as well get on with it and perform the marriage ceremony, don't you think?"

"…Uhh…."

"This way," Megan said, with that smile of hers, taking Justin by the hand and leading him to the right-hand door in the far wall.

She pushed a button to open the door, then Justin followed her into a small room which had a wooden, antique-looking table and an antique-looking chair, both of which were placed to the right side. There was also as a large, flat screen TV – like the one up in the round room – occupying the center of the wall which faced the door. The only other decoration in the room was an eight by eleven inch door – apparently the door to a safe – built into the right-hand wall. As Megan led Justin inside, Baker's face flashed onto the TV screen.

"This will be your office, your special room, where you and I will communicate in private," Baker explained to Justin. "You'll notice that there aren't other screens in that second-story section of the shuttle. The rest of that section is the private residence of the ruling family of Mars. But there is this one screen in this room, which you and I will use for our discussions. And today, right now, this room is also serving as the wedding ceremony chamber."

Baker smiled his lips-pressed smile, and then he said, "So, here we go."

Megan had continued holding Justin's hand after she'd lead him into the room, and now she squeezed that hand, looked up at him, and smiled. He smiled awkwardly in response.

"By the way," Baker added, "I should probably first point out that I do in fact have a Nevada marriage officiant's license, so this is all entirely legal."

That point clarified, he proceeded:

"Dearly beloved, we are gathered here today – you up there on Mars, me in an undisclosed location in Nevada – to witness the joining together in matrimony of Megan Babayev and Justin Jones. These two people, having found themselves in unique circumstances, and wishing to lead enjoyable lives as well as to act on behalf of the survival of the human species, have decided to make the following vows to one another, here today, before me as their witness. Now, Megan, if you would please get the rings."

Megan let go of Justin's hand and picked up a small ornate box off the antique wooden desk. Opening the box, she took out two rings, set the box back on the table, then gave one ring to Justin and kept the other in her right hand. This done, she re-clasped his right hand with her left.

"Great," Baker said. "Now, Justin, if you will please repeat after me: I, Justin Jones...."

"...Uhh...." Justin said, still stunned, still feeling as if he wasn't fully within the moment, and instead was watching things play out around him like a spectator," I...Justin Jones...."

"Do solemnly swear...."

"...Do solemnly swear...."

"To be Megan's husband...."

"To...be Megan's husband...."

"As long as I shall live...."

"Uhh...." And he looked at Megan, his legs going weak beneath him, "as long as...as long as I shall live...."

"For better or for worse...."

"For better or for worse...."

"In sickness and in health...."

"In sickness and in health...."

"And regardless of anything else that may occur."

"And..." Justin looked at the screen, then he glanced at Megan, then he looked back at the screen again, "and regardless of anythin' else, that may occur."

"Excellent. Now Justin, if you'd be a gentleman and put that ring that you're holding there on Megan's finger."

Justin did as instructed, very awkwardly.

When this was completed, Baker asked Megan to repeat back the same lines, with regard to Justin, at the end of which she slipped the ring that she was holding onto Justin's finger.

"Now then," Baker finished, with a dramatic flourish in his voice, "by the power invested in me by the state of Nevada, I pronounce you man and wife. You may kiss the bride."

Justin hadn't kissed a woman in a long time. And as he did so all the emotional resistance which he'd been generating in response to his present circumstances simply collapsed. The power of Megan's kiss, the way she looked, the stylish manner in which their residence was decorated, the fact that he was going to be the ruler of a planet, it all definitely had an appeal. So he gave in.

'Yeah,' he figured, 'why not?'

After the kiss was completed, Baker announced, "And now the honeymoon can begin! Before that gets underway, however, I do think it'd be best, Justin, if you first went and buried those two bodies."

III

The other room on the shuttle's second level – the room from which Megan had first emerged – was the master bedroom. It came with an actual bed as opposed to simply a hibernation unit, although there was one of those in there as well, set against the far left wall. Aside from that the room looked like a typical, stylishly decorated apartment bedroom, with a modernist metal bed frame, a large, metallically framed mirror on one wall, two wood-and-metal chests-of-drawers, and a walk-in closet. A door on the far wall led into a tiled bathroom, complete with a tub.

"Nice," Justin commented, as Megan led him in by the hand.

"I'm glad you like it."

"You choose the decorations?"

"Mmhm. It was all packed in boxes for the trip and then I unloaded it after I was woken up."

"I'm glad my wife's got good taste." He felt compelled to sweet talk her despite the fact that the marriage was a done deal.

She smiled her chef's knife smile. "I'll wait here for you while you bury those bodies."

He nodded. "Right."

And so off he went….

And then the following morning, at 10:00, Megan told him, "You need to go check in with Bill. With Baker. In the study."

"What?"

"You need to check in with him. It's 10:00."

"Now? But it's our honeymoon."

"I know, but it's important for you two to talk. The others will be here in three weeks. You need to start your training."

"My training?"

"Mmhm. Don't worry, I'll be here when you get back."

"Seriously? I gotta go talk to him now?"

"Mmhm."

Justin considered this, then he exhaled, nodded reluctantly, and rose from the bed.

Baker was waiting for him there on the TV screen when Justin entered the room with the antique table and chair.

"Good morning, Justin."

"Hey there, Baker."

"Enjoying your honeymoon?"

"Oh yeah."

"Glad to hear it. Now if you'll please take that antique table and set it between the two of us. And then place that chair behind it, so that you can sit at the table facing me."

Justin did as instructed.

"Great. Now please shut the door behind you."

"You want me to shut it?"

"Yes. Megan already knows that the discussions you and I are going to have in here will be private."

"Okay...." And Justin shut the door.

"Now please make yourself comfortable in that seat there."

Justin sat down.

"So now, here's my first question for you: why do you think I just asked you to shut that door behind you? Why do you think this is going to be a private conversation? More generally, why is it that you and I are going to be having lots of private conversations in here?"

Justin thought for a minute. Before he had a chance to answer, Baker asked him, "Do you think it's because Megan can't be trusted? Or, let me put it this way: do you think that I trust you more than I trust her?"

"Uh...."

"That wouldn't make a lot of sense, would it? After all, I know her quite a bit better than I know you. She and I have known each other for years, in fact. In addition to which, her father was a friend of mine. So no, it's not about trust. Do you think it's because you're smarter than she is, that she wouldn't understand certain subjects we might discuss?"

"I doubt it."

"Right. If anything, she's smarter. She's certainly much better educated than you are – no denying that."

Justin nodded.

"So then why did I ask you to close that door?"

Justin shrugged. "Why?"

"Because what we're going to be talking about in this room, in our study sessions together, is politics. Real politics. Not the fairytales that people tell themselves. We're going to be talking about hard and difficult decisions. Decisions about life and death. Decisions that you, as the ruler of Mars, will need to make, and that you will ultimately need to make alone. And so this training needs to be focused on you, and only you."

Justin nodded.

"Do you remember," Baker continued, "what I told you and the other men, about why I chose death row inmates to send to Mars? Do you remember all the reasons?"

Justin nodded again. "Yeah, you said it was 'cause we were willin' to do whatever it takes to survive. And we were used to confined spaces. And we'd be less upset 'bout gettin' kidnapped than other people would."

"Right. And that if you died up there, then no one down here on Earth would need to be informed."

"Yeah."

"Now, which of those do you think was the primary reason?"

Justin answered without hesitating. "The one 'bout bein' willin' to do whatever it takes."

"Precisely!" Baker was pleased with Justin's clear grasp of this point. "You're willing to do things that most people won't even consider. And obviously that particular character trait played a rather central role in the fact that you're still alive. You took the knife before anyone else considered doing so. You poisoned Tristan – or at least allowed him to poison himself – before he even came after you. And you didn't try to rescue Byron. You calculated that Tristan might well kill you in a knife fight, so you let the poison do its work, and in the process you left Byron to his fate. Point being: you're willing and able to think tactically and strategically in terms of life and death. And that is an essential quality not simply for surviving on Mars but for ruling Mars. For ruling other people on Mars."

Justin sat quietly as Baker spoke. In truth, he wasn't nearly as comfortable with killing as Baker made out. The nightmares and guilt still came from killing Tobey Williams in the parking lot of that bar. And he knew there'd be nightmares about Byron too, although they probably wouldn't be as intense as his nightmares about Tobey. After all, he hadn't murdered Byron, and he likely couldn't have saved him. As for what happened to Tristan – he didn't anticipate any lingering emotional anguish about that.

"Now I don't think I need to spend a lot of time," Baker continued, "explaining to you why scientists – the sort that I'm surrounded by down here; the ones who spend their lives studying space and how to get there – aren't the most obvious candidates for ruling a Martian colony.

"For one thing, they're typically extraordinary, in terms of their intelligence, which means that the way they relate to the world and the way that it relates to them is very much out of the norm. Added to that is the fact that they spend their adult lives working inside highly sanitized laboratories or up in ivory towers, focusing on abstract equations while dealing with the relatively iron laws of biology and physics. The messy here-and-now of political order is rarely their concern. For them, political drama is what transpires in the process of applying for and administering government grants."

Justin nodded.

"And as for professional astronauts – the people who typically get sent into space – they're not ideal candidates for setting up and running a colony either. They're usually boy scouts – or girl scouts, as the case may be – and boy scouts are trained to preserve societies, not to create them. Whereas what we're engaged in is very much a creative act. An act which will require doing things that a boy scout would never do."

Justin nodded.

"Which therefore brings us back to you, and to your particular skill set. Now, tell me this: have you ever heard of someone named Romulus?"

"…Romulus? Uh, yeah, I think so…."

"He was the legendary founder of Rome."

"…Yeah."

"Do you know anything about him?"

"…Didn't he kill his brother or somethin'?" This random fact had somehow survived the general purge that Justin had conducted towards the majority of information which he'd acquired in high school.

"Excellent. Right. He did. He killed his brother Remus."

"Yeah, I remember that."

"He was also cared for by a wolf when he was a baby."

"No kiddin'?"

"It's all just legend, of course, but legends are more important than facts when it comes to understanding fundamental truths. And the legend is that when Romulus and Remus were babies, they were abandoned, and then they were found by a wolf who looked after them.

"Another interesting biographical note: Romulus' parents were a mortal woman – that is to say, a human – and a male god."

"No kiddin'?"

"Indeed."

"Interestin' guy."

"He was. Now, answer me this: what do all those bits of legend tell us about Romulus? What's the essential point about his character that is being conveyed?"

Justin considered the question. "That he was...unusual? That he wasn't typical?"

"Correct. Not typical how?"

"Whad' ya mean?"

"All those stories, they point to one, overriding idea, don't they? That Romulus stood outside the bounds of society. That the founder of Roman civilization was himself uncivilized. Conceived in part by a god, he was better than a normal human. Suckled by a wolf, he was wilder and more savage than a normal human. The man who could kill his brother – who could break a fundamental taboo – also went on to create one of the strongest societies, with one of the strongest set of laws, that mankind has ever produced.

"The larger point, beyond simply considering Romulus, is that the creators of civilized society cannot be bound by civilized society. After all, a creator cannot – almost by definition – be bound by the limits of his own creation."

Baker paused for effect. Then he continued.

"That, my dear Justin, is, quite simply, why I chose you. That is why you are up there on Mars. You're not just going to preside over that colony like a president; you're going to rule it, like a founding monarch. Your role is to be the Romulus of Mars."

Justin nodded, feeling simultaneously attracted and repulsed by Baker's words. "...It does have a certain ring...."

Baker smiled. "Now, as for me, I don't claim to be a politician. I made my career in finance. And that's what I majored in when I went to the University of Chicago. But when I was at Chicago I wound up in a political science course during the second semester of my freshman year called "Introduction to Political Philosophy." I only took it because it satisfied an elective. At the time I didn't have the slightest interest in politics. But the professor was exceptional. His name was Jeremy Godwin. A Brit, and very well educated, and in that peculiarly British way where it doesn't seem like any effort was expended to acquire a truly masterful level of erudition. It was as if it had simply just happened. Anyway, he hooked my mind in a manner that no other teacher ever has, and even though I still majored in finance – I was determined to get rich, after all – political philosophy became a hobby for me, and it has been ever since.

"My reason for mentioning all this is that, thanks to Dr. Godwin, there're a whole host of mistakes we're not going to make up there when it comes to you running that colony. And the major mistake we're going to avoid is the one of having you run it like as a democracy."

"So…not as a democracy?"

"Correct."

"Why not?"

Baker smiled. He'd been waiting for that question, and clearly relished the opportunity to provide an answer.

"Let's consider recent events, shall we? Consider what happened with you and the other four men, pretty much right from the start. What happened is that the five of you formed factions. There was the Tristan-Troy faction, and the Byron-Calvin faction, which you eventually joined, more or less. Why did those factions occur? Because there was no power preventing them from occurring. Or to put it another way: everyone was empowered. And what did that produce? A fight. A civil war, if you will.

"The problem with democracy is that, when the general populace is empowered, it naturally divides up into competitive factions. That then typically results – as it did in the early historical cases of democracy, such as ancient Athens and so forth – in either the permanent domination of one particular faction or in competition between the factions. And that competition can become highly destructive. Furthermore, the first option – of domination by one faction – often leads to the second option – of destructive competition between factions – since factional dominance is rarely permanent or all pervasive.

"So then the puzzle is how to set up a stable democratic regime, given the problem of factions. As you might imagine, numerous political philosophers have sought to solve that puzzle in numerous ways.

"Then along came us yanks. And in our homespun yet brilliantly practical way, we – and more specifically, Mr. James Madison – figured something out: that you can solve the factional problem if you have a large state. Why? Because in a big state no single faction can dominate all the other factions for very long. As a result, various factions which have very little in common with each other are obliged to band together to promote a collectively watered-down agenda, which is then pursued, in turn, by elected representatives rather than via direct democracy. And, given the challenge of permanently persuading a large electorate to vote for any one factional coalition, none of the coalitions is able to guarantee that its elected representatives will be able to hold onto power for too long.

"The end result is that extremism is dulled and typically nothing too momentous gets accomplished in the political realm. What this looks like in practice, ultimately, is essentially what we've got with the major American political parties.

"It's exceptionally effective. The state remains intact, civil wars are avoided, for the most part, and everyone can focus on making money rather than worrying too much about politics. Make sense?"

"…Uh, yeah, actually."

"Good. Now obviously it's going to take decades – at least – to grow our Martian colony to the point where it's large enough to solve the factional problem via this method of scale. In fact, if anything, the usual factional issues would be amplified if we tried to establish a democracy up there in the near term, since, given the truly tiny population and the extraordinarily tight quarters, it'd be all but impossible to "dilute" the factions, and it'd likewise be difficult for one faction to entirely overpower another faction, especially since the opportunities for violence between the factions would be more or less constant.

"That therefore means that, until the day comes when we have a large population up there, we're left with a choice: either we institute a monarchy – the rule of one person – or an oligarchy, which is the rule of the few. I've opted for monarchy since the rule of the few would likely be even more untenable up there than the rule of the many, for the reasons just mentioned regarding the difficulties of maintaining single-faction dominance. Besides which, oligarchies typically collapse from infighting eventually anyway.

"We are therefore going to concentrate executive authority in the hands of a single ruler so that he can dominate that colony for the long-term benefit of the colony. And by "executive authority" I mean, quite literally, the authority to execute not just the laws but people. That is an authority that I – as both the creator and funder of this project – am now bestowing upon you. But it's also something that you're going to have to establish by will and skill over the other colonists we're sending up there.

"And of course that's going to be a challenge since those colonists are products of modern society, with all its knee-jerk assumptions about the legitimacy of democratic governance. Those assumptions are going to influence the other colonists' behavior even though they've all been told that the mission leader – you – will be permanently in charge. Your core job, therefore, will be to iron those assumptions out of them so that they, in turn, will then help facilitate your ability to dominate the next group that arrives, and so on."

Justin rolled all this around in his mind. "...You said the second spaceship is gettin' here in three weeks?"

"Indeed. Admittedly that doesn't give us a lot of time to get you trained up as a monarch, but we didn't have any choice due to something called the Mars Opposition. It's a period of a few months which occurs every two years when the elliptical orbits of Earth and Mars bring the two planets within relatively close proximity of each other. Essentially it's the best window of time during which to launch a Mars mission. And so we arranged for your ship to arrive at the beginning of the Opposition period and for the second ship to arrive towards the end, giving us the longest possible stretch of time in which to allow you to outlive the other four men and then to begin prepping for your ruler-ship."

Justin cogitated about this. "You know...you know I've never led a group a people before, right?"

"Oh yes, I'm well aware. Which is why we need to get cracking. Luckily we have something onboard there, in that safe in the wall to your right, that will make your job infinitely easier. With it in-hand you'll be able to keep the rest of the group very much in line."

"What is it? A weapon?"

"Indeed."

IV

The face of the safe was filled by a digital screen, which Baker now asked Justin to approach.

"That safe has three security measures," Baker explained. "First there's a fingerprint and palm scanner. To activate it please place your right hand against the screen."

Justin did so.

A series of horizontal red lines appeared and ran down the length of the screen, reading the details of Justin's hand.

Then a red circle – the size of an apple – appeared on the screen with words above it which read, "Place right eye here."

"The second security measure," Baker continued, "is an iris and retina scanner. Please place your right eye in front of that circle like the screen says."

Justin proceeded to do so. After five seconds the circle and the words above it were replaced by the image of a keypad which contained the numbers 1 through 9.

"The third security measure is a numerical code. Please choose a passcode which includes all nine of the numbers on the keypad."

Justin raised his eyebrows, thought for a moment, then chose a code which he knew he could remember: 654321987. Or in other words, the numbers running right-to-left on the middle row, then the same for the first row and the same for the last row.

After he completed this the image of the keypad was replaced by the image of a rectangular red button with the word "ENTER" written on it in black.

"So now," Baker said, "even if someone forces you to place your hand and your eye against the screen, that won't do them a whole lot of good since they'll still need to figure out the code, and that will be highly unlikely, even if they do a fingerprint stain analysis of the keypad, since all the numbers are being used. Their only option will be to convince you to give them the code. And under no circumstances, whatsoever, can you ever tell anyone that code."

"What's in here? A gun?"

"Something much deadlier than a gun. Besides, shooting a gun off inside a space shuttle would be counterproductive."

"Is it a lightsaber?"

"Better than a lightsaber."

"Seriously?"

"Oh yes."

"Can I open this thing now?"

"Please do."

So Justin did. He pushed the ENTER button and the safe's door slid open. What he saw inside, to his great surprise, was a very thin little leather-bound book. Nothing more.

"A...book?"

"Not just any book."

"Can I take it out?

"Yes."

Justin reached in and pulled it out. The book was titled *The Prince*. The author's name was Niccolò Machiavelli.

"This is *it*?" Justin asked.

"My dear Justin, do you have any idea what "it" is? Have you ever heard of "it" before?"

"No."

"I see. Well, "it" is one of the most dangerous books ever written. Its author, Mr. Niccolò Machiavelli, established the foundation for modern political philosophy, and he did that, in no small part, with that book. Your ability to understand "it" is going to determine whether your rule up there on Mars is successful or not."

"When was it written? How come I never heard of it?"

"The answer to your second question is: the state of American education. The answer to your first question is that it was written in the 1500s."

Justin was shocked. "The 1500s?"

"That's correct."

"You want me to run a colony on Mars in 2018 by readin' a book that was written by some dude in the 1500s?"

"That is precisely what I want you to do."

Justin shook his head. Then he said, "…Okaaay…." The word was laced with skepticism.

"Good. Now please take a seat and place that book on the table. Before we delve into it I need to properly introduce you to Machiavelli."

Justin did as directed, although he slouched into his chair, like a reluctant pupil.

Baker's face was replaced on the screen by the painting of a thin man in a black and red robe, who had tight facial features and a close-cropped haircut and whose thin lips formed a small, tight smile.

"That's the man himself. He was born in 1469 and died in 1527. Almost all his life was spent in or near the city of Florence, Italy."

The painting of Machiavelli was replaced on the screen by a map of Italy, with a star over the location of Florence. Then the map zoomed down to street level, showing Florence's central square, the Piazza della Signoria.

"Florence at the time was its own independent state; a city-state. And Machiavelli was a bureaucrat, a political operator in the Florentine power structure. Among other things he was in charge or organizing the city's militia. This was all during the time when Florence was a republic, which means that it was quasi-democratic in nature, and thus subject to factional competition. One of these factions was led by the De' Medici family. Ever heard of them?"

Justin shook his head.

"They were exceptionally rich bankers who helped bankroll the Renaissance. And, after they got control of political power in Florence, they thought Machiavelli might be plotting against them so they had him locked up and tortured."

"This dude did time?" Justin asked, tapping the book's cover with his finger. His opinion of the author suddenly improved.

"Indeed. And he was tortured. The way they did it was called the "strappado." They tied his wrists together behind his back with a rope, then threw the rest of the rope over a beam, up above him, and pulled on the rope so that he was lifted off the ground. Apparently it's extremely painful and can separate a person's shoulders from their sockets."

"Nice."

"Right. Anyway, after that he retired from direct involvement in politics and spent the rest of his life writing about politics instead. That's why we have *The Prince*."

Justin nodded.

"Now, the first thing you need to know about reading *The Prince* is that you can't read it like you would a normal book." As Baker spoke his face reappeared on the screen.

"Whad' ya mean?"

"Think about it this way: do you trust me?"

"Trust you?"

"Right."

"Uhh...."

"I've lied to you several times already, haven't I?"

"Yeah...."

"Yet I also rescued you from being executed back in Ohio; I gave you an advantage over the other four men up there on the ship; I arranged for you to marry the alluring Megan; and now I'm giving you the job of being the ruler of an entire planet. So, again, simple question: do you trust me?"

Justin shrugged. "I...."

"Right. You do and you don't – correct? You know that you can't believe everything I say, that you can't take it on face value, yet you also know that I appear to be looking out for your best interests. In fact I've probably done more for you than anyone else has ever done for you, with the possible exception of your mother.

"You should think about Machiavelli in the same way. He wants you to understand how to be a prince, but in the process of conveying the necessary information in that regard, he's going to say things in his book that he doesn't actually mean, he's going to appear to contradict himself, and in general he's going to play with your mind."

Justin smiled ironically, skeptical of the book's power.

"You doubt me, I can see that. And of course only the experience of reading *The Prince* can truly persuade you in this regard. Nonetheless, allow me to note the following: Machiavelli is known to be an evil man; a man who wrote about things and advocated for things that are, by any general standard of civilized mores, unethical. And yet – and yet – despite that reputation, he managed to lay the groundwork for modern politics. People think that they can read him and then set him aside. That they can resist his spell. And yet...."

Baker let those words hang in the air, using silence as a flourish. Then he continued, "A good way to begin to understand how to read him is to listen to a letter which he wrote to a friend of his after he retired from politics. In it he explains how he spends his days involved in household chores, which he hates, but then in the evenings he goes into his study and reads and thinks and writes. This is what he tells his friend."

Baker's eyes cast downwards, and he began reading from a text.

When evening comes, I go back home, and enter my study. At the entrance to that room, I take off my work clothes, which are covered in mud and filth, and I put on the clothes that an ambassador would wear. Decently dressed, I sit and read ancient texts, and through them I enter the courts of rulers who have long since died. There, I am warmly welcomed, and I feed on the only food that I find nourishing and was born to savor. I am not ashamed to talk to these ancient rulers, and to ask them to explain their actions, and they, out of their kindness, answer me. Four hours go by without my feeling any anxiety. I forget every worry. I am no longer afraid of poverty or frightened of death. I live entirely through them.

Justin nodded after Baker finished reading, not sure what he was supposed to get out of that, or even what Machiavelli was talking about.

"Machiavelli went into his study," Baker explained, "to learn from the ancients. He read books about politics, history, philosophy. He spent hours alone, learning from the master texts. Learning about power, and how to wield it. And like Machiavelli you now come into that room there, you close the door behind you, you sit at that antique table, and you will read and learn from him just as he learned from great minds who wrote books hundreds of years before he lived.

"Nothing could be more serious, more important, than what you are going to do in that room, Justin. Just like Machiavelli read very, very carefully, we too are going to read his book very, very carefully. The fate of the colony depends on it."

Justin nodded.

"Now," Baker said, with drama in his voice, "I want you to open that book and go to the page right at the beginning which is titled, "To the Magnificent Lorenzo Di Piero De' Medici". As Baker spoke a portrait of Lorenzo – a large-nosed man with a woman's "bob" haircut – appeared on the screen.

Justin opened the book as directed.

"It's the dedication of the book," Baker explained. "Machiavelli is dedicating it to Lorenzo De' Medici. Two things of note in that regard: Lorenzo was the dominant figure in the politics of Florence at the time, and Lorenzo was also, obviously, a De' Medici – which is to say, a member of the very family responsible for getting Machiavelli kicked out of office, jailed, and tortured."

Justin's brow creased with confusion. "So this Machiavelli guy dedicated his book to the people who tortured him?"

"That's right. He dedicated it to his enemies."

"...Why?"

Baker smiled his pressed-lips smile. "Let's have you read that dedication, shall we?"

"Okay. You want me to just read it now?"

"Yes. Out loud, please."

"Uhh...okay."

So Justin read, somewhat haltingly at times, as follows:

To the Magnificent Lorenzo Di Piero De' Medici:

Those who wish to obtain the good graces of a prince are accustomed to come before him with things they hold most dear, or in which they see him take most delight; thus one often sees horses, arms, cloths of gold, precious stones, and similar gifts presented to princes.

Wishing to present myself to your Magnificence with some sign of my devotion towards you, I have not found among my possessions anything which I hold more dear than, or value more than, the knowledge of the actions of great men, which I accumulated by a long experience in contemporary affairs, and by continual study of antiquity. Having reflected upon this subject with great and prolonged diligence, I now send my thoughts, condensed into this little book, to your Magnificence.

And although I consider this work to be unworthy of your attention, nevertheless I do trust much to your generosity that it may be acceptable, since it is not possible for me to make a better gift than to offer you this opportunity of understanding, in the shortest possible time, all that I have learned over so many years and with so many troubles and dangers.

I have not embellished this text with flowery words, nor filled it with rounded periods, nor with any other decorations, with which so many authors are accustomed to embellish their works; because I wish that no honor should be given to my book unless the truth of its teachings and the significance of its theme shall make it acceptable.

Nor do I agree with those who think it is presumptuous if a man of low and humble condition should dare to discuss the concerns of princes. After all, just as those who wish to draw landscapes place themselves below, in the plain, in order to contemplate the nature of the mountains and lofty places, and, in order to contemplate the plains, they place themselves on mountains, so too, in order to understand the nature of the people it is necessary to be a prince, and to understand the nature of princes it is necessary to be of the people.

Take then, your Magnificence, this little gift in the spirit in which I send it to you; so that, if it be carefully read and considered by you, you will learn my extreme desire that you should obtain all the greatness which fortune and your many virtues promise. And if your Magnificence, from the summit of your greatness, will sometimes turn your eyes to these lower regions, you will see how undeservedly I suffer from a great and continued malignity of fortune.

"Thoughts?" Baker asked, after Justin finished reading.

Justin shrugged. "I, uh...."

"What's the primary thing that strikes you?"

Justin shrugged again. "He...he seems to be actin' real nice to a guy whose family tried to rip out his shoulders. He's all complimentin' him and everythin'."

"Why do you think he's doing that?"

Justin shrugged again as he contemplated that question. "At the end, he says how, he like, he wants this other dude, this Lorenzo, to pay attention to him."

"Why do you think he wants Lorenzo to do that?"

"I guess because...Lorenzo is this really powerful guy, and so he wants Lorenzo to, I dunno, maybe let him get back into politics again.

Maybe give him his job back."

"Does that seem plausible, that Lorenzo would do that? If you'd had someone fired, jailed and tortured, would you feel comfortable hiring them back to work for you?"

"Guess not."

"Right. So then why is he really being so nice to Signor Lorenzo De' Medici?"

Justin shrugged. "Why?"

"Let's look at the text again, and specifically at the second-to-last paragraph that you just read. According to Machiavelli, why is it that he – Machiavelli – assumes that his insights might be useful to Lorenzo?"

Justin returned to the text and examined that paragraph. After a time, he replied, "'Because, he's sayin' that…he can see the mountaintop better than Lorenzo, 'cause Lorenzo's standin' on the mountain, but this Machiavelli is down in the plains."

"Precisely. So what's he actually saying to Lorenzo?"

"Whad' ya mean?"

"What's he saying to him? What's he really saying?"

"He's sayin' that…I guess he's sayin' to Lorenzo that he knows more 'bout Lorenzo's job than Lorenzo does."

"Precisely! Now think about that. Here's Lorenzo De' Medici, the most powerful man in Florence. He could ruin Machiavelli with a word, by issuing a single order. And he already has reason to be suspicious of Machiavelli, based upon past history. And so what does Machiavelli do? He sends Lorenzo that book, telling Lorenzo that he, Machiavelli, knows more about how to be a prince than Lorenzo does. And he claims that he acquired that knowledge, in part, by being sent down to the proverbial plains, by being kicked out of power and having to spend his time with the commoners. Or in other words, that he's become a better student of power than Lorenzo precisely because of what Lorenzo's family did to him.

"Even more audaciously, he's making that claim right up front, at the beginning of this book about power, which he expects other people to read as well. And some of those other people, Machiavelli hopes, will be other princes and would-be princes. In fact by the time you finish reading this book you'll see that Machiavelli's ultimate goal is to inspire a prince or would-be prince to do nothing short of reconstituting a version of ancient Rome, in order to make Italy strong again.

"Now, do you really think he wants the De' Medicis to lead that project? The people who ruined his life? Clearly not. He wants another prince to take on that task. And what will that task require? Among other things, the conquering prince will need to dominate the De' Medici clan.

"So, in other words, this whole book is one big slap in the face to Lorenzo and his family. And what does Machiavelli do? He not only sends this little book to Lorenzo, but he dedicates it to him, so that he – Mr. Machiavelli – can insult Lorenzo directly and publicly. And yet you read it, and unless you read it very, very carefully, you think that Machiavelli is being excessively nice to Lorenzo, when in fact what he's calling for is someone else to step forward to become the new Romulus."

"Huh...."

"That's Machiavellian writing in a nutshell. No doubt that's the primary reason why Machiavelli put that dedication in there – to alert the careful reader about the type of book they're about to encounter, and thus to prepare them to encounter it properly."

"He's a tricky guy."

"To say the least."

"So you want me to read the next section now?"

"No, I'd like you to read chapter fifteen next, but on your own, and then we'll discuss it tomorrow at 10:00."

Justin nodded. "Yeah, okay."

"One more thing...."

"Yeah?"

"Speaking of Romulus – of the new Romulus that Machiavelli is calling forth – there's an important question you didn't ask me, when I was telling you about the original Romulus and his background."

Justin shrugged. "What should I of asked you?"

"You know how I mentioned that Romulus' lineage was unusual – his mother was human but his father was a god?"

"Yeah."

"You should have asked me who the god was."

"...Okay. Who was the god?"

"Want to take a guess?"

Justin thought for a moment. There was only one Roman god that he knew of, and that Baker would expect him to know. So he said, "Mars?"

Baker nodded, then smiled. "Isn't that convenient?"

V

The rich, thick scent of stuffed tortillas wafted up Justin's nostrils after he locked *The Prince* back in the safe, pushed the button to open the study's door and then stepped out into the main room.

"Greetings my prince," Megan said, standing at the kitchen counter and smiling at him as she finished preparing the tortillas.

Justin smiled widely. "Mexican food!"

"Baker told me you liked it. He said you'd said that to the others."

"I love Mexican food!"

"It'll be ready in a sec. Have a seat."

Justin obeyed, settling into a chair at the metal-and-wood dining table. "I can see already that you're the right kind a princess for me."

Megan added pepper to the tortillas and then placed two tortillas each on two plates and set the plates on the table. It'd been so long since Justin had eaten with "civilized" company that he nearly grabbed hold of a tortilla and bit into it before Megan sat down. But then he caught himself, smiled sheepishly, and waited as she took her seat.

As soon as she bit into one of hers, he proceeded to wolf down his first tortilla.

"This is delicious!" He announced, between mouthfuls.

She smiled. "Glad you like it."

"Where'd you learn to cook Mexican like this?""

"A cookbook."

"Seriously?"

"Mmhm. I've been perfecting it over the last couple days."

Justin nodded. "So my wife's a nurse from New Jersey who can cook like a Mexican woman. Tell me more 'bout yourself."

He meant the question as a compliment but he could instantly see that she didn't take it that way. She didn't look offended, exactly, but she did set her tortilla down and scrunch up her nose in reply.

"I've been thinking," she said, placing her elegant hands on the table. "Thinking about something a lot, actually, while I've been waiting down here for you these last few weeks."

"Yeah?" He put the remainder of the first tortilla in his mouth. Whatever she was about to tell him was obviously important to her, but the tortillas were just too tasty for him to keep from eating while he listened, so he picked up the second tortilla and bit into it.

"I'm your wife now, and you're my husband. I'll tell you anything you ask me about myself and I'd expect you to tell me about anything I ask you."

"'Course."

"And since we're strangers to one another, there's a lot we could ask each other about about our pasts and all of that."

"Sure."

"But the thing is, whatever I would tell you about myself, about my past, doesn't really matter anymore. Because I'm not the same person that I was back on Earth. Everything has changed. I mean I'm – we're both – in a completely different place now, a completely different environment. We're not even breathing normal air or part of a natural ecosystem. And who we're supposed to be up here has hardly any connection to who we were before."

Justin nodded, and took another bite of the tortilla.

"You – you were technically executed," she said. "And now it's almost like you've been reborn, in a really profound and fundamental way. It's the same for me, even though I didn't get sent to an execution chamber. What I'm saying is, now you're supposed to be the prince of Mars, of all things. And I'm supposed to be your princess." She smiled as she enunciated this title. "So...why don't we just be that? Let's just be who we are now. Let's treat each other like that, and become who we're supposed to be, who Baker wants us to be. If you treat me like that, and I treat you like that, then we'll become that. And you'll find out about me while I'm finding out about me, and vice versa. Does that make sense?"

Justin nodded as he polished off the second tortilla. "Yeah, sure." He was impressed by the level of intelligence she conveyed as she spoke.

Megan smiled. "So then let's not ask each other questions about the past, alright? Let's just assume we're as mysterious to ourselves as we are to each other. And let's become who we are, together, naturally, as time goes by for us up here together."

Justin nodded again. "Works for me."

"Really?"

He shrugged. "Yeah, I can dig it."

She smiled.

"One a the things I'm findin' out 'bout this new you," he told her, "and I'm bettin' it applied to the old you too, is that you're probably the smartest chick I've ever met."

Megan smiled still wider. Then she raised her eyebrows, as if to say, "I'll bet."

VI

Lunch was to be followed by gardening, but Justin asked Baker a question before he and Megan headed outside.

"Since there're only two of us on this shuttle now, is there just gonna be one of us goin' outside at a time, so the other one can handle the airlock? And what 'bout havin' someone on backup in the cockpit?"

"Those measures were for when we had five modestly educated death row escapees working together up there. Now those precautions can be largely dispensed with, especially since we know that all the instruments and the spacesuits are working. But speaking of security backups, there are remote controls on the shuttle that you can fasten to your spacesuits which will allow you to operate the airlock's doors from the outside."

Justin couldn't help thinking of the difference it would have made – to Byron in particular – if those remotes had been made available earlier. "Seriously? We've got remotes?"

"Indeed."

Baker told them where the remotes were stored, and after they suited up they clipped the remotes onto their spacesuits. Then they stepped outside for Megan's first Martian walk.

It didn't take her long to get used to the gravity change, and then Justin led her into the garden and explained how to conduct analyses of the various planter boxes' contents by using the hand-held scanner.

One of the planter boxes in the gravity-testing room now had two plant stalks in it, the other planter box in that room had one stalk, and the planter box located under the filtered skylight in the radiation-testing room now had a second shoot as well. Given the lack of progress in the planter boxes which contained Martian soil, Baker directed the duo to mix a few tablespoons of nutrient-rich liquid into those boxes.

This done, Justin and Megan went back inside the shuttle, into the cockpit, and he showed her how to read the instruments and enter data into the onboard computers. She was a quick study, accustomed as she was to medical analysis, and this endeared her still further to Justin; he was pleased to be married to such a capable woman.

Later that evening, when it came time for dinner, she taught him how to prepare a dish of fettuccine. Evidently they were both going to be responsible for doing the cooking in this relationship. In the course of this demonstration she showed him that there was a large container space located at the front of the ship on the second level where more food items were stored.

After they'd eaten Justin excused himself, entered the study, shut the door behind him, unlocked the safe, grabbed the book, sat down at the antique table and then opened *The Prince* to chapter fifteen as Baker had instructed.

'Why am I startin' at chapter fifteen?' He wondered.

Then he read.

It remains to consider what ought to be the rules of conduct for a prince towards his subjects and friends. And as I know that many others have written on this point, I expect that I shall be considered presumptuous in mentioning it, especially since, in discussing it, I shall depart from the methods that are by used other people.

But it being my intention to write something which will be useful to him who can understand it, it appears to me more appropriate to present the reality of the matter rather than to describe merely an imaginary world; for many theorists have designed imaginary republics and principalities which have never been known or seen, because the way that one lives is very far different from how one ought to live.

Therefore he who neglects what is done for what ought to be done, sooner brings his own ruin than his success; for a man who wishes to act entirely in accordance with virtue will soon meet with destruction among so much that is evil. Thus it is necessary for a prince who wishes to maintain his power to know how to do what is morally wrong, and to make use of this knowledge or not, according to necessity.

Therefore, putting aside all imaginary things concerning a prince, and discussing only things which are real, I say that all men when they are spoken of, and in particular princes, since they hold positions of public authority, are particularly notable for some of those qualities which bring them either blame or praise.

Therefore one prince is known to be liberal, and another is considered miserly; one is reputed generous, and another is considered rapacious; one is cruel, and one is compassionate; one is faithless, and another is faithful; one is effeminate and cowardly, another is bold and brave; one is affable and another is haughty; one is lascivious, another is chaste; one is sincere, another cunning; one is hard, another easy; one is grave, another frivolous; one is reputed religious, while another unbelieving, and the like.

And I know that everyone will claim that it would be most praiseworthy for a prince to exhibit all the above qualities that are considered good; but because those qualities can neither be entirely possessed nor observed, since human conditions do not allow for it, it is necessary for a prince to be sufficiently prudent that he may know how to avoid the criticism which results from having those vices which would lose him his state; and also to keep himself, if possible, from those which would not lose him it. But since this is not possible, he may with less concern indulge himself in the latter type of vice.

And again, a prince need not worry about being criticized for having vices which enable him to more securely hold onto power, for if things are considered carefully, it will be found that something which looks like virtue, if followed, might lead to his ruin; while something else, which looks like vice, when it is followed, brings him security and prosperity.

Thus ended the chapter.

Justin thought for a few seconds about what he'd just read, then he shook his head and put the book back in the safe.

VII

The image was crystal clear and yet blurry at the same time: three men, all seated at a table. Soon it became apparent that they were playing cards. One of the men was Tobey Williams, whom Justin had run over in the parking lot of that bar back in Cleveland. Another was Tristan Martin. The third was Byron Carruthers. They were talking among themselves, evidently unaware of Justin's presence.

"I *got* this!" Tristan was saying. "I so got this!"

"Man, that's what you said last time," Byron replied. "And look what happened then."

"I live in the present, I don't worry 'bout the past."

"You don't live nowhere," Tobey said. "Remember?" A solidly built man, somewhere between Tristan and Byron in terms of size, Tobey sat with his shoulders pressed straight against the back of his chair.

"Yeah well neither do you, so don't get on 'bout it!"

At which point Tobey turned and looked at Justin, who'd been approaching them, moving closer and closer with every passing moment. "See what you did to me, Justin?" Tobey complained. "Not only did you run me over in a parkin' lot. Not only did you kill me and leave my kids without a dad. But you made it so I'm stuck here forever playin' cards with this joker." He nodded at Tristan.

"Oh, like you're the one sufferin'!" Tristan retorted. "You think playin' cards for eternity with you two fools is my idea of a good time?"

Byron rolled his eyes and set his cards face down on the table in exasperation. "Justin, man, seriously? You couldn't a just gone into the cockpit, hit that one little override button, and let me get back on the ship 'fore my oxygen ran out? Seriously? This dude had a knife. You had a knife. It was even-steven. Fifty-fifty shot."

"Fifty-fifty?" Tristan protested. "What're you talkin' 'bout? You know how many knife fights I been in? How many dudes I wasted in total? With a knife? With a gun? With my bare hands?"

"I really don't care," Byron replied.

"Neither do I," Tobey concurred. "Look, Justin, okay, I get it – with these two jokers, you didn't have a choice. You're on a spaceship. Oxygen's runnin' out. Food and water, they won't last forever. Man's gotta do what a man's gotta do. But Justin, man – we was in a bar fight. It was just a bar fight! It was like – nothin'. Who cares? Did you ever see that woman again? No. Did she call you when you were in prison? No. Did she try to save you from gettin' executed? No. So what were ya thinkin?"

Justin tried to reply, to explain his actions as best he could, or at least apologize, but no matter how hard he tried no words came out of his mouth. There was only muffled silence.

"Cat got your tongue?" Tristan smirked. "Or maybe it's that fine lady you've hooked up with."

"Wish I'd been the one who survived," Byron said. "Her and me, we could a really cooked some fettuccine, you know what I'm sayin'."

"If I'd been up on that spaceship you know I'd be the one with the lady," Tobey insisted.

"Man," Tristan said, shaking his head, "dude took you out in a parkin' lot. You didn't even make it to your car – how you gonna survive up in space?"

"I'd a been great in space."

Byron rolled his eyes again. "Can we get on with this game?" He picked his cards up off the table. "I'd like to beat you two 'fore eternity is over with."

Tobey and Tristan both nodded, and so the game resumed. Their conversation continued as well, but the sounds of their voices grew fainter and fainter as the image of the three of them sitting at the table receded further into the distance. Amidst the dwindling sounds, the last words Justin was able to discern were,

"That Justin did us in real good." It was Tobey's voice.

"Yeah," the other two responded simultaneously.

Then everything faded to black.

"Justin!" This was Megan's voice. "Justin!" She was lying beside him, shaking him gently.

"Wh-what? What is it?" He asked, rolling back into consciousness.

"You were making strange noises."

"What?"

"Like you were trying to yell, but you couldn't."

"…I was?"

"Mmhm. And look at you – you're all sweaty. I think you were having a bad dream."

Justin took a deep breath. "…Yeah, maybe I was."

"Do you want to talk about it?"

"Uh…naw. It was just a dream. You know – no big deal."

"Then why are you sweating?"

He smiled at her. "Maybe I was dreamin' 'bout you."

She smiled in return. "You don't have to dream. I'm right here."

He smiled still wider. "Good point."

VIII

"Thoughts about what you read?" Baker asked, as Justin settled into place at the antique table. *The Prince* was lying in front of him, opened to chapter fifteen. It was 10:02 the following morning.

Justin shrugged. "He's kind a hard to follow, the way he writes. But I guess…he's just sayin' that he's gonna tell it like it is. He's not gonna make stuff up."

"Right. So on the one hand, we know, given what he wrote in the dedication to Lorenzo De' Medici, that Machiavelli is going to mess with the reader's mind, play around with his writing, and sometimes hide the true message he's trying to convey in a lot of conflicting statements. But on the other hand he's not going to talk about things that aren't real, that are simply wishes or fantasies. And in fact it's precisely because he's going to be giving us the real, politically incorrect version of reality that he sometimes needs to mask his meaning. Does that make sense?"

Justin shrugged. "…Yeah."

"Good. And what he tells us, in that chapter you read for today, is that, given the nature of reality, a prince is going to need to do things that, in normal circumstances, would be considered bad. Because some of those bad things are necessary in order to maintain his state. And if that unsavory behavior does in fact allow him to hold onto power then he shouldn't worry too much if he has a reputation for being bad."

Justin thought about this. "Huh."

"There's also something else that's going on in this chapter which is useful to point out. He talks about other political theorists who have designed fantasy states that could never work in real life. And in that regard Mr. Machiavelli probably has someone very specific in mind."

"Oh yeah? Who's that?"

"Plato."

Justin nodded. "I heard a him."

"He's the founding father of western political philosophy."

"Sure."

"And the most influential book that Plato wrote is *The Republic*. Have you heard of it?"

"Not recently."

"It is arguably the most important book ever written about politics. And it is, in all likelihood, that book that Machiavelli is taking issue with. The whole point of *The Republic* is to try to design an ideal state. The end result, however, is that what gets designed is a fantasy state that can never really be achieved.

"Machiavelli is rebelling against all that. Against that whole Greek approach to life; too much philosophy and too much abstraction. That's why he prefers the Romans. The Romans were second-rate philosophers but they knew how to set up and run a real, long-lasting state. They knew how to build a strong army, and they knew how to use that army to crush everybody else around them."

Justin nodded, appreciating that point. He'd never been all that into philosophy himself.

"A primary focus for Plato is the concept of virtue. He's always wondering what virtue is, what the best virtue is, how to cultivate it, how to live the best possible life and be truly happy. Machiavelli dispenses with all that. For him virtue is synonymous with being able to run your state well and to conquer your enemies. As far as he's concerned, virtue, in its classical formulation, is an unaffordable luxury and therefore an illusion.

"For instance, the most famous part of *The Republic* is something called "the allegory of the cave." Human beings are described as living in a cave, in semi-darkness, mistaking shadows for reality. The process of education, of enlightenment, is meant to draw people out of the cave and into the light so that they can live truly good and philosophical lives. Machiavelli is laughing at all of that. As far as he's concerned humans are and always will be cave dwellers, one way or another. Human life is about figuring out who rules the cave."

"Like in prison," Justin noted, nodding.

"Like everywhere," Baker replied.

A few moments of silence passed between the two men, as Baker allowed this thought to fill up the empty space in the room.

Then he continued, "So now let's turn to chapter one."

Justin did accordingly. The chapter title was "How Many Kinds of Principalities There are, and by What Means They are Acquired."

"The first five chapters of *The Prince* function as a sub-section of the text," Baker explained. "And in this sub-section Machiavelli is describing a situation in which a new prince is obliged to rule when that prince doesn't have absolute control.

"This prince has not simply inherited his power, and therefore he can't count on tradition to maintain his position. And this prince is also ruling a state that is outside his native homeland, in some distant place, with different customs and manners, which means that he can't simply rely on cultural affinities and sympathies to maintain his power there. Furthermore he's ruling in a place where there are lots of people with varying degrees of power, which means that he can't just dominate everyone outright. And he's ruling people who are accustomed to being free, so they're going to be offended if he simply starts issuing orders to them.

"In other words, Machiavelli is describing a situation in which a prince has to use all his skill, all his cunning, all his ruthlessness to run the state and retain his power. And, as may have already occurred to you, he's describing a situation which is very much like your own.

"You won't be able to rule that colony up there based upon some hereditary claim. Indeed, quite the opposite – it's going to be essential that we don't tell the rest of the colony about your true past. Yours or Megan's.

"You are also, quite obviously, in a very distant land; in a place where the customs and patterns of life which exist on Earth are, in many ways, no longer relevant. Which means that you can't simply build your power off of existing ways of doing things.

"And of course everyone up there will possess a certain amount of power insofar as they have free will and two hands. And given that the community will be so small, each individual personality will have some impact upon the whole. Certain personalities, furthermore, will inevitably become more dominant than others. You'll need to make sure that none of those personalities becomes *too* dominant.

"Finally, and most fundamentally, you'll be ruling over people who are used to being free. As mentioned, the other colonists have all been told that you're the team leader, but they'll still think of themselves as participating on precisely that – a team, in which the captain of the team is merely the first among equals. They are completely unaccustomed to being ruled. And you are going to need to rule them. Otherwise we'll get dominant and minority factions and those factions will either start a civil war or the dominant faction will eventually implode. Then the colony will be lost and along with it we'll lose humanity's best option for surviving some potential man-made catastrophe down here on Earth.

"Now, in order to truly rule, you're going to need to make some very hard decisions. Which is precisely why it's essential for you to take Machiavelli's dictum to heart: sometimes it is necessary to do bad things in order to preserve the state."

Justin thought this over. He didn't nod. But he didn't shake his head either. He simply rolled this information around in his mind.

"What I want you to do now," Baker continued, "is to read those first five chapters. You don't need to read the first four of them out loud. You can just read them to yourself. But I'll be right here, and if you get to any point in the reading that doesn't make sense, just ask me, and I'll go over it with you."

"Okay."

And thus Justin began to read.

He had to admit, this Machiavelli guy was beginning to intrigue him. The idea of fighting for the here and now – as opposed to dreaming up some ideal state – resonated with him, given the hardscrabble existence to which he'd been accustomed for most of his life. Likewise, the fact that the first five chapters of the book – a book written in the 1500s – dealt precisely with his own situation, was compelling.

Chapter one was short – just a brief paragraph – and it noted that there are two types of states: republics and principalities.

"So wait," Justin said. "What's a republic?"

"In Machiavelli's terminology, it's basically any type of state that isn't a principality. And a principality is a state that's run by a prince."

Justin nodded, then continued reading.

Soon he came to an unusual name. "Who's Francesco…Sforza?"

"A prince who ran the city-state of Milan. We'll talk more about him later. And in general I'll let you know if there are specific people you need to remember."

"Okay."

Justin read on through chapter two, which was likewise short and was titled "Concerning Hereditary Principalities." When he came to the following line, he was confused.

We have in Italy, for example, the Duke of Ferrara, who could not have withstood the attacks of the Venetians in 1484, nor those of Pope Julius in 1510, unless he had been long established in his dominions.

Justin read the sentence out loud and then looked up and asked Baker, "Dude got attacked by a pope?"

"Oh yes. Back in those days popes didn't simply run the Vatican; they ran the Papal States, which took up a whole portion of central Italy. Essentially the popes were like princes themselves. We'll come back to that point later on – it's quite important."

Justin stuck out his lower lip in surprise, then continued with his silent reading, moving on to chapter three, which was titled "Concerning Mixed Principalities." This chapter began by considering the challenges that typically face a newly established principality, then addressed the issues which come from creating a new principality in a foreign territory. Justin noted how much Machiavelli stressed the importance of setting up colonies, and how he praised the Roman methods of establishing such.

There were also people whom Machiavelli held up as negative examples. "Apparently he thinks this one guy, King Louis, is an idiot," Justin noted. "Says he did everything opposite a what he should a done."

"Louis XII? Yes, indeed. You'll note the contrast with how he talks about the Romans."

"Yeah, he definitely likes those guys."

Chapter four was titled, "Why the Kingdom of Darius, Conquered by Alexander, Did Not Rebel Against the Successors of Alexander at His Death." In this chapter Machiavelli noted that Alexander the Great and his generals were able to retain control over the lands of the Persian Empire without much difficulty, even though they were ruling in foreign territory. Machiavelli's explanation was that, because the Persian king ruled as an absolute despot, whoever defeated him in battle instantly became the despot in his place. By contrast, in other types of states where the nobles have some authority – where there are multiple nodes of power, in other words – you can't simply kill the king and then expect things to go smoothly.

Finally Justin arrived at chapter five: "Concerning the Way to Govern Cities or Principalities Which Lived under Their Own Laws before They Were Annexed."

When Baker saw that Justin had reached this point, he said, "Now you're at chapter five? Best to read that one out loud."

"Okay."

So Justin read.

Whenever states have been accustomed to live under their own laws and in freedom, there are three options for those who have newly acquired these states and who wish to hold them: the first is to ruin them, the next is to live there in person, the third is to allow the inhabitants to live under their own laws, while you collect payments from them, and you should also establish within that state an oligarchy which will keep the state friendly to you. That oligarchy, being created by the prince, knows that it cannot survive without his friendship and interest, therefore it will do its utmost to support him, and thus he who would keep a city which is accustomed to freedom will hold it more easily by the means of its own citizens than in any other way.

However, if we look at the examples of the Spartans and the Romans, we see that even though the Spartans held Athens and Thebes, and established ruling oligarchies in those states, nevertheless the Spartans lost control of them. The Romans, in order to hold onto Capua, Carthage and Numantia, dismantled them, and did not lose them. But when they wished to hold Greece as the Spartans had held it, making it free and permitting it to have its own laws, they did not succeed. Thus, in order onto hold Greece, they were obliged to dismantle many cities in the country, for in truth there is no safe way to retain cities which are used to being free other than by ruining them.

Therefore he who becomes the master of any city that is accustomed to freedom, and does not destroy it, may expect to be destroyed by it, for in a rebellion it has always the inspiration of its former liberty, and its ancient privileges serve as a rallying point, which neither time nor benefits will ever cause it to forget. And no matter what you may do or prepare for, the inhabitants of such a city never forget their liberty or their privileges, unless they are disunited or dispersed; if they are allowed to remain united, then with every chance they get they will immediately rally to the cause of freedom, as Pisa did after the hundred years she had been held in bondage by the Florentines.

But when cities or countries are accustomed to live under a prince, and his family is exterminated, then the inhabitants, being on the one hand accustomed to obey and on the other hand not having the old prince around, cannot agree about choosing a new prince from among themselves, and they also do not know how to govern themselves either. For this reason, they are very slow to take up arms, and a prince can win them to himself and secure them much more easily. In republics which have previously enjoyed freedom, on the other hand, there is more vitality, greater hatred, and more desire for vengeance, which will never permit them to allow the memory of their former liberty to rest; so that the safest way is to destroy them or to reside there.

"Thoughts?" Baker asked, after Justin finished reading.

Justin shrugged. "If people are used to bein' free, they're gonna wanna be free. Simple as that."

Baker nodded. "Simple as that, indeed. Which is why it's going to be important to eradicate your impending subjects' freedom-formed habits as quickly as possible."

"But...Machiavelli says that once people are used to bein' free, they'll always wanna go back to it even if you take their freedom away."

Baker smiled, pleased to see Justin engaging intellectually with the text. "True, but he tells us something else as well, something that will be particularly helpful to you as you transition the others away from their freedom-wanting ways. What does he tell us that you ultimately have to do with a state that is accustomed to being free?"

Justin reviewed the text for a few moments. "He says that you basically either gotta go live in the state you're takin' over or you gotta destroy it."

"Right. Now obviously you're already living there. You're the founder of that state. So that'll give you an edge. But the larger point is this: the states of reference for the other people who'll be arriving there will, for all intents and purposes, have been destroyed. Destroyed as far as they're concerned, since they've left those states behind permanently. Which means that they're all going to be politically disoriented and thus vulnerable when they first get there. Your task will be to capitalize upon that fact and make it abundantly clear to them that their democracy days are over. Even if they're excited to be there, they're going to be frightened. You'll need to take that fear and make it work for you."

IX

Baker didn't assign Justin any homework for that evening – he told him that they'd do the next reading together the following morning – which caused Justin to feel the way he'd always felt when he managed to dodge homework in high school.

Stepping out into the main room, Justin found Megan lounging on the gray leather couch, waiting for him. She flashed her knife of a smile.

They'd woken up around 9:00 that morning and eaten breakfast before Justin's session with Baker, so neither of them were hungry now. Which meant that they could head straight outside and tend the garden. Although that could wait a little while.

He countered her smile with a grin and slid down onto the couch next to her feet. She had thin, elegant feet, and he began playing with her toes. As he did so she smiled at him some more.

The question on his mind was, could he trust her? She was his wife, true, but this wasn't a typical marriage. And there was of course the fact that she'd engaged in criminal activities back on Earth. Apparently she'd gotten started in that by selling painkillers, which she might have done – at least initially – out of a sense of compassion. Or not.

And there was another thing: right after his first study session with Baker, she'd called him her prince, as if she knew what book he'd been reading. So had Baker shown the book to her already, even though he told Justin that the book was for Justin's eyes only? Were she and Baker just playing with him? Were they holding secret sessions behind his back? Or were secret sessions superfluous because they'd already planned out all the details of this little extraterrestrial undertaking? Of course Baker was far away, on a planet that Megan would never see again, whereas Justin was right here with her, in a forbidding environment, and they were going to have children together. Which all presumably counted for something.

'Hmm,' he thought. Maybe he couldn't trust her now but maybe he could trust her later.

Yet this issue of trust had taken on an immediate quality as soon as he'd realized that she might be able to decipher his nightmares. He couldn't hide from her the fact that he was having them. And he might not be able to hide what they were about either. If he was talking or yelling in his sleep then pretty soon she'd figure out what he was yelling about. She might have figured it out already. And he knew that there'd be many more of those dreams. Especially now that the image of Tobey was accompanied by the new additions of Tristan and Byron. The fact that some of the images in his dreams were ridiculous – three dead men playing cards, for instance – didn't make the nightmares any less intense. If anything the absurdity made the dreams all the more terrifying.

This all thus posed a potential problem if the reason he'd been "hired" for this job was his supposed willingness to do very bad things, including kill people. Baker expected him to be a Machiavellian prince, but if Megan told Baker that Justin was having nightmares about those people he'd already killed, what would Baker do? Send up a replacement prince to rule Mars and make babies with Megan?

Under different circumstances, of course, the logical thing to do would be to ask Megan some casual yet probing questions in order to find out more about her and especially about her past connections to Baker. But he'd already agreed to not ask her about any of that. In the moment when he'd agreed to that condition he'd been pleased by her suggestion. After all, his own past wasn't glamorous and he was inclined to trade it in for the exponentially more exotic present. But....

"Are you curious, 'bout what I'm doin' in there?" As he asked her this, he nodded his head towards the study's door.

"I know what you're doing in there."

"You do?"

"Mmhm. You're training."

"Yeah, but like, do you know how? Like, what I'm doin' in there specifically?"

She nodded. "Mmhm. You're reading *The Prince*."

Justin was surprised and pleased by her candor. "I thought it was supposed to be a secret."

Megan shrugged. "I've never read it. I've never even seen it. Baker told me it was in there. He said the two of you would be reading it together. He said that what you read and discuss in there will be just between the two of you. That's all."

Justin nodded. He liked her answer. It made sense. It meant that what Baker had told him was still true, potentially. And it explained why she'd called him her prince.

He began studying her big toe. "Does that bother you? That it's just 'tween me and Baker?"

She shook her head. "No." Then she smiled as he pulled on her toe. "I want you to be the prince of this planet, and I'm glad he's preparing you for that. I'm sure he knows what he's doing."

"Yeah but...don't you wanna get trained too? To be the princess? You're not jealous?" He asked this question playfully, as if he was teasing her.

She shook her head, continuing to smile as she lounged back more deeply into the couch's leather pillows. "I don't need any more training for that."

X

The rover was back at the base camp. Justin was surprised to see it parked near the garden as he descended the shuttle's exterior staircase and stepped onto the Martian ground.

"Baker," he said, speaking into his helmet's intercom, "the rover."

"Indeed."

"How'd it get there?"

"My people down here drove it back, using remote control."

"So, what, it's fixed?"

"It is."

"How?"

"I have the super-genius equivalent of a mechanic on staff. He did it via remote as well."

"So…what was wrong with it?"

"It's complicated. The short version is, a steering valve."

"…Huh." Justin considered this information, while a shiver slid down his spine. "So there really was somethin' wrong with it then?"

"Oh yes."

"Huh," Justin said again.

"And now that it's back and in working order we can get on with phase two, I'm happy to say."

"Phase two?"

"Correct. I'll explain it to you and Megan after you finish working in the garden."

And thus later that afternoon the newlyweds sat in the round room on the top floor of the shuttle, looking at the TV screen where Baker had appeared so many times before to the group of five.

As soon as Baker's image appeared on the screen, he announced, clearly enthused, that "Phase two entails exploration near the base of Arsia Mons."

"Near the base a what?" Justin asked.

"Arsia Mons. You know that big mountain, the one that Calvin reached on the rover?"

"Yeah."

"That's Arsia Mons."

"It's the name a the mountain?"

"Correct."

"Arsia…Mons?"

"Exactly. "Mons" is the Latin word for "mountain." And "Arsia" was the name of a forest near ancient Rome."

As Baker spoke his face was replaced by a topographical map of Mars, which was centered on three volcanic mountains. To the northwest of those mountains lay another, much larger mountain.

"Arsia Mons is the most southerly of those three mountains that form a diagonal line running from southwest to northeast. To the north of Arsia Mons is Pavonis Mons, which is Latin for "Peacock Mountain," and north of that is Ascraeus Mons, named after a mountain in Greece."

He paused to give Justin and Megan time to examine the map.

"All these mountains are located on a massive plateau known as the Tharsis region. You'll note that, to the northwest of this region, towards the top left of your screen, is another mountain which is much larger than the other three. It technically lies just off to the side of the Tharsis plateau. It's called Olympus Mons."

"Mount Olympus," Megan said.

"Precisely. It's named after that mountain in Greece which in both ancient Greek and Roman mythology was supposed to be a home for the gods. Now as it turns out, the original Mount Olympus can't hold a candle to the Mount Olympus that you've got up there. Not only is your Mount Olympus much bigger than the one in Greece but it's also much taller than Mount Everest; about three times as tall. In fact it is, by far, the largest mountain in the solar system, bigger than any other mountain on any of the eight planets."

Baker paused for effect, then continued. "Think about that: your colony, the society that you two are going to create, is going to be born and develop in the shadow, as it were, of the largest mountain in the solar system. If that's not a claim to distinction I don't know what is."

Megan and Justin both nodded and smiled.

"Now this whole region," Baker continued, as the perspective on the screen pulled back to reveal Mars in its entirety, "is right near Mars' equator. You can see it there." The Tharsis region was highlighted green.

"Aside from having some impressive mountains, this region is interesting to us for two other reasons. Reason number one: it happens to be in the middle of two regions which have shown possible evidence of water." An area to the east of Tharsis lit up in red. "This region you see lit up there is Meridiani Planum. And what's so interesting to us about Meridiani Planum is that it has hematite, and hematite, when we find it here on Earth, is often formed in water. Which is why NASA landed its *Opportunity* rover in Meridiani Planum back in 2004. They haven't found any water there yet, however.

"And over here" – the region to the west of Tharsis lit up in red – "we have the Gale Crater, which is where NASA has located evidence of possible recurrent water flows along certain ridges, known as recurrent slope linae, or R.S.L.s. That's the area where NASA sent its *Curiosity* rover in 2011. What they've found there so far, however, doesn't suggest that there's a potential water source in that area that could support our colony. Basically, we're not sure if there is enough water in that area, and there's also some concern about its salinity.

"Now, we do know that there is water on Mars in the form of ice caps at the two poles, but the weather conditions in those places are so difficult that we decided against setting the colony up anywhere near them.

"And so, in light all these water-related data points, we've decided to concentrate on the region around the Martian equator, and on the Tharsis region in particular. Now as far as anybody can tell, most of the water in that region – to the degree that it's actually there – is probably below the surface. The good news is that, in all likelihood, it's probably not that far below the surface. But it'll still be hard to get at if you're simply digging into the ground. Which brings me to the second reason why the Tharsis region is the best place to be: it has caves. Vertical caves, as far as we can tell. Big ones. And guess where in the Tharsis region the caves are located."

Baker paused for effect. Then he told them, "At the base of Arsia Mons. Right near where we landed you."

Megan and Justin both nodded and smiled, impressed by all this information.

"So now you know why you are where you are. And we would've landed you even closer to the base of that mountain but we didn't want to cause any damage to the caves, and we also needed to land your shuttle on a relatively flat surface. Now then, the caves – are here." While Baker spoke the perspective on the map zoomed in to a closer shot of Arsia Mons and its immediate environs. As the zooming continued, seven black dots appeared, located around the edges of the mountain.

"Since Arsia Mons has functioned in the past as a volcano, with lava flows and the like, certain geological opportunities were presented for caves to form. The cave that we're particularly interested in is named "Jeanne."" As he spoke, the perspective zoomed in still further, towards the black dot which was located furthest from the mountain, to the north.

"Seriously?" Justin asked. "Jeanne?"

"Indeed. All seven of the big caves near Arsia Mons were given female names by the scientists who discovered them: Dena, Chloe, Wendy, Annie, Abby, Nikki, and Jeanne. Jeanne is our favorite because, as you can see, although it's close to the mountain it's not actually on the mountain's slope. That means it's on relatively low ground and therefore nearer to a potential water source. Jeanne is four hundred and ninety-two feet across and – we're estimating, based upon satellite imaging – it's approximately five hundred and eighty-four feet deep."

Justin whistled. "That's big."

"That is. And it may in fact be even bigger. Our fondest hope is that it has caverns and tunnels stretching out from it which will then take us still deeper into the planet's surface crust."

"So we're doin' some explorin'."

"Spelunking, yes. The farther down we can go without needing to drill or blow things up, the better. And given what NASA found over in Meridiani Planum and around the Gale Crater, and considering the relative proximity of those regions to the Tharsis plateau, we have reason for being cautiously optimistic about finding water down there somewhere.

"You'll note, for instance," and the perspective on the map pulled out again, showing the three regions along with a massive rift valley which ran from Tharsis to Meridiani, "that long canyon there." The valley lit up in red. "That's Valles Marineris. You can see that it serves to connect the two regions. It's enormous. If it was in the US it would run from the west coast to the east coast. And what's important is that the geological connectivity that it provides between the two regions leads us to think that what happens in Meridiani may happen in Tharsis.

"Obviously we're hoping that that's the case. Finding water is now your primary objective. If you find it then that means you not only have a secure water supply for the colony but that – via electrolysis, as I've mentioned before – you'll have a steady oxygen supply as well."

"And if we don't find it?" Justin asked.

Baker's face now reappeared on the screen. "The second ship is carrying more oxygen and water supplies. In fact that's practically all its carrying aside from the ten new colonists and more food supplies. Those additional supplies will last you all for a little while, but certainly not for the next few years; not even long enough for us to get a third ship to Mars if we chose to launch one ahead of schedule. Which means that if you don't find a local water source relatively soon, then you, Justin, are going to have to make some rather tough decisions up there."

XI

Later that evening the two newlyweds went for a drive. Baker had recommended that they take the rover for a spin in order to get used to handling it. Thus as the Martian sunset began settling into place, Megan and Justin climbed onto the rover – he in the driver seat, she in an added seat which Baker had explained how to lock in place – and they began slowly cruising around the periphery of the base camp. It was romantic.

Justin still felt compelled to woo her – something in his nature necessitated it – and he liked the fact that his efforts would inevitably be successful since the marriage was already a done deal. It actually made the courtship all the more enjoyable, and, in a way, more meaningful, since he didn't have to do it. And what better way to woo a woman than to take her for a drive in your car.

They circled the base camp a few times and then headed out farther into the periphery. It'd been years since Justin had driven a vehicle of any sort, much less cruised in one with a lady. And the most expensive car he'd ever driven was a Ford. He figured this rover had to be about ten times as expensive, at least. It was tempting to ask Baker how much it cost, but he didn't want to break the silence which he and Megan were sharing, and more fundamentally, he didn't want to invite Baker into this moment.

Eventually he asked Megan if she wanted to drive, and she did, so they switched places and then she drove them around until the Martian sunset faded away.

Justin didn't have any nightmares that night, as far as he could remember, and then the following morning, feeling rested, he walked into the study – Baker was waiting for him on the screen – at 10:00 sharp.

It was time to consider chapter six. Baker asked him to read out loud, and so he did.

> *Let no one be surprised by the fact that, when discussing new principalities as I shall do, I consider the most notable examples, both regarding princes and states; because men,*

who almost always follow paths that are beaten by others, and thus follow by imitation those others' deeds, are yet unable to keep entirely to the ways of others or to attain the power of those they imitate.

A wise man ought, therefore, to always follow the paths beaten by great men, and to imitate those who have been supreme, so that, if his ability is not equal to theirs, at least it will have a similar quality. Let him behave, that is to say, like those clever archers who, wishing to hit a mark which appears far distant, and knowing the limits of the strength of their bow, take aim much higher than the target, not in order to reach with their arrow to so great a height, but to be able, with the aid of so high an aim, to hit the mark they wish to reach.

"So far it's clear, yes?" Baker asked.

"Yeah. Got it."

"Good. Please continue."

I say, therefore, that in new principalities, where there is a new prince, more or less difficulty is found in holding onto that principality, accordingly as there is more or less ability in him who has acquired the state. Now, since the act of a private person becoming a prince requires either ability or fortune, it is clear that one of these two things will reduce to some degree the difficulties that will likely be encountered. Nevertheless, he who has relied the least upon fortune will enjoy the strongest position as a prince. Furthermore, it makes things easier when the prince, having no other state, is compelled to reside in his new state in person.

"No problems?"

"Uh, yeah, I think we're good."

"Great. Now from here on out you'll need to read very carefully. What he's going to say pertains directly to your situation up there and to what we talked about yesterday, about using the opportunity presented by the other colonists' fear to consolidate your rule. Please proceed."

Justin raised his eyebrows, then continued.

But to come now to those who, by their own ability and not through fortune, have risen to be princes, I would say that

Moses, Cyrus, Romulus, Theseus, and rulers like them are the most excellent examples.

"Cyrus was the first notable ruler of the Persian Empire," Baker explained, "and Theseus was the king of ancient Athens."

Justin nodded, then continued reading.

And although one should not discuss Moses, since he was a mere instrument of the will of God, nonetheless he ought to be admired, if only for those qualities which made him worthy to speak with God. But if we consider Cyrus and the others who have acquired or established kingdoms, all of them will be found to be admirable; and, if their particular deeds and conduct shall be considered, these will not be found inferior to those of Moses, although he had so great a teacher.

In examining their actions and their lives, one does not see that they owed anything to fortune, aside from their initial opportunities, which provided them with the raw material which they could mold into the form which seemed best to them. Without the initial opportunities, their abilities would not have amounted to much, while without their inherent abilities the initial opportunities would have come in vain.

"Thoughts?" Baker asked.

Justin reflected for several seconds on what he'd just read. "So you gotta seize the opportunity, basically, is what I guess he's sayin."

"That's part of it. Like we talked about yesterday. Does anything else strike you about what Machiavelli just said?"

Justin re-read the section. Then he noted, "What he's sayin' 'bout Moses doesn't seem to totally make sense."

Baker smiled. "How so?"

"Well, so first he's sayin' Moses was different than the other guys and then he's basically sayin' that those other guys did the same things as Moses."

"Precisely. And which do you think it is? Is Machiavelli saying that Moses is essentially the same as the other rulers or is he saying that Moses is different because he had divine guidance for his activities?"

Justin shrugged. "I'm thinkin'…he's sayin' Moses is basically the same."

"Indeed. Please read on."

It was necessary, therefore, that Moses should find the people of Israel enslaved and oppressed by the Egyptians, so that they would be inclined to follow him and thereby be delivered out of bondage. And it was necessary that Romulus should not remain in Alba, and likewise that he should be abandoned at his birth, in order that he should eventually become King of Rome and founder of the fatherland. It was necessary that Cyrus should find the Persians discontented with the government of the Medes, and that he should also find the Medes soft and effeminate as a result of their long peace. Nor could Theseus have shown his ability if he had not found the Athenians dispersed.

These opportunities made all these men fortunate, and their great ability then enabled each to recognize the opportunity they had been given, with the end result that their countries were ennobled and made famous.

"It was necessary," Baker emphasized, "for Moses to find all the Israelites enslaved in order for him to have the opportunity to "become" Moses. He saw the opportunity and he took it. Likewise it was necessary for Romulus to be put into all sorts of bizarre situations so that he could become Romulus. So too it was necessary for you, Justin, to get led to the execution chamber, then shipped up on a shuttle to Mars and be the sole survivor of the five, just as it's necessary for the next group of colonists to arrive there feeling disoriented and afraid, in order for you to become what you are now becoming – the first prince of Mars."

Justin nodded, still finding it difficult to process this point which he'd been told repeatedly: that his role was to be the founder of the first Martian society. Instead his mind latched onto the other point which Baker raised.

"So then…why'd he talk 'bout Moses like that? First he's sayin' he's different than the others and then he's sayin' Moses is pretty much the same. Why not just say they're all the same?"

"Why do you think?"

Justin thought for a few moments, then shrugged. "Was it 'cause Moses was like, a religious person, a religious leader, so he couldn't talk 'bout Moses the same way he could 'bout the other leaders? Or at least he couldn't seem like he was doin' that? Maybe he had to cover himself, so that no one back then could accuse him a bein' blasphemous?"

"Precisely."

"But then why's he mention Moses at all? Why not just talk 'bout the others?"

"Why do you think?"

"Was it 'cause…he wanted to show that all great leaders are like this, even if we don't think they are?"

Baker nodded. "Excellent. Clearly you are learning how to read Machiavelli. Now, next question: why did he want to show us that?"

"…Whad' ya mean?"

Baker shrugged. "Let's have you read the next few paragraphs and then we'll return to the question."

"Okay."

Those who, by virtue of strong character, become princes like these men, acquire their principality with difficulty but they keep it with ease. The difficulties they experience in acquiring their principality arise in part from all the new rules and methods which they are obliged to introduce so as to firmly establish their government and its security.

There is, after all, nothing more difficult to accomplish, more dangerous to undertake, and less certain of success, than to introduce a new political order, because the innovator has as his enemies all those who have done well under the old conditions, and he will have only lukewarm defenders in those who may do well under the new conditions that he introduces. This lukewarm quality arises partly from fear of the new prince's opponents, who have had the laws on their side, and partly from the incredulity of men, who do not readily believe in new things until they have had a long experience of them.

Thus it happens that, whenever those who are hostile to the new prince have the opportunity to attack him, they do so aggressively, while his supposed supporters only defend him lukewarmly, with the ultimate result that the prince is endangered along with his supporters.

It is necessary, therefore, if we desire to discuss this matter thoroughly, to inquire whether these innovators should rely solely upon themselves in securing power, or whether they should depend upon others: that is to say, in other words, whether it is necessary, in order to successfully reach their goals, for them to use prayers or to use force?

In the first case, when they rely upon others, they always do badly, and never achieve anything; but when they can rely upon themselves and they can use force, then they are rarely endangered. Therefore all armed prophets have conquered and all the unarmed prophets have been destroyed. That is because the mood of the public changes very frequently, and while it is easy to persuade people of something, it is difficult to fix them steadfastly in that persuasion. And thus it is necessary to take certain measures so that, when the people no longer believe, it will be possible to force them to believe.

"It will be possible to force them to believe," Baker emphasized.

"…Right," Justin nodded, cautiously.

"You can't simply hope for divine assistance. You need to seize the opportunity and you need to be ready to use force to hold onto it."

"Uh-huh."

"So then, once again, why does Machiavelli want to show us that Moses is like other great men who rule states well?"

"'Cause…Moses would a got what he wanted one way or another, even if he had to do it on his own, 'cause he was willin' to use force."

"Precisely."

Justin nodded, although truth be told this discussion was making him uncomfortable. It was causing his mother's religious sermonizing to echo in his ears.

"Please continue," Baker said.

If Moses, Cyrus, Theseus, or Romulus had been unarmed, then they would not likely have been able to enforce their constitutions for very long—as happened in our time to….

Justin ran into a name which he had difficulty pronouncing, so Baker did it for him.

"Fra Girolamo Savanarola. He was a monk and religious leader back in Renaissance Florence – a puritan of sorts, who railed against some of the noblemen and powerful religious figures. He was a prophet of the unarmed variety, in other words, and what he got for his troubles was the honor of being burned at the stake."

Justin nodded, then continued reading.

Fra Girolamo Savonarola. Savonarola was ruined, along with his new order of things, as soon as the multitude no longer believed in him, since he had no means of making sure that the faithful continued to believe, or of making the unbelievers believe.

In contrast, armed prophets often have great difficulty in completing their acquisition of power, because all of their dangers must be faced during the ascent to power, but, thanks to their ability, they are ultimately able to overcome those dangers. However, when these initial challenges are overcome, and those who envied them their successes are exterminated, then these new rulers will be respected, and they will remain powerful, secure, honored, and happy.

To these famous examples I wish to add a lesser one; still it bears some resemblance to them, and I wish it to serve as a general example of my point: it is Hiero the Syracusan. This man rose from a private station to be Prince of Syracuse, and he did not owe anything to good fortune, other than his initial opportunity; for the Syracusans, being oppressed, selected him to be their captain, and afterwards he was rewarded by being made their prince.

Hiero was of so great ability, even as a private citizen, that one who writes of him says that he lacked nothing but a kingdom in order to be a king. This man abolished the old soldiery, organized the new, gave up old alliances, made new ones; and, since he had his own soldiers and allies, on that solid foundation he was able to build a strong edifice: thus, although he endured much trouble while acquiring power, he had but little trouble keeping it.

Having reached the end of the chapter, Justin looked up at the screen.

"That part there about Hiero is worth noting," Baker pointed out. "Hiero was not merely the ruler of the ancient city-state of Syracuse – which is located on the island of Sicily – but he was also the subject of a famous dialogue written by a gentleman named Xenophon, who was an

Athenian, as well as a contemporary of Plato. Xenophon's dialogue, titled *Hiero*, is the classic argument in defense of tyrannical rule – that is to say, essentially, unlimited rule by a single individual. In *Hiero* all sorts of arguments are raised about why it's better to be a private citizen than a prince; that you'll live a happier and far more peaceful life as a private citizen, etc. But these arguments are then countered by the claim that the honor and glory that go with being a prince outweigh all the problems that come with a public career. And that, of course, is a line of thinking with which Machiavelli would very much agree."

Justin nodded, thinking this point over.

"You, for instance," Baker continued, "are going to have a lot of difficult things to do up there, Justin. There will be a lot of challenges, a lot of problems. But it's all going to be worth it. It's all going to be well, well worth it. I guarantee."

XII

No gardening was done that afternoon. Instead Megan and Justin loaded up the rover with extra oxygen tanks and some plastic boxes which Baker directed them to take, then they drove away from the base camp heading towards the cave.

They followed the tracks that Calvin had made until they reached Calvin's makeshift grave. When they arrived at the grave, Baker instructed them to stop.

As the rover rolled to a halt, Baker explained, "We're going to be using these tracks a lot. Not only the two of you, but the other colonists will be taking this route to the cave. And we can't have the others seeing Calvin's grave since they can never know that there was anyone on Mars before them other than the two of you. That means that I'm going to need you – Justin – to go kick over that pile of rocks that you stacked there to mark where Calvin is buried."

This seemed genuinely cold-hearted, but Justin didn't see how he had much of a choice, so he climbed off the rover and walked over to the stack of rocks and kicked it.

"And if you could push around the sand and rocks there," Baker said, "so that it doesn't look like the area was cleared away intentionally, that'd be great."

Justin did as directed, then climbed back on the rover and turned on the engine.

As he and Megan continued on their journey, he asked Baker, "So I guess we're gonna need to kick over the rocks where the other three are buried too, back at the base camp, right?"

"That's true, yes."

"But aren't you worried that with all the people that'll be hangin' 'round the base camp, someone'll dig up those bodies by accident?"

"No, because after the second ship lands it will be drivable for a short distance and we're going to park it on top of those buried bodies. Conveniently, you chose an ideal place for us to put that second ship, so that'll take care of that."

This seemed even more callous than kicking over Calvin's burial marker, but Justin kept his thoughts to himself.

A few minutes after leaving Calvin's grave, Baker asked them to veer left at a forty-five degree angle, away from Calvin's trail, such that they began heading northeast, with the base of the mountain now lying off to their right. Without a trail to guide them, Justin slowed their speed, making sure to drive carefully over the sand dunes and around the larger rocks.

Thirty more minutes passed before they caught their first glimpse of Jeanne the cave. It was, as Baker had described, a massive round hole in the ground.

"There!" Megan announced, rising up from her seat and pointing ahead of them, beyond some low lying clumps of rocks.

"And thusly we arrive!" Baker declared, able to see what Megan was seeing via her helmet's video-camera. "There she is! Excellent!"

Justin maneuvered the rover around some rock clumps and then he too could see it. It looked to him like a giant, four hundred and ninety-two-foot diameter sink hole. "How close should I get?" He asked.

"You'll want to park a couple hundred feet back. We're not sure how stable the ground is there around the cave's rim."

"Got it."

"It's huge!" Megan exclaimed as Justin slowed the rover to a full stop and then switched off the engine. "Somehow I didn't picture it being this big."

"The Astrodome in Houston," Baker noted, "has a diameter at its base that's not all that much bigger than that hole there in front of you."

Megan and Justin climbed off the rover.

"How's the ground feel there?" Baker asked.

"Solid," Justin confirmed.

"Good. Then we'll drop an anchor from the rover into the ground."

Baker instructed Justin to open a compartment door on the rover's side, then to turn a switch which caused an automatic drill to shoot down from the rover's undercarriage and burrow three feet into the ground. Once the drill reached that depth it pushed out four smaller drills which extended horizontally into the surrounding rock and sand.

"That should hold it," Baker confirmed. "Now, I'd like you to locate the rubber ropes that are in one of those boxes you loaded onto the rover. Once you've found them, you'll see that they have hooks with safety catches at either end. I want you to connect one hook to one of the hand clasps that are there on the side of the rover, next to your seats, and then connect the other hook to the clasp on the back of your packs. You'll have to do that for each other."

Justin and Megan proceeded accordingly. When the hooks were connected to the respective clasps, Baker told them, "Great. Now off you go!"

"You want us to walk towards the cave?" Justin asked.

"Of course."

Jeanne had an inherently forbidding quality about it, and Justin felt protective of his wife. "You sure we should both be approachin' that thing? Maybe Megan should hang back in case somethin' happens."

"No, don't worry, you'll be fine."

"...Okay."

So they walked cautiously towards the cave, testing the ground with every step to make certain it was stable. The solidity of the terrain didn't appear to change.

"Excellent, excellent," Baker kept repeating, encouraging them forward.

When they were about a hundred feet from the cave's rim, Baker instructed them, "Now we're going to want to slow down. Let's take this very, very slowly from here on out."

If Baker was wary, there must be a reason. Justin glanced over at Megan, she nodded back at him, then they both proceeded forward.

As they approached the cave they could see that its interior sand-and-rock wall was folded and cleaved into intriguing patters which had evidently been formed by some ancient lava flow. But it was only when they walked up close to the edge that they began to truly appreciate just how deep the cave actually was, although even then their sense of its depth remained vague, since after two hundred feet down the interior light within the cave became progressively hazy.

"What sort of visual range are you getting down into it?" Baker asked, not able to get an accurate sense of things from the helmet cams.

"We can't see too much beyond a certain point," Megan reported. "I'm thinking after about two hundred feet."

"Yeah, same," Justin confirmed.

"Can you please, both of you, grab hold of your rubber ropes and then very carefully step up to the edge and look straight down into it."

They did as directed.

"Hmm…Yes.…" Baker muttered, as if he was trying to "read" the murkiness. Then he asked them, "You do realize what you're looking at, don't you?"

"…A big hole?" Justin replied.

"The future of the human race," Baker said. "The future of the human race. Whatever is down there is key to the survival of our colony, and the survival of our colony could be, in my humble estimation, key to the survival of our species. Whatever's down there…that's what we came here to find."

"So then whad'a we do now?"

"Now – we investigate!"

Baker directed them to walk back to the rover, open one of the black plastic boxes and take out a foot-long, rectangular piece of metal which had horizontal grooves. Then he asked them to take a small metal control panel out of the same box. The control panel had two buttons and a screen.

"Please push the green button on that control panel," Baker said.

Justin pushed it and the grooves in the metal rectangle suddenly buzzed to life, emitting a red light.

"That rectangular device is an extremely hi-tech sensor," Baker explained. "When you lower it into the cave it will tell us what's down there in terms of elements, water, and so forth. All that information will be relayed back to the control panel and from there back to the shuttle and from the shuttle back to my people here on Earth."

There were several very long and thin, exceedingly light-weight rubber ropes stored in the other black boxes, and Baker instructed Justin to carry those ropes – taking multiple trips – over to the edge of the cave. Meanwhile Megan carried over the sensor and the control panel and two metal stakes. Once everything was delivered to the cave's edge, Baker asked them to hook the ropes up end-to-end and then to hook one of the two final ends to the sensor, which had a little clasp on it. This done, the other end of the long rope line was staked securely into the ground.

"Now then, this…this is a very big moment," Baker announced.

"Whatever happens next is…well…okay, off you go then, lower it in there, gently."

Justin and Megan exchanged glances, then Justin began lowering the sensor down into the vast hole. The sensor bounced against the edges of the wall as it descended and eventually – after it'd cleared the first two hundred feet – disappeared into the deep inky haze.

A thought occurred to Justin while he was lowering in the sensor. "Hey Baker?"

"Yes?"

"You're sayin' there might be water down there, right?"

"That's the idea."

"So if there's water then there could be things livin' down there too, right?"

"That's technically possible, yes."

"So by me lowerin' this thing down into this hole, I could end up disturbin' somethin' that's livin' down there and that ain't been disturbed before. Like, ever. Right?"

"It's possible."

"…Is that a problem?"

"Potentially."

"So whad'a we do if somethin' suddenly flies out a this cave and comes after us?"

"If something's down there chances are it won't be able to fly. If it has locomotion at all it'll most likely be by swimming."

"Huh," Justin replied, and continued lowering the sensor.

And the lowering continued. And continued….

"Interesting…." Baker said, after a time.

"What's that?"

"Because of the relay signal that the sensor sends back up to the control panel, we're able to tell how far down the sensor has gone. And it looks like it just passed 600 feet."

"No kiddin'."

"You may run out of rope before it hits bottom."

Justin kept lowering.

Eventually Baker announced, "You're there!"

"I am?"

"Yes. The sensor just stopped descending."

The sensor was so far down by this point that Justin wasn't able to tell if the weight pulling on the rope – a gravitational pull which was far less than the pull would have been on Earth, in any case – was caused by the sensor's own weight or the rope's, and thus he couldn't tell whether the sensor had stopped descending or not.

"643 feet!" Baker announced. "That's quite a cave!"

Justin looked down at the remainder of rubber rope which lay on the ground near his feet; there were only a handful of yards left.

"…So?" Justin asked after a minute passed in silence. "Is there any water down there? You pickin' up anythin'?"

"There's a lot of data coming in, and my people are analyzing it furiously, as you can imagine."

Several more minutes passed….

Justin and Megan stood in silence, peering into the murkiness, waiting to hear whether the colony would in fact be able to survive thanks to a located water source. Several times they glanced at each other, and each time they did so they raised their eyebrows.

When Baker eventually came back on the line, he informed them, "We're still reviewing the data. Why don't you set the control panel in a secure place there on the ground, maybe between some rocks. Then you can head back to the rover and switch out your oxygen tanks for new ones."

They nodded and did as directed.

After replacing the oxygen tanks on each other's packs, Megan and Justin took their seats on the rover, and waited.

"Wanna make a bet 'bout whether there's gonna be any water down there?" Justin asked her, trying to break the tension.

"Don't jinx the mission," Baker cut in.

Justin rolled his eyes, and Megan smiled.

Another half hour crawled by amidst the Martian silence….

Eventually Baker came back on the line and informed them that, "We're not picking up any water readings yet. That's not particularly surprising. The expectation is that the water will be underground, and the sensor can only pick up water that's located a few feet below the surface. So tomorrow we'll come back with the robots, which have much more powerful detection capacities, and we'll also get the whole cave lit-up with floodlights.

"Now, if you could go back and pull up the sensor and then leave it, along with its rope and the control panel, near to where you're parked, that'd be great. You can also leave your security ropes. Once that's all set you can head back to base camp."

"We've got robots?" Justin asked.

"Yes. They're basically like mini-rovers but they're also able to stand vertically and to a limited degree they can climb rocks. And unlike your rover they have a single tank-style tread running around the wheels rather than having each wheel treaded individually."

"It'll be interesting to see what's down there," Megan said, "when we light the space tomorrow."

"It will indeed," Baker agreed.

XIII

Later that evening, while sitting in the study, Justin read chapter seven of *The Prince* – having been instructed to do so by Baker – and he was disturbed by what he read. He knew what would be coming the next morning; he knew precisely the part that Baker was going to emphasize.

And that's what Baker did. He asked Justin to skip the first two paragraphs and to begin reading out loud at the third.

> *With regard to the two methods of rising to be a prince by ability or by fortune, I wish to note two examples within our own recollection: Francesco Sforza and Cesare Borgia.*
>
> *Sforza, by his own means and with very great ability, even though he was a private person, rose to be Duke of Milan, and that which he had acquired with countless difficulties he managed to keep with little trouble. On the other hand, Borgia acquired his state as a result of the power of his father, and once his father was gone then he lost his power, notwithstanding that he had done everything that ought to be done by a wise and capable man to firmly set his roots in those states which the arms and fortunes of others had bestowed upon him.*

"So what Machiavelli is saying," Baker noted, "is that there are these two recent examples – recent for the Renaissance period during which Machiavelli lived – of men becoming new princes. He's already talked about famous examples of the past – Romulus, Cyrus, Moses, and the like – and now he's going to point out two examples from his own era. The difference between these two men – Sforza and Borgia – is that one did everything on his own, while the other one – Borgia – was given power by his father. And because he was given his power by his father, rather than seizing it himself like Sforza, ultimately Borgia lost everything when his father died. By the way, Borgia's father was Pope Alexander VI."

"Wait. What? His father was a pope?"

"Indeed."

"How's that possible?"

"It was the Renaissance."

Justin's brow creased. "…Huh."

Then he continued reading.

As stated above, he who does not lay his own foundations may be able, with great ability, to lay them afterwards, but they will be laid with difficulty by the architect and with danger to the building.

If, therefore, all the steps that were taken by Borgia are considered, it can be seen that he laid solid foundations for his future power, and I do not consider it useless to discuss them, because I do not know what better advice to give a new prince other than the example of Borgia's actions. And if his efforts were ultimately to no avail, this was not his fault, but was caused by the misfortune of having been given these lands by his father.

"So," Baker said with an element of energy in his voice, "there are two examples – Sforza and Borgia – and Sforza did everything right and he therefore succeeded, whereas Borgia did everything right except that he had his power given to him, and thus ultimately he failed. So why does Machiavelli tell us that he's now going to spend time considering the deeds of Borgia rather than Sforza?"

Justin shrugged, even though he knew the answer. "Is it 'cause this Borgia guy was sort of a sick dude?"

Baker smiled. Then he said, "Please skip the next two paragraphs and continue reading at the subsequent paragraph where it talks about how Borgia solidified his power over the Italian region known as the Romagna."

Justin took a deep breath, then read as directed.

When Borgia occupied the Romagna, he found it under the rule of weak masters who plundered their subjects rather than ruling them, and who gave their subjects more cause for disunion than for union, so that the country was full of robbery, quarrels, and every kind of violence.

Wishing to establish peace and obedience to authority in the region, therefore, Borgia considered it necessary to select a good governor. For this purpose, he chose Ramiro d'Orco, an efficient and cruel man, to whom he gave the fullest power. And in a short time d'Orco restored peace and unity with great success.

Afterwards, however, Borgia decided that it wasn't advisable to give so much authority to d'Orco, for he had little doubt that d'Orco would become odious. Therefore Borgia set up a court of judgment in the Romagna, under a most excellent president, wherein all the cities had their advocates. And because Borgia knew that d'Orco's severity had also caused a degree of hatred against Borgia himself, and because he wished to clear himself in the minds of the people and to gain their loyalty entirely, he decided to show that, if any cruelty had been practiced by d'Orco, it had not originated with Borgia, but from the innate cruelty of his minister.

Under this pretense, he had d'Orco seized, and one morning he arranged to have d'Orco cut in half, and the two parts of his body were displayed in the central square in the city of Cesena, with the chopping board and the bloody knife lying at his side. This ferocious spectacle made the people of the Romagna simultaneously happy and dumbfounded.

Justin took another deep breath, then looked up from the reading. Baker was staring at him, smiling.

"Thoughts?" Baker asked.

"Tough guy to work for," Justin observed.

"Clearly. Other thoughts?"

Justin shrugged. "Did this Borgia guy kill a lot of people?"

"That depends on what you mean by "a lot." It's widely believed that he arranged his brother-in-law's murder, and it's also suspected that he killed his own brother."

"Like Romulus killin' Remus."

"Precisely."

"But it all still failed in the end. He lost his power when his dad died."

"Correct. So then, again, the question – why does Machiavelli spend time discussing the career of Cesare Borgia? If there is one person that people remember Machiavelli assessing and praising in this book, it's Borgia. So, again, why? Well as you say, he was a "sick dude." More to the point, he was a recent example of a man who used cruelty well.

After he killed off d'Orco he had the people eating out of his hand.

"Still, because of how he originally came to power, all his political machinations were ultimately for naught. Borgia also wasn't particularly skillful when it came to military affairs, so his reputation as a soldier wasn't going to secure him a notable mention in the history books either. In fact if it wasn't for Machiavelli, Cesare Borgia would probably be just a footnote in history.

"It's worth noting, moreover, that Machiavelli wrote *The Prince* shortly after Borgia's career had come to a quick and violent end. Which meant that Borgia was just beginning to fade from the public's collective memory. Machiavelli, of course, was aware of that progressive fading; in fact he refers to Borgia's downfall in that book. Thus he clearly realized that he could mold Borgia's reputation as he wished. He could never do that with a Romulus or a Moses but he could do it with a relatively minor figure like Cesare Borgia. As a result, the Borgia we remember is very much the Borgia that Machiavelli serves up to us.

"And why does he serve him up? To illustrate this dramatic act of cruelty well used. By putting d'Orco in charge, letting d'Orco crack down on the populace, and then slicing d'Orco in half, Borgia gained control over a very difficult region."

While Baker spoke, his image on the screen was replaced by the painting of a bearded man with an intense gaze who was wearing a large beret and a blue dress.

"Is that Borgia?" Justin asked.

"It is."

"So the other guy – Lorenzo De' Medici – had a woman's haircut and this dude's wearin' a woman's dress."

"Styles change. No doubt back then they both looked like tough guys. Although your comparison of the two men is worth commenting on in the following respect: the Borgias and the De' Medicis were rivals in all sorts of ways. So the fact that Machiavelli is praising Cesare so highly probably didn't sit all that well with Lorenzo, to whom, as you'll recall, *The Prince* is quote-unquote dedicated."

Justin nodded. "Guess not."

"But to return to the point about cruelty well used: this is an idea which pertains directly to you. You, Justin, are going to need to select one of the new colonists to be the d'Orco. Someone to serve as your right hand. And then you're going to need to dispense with that person."

"…Dispense…with…."

"That's correct. Kill."

"You want me to kill somebody?"

"Of course. As I've already told you, I selected you precisely because you're willing to kill people."

Justin had known this discussion was coming, but Baker's blunt statement still hit him like a punch to his stomach. "…So, what then? You literally want me to pick one a those ten people who're showin' up here in a couple weeks, and have that person be the d'Orco, to act strict with everybody and all, and then you want me to kill him?"

"Him or her – yes."

"Well I ain't killin' no lady."

"Then choose a man. That'll probably work better anyway."

Justin shook his head and exhaled, feeling shocked and yet not-shocked simultaneously.

"We need that colony to survive up there, Justin. It won't work as a democracy. It therefore needs to be run by a prince. In order to run it that way you need to be able to keep people in line when they no longer want to follow your lead. You need to be an armed prophet; all unarmed prophets fail. At the same time, if you simply lord it over them they'll eventually get sick of you. But if you relieve them of the dominance of someone else whom they find odious, if you kill that person, then they'll be drawn to you and they'll also be afraid of you. Which will make them relatively easy to rule. It's all just simple logic. For the sake of the colony, and for the sake of your children which Megan will bear, you need to do this."

Justin took another deep breath before replying. "It's easy for you to talk 'bout all that, sittin' down there in Nevada." He said this last word dismissively. "But you've never actually killed anybody, have you?"

"Haven't I? I sent five men to Mars knowing that only one of them would survive."

Justin stared hard into Baker's eyes, trying to read them, but he couldn't see anything in them, so he decided to just ask Baker point blank, "Okay, then tell me this: did you mess with the rover when Calvin drove it to the mountain? Is that what happened? Did you cause somethin' to go wrong with it by remote control?"

"Yes, I did."

"So…you murdered Calvin?"

"Yes."

"Why?"

"To set in motion the train of events which culminated in only one of the five of you being left alive, of course."

Silence ensued, as the two men stared at each other. After a time, Baker smiled. "Now," he said, "I have a question for *you*."

"…What?"

"Did I just lie to you?"

"What? Just now? 'Bout Calvin?"

"Yes. Was that a lie?"

"Why would you lie 'bout somethin' like that?"

"Ahh, but why wouldn't I lie? After all, I want you to play the role of Cesare Borgia up there. I want you to be the Renaissance prince of the red desert planet. And you just asked me if I've ever killed anyone; you asked it as a form of reproach, as if I'm directing you to do something which I myself would never do. So of course I would lie, to persuade you that, were I in your position, I would indeed play the role of Borgia, and I would in fact select a d'Orco."

"So…what? You literally just lied to me, 'bout killin' Calvin?"

"I didn't say that. I asked you, did I lie?"

"Man," Justin declared, shaking his head in exasperation, "how should I know? I don't know what your deal is!"

"Precisely."

Silence once again filled in the space between them. After a few seconds Baker continued, "Justin, tell me this – do you think that Tristan was a dangerous person?"

Justin shrugged. "…Yeah. Apparently he killed who knows how many people."

Baker nodded. "Yes, he did. Many more than I have, no question. But now answer me this: who do you think is – or in Tristan's case, was – more dangerous: me or him?"

Justin considered the question. "I guess I'm not sure."

"Allow me to suggest that I'm a far more dangerous person than Tristan ever was. You see, all his life, Mr. Tristan was just reacting to the non-ideal circumstances into which he was placed. As a boy he reacted in a relatively rational manner to the abusive men that his mother brought into his life. And so he developed a habit of violence as a result of that upbringing. That habit then prompted other people, as he grew older, to react against his violent tendencies in turn. He then reacted against their counter-violence, and so on. In a way you might even say that there was something innocent about how he lived his life. He didn't choose to be that way – he simply responded to the world into which he was placed.

"I, on the other hand, was born into comfortable circumstances. I never had to struggle, I never had to fight, if I didn't want to. The great exertions of my youth all played themselves out on prep school rowing teams and in economics classes and the like. And later on, when I reached college age, I didn't find it difficult to get into a reputable university and I didn't find it difficult to land a high-paying job after I graduated. But at a certain point I realized something: I realized that if I was going to get really rich – and I mean, really, really rich; the kind of wealth that moves mountains – then I was going to have to learn to play mean, and dirty. And that's what I did. I chose that. Similarly, when I began considering what it was going to take to make a colony succeed up there on Mars, I realized I was going to be obliged to make decisions that would cost people their lives. And I chose that too. I chose all of it."

Baker paused for effect, then added, "Justin, allow me to suggest that I'm the most dangerous person you've ever met. And when I tell you that there will come a time when you need to kill people to maintain that colony up there, allow me to suggest that I mean it."

Justin didn't doubt it; still, he couldn't resist asking, "But how can I believe you? Everythin' you just said could be a lie."

Baker smiled. "True."

The two men stared at each other.

Then Justin asked, "So how'd you get so good at lyin', anyways?"

Baker shrugged. "The same way you will. The same way anyone gets good at anything."

Baker waited for a few seconds, to see if Justin would complete the thought. When Justin didn't do so, Baker did, with a word:

"Practice."

XIV

Megan and Justin did a quick scan of the garden and found that all the planter boxes – except the ones with Martian soil – were now showing plant sprouts. So Baker asked them to add more growth formula to the Martian soil.

When this was done he directed them to load several boxes onto the rover. Two of the boxes contained the robots, while the other boxes contained floodlighting lamps and extension cords and other equipment. Once all this was loaded they headed out to the cave and reached Jeanne a little after 14:00.

"First we need you to secure yourselves with your safety ropes," Baker instructed, after they'd parked in the same spot as before, "and then let's start by lowering in the floodlights."

Megan carried two lamps and two securing stakes to the cave's rim and then returned to collect two small boxes which would supply the lamps with energy, while Justin made multiple trips carrying power cords. Once the cords were all connected to each other and then to the lamps and to the power boxes, and after Megan used the stakes to secure the cords into the ground in front of the boxes, the two lamps were slowly lowered down into the vast hole. The cords extended 400 feet, and when that depth was reached Megan pushed the buttons on the control boxes and turned on the lamps.

The deep inky haze – at least the part of it that was nearest to this portion of the cave's diameter – evaporated. The lamps were so powerful that all at once Justin and Megan – and therefore Baker – could see straight down to the cave floor. What had been shrouded in dimness for millions of years was instantly brought into the light, and what they saw there before them was…the bottom of a cave.

As best they could tell, the cave's floor appeared to be filled with ridges and dips, presumably carved endless ages ago by lava, but overall the bottom of the cave was generally all on one level.

Megan and Justin stood there at the cave's rim, staring into the massive hole, waiting for Baker to provide his professional assessment of the view. Eventually he said, simply, "Now then, time for the robots."

The pair returned to the rover and unloaded two boxes which each had wheels on one end, like pieces of luggage, and which also had doors that could be opened by a remote control. The remote had been stored in the box that contained the floodlights. Justin grabbed the remote and then he and Megan wheeled the two robot boxes over to the cave's rim, after which they made multiple trips between the rover and the cave to collect some very long thin ropes out of the other boxes.

Baker instructed them to attach the hook at the end of one of the ropes to a clasp on the top of one of the robot boxes, and then, together, Megan and Justin slowly lowered the box down into the flood-lit hole. When the box finally reached the bottom Justin pushed a button on the remote control to open the box's side. Then they lowered in the second boxed robot.

After this was completed Baker asked them to return to the rover and unpack yet another box, which contained a signal transmitter – it was roughly the size and shape of two stacked shoeboxes – and to carry that over to the cave's rim. With this transmitter in place, the signals sent from the robots down in the cave could be transmitted back to the shuttle and from there back to Nevada.

Once the transmitter was situated, Justin and Megan sat down on the edge of the cave, staring into it, trying to catch sight of the two robots which had now begun roaming around the cave's floor. The distance was such, however, and the overall lighting of the cave too incomplete, for them to be able to spot the robots more than a couple times.

"Do those robots move on their own, or are there people driving them?" Megan asked.

"Both," Baker explained. "They generally move on their own – they're programmed to carry out certain inspection tasks without needing any external direction – but if there's something specific we want them to do then we can control them by remote."

"Are they pickin' up any signals yet?" Justin asked.

"Lots of signals. But none so far for water."

Justin and Megan exchanged glances.

"This is going to take a while," Baker informed them. "There's a lot of ground to cover down there, lots of cracks and corners to inspect.

So you two can stay there or you can head back to camp. Whatever you prefer."

The pair chose to stay at the cave's edge for a little while longer. Then they walked back to the rover, switched out their oxygen tanks for new ones and sat on the rover for another hour or so, waiting to hear any news pertaining to the robots.

There was a part of Justin that wanted to talk to Megan about what he and Baker had discussed earlier that morning, regarding Borgia and d'Orco and Justin's "assignment" to pick a right-hand man whom he'd eventually be obliged to kill. He felt a strong inclination to confide in her, simply to be able to share his thoughts and feelings with someone other than Baker.

But of course he couldn't talk to her about any of that while they were wearing their spacesuits and thus connected to the intercom system. In fact he couldn't do it at all unless he whispered to her in their bedroom. And even if he did tell her, could he be sure that she wouldn't tell Baker what he'd said? Besides, she might not like hearing him complain about this murderous job he'd been given. She was the princess, after all, and he was the prince, and she might simply expect him to buck up and do what he needed to do. And what would happen if she concluded that he wasn't up to the task? What would happen if she and Baker both arrived at that conclusion?

These thoughts all rolled around inside his head as he sat there in silence, saying nothing.

Eventually the newlyweds headed back to base camp, and then later that evening Megan taught him how to make lasagna.

XV

The lighting was dim – provided as it was by stadium-style lights which were situated high up and far away – and he could only see a few feet in any direction. The sound of men frantically conversing caught his attention, so he moved towards them, feeling his way through the murky air. The men eventually came into view: Tobey, Byron and Tristan. They were each tied to a separate table, each one with a chef's knife lying on a chopping board beside them.

"Man, this is *bad*!" Byron was saying.

"Did you see what that dude was wearin'?" Tristan added.

"What sort a accent did he have?" Tobey asked. "I could barely understand what he was sayin'."

As Justin approached the three men, Byron declared, derisively, "Well, well, well, look who's here."

"Hello, hello," Tristan said, the anger evident in his voice as well.

"Justin!" Tobey declared, angry but also relieved. "Justin, man, you gotta untie us! Do it now! You gotta hurry!"

"Yeah, seriously Justin!" Byron nearly yelled. "Untie these ropes! The dude's comin' back!"

"What…dude?" Justin asked, although it took some effort to form the words.

"The dude, man!" Tristan explained. "The killer in the blue dress!"

"…What?"

"With the beard and the hat," Tobey elaborated. "He's crazy, and he said he's gonna cut us in half!"

Justin felt confused. He glanced around several times, trying to get his bearings by staring harder into the murky darkness. "Where are we?"

"Dude, what's wrong with you?" Tristan shot back. "Don't you know nothin'? We're in the Astrodome!"

"We are?"

"Yeah, man," Byron confirmed. "Now untie these ropes! I'm not kiddin' – you gotta get us out a here!"

"How'd we get in the Astrodome?"

"How should we know – it's your dream!"

"Justin," Tobey said. "Justin, look at me, man! Alright, please. Look at me."

Justin looked at Tobey.

"You killed me. Okay. You did it. But now you can start to make things right. You can untie me and keep me from gettin' chopped in half. You gotta! After what you did to me in that parkin' lot, you can't just leave me here to get cut into pieces in the middle a the Astrodome! You owe me this! You gotta untie me!"

Justin began walking slowly towards the wooden table to which Tobey was bound. "Who did this to you?"

"Like we was tellin' you – the guy with the beard and the hat and the dress."

"A seriously freaky dude," Byron added. "He kills people for fun. He killed people in his own family!"

"You mean...Cesare Borgia?"

"That's it! That's the dude!" Byron confirmed. "Borgia! And he's comin' back!"

"...Cesare Borgia's at the...Astrodome?"

"Yeah, man! Now hurry up and untie these ropes 'fore he gets here! He'll be back any minute!"

Justin nodded, and stepped still closer to Tobey's table, but for some reason he couldn't quite reach it.

"C'mon man!" Tobey yelled at him. "Untie me! You owe me! You owe me! Don't let me die again!"

Justin kept forcing his legs forward, trying to reach Tobey's table, but it just wasn't happening.

"Man, what's wrong with you?" Tobey nearly shrieked.

At which point the three bound men became hysterical and began yelling at Justin in unison to untie the ropes. This seemed to go on for a while, until all at once their yelling stopped and they turned to look to their left, at a man who'd emerged from the darkness, wearing a blue dress and a large beret. This person had an intense look in his eyes and his face was covered by a thick beard. But it wasn't Cesare Borgia's face. It was Justin's.

"Aaaa!" Justin woke up with a gasp.

He was sweating.

Megan was lying beside him, on her side, studying him.

"...Hey," he said, as he tried to catch his breath.

"Hey," she replied, quietly.

He stared at the ceiling for several seconds before turning to look directly at her.

Then he asked her, "You been awake long?"

"A couple minutes. All the sounds you were making, they woke me up." She spoke very softly.

He wasn't sure what to say. He wasn't sure what she might have heard.

The seconds passed between them in silence.

Then, in an even quieter voice than before, barely a whisper, she told him, "I know what your nightmares are about."

Their eyes locked. Justin froze. He didn't know how to reply.

Megan studied his face for a little bit longer, until her own facial features shifted, conveying a feeling of disappointment. She just lay there like that, letting him see what she was feeling. Then she turned onto her other side to face away from him and eventually drifted back to sleep.

XVII

"As you may have already surmised," Baker said, when he and Justin settled into their morning discussion, "Cesare Borgia is hardly the most dangerous person presented to us in *The Prince*."

Justin said nothing in reply. Images of his most recent nightmare were still flitting in front of his mind's eye.

"As I mentioned yesterday, Borgia – in the pages of this book – becomes Machiavelli's tool. And that tool is used for multiple tasks. One task is to introduce the idea of cruelty well used; and in this case, well used by someone from Machiavelli's own era. But Borgia is neither the sole nor even the supreme example of that particular talent. In chapter eight Machiavelli introduces us to someone who is far worse, or better, as the case may be. His name is Agathocles and he ruled the city-state of Syracuse starting in 317 B.C."

Justin nodded, bracing for what came next.

"Agathocles," Baker noted, "makes Cesare Borgia look like a piker, frankly, when it comes to killing people."

"So then Machiavelli liked this other guy even better?"

"Let's see what he has to say. If you could read out loud, starting with the second paragraph."

Justin took a deep breath, then began to read.

Agathocles became the King of Syracuse after starting out in life from not only a private but from a very low and abject position. This man, who was the son of a potter, through all the changes in his fortune, always led an infamous life.

Nevertheless, he combined all his infamous behavior with so much ability of mind and body that, having devoted himself to the military profession, he rose through its ranks to be Praetor of Syracuse. Being established in that position, and having decided to make himself prince, and to seize by violence, without obligation to others, that which had been already conceded to him by assent, he decided to establish a temporary peace with his primary enemy, Hamilcar the Carthaginian, who, with his army, was fighting in Sicily at the time.

Thereby secured against that external enemy, Agathocles proceeded one morning to assemble all the people and the senate of Syracuse, as if he intended to discuss with them things relating to the Republic. However, at a given signal from him, the soldiers killed all the senators and the richest of the people. With these dead, Agathocles was able to then seize and hold the princedom of that city without any civil disturbances.

And though he was twice routed by the Carthaginians in battle, and ultimately besieged, yet not only was he able to defend his city but, leaving part of his men for its defense, he went with his other soldiers to attack the Carthaginians in Africa and, as a result, in a short time he managed to end the Carthaginian siege of Syracuse. The Carthaginians, thus reduced to extreme necessity, were compelled to come to terms with Agathocles, and, leaving Sicily to him, had to be content with the possession of Africa.

"Thoughts?" Baker asked.

Justin shrugged, reluctant to talk about what he'd just read. "So this guy, Agathocles, was basically like a mass murderer?"

"With a purpose. Yes."

"And that's just fine then, far as Machiavelli's concerned?"

"Let's see what he says. Please continue."

Thus he who considers the actions and the genius of this man will see nothing, or very little, which can be attributed to fortune, inasmuch as he attained pre-eminence not by the favor of anyone, but went step by step in the military profession, and these steps were gained with a thousand troubles and perils, and were then afterwards boldly held onto by him in the face of many dangers.

We cannot, of course, call it "virtue" to massacre one's fellow-citizens, deceive friends, to be without faith, without mercy, or without any religion; such methods may gain an empire, but not glory. Nonetheless, if the courage of Agathocles in entering into and then extricating himself from dangers is considered, together with his greatness of mind in enduring and then overcoming difficulties, it cannot be seen why he should be held in less esteem than the most notable ruler. Nonetheless, his barbarous cruelty and inhumanity do not permit him to be celebrated among the most excellent men. In any case, the things he achieved cannot be attributed to either fortune or genius.

"So does Machiavelli think he's great or not?" Justin asked.

"What do you think?"

Justin re-read the text briefly. Then he noted, "He says this guy is as good a ruler as any other great ruler, but that he isn't "excellent," whatever that means."

"Whatever that means indeed."

"And he says he isn't a genius."

"He says that at the end there, but a little above that he says that Agathocles does in fact have genius."

"So…Machiavelli's bein' Machiavelli."

"Clearly. Please skip the next two paragraphs and pick up where he returns to the subject of Agathocles."

Justin did as instructed.

Some may wonder how it was that Agathocles, or someone like him, after having committed countless treacheries and cruelties, could nonetheless live for such a long time, secure in his country, and be able to defend himself from external enemies, without ever being conspired against by his own citizens; especially since many others, by means of cruelty, have not been able even in peaceful times to hold the state, and still less to do so in times of war.

I believe it depends upon cruelty being badly or properly used. Cruelty may be said to be properly used, if of evil it is possible to speak well, when it is applied at one blow and necessary to one's security, and when it is not persisted in afterwards unless it can be turned to the advantage of one's subjects. Badly employed cruelty is that which is very limited in the beginning but then multiplies with time rather than decreases.

Those who take the first approach are able, by aid of God or man, to mitigate in some degree their cruelty over time, as Agathocles did. However, it is impossible for those who follow the other approach to maintain themselves in power.

"So he's approvin' of Agathocles," Justin stated. "It's clear."

"It would appear so. Please read the final paragraphs, to wrap up the point."

Thus it is to be remarked that, when it comes to seizing a state, he who does so ought first to carefully consider all those injuries which it is necessary for him to inflict, and to do them all at once, so that he will not need to repeat them daily; and thus, by not unsettling people, he will be able to reassure them, and win them to himself by all the benefits which he bestows upon them.

He who does otherwise, however, either from timidity or evil advice, is always compelled to keep the knife in his hand. Since he cannot rely upon his subjects, nor can they attach themselves to him, owing to continued and repeated wrongs which he commits against them. For injuries ought to be done all at once so that, since they are tasted less, they offend less. Benefits, however, ought to be given out little by little, so that the flavor of them may last longer.

Justin looked up, and closed the book. "I'm not doin' it," he stated matter-of-factly. "If that's where this is goin', forget it. I'm not killin' off a whole bunch a people just to scare them into doin' what I want them to do. No way. Period!"

Baker studied him for a few moments, then replied, very calmly, "Justin, it's not simply a matter of doing this or doing that specific act. It's not about how many you kill or don't kill. It's about doing what's required to maintain the state, to maintain the colony."

"I'm not committin' mass murder for this colony! That's it! Not gonna happen!"

"Justin, if you had to kill ten people to save the human race, would you do it?"

"We're not talkin' 'bout that!"

"That's precisely what we're taking about. Here on Earth, nuclear weapons are proliferating, religious fanatics are butchering whole towns and cities, the ocean levels are rising. What you need to recognize, Justin, is precisely what's at stake in our little experiment up there."

Justin shook his head, exasperated. "First you're tellin' me I gotta choose some dude in order to kill that dude, and now you're tellin' me that I gotta be ready to kill off a whole crowd a people! What's next, man?"

"It's not a question of what's next. It's a question of what you're prepared to do in order to deal with whatever comes next. Which is to say, more fundamentally, that the real question is this: are you a ruler or aren't you? Are you still a mailman, or are you the prince of Mars?"

"Man, this is...." Justin said, shaking his head. "This is just too much."

Baker said nothing in reply. Instead he studied Justin for a few seconds, in that way he had of looking not just at but through people. Then his expression shifted, displaying his disappointment, and the TV screen switched to black.

XVIII

Justin stepped numbly out of the study, wondering if something important – something bad – had just transpired.

Megan was making them a lunch of tofu hotdogs and he helped her finish getting things prepared. After they ate they briefly checked up on the garden; all the planter boxes – except the ones with Martian soil – continued to have plants growing in them. Then they loaded up the rover with more boxes – as instructed by Baker – and headed out to the cave. Megan offered to drive this time and Justin was glad to have her do so since it was easier for him to let his mind wander if he didn't need to keep an eye out for rocks and ditches.

As they rolled along, Arsia Mons loomed in the distance to their front and right; a huge, lonely mountain on a barren, lonely planet....

Justin stared at the mountain, feeling similarly stranded, marooned, all alone. The only individuals he could talk to were a rich white guy who wanted him to kill people and this lady – his wife – who claimed to know what his nightmares were about.

He couldn't help wondering whether the two of them had already decided that he hadn't met their expectations, that he wasn't the sociopath they'd been hoping for. Perhaps they'd reached that conclusion – together – while he was taking a quick shower after lunch.

His darkening thoughts turned altogether black when they arrived at the cave and Baker informed them that, "One of the robots has broken down. Its tread snapped off its wheels on one side. Justin, that means we need you to go down into the cave and fix it for us."

"A robot is…broken?"

"That's right. And we can't fix it by remote, which means we need you to go down in there and take care of it for us."

"How'd the tread snap off?"

"It looks like a rock shard slid between the wheels and the tread and got stuck in there, and when the rover kept going forward that shard pulled the tread off."

"But how do you expect me to get down there?"

"The components of a specially designed repelling system are in the boxes that you loaded on the rover today. There are several notched, rubber ropes which join together like the other ropes you've used at the cave, and there's a motorized mechanism that hooks onto that rope line and then slides down the line from one notch to the next. That mechanism, in turn, hooks up to a leather strap which will be your seat. There's also a remote control device which will remain up on the surface at the descent point, which can likewise be used to control the motorized mechanism and which can override the controls on the mechanism if for any reason that's necessary. After the two of you unpack all that and carry it over to the cave I'll walk you through how to set everything up."

Justin and Megan exchanged glances, then began unpacking the boxes. The motorized mechanism was small – only a foot long and a few inches tall and wide – and the remote control device was even smaller, about the size of a large television remote. Megan carried these and the leather seat, which she threw over her shoulder, while Justin carried some of the notched ropes. As they walked he looked over at her a few times, trying to gauge from her expression what she was thinking, what she was feeling.

She looked quietly concerned, but he just couldn't read anything beyond that. Was she concerned because she cared about him and was worried about him repelling hundreds of feet down into the incompletely lit cave, yet she didn't want to voice this concern because she didn't want to cause him undue nervousness? Or was she concerned because she and Baker had decided to kill him off by leaving him stranded down there, and she was wondering if he was going to figure that out in time to stop it from happening, perhaps by refusing to be lowered into the cave, or perhaps by grabbing hold of her and then threatening to throw her in?

The simple fact was that he didn't know her well enough to be able to tell for certain whether she wanted him dead or she was afraid that he might die. Evidently this was one of the drawbacks of a shotgun marriage.

He made multiple trips between the rover and the cave to gather all the ropes, then connected the ropes together, and once this was done Baker explained how to set up the repelling system. First the motorized mechanism was attached to the notched rope and to the leather strapped seat, then Justin lowered the other end of the rope into the cave until that rope was fully extended. Next, following Baker's instructions, Megan unlatched the safety rope from Justin's pack – while the other end of that rope remained hooked to the rover – and attached the safety rope to the notched rope. This done, she picked up the repelling mechanism's remote control.

Justin stared at his wife while he pulled the leather seat up to his waist; he was waiting for her eyes to make contact with his. As their pupils drew even, he tried to see deeply into her, to read the depths of her soul, the way that Baker looked into people. But he couldn't.

For a few seconds he contemplated the option of grabbing hold of her and taking her with him into the cave for the sake of bargaining leverage. Presumably Baker wouldn't want to sacrifice both of them. But maybe he would. And the thought of causing Megan's death was appalling to Justin. He'd rather go to his death than risk her life, even if she was currently cooperating in killing him. This surprised him – he realized that he cared more about her than he did about himself. Or maybe he was just disinclined to cause any more people to die.

Whatever the reasoning, he stepped carefully off the ledge and then allowed the repelling mechanism to begin its work of lowering him slowly down into the enormous cave. His eyes watched hers for the first few seconds until the cave's wall absorbed his entire line of vision and then she was gone.

He was now completely vulnerable. At any moment Baker might order Megan to detach the notched rope from the safety rope and send Justin plunging to his death, and this thought naturally amplified the sense of dread which he was already experiencing as a result of repelling into a vast Martian cave. It was important to him, however, to prevent the other two from realizing how frightened he was.

Of course if they were planning to kill him then who cared if they knew he was scared? And if they weren't going to kill him then who cared all the same? But for some reason he didn't want them to know.

This was hard to pull off, since it turned out that facing death the second time wasn't any easier than the first. If anything it was worse because he knew the fears that flow through the human body when death is coming straight at you down the line. He didn't want to feel those fears ever again. And if they came on full bore then he knew he'd panic and lose control, and who knew what would happen then.

All he could do for the moment was keep his breathing slow and wrap his space-gloved hands around the notched rope, tight enough to steady himself but loose enough to allow the rope to slide through his grip as he went down.

Silence rose up higher and higher around him as he descended. Somehow the inside of the cave was even quieter than the planet's surface. It was as if he was entering a whole new dimension of silence, which grew thicker in proportion to the increasing depth.

Eventually he reached the point where the floodlights hung – at 400 feet – and then kept going. Beyond this point the lighting in the cave became surreal – a mixture of manufactured light and a few remaining strands of sunlight – which created strange shadows, all playing together on the cave's lava-sculpted walls. The visual effect didn't help Justin hold back his panic, and now his breathing became loud enough to echo inside his helmet.

"Doing alright in there?" Baker asked, in a monotone voice, as if he wasn't particularly interested in the answer.

"Fine," Justin replied, trying to sound equally disinterested in the topic of his well-being.

At long last his feet touched the bottom of the cave. "I'm there," he announced. Then he stepped out of the seat.

"Okay now," Baker told him, "the robot is a couple hundred feet from where you're standing. It'll be in a relatively straight line from you, if you walk directly forward from the cave wall."

Justin took a few steps in the recommended direction and then stopped, waiting to hear if the repelling mechanism would start climbing back up the notched rope and leave him stranded where he stood. But the mechanism remained in place. So he continued walking.

The floor of the cave, he now realized, was very uneven; much more so than it appeared when viewed from six hundred feet away. The rocky folds and ditches were all contorted into bizarre shapes, and several times he slipped as he stepped from one fold to the next, which didn't do anything for his hard-pounding heart. More than once he gazed up at the cave-framed sky, as if pleading with the powers-that-be not to abandon him in this truly forsaken place; a place so forsaken that no one had ever had the opportunity to forsake it.

It occurred to him that the last time he'd felt this alone was when he was back in prison, getting ushered from the final holding cell to the execution chamber.

"Those robots found any water yet?" Justin asked Baker, thinking that if he was going to get left down here, at least he might have a water supply.

There was a brief silence on the line. Justin stopped walking. So this was it. He'd been abandoned.

But then Baker said, "No, no water yet."

Justin nodded, took a deep breath and continued making his way in the direction that Baker requested. After he'd cleared a few more folds the robot came into view.

And – it wasn't broken. Its treads were in place.

Justin smiled, tragically. Then he sat down on a rocky fold, about ten feet from the rover. His breathing relaxed now. Knowing that he was dead brought with it a sense of calm. Calm combined with dread, but calm nonetheless. So this was it. At least now he knew. He wanted to take a few moments and get his thoughts together.

He wasn't going to say anything to Baker. He wasn't about to give that guy any satisfaction by begging for his life, or even by acknowledging him. But he did want to say something to Megan. She was his wife, after all, and she'd been good to him for their short marriage, at least up until this point. Besides, if she was pregnant then he wanted her to take good care of their child, and he wanted to say something special to her now, something that would cause her to regret killing him and thereby further ensure that she'd look after his offspring.

"Megan…." He began.

"Justin, what's going on?" Baker cut in. What's wrong?" "Why have you stopped?"

"Megan," Justin repeated, trying to ignore Baker, "I…."

"Justin, what are you doing?" Baker cut in again, the confusion registering in his voice. "The robot's right there. Go up to it. Examine the treads."

"The treads are just fine, Baker. The treads are just fine."

"No they're not. One of them is off in the back, wrapped around the wheels. Go up closer to it and you'll see."

"…What?"

"The tread in the back, it's wrapped around the two back wheels.

We didn't send you into that cave to look at a perfectly functional robot."

Justin shook himself out of his waiting-for-death trance and rose to his feet. "…Oh," he replied.

Sure enough, as he walked up beside the robot he saw that one of the treads had been pulled off two of its three wheels and it was wrapped around them.

"Ha!" He yelled out, ecstatic.

"What?" Baker asked. "What do you see?"

"It got wrapped around the wheels, just like you said!"

"Of course it did. Now we need you to fix it."

"Ha!" Justin exclaimed again.

Then, gathering his composure, though giddy, he bent down and gripped the edge of the tread as best he could with his gloved fingers. For the next few minutes he pulled and pushed and stretched the tread until it fit back around the two wheels' grooved edges.

"Done," he announced at last, as he sat down on a fold of rocks, feeling exhausted, more so from the fear he'd been entertaining than from the exertion of working the tread back into place.

"We'll try it on our end," Baker said.

A few seconds later the robot's six wheels began to spin, as both its treads spun properly around, causing the robot to lurch forward a few feet before coming to a stop.

"Excellent!" Baker announced. "Justin, it looks like you did it. Good work!"

"Great," Justin replied, not really caring at this point, still basking in the relief of not being dead. While he sat there, the robot started up again and quickly sped out of sight, disappearing around the edge of the rocky fold on which it had stalled.

After it was gone, Baker asked Justin, "So, what's it like down there?"

"It's…quiet. Real quiet. It's even quieter down here than it is up on the surface. It's just like…pure silence."

"That silence is the sound of hope. Our great hope. Hope for what we can find down there."

Justin glanced around. "I'll be honest with you – I don't see a whole lot down here other than a bunch a weird lookin' rocks."

"It's what's below those rocks that interests us."

"But you said the robots ain't picked up anythin' yet with their sensors."

"Yes, well, "yet" is the operative word. It'll take us a couple weeks to do a full reconnaissance of the cave and to send signals down into the rocks below it. We have to think positively. Optimism is an asset."

Justin glanced around again, then nodded. "Yeah, okay."

"Do you want to walk around for a little while down there and do some exploring?"

"Naw, I'm good. I've had enough a bein' down here in this thing for one day. I'm ready to go up."

"Alright then."

So Justin walked back to the cave's wall, stepped into the seat of the repelling system, then allowed the motorized mechanism to lift him out of the giant hole in the ground. Going up seemed to take much less time than going down, although that was probably just his imagination.

As he arrived back at the cave's rim he let go of the rope, placed his gloved palms on the ground and pushed himself up onto the Martian surface. In the process he felt Megan's hands grab him under his armpits and help him with the final lift. He rolled onto his side and from there onto his knees and then, as she held his shoulders to steady him, he rose to his feet.

She threw her arms around him and embraced him as soon as he straightened up. And while they stood there, holding each other, he noticed that she'd set the repelling mechanism's remote on the ground, tucked between two small rocks.

Later that evening, when they were lying in bed, on their sides, facing each other, he spoke to her in a whisper. "So you know what I've been havin' nightmares 'bout?"

She nodded. And replied likewise in a whisper, "I don't want you to suffer, but there's a part of me that's glad you're having them."

He wasn't sure what she meant.

"If you weren't bothered by people dying," she explained, "it'd mean that you weren't entirely human. That you were a monster, or you were becoming one. And I don't want that to happen."

Justin nodded, feeling deeply relieved, once again, on this day full of fear and relief. "I thought," he whispered, "that you were disappointed that I wasn't stronger. That I wasn't handlin' it better."

She shook her head. "I was disappointed that you didn't want to talk to me about it."

He smiled, gratified. But then his smile disappeared. "There are things…" he said, "that Baker wants me to do up here. I.…" He hesitated. "I think there're gonna be things that might be…tough."

She nodded. Then she ran her hand through his hair and down his cheek.

His smile returned.

This was, to be sure, an atypical relationship. He wooed her when there wasn't any need to and as a result the wooing seemed all the more meaningful. He had thought that she was going to kill him and when she didn't, when she didn't abandon him at the bottom of a Martian cave, he concluded that she was a wonderful person. And now, when she told him that she was happy he was having nightmares, he experienced the most profound sense of gratitude.

Who knew – maybe all his positive responses to her were just a product of her being the only other person on the planet. Yet he couldn't help thinking that maybe this was in fact the real thing, after all. Maybe this was it. Maybe this was love.

XIX

"Now we come to a truly intriguing chapter," Baker declared the following morning after Justin had read through chapters nine and ten in silence. "Chapter eleven. This one you're definitely going to want to read out loud."

So Justin read.

It is time to discuss ecclesiastical principalities....

"...What?" Justin asked, stopping mid-sentence.

"Ecclesiastical principalities," Baker explained, "are states ruled by religious leaders. For example, a state run by a pope, or in Islam by an ayatollah. That sort of thing."

"Oh, okay."

It is time to discuss ecclesiastical principalities, regarding which all the difficulties occur before you get possession of them, since they are acquired either by capacity or by good fortune, yet they can be held onto without either; for they are sustained by the ancient decrees of religion, which are so powerful and of such a character that these principalities may be held no matter how their princes behave and live.

These princes are the only ones who have states and do not need to defend them; they have subjects and do not rule them; their states, although unguarded, are not taken from them, and their subjects, though not ruled, have neither the desire nor ability to betray the state. Only these principalities are therefore truly secure and happy.

But, since they are upheld by powers to which the human mind cannot aspire, I shall speak no more of them here, because, being exalted as they are and maintained by God, it would clearly be the act of a very presumptuous and rash man to discuss them.

212

"So what did he just say?" Baker asked.

"He's sayin'…that if you're a religious leader, it's easier to hold onto power."

"Correct. Why is that?"

"Because people believe, ya know, people think you're actin' in the name a some sort a higher power."

"Exactly. So then do you suppose he's going to tell us anything more about these sorts of states?"

"Well he just said they're somethin' that shouldn't be discussed 'cause a the whole higher power thing."

"Indeed. So do you think he's going to discuss them?"

Justin shrugged. "He *is* Machiavelli."

"Right. So of course he is. Please continue."

Yet someone might ask how it came about that the Church has now attained such greatness in temporal power….

"What's temporal power?"

"Earthly power. As opposed to power in heaven."

"Oh."

…in temporal power, considering that, prior to the time of Alexander VI, all the powerful Italian rulers (not only those who have been called rulers, but also every baron and lord) have valued the Church's temporal power very slightly. Yet now a king of France trembles before the Church, and the Church has been able to drive him from Italy, and to ruin the Venetians. Although it may be obvious how this change occurred, it does not appear to me superfluous to recall it in some measure to memory.

"Alexander VI, remember," Baker noted, "was the pope who also happened to be Cesare Borgia's father. And what Machiavelli is pointing out is that, prior to the time of Alexander, the Church's earthly power was quite limited. Please continue."

Before Charles, the King of France, entered Italy in force, the Italian peninsula was under the dominion of the pope, the Venetians, the King of Naples, the Duke of Milan, and also the Florentines. All these rulers had two principal concerns:

to ensure that no foreigner should enter into Italy with his military; and to ensure that none among themselves should seize more territory than they already held.

Among themselves, those about whom there was the most anxiety were the pope, on the one hand, and the Venetians, on the other. To keep the Venetians in check, it required the union of all the other Italian rulers; and to keep the pope in check, the other Italian rulers made use of the barons of Rome, who, being divided into two factions, the Orsini and Colonnesi, always had excuses for causing disorder, and since they were standing with weapons in their hands, near to the pope, they kept the pope weak and powerless.

Though there sometimes arose a courageous pope, such as Sixtus, neither fortune nor wisdom could rid him of these constraints. Furthermore, the short life of a pope is also a cause of weakness; for in ten years, which is the average life of a pope, he can only with great difficulty reduce the power of one of the factions; and yet, if one should almost destroy the Colonnesi, then some other faction from among the general populace would arise, hostile to the Orsini, and would support the Orsini's opponents, and yet this new faction would not have the capacity to ruin the Orsini. This was the reason why the temporal powers of the pope were little esteemed in Italy.

Alexander VI, however, of all the popes that have ever lived, showed how a pope with both money and arms was able to prevail; and, via the actions of his son, Cesare Borgia, and by reason of the entry into Italy of the French, Alexander brought about all the things which I have already discussed relating to Cesare. And although Alexander's intention was not to aggrandize the Church, but rather his son, still he contributed to the greatness of the Church, which, after his death and after the ruin of Cesare, became the heir to all his achievements.

"So the previous popes," Baker summarized, "hadn't managed to establish the Vatican as a real political powerhouse, but Alexander VI, with the help of Cesare, did manage to do so. And he did that with money and a military."

"Right."

"Please continue."

Pope Julius came next, after Alexander VI, and found the Church strong, possessing all the Romagna, the barons of Rome reduced to impotence, and, thanks to the actions of Alexander VI, the factions subdued. He also found the way open to accumulate money in a manner such as had not been practiced prior to that time.

Such methods Julius not only followed but improved upon, and he intended to obtain the city of Bologna, to ruin the Venetians, and also to drive the French out of Italy. All of these enterprises prospered with him, and this was all the more to his credit, since he acted in order to strengthen the Church and not any private person.

He likewise kept the Orsini and Colonnesi factions within the bounds in which he found them; and even though there were among them some who wished to cause disturbances, nevertheless he always held firmly to two principles: one of these principles was the supreme greatness of the Church, with which he terrified the factions; the other principle being, to never allow the factions to choose their own cardinals, since such choosing of cardinals always caused disorders among them. For whenever the factions have their cardinals, they do not remain quiet for long, because cardinals foster the factions both in Rome and outside of it, and the barons are compelled to support them, and thus from the ambitions of cardinals arise disorders and tumults among the barons.

Thus for all of these reasons, his current Holiness Pope Leo found the pontificate so powerful, and it is only to be hoped that, if others made it great in arms, he will make it all the greater and more venerated as a result of his goodness and infinite other virtues.

"A few points to note," Baker stated, after Justin finished reading this section. "First, and most obviously, we can see from the reading that Machiavelli is of the opinion that the Papal States in his day were not run entirely by following divine revelation. Also worth noting: the popes who ran the Papal States during this time were not exactly exemplars of the papal ideal in their personal lives either. Both Alexander VI and Julius II fathered children, and Leo X – whom Machiavelli refers to at the end – was, by some accounts, an atheist."

"The pope was an atheist?"

"Evidently."

"How's that possible?"

"It was the Renaissance."

"Huh. You'd think they'd weed those out in the selection process."

"Yes, well, it didn't hurt that he had a very powerful father."

"Who was that?"

"Lorenzo De' Medici."

"The guy who Machiavelli dedicated this book to?"

"The very one."

"Huh."

"The story is that when Leo X became pope, he announced, "Since God has given us the papacy, let us enjoy it." And enjoy it he did. He threw wild parties, hosted bizarre festivities involving a pet elephant, you name it."

"Seriously?"

"Indeed. He was also very interested in art. Which he paid for by granting indulgences. Which is to say that if you paid him or the people working for him then he'd help you avoid getting sent to hell. As you might imagine, that was a system rife with corruption. And by presiding over that system Leo helped trigger the Protestant Reformation."

"What's that?"

Baker smiled. "You were raised by a single mother, yes?"

"…Yeah."

"She was religious?"

"Very."

"Baptist, yes?"

"Yeah."

"The Baptist Church is a protestant church."

"Uh-huh."

"Protestantism, as a phenomenon, happened when certain people became sufficiently unhappy with the Catholic Church that they decided to break away from it."

"Uh-huh, yeah, okay."

"And all that really came to a head during the reign of Leo X."

"So…the guy this book is dedicated to – his son basically broke up the church?"

"He played a major role, yes."

"Huh."

"Here's a picture of Leo." As Baker spoke his image on the screen was replaced by a painting of an overweight man who was wearing a red robe and had a less-than-pleasant countenance.

"That's him?"

"It is."

"Not too friendly lookin'."

"Not very, no."

Justin reviewed the last paragraph he'd read. "Machiavelli talks 'bout this Leo havin' "goodness and infinite other virtues." So that's just Machiavelli bein' Machiavelli again?"

"Clearly. And of course, as we discussed, the way in which that book is quote-unquote dedicated to Leo's father makes that entire text an exercise in manipulation, not to mention an extended study in irony."

"These dudes in the Renaissance...." Justin shook his head.

Baker smiled. "There's a larger point at work here, however. The point is that the influence of religion, combined with the willingness of certain popes to use some very earthly means to get what they wanted, allowed the Papal States to become quite powerful. Which is simply to say that if you're resourceful and you have religion on your side or can make a claim in that direction then you can accomplish big things."

"Yeah, I guess."

"It's something for us to consider very closely while we wait for the other colonists to arrive."

"What – you mean usin' religion? To rule?"

"Correct."

Justin was surprised. "But...how could that work? On Mars? In the 21st century?

"Because the colonists we're sending up there are very religious people."

"Seriously? Which religion?"

"The religion of science."

"The what?"

"The religion of science. Their god is the big bang, their creed is evolution, their saints are physicists and biologists and their miracles are all technological devices."

"What're you talkin' 'bout?"

"I'm talking about the dominant faith of our times, Justin. These people think science can explain everything. Can bring them everything. For them the exploration of the universe is a holy quest and their holy grail is the discovery of alien life forms. That is what I'm talking about."

"The religion of science…?"

"Precisely. And the people we're sending up there for you to rule are its dedicated disciples. They're fully convinced that the advancement of science ought to give their lives meaning. It's why they signed up for this mission in the first place. And the thing they want to find up there, more than anything else, is alien life."

"But…is there any alien life up here?"

"I doubt it. Not intelligent life at any rate. I'm a hundred percent certain that there isn't intelligent life anywhere in our solar system aside from human beings. That said, there might be some low-level life forms swimming around in the water that's buried under the Martian crust. After all, water is the key when it comes to life. So who knows? The fact of the matter is, I don't care. As far as I'm concerned, a fish is a fish is a fish. Unless you happen to find it sitting at a desk composing poetry or math equations, I really couldn't care less."

"But if you don't care 'bout any a that, then how does that relate to us usin' religion to run the colony? What's the point?"

"The point, my dear Justin, is that we're going to lie."

XX

A new image appeared on the screen; it was a painting of a woman. Justin recognized it – he'd seen the painting before.

"No doubt you're familiar with the *Mona Lisa*," Baker said.

"I've seen that paintin', sure."

"Do you know who painted it?"

Justin thought for a moment. "Can't remember."

"Have you ever heard of Leonardo da Vinci?"

"Oh right. Like *The Da Vinci Code*. He was another one a those Renaissance guys, wasn't he?"

"He was. Arguably *the* Renaissance guy. And as it turns out he was also an associate of Machiavelli."

"No kiddin'."

"Indeed. At one point the two geniuses joined forces – this was when Machiavelli was still a government official – to figure out a way to divert the course of the Arno River. The Arno runs through the center of Florence and from there to the city of Pisa, after which it empties into the sea. Pisa was a rival of Florence, so Machiavelli and da Vinci tried to alter the course of the river away from Pisa in order to remove that city's fresh water supply. In addition to being a brilliant painter da Vinci also happened to be an extraordinary engineer."

"Did it work?"

"No. But it would've been fun to listen in on their conversations. Even more fun would have been to tag along for the ride when the two of them teamed up with Cesare Borgia to inspect the Romagna region."

"That actually happened?"

"It did. Can you imagine the small talk? In any case, what I want you to do is to look at this painting and tell me what you see. Obviously it's a woman, but what is it that strikes you about her? This is, arguably, the single most famous painting on Earth. So what do you see when you look at it?"

Justin studied it carefully. "Is she smilin' or not?"

"Nobody knows. It's that enigmatic quality, in part, that makes the painting so famous. But that's not all there is to it. Keep looking at it and tell me what else you see?"

Justin stared at the painting for over a minute. Then he noted, "Her eyes. That look in 'em. It's like she's lookin' right through whoever it is she's lookin' at."

"Precisely. Excellent, Justin. That's it precisely. As we proceed here I'm going to teach you how to lie, to lie like a prince, and the ideal I want you to keep in mind is this portrait. The woman – her actual name was Lisa del Giocondo – gives away nothing with her expression; at the same time her eyes penetrate right into and through whoever it is she's looking at. She gives away nothing and nothing is kept from her."

"So then I gotta keep my face lookin' like that all the time?" Justin tried to mimic the *Mona Lisa's* expression.

Baker smiled. "No, let your face do what it wants. Just be sure that you know what it's doing. Control your facial features. Don't give away your true intentions. Smile when you're angry, frown when you're happy. And while you're doing that, see through other people's facial expressions, see through their masks."

"How?"

"The seeing is simple; it's merely a matter of focus. But preventing other people from seeing what you're thinking is a matter of technique."

"Technique?"

"Correct. Here, let's practice. Ask me a question."

"A question? Any question?"

"Any question."

Justin shrugged. "Alright. What's your wife's name?"

"Sophia."

"Is that true?"

"Is it?"

Justin studied Baker's face. "It's true."

"You're right."

Justin smiled.

"Now, here's my question for you," Baker continued.

"Okay...."

"When you decided just now that I was telling the truth, did you know that I was telling the truth or did you guess?"

"I knew."

"You're lying."

Justin smiled sheepishly. "How'd you know?"

"Because I focused on your features, and, since you lack proper lying technique, since you haven't practiced enough, that degree of focus provided me with everything I needed to know."

"So then how do I develop this technique?"

"It's quite simple. The fact is that most people, most of the time, tell the truth. They're not accustomed to lying. As a result, when they do lie it feels unnatural to them, thus their facial features reveal that fact. The way to get around that is to lie all the time. Lie even when there's no reason to lie. Not only will that get you accustomed to the experience but it will make it difficult for other people to determine when you're lying and what you're lying about since there won't be any difference between the times when you're wearing a mask and when you're not."

"But...if I'm always lyin', then why is anybody gonna believe anythin' I say?"

"For the simple reason that they're not going to know that you're lying. You only found out that I was lying to you because I let you find out. If I hadn't, you never would have known that I was lying. Similarly, the colonists who join you on Mars must never be allowed to realize that most of what you tell them is a lie."

Justin nodded, thinking all this over. He could only imagine what his mother would be saying if she was overhearing this conversation.

"Now let's try again," Baker said. "You tell me something and I'll say whether I think it's true or not."

"Okay. Uh...when I was a kid I had a dog named Ralph."

"That's true."

"You're right. It is."

"I know. Tell me something else."

"My first girlfriend's name was Jenna."

"True."

Justin nodded. "Right."

"Another."

"Uh...I hate cheeseburgers."

"Lie."

Justin smiled, embarrassed, and nodded. "You're right."

"You'll need to stop with that embarrassed smiling business. From this moment forward nothing is more dangerous for you to do than that."

"Okay."

"And everyone likes cheeseburgers. Don't make it so easy."

"Vegetarians don't like cheeseburgers."

"That's a lie."

Justin smiled. "Probably true."

"Tell me something new."

And Justin did. For the next half hour it went on like this. And Baker was right, every single time. Then they switched roles.

"I robbed a candy store when I was ten," Baker said.

"I'm thinkin' that's a...I'm thinkin' that's true."

"It's a lie. I cheated on my wife with one of my secretaries when I was forty-three."

"True?"

"Lie. I never drink milk."

"Lie?"

"True. I love jazz music."

"True?"

"Lie – I can't stand jazz music."

And so it went.

At least half an hour passed in this fashion until Baker saw that Justin was becoming psychologically fatigued, so he ended the exercises for the day. "That's enough for the time being. We'll continue the training tomorrow."

"I'm guessin' you're not lyin' now."

Baker smiled. "True."

Justin shook his head. "I'm thinkin' lyin' isn't a talent a mine."

"It doesn't have to be. It's all about practice. Besides, you're not going to be lying to me. You'll be lying to people who aren't accustomed to lying or thinking that they're being lied to. Quite the opposite – they're going to want to believe everything you say. Especially when you tell them that you can't wait to find alien life on Mars and that you're convinced it's there."

"That's really that important?"

"Oh yes. The fact is that if we don't find water up there either before or shortly after those other colonists arrive then you're going to have to kill some of them. Maybe all of them. But if we do find water then that colony's chances for long-term survival will be quite good, provided that you're the right kind of prince and you use cruelty well. But even if you do use cruelty with aplomb it'll still be useful to inspire your subjects. After all, if they start getting bored up there then it's going to be challenging to keep them in line no matter how effective your cruelty happens to be. But if you simultaneously scare them and inspire them, if you give them hope, give them some grand objective, then you'll be able to get them to do almost anything."

XXI

That afternoon, following lunch and a little gardening, Megan and Justin loaded up the rover with more boxes and headed out to Jeanne. As Justin drove, Baker explained that the boxes contained more floodlights along with the necessary extension cords. The task for the afternoon was to lower those lamps down into the cave at various points along the cave perimeter, away from the other lamps they'd already lowered in. Once the lamps were in place then most of the cave's wall-space would be lit, as would be the bulk of the cave's floor.

The newlyweds proceeded as Baker directed. It was slow work, driving around the cave's rim, keeping the rover back about one hundred yards in case any of the area near the rim was porous, then lowering the lamps into position in different places. When all the lamps were eventually hung, Megan and Justin switched out each other's oxygen tanks for new ones, then spent a while sitting on the cave-edge and peering down into the vast hole, occasionally spotting one or the other of the robots.

"So no signs a water yet, I'm guessin'?" Justin asked.

"Not yet," Baker replied.

Later that evening, before dinnertime, Baker asked to see the two of them up on the top floor of the shuttle, and when they walked into the round room his image appeared on the big screen.

"It won't be long before the others get there," he told them. "And in anticipation of their arrival there are certain topics that we should begin reviewing."

The first details for discussion were the names of the impending colonists: Robert Olambayo, Edgar Allen, Cynthia Wu, Maria Manfredi, Mukesh Mishra, Georges Morel, Adiba Al-Arabi, Oscar Suarez, Olga Malenkov and Suzanne Ritter. Photos of each one appeared on the screen as Baker named them.

"Now these are not your typical sixty-plus-ers," Baker explained. "They're all in pretty good shape. None of them run marathons but they'll be up for all sorts of tasks that you might give them."

"They're all from different countries?" Megan asked.

"They are. Allen is from the U.K., Wu's from Taiwan, Manfredi's from Italy, Mishra's from India, Olambayo's from Nigeria, Morel's from France, Al-Arabi's from Egypt, Malenkov's from Russia, Ritter's from Germany, and Suarez is from Mexico."

"If they're not reproducing," Megan observed in a questioning tone, "then there isn't any biological rationale for spreading out the gene pool geographically."

"No, that's true. But as you're aware the idea is that our little colony will function as a back-up option if things get really out of control down here on Earth. And in that spirit we want to have the whole world represented up there, so to speak, to the degree that we can."

Megan nodded.

"Now, Allen, Olambayo and Malenkov are biologists. Morel and Suarez are geologists. Mishra and Manfredi are astrophysicists. Ritter and Wu are computer programmers as well as general tech gurus. Al-Arabi is a horticulturalist."

Baker paused, allowing this information to sink in.

"To a certain degree," he continued, "their professional skill sets will be useful. But in the long run we really don't need them. All we really need up there for the time being are the two of you, to grow and scan the plants and to fix the robots when they break. Almost everything else – everything, for instance, that is found by the robots – can be analyzed via remote by my people down here. Which means that the most useful thing about these other colonists' skills is that they give you excuses to come up with jobs to keep everyone busy and occupied."

Justin nodded.

"Something else that you should know about these people: none of them have had particularly stellar careers back here on Earth. They didn't become standouts in their fields. None of them ran some large research lab somewhere. They were good or at least decent at their work but ultimately they're functionaries. They've spent their careers following someone else's orders, riding along on the coattails of someone else's research projects, benefiting from someone else's government grants.

"We looked for that when we selected them. We wanted people who were professionally unfulfilled. People who hadn't gotten what they wanted out of their professional lives and who would jump at the chance to do something really groundbreaking in their fields of study. A chance for which they'd be willing to leave behind their friends, their families, and Earth itself. Of course they want recognition for what they're doing, so they've all been assured that when the time is right this mission will go public and their research findings will be available for all the world – this world, down here – to see."

Justin assumed that that promise was a lie. "So does anyone else know that they're comin' up here other than the people you got workin' for you?"

"No. It's been arranged so that they quote-unquote disappeared. Some left notes saying that they'd decided to run away and start a new life. In other cases we made it look like they'd been kidnapped. A few of them simply walked out of their house one day, got into a car that we had waiting for them and left their old lives behind."

Baker paused before continuing.

"These are dedicated people. Dedicated to the future of science, and to their legacy in the history books of that future world."

He paused again, then added,

"By the way, it's important for you to know the following: all of their spacesuits – like yours – are equipped with microphones that will allow them to project their voices so that they can be heard outside their helmets. But those microphones won't project into the general intercom system up there, even though we – my people and I – will be able to hear everything they say. And we'll be switching off the intercom feeds on your two helmets as well when those others get there.

"Another key point: none of the other colonists will communicate directly with me, and none of them will know that my people and I are watching and listening in. Which means that, after the others arrive, the only time I'll talk to you two is when I talk into your specific helmets or when you're in your private quarters. Understand?"

Megan and Justin nodded.

"Also, there isn't any video feed built into those other colonists' helmets. We did that for two reasons. First: whereas the audio link can be camouflaged inside the helmet microphones – since the same device that amplifies the sounds of their voices will also be transmitting into the shuttle's system – we can't really hide a camera in those helmets. The people we're sending up there aren't idiots, and they will be constantly wearing their helmets, taking them on and off and so forth, so it's likely that they'd eventually discover the cameras and then they might start to wonder what was going on.

"Second: as you're well aware, there are already a collection of cameras hidden on your shuttle, and there will also be more on the second spacecraft. Which means we don't need many more. Having the existing cameras plus another ten – one for each new colonist – would be a bit of overkill."

Baker paused, then asked, "Any questions about anything?"

"Will that other spaceship be just like this one?" Megan asked.

"Important question, to which the answer is no. I was able to save the shuttle you're on just in time, before NASA had it permanently moth-balled. That's the old version, the shuttle design we're all familiar with, like *Challenger* or *Atlantis*. NASA's new spacecraft design is called the *Orion*." As Baker spoke a 3D diagram of an *Orion* appeared on the screen.

"The first successful *Orion* test flight into low Earth orbit took place in 2014, and now that's the only model NASA is making. But they haven't sent one into deep space before, and because of that my NASA friends were inclined to accept my offer to run a top-secret and privately funded deep space test of the new *Orion* model in order to see how it worked. As you can imagine, the reports I've been sending back to them are quite limited. For instance, I haven't mentioned to them that I've any intention of sending an *Orion* to Mars.

"Now, when an *Orion* launches what you see looks like a rocket. But after launch some parts of that rocket progressively disengage and then what you're left with, flying through space, looks like an enlarged version of those pods that the astronauts back in the '60s used to return to Earth in. You remember those famous images of astronauts getting picked up at sea, floating around in those cone shaped vessels? An *Orion*, as you can see on your screen, looks like an enlarged version of one of those pods. Of course everything else about an *Orion* is different technologically.

"Now the thing is, the *Orion* model is designed to hold only six crew members. So I told the NASA people that I wanted a slightly bigger version; I told them that I was interested in long-term storage capacity in the event that I might someday choose to send a manned mission out into deep space. And my NASA friends obliged. Then I had my people retrofit our *Orion* so that it would be able to hold ten of our incubation beds, and there you go. That's what's hurtling through space and heading right at you as we speak, carrying our next ten colonists."

"How much do those others know about us?" Megan asked.

"Very little. And nothing that's real. They haven't even been told your names, although you should feel free to use your real names with them. The story they've been told is that, prior to volunteering for the trip to Mars, the female founder – that would be you, Megan – was a medical researcher for a top-secret government program, and that the male founder – you, Justin – was part of an elite, top-secret military group. Now the nice thing about those cover stories is that they provide a built-in excuse for you two to refuse to talk about any aspects of your pasts. In fact the other colonists have been told that the two of you are legally prohibited from talking about any part of your previous lives."

"An elite, top-secret military group," Justin said, smiling as he repeated the phrase.

"Yes, well, there is one issue with that backstory, which is that the other colonists will likely expect you to have had a bit more schooling, a bit more polish, than you've actually had. The main things we're going to need to work on in that regard are a few points of grammar."

Justin was deeply embarrassed. "...Whad' ya mean?"

"For starters, I'd recommend that you expunge the word "ain't" from your vocabulary."

"You're sayin' I shouldn't say "ain't"?"

"Right."

"Okay...."

"And it also wouldn't hurt to try tacking the "g" back onto your gerunds and present participles."

"What?"

"Words ending in i-n-g. You typically drop the "g.""

"Oh. Okay...."

"Great. Now then, when those others arrive we'll be landing their ship a couple miles from your base camp. That's a safety precaution, in case anything malfunctions during the landing sequence or the *Orion* kicks up some big rocks with its landing rockets.

"One nice thing about that *Orion* model is that it's designed to conduct vertical landings straight down onto rugged surfaces, unlike that shuttle you flew in on which was designed to land on a runway like a plane. For your Mars arrival we had to engineer some extremely hi-tech hot air balloons, which deployed as you came in for a landing, and which, by the way, are lying a few miles to the west of you. We also had to retro-fit some landing rockets onto the shuttle, and then send the shuttle into a controlled gliding drop towards Arsia Mons and the Jeanne cave. Trust me, it wasn't easy. You were much better off being asleep during that little operation. But with the *Orion* the landing will be a simple downward drop from a predetermined orbital point.

"Another modification that NASA made for us is that this *Orion* pod has retractable tank-treaded wheels. After it lands those treads will come out and we'll be able to drive that pod – very slowly – over to the base camp. That drive could take a couple days. Once the colonists arrive at the base camp we'll wake them all up and then from that point forward five of them will take the bedrooms on the top floor of the shuttle and the other five will continue to sleep each night in the *Orion* pod."

"If we're going to have a little village," Megan said, "with more and more people, then we ought to give this place a name instead of just calling it the base camp."

Baker nodded. "I agree. And we should choose the name carefully because that locale is going to serve as the capital of the entire civilization we're starting up there."

"I'm guessin'" – and then Justin caught himself – "I mean, I'm guessing, that you've already got a name in mind."

"I do indeed. And as the individual who thought up and financed this entire venture, I wish to claim a certain proprietary privilege. Which is to say that I would like the name of our capital city to be Bakersville."

XXII

The next several days passed without any visits to the cave. Instead they were spent in and near the shuttle. The duo gardened; all the planter boxes, save for the ones filled with Martian soil, now had leafing shoots. There were cooking lessons, with Megan showing Justin how to prepare a variety of fish dishes. And Justin also worked on his grammar, practiced the art of lying, and continued reading *The Prince*.

He read chapter twelve – about the importance of using one's own soldiers rather than paying foreign mercenaries – and chapter thirteen – about the importance of not employing the troops of a foreign ruler – and chapter fourteen – featuring Machiavelli's general thoughts on the topic of war – and, since chapter fifteen was the first chapter which Baker had asked him to read when they began this process, he skipped ahead to chapter sixteen, which advises that a prince should not be generous since it's impossible to be generous forever.

Thus Justin arrived at the end of the second week of his princely training phase.

The first morning of the third week began with a particularly quiet desert dawn, which rose slowly over Bakersville. Then a few hours later, Justin – who'd been up late with Megan the night before – rose slowly as well. As 10:00 rolled around he still felt a little groggy.

"I have news," Baker informed him.

Justin was opening *The Prince*. "Oh yeah?"

"Yes. The robots have found something in the cave that might be of interest."

"Water?"

"No, no water yet. What they've located are what look to be two small openings in the cave wall. Those openings are too narrow for the robots to enter so we're going to send you down in there this afternoon with tools that will help you break through the wall, in order to see if the openings lead anywhere."

Justin nodded, his grogginess instantly fading. "Yeah, okay." This mission sounded intriguing, and since he was now fairly certain that Baker and Megan weren't plotting to kill him, he felt much more comfortable about descending back into the cave.

"But first," Baker said, "we need to read what is, by far, the most famous chapter in Machiavelli's text: chapter seventeen."

"The most famous?"

"Certainly the most quoted."

Justin nodded. "Interesting."

"Indeed. Please read."

Coming back now to the other qualities mentioned above, I say that every prince ought to desire to be considered kind and not cruel. Nevertheless, he should also take great care to not misuse kindness. Cesare Borgia was considered cruel; nonetheless, his cruelty helped pacify the Romagna, unified it, and brought the region peace. And if this is correctly considered, then Borgia will be seen to have been much more merciful than, for example, the Florentine people, who, in order to avoid a reputation for cruelty, permitted Pistoia to be destroyed.

Therefore a prince, so long as he keeps his subjects united and loyal, should not worry much about being considered cruel; because, by making a few examples of people, he will be more merciful than all those who, by being too merciful, allow many disorders to arise, from which follow murders or robberies; and these latter sorts of injuries often afflict the whole people, while those executions which originate with the prince only harm an individual.

In fact it is impossible for a new prince to avoid the reputation for cruelty, owing to new states being full of dangers. Hence Virgil, through the mouth of Dido, excuses the inhumanity of her reign owing to it's being new, saying....

"At this point in the text," Baker interjected, "Machiavelli quotes some Latin. It's by the Roman poet Virgil, who wrote some lines in which he has Dido, the legendary founder of Carthage, saying that she may have been cruel but that's because a girl's got to do what a girl's got to do."

Justin nodded, and skipped over the following:

"Res dura, et regni novitas me talia cogunt

Moliri, et late fines custode tueri."

Then he continued reading.

Nevertheless, a prince should be slow to believe things he hears, and slow to act, and he should never himself show fear, but proceed in a temperate manner with prudence and humanity, so that an excess of confidence may not make him incautious, and too much distrust of others render him unbearable.

"Now we come to Machiavelli's famous insight," Baker declared.

Thus a question arises: whether it is better to be loved than feared or feared than loved? It may be answered that one should wish to be both, but, because it is difficult to inspire both of these feelings towards the same person, it is much safer to be feared than loved, when, of the two emotions, one of them must be dispensed with.

This is because it may be said in general of men, that they are ungrateful, fickle, false, cowardly, and covetous, and as long as you succeed they are yours entirely. They will offer you their blood, property, life, and children, when the need is far distant; but when the need approaches, they will turn against you.

And that prince who, relying on other men's promises, has neglected to make his own precautions, will certainly be ruined, because friendships that are obtained by payments, and not by greatness or nobility of mind, may be earned, but they are never secured, and in time of need they cannot be relied upon.

Men have less scruple in offending one who is beloved than one who is feared, for love is only maintained by the link of obligation which, owing to men's baseness, will be broken at every opportunity; fear, on the other hand, preserves you by a dread of punishment which never fails.

"Seems like pretty much what he's been saying all along," Justin noted.

"True. But here comes the clever part. Please continue."

Nevertheless a prince ought to inspire fear in such a way that, if he does not win love, he at least avoids being hated; because he can manage to be feared and not hated if he does not touch the property of his citizens and subjects, and if he does not touch their women. And when it is necessary for him to proceed against the life of someone, he must do it with proper justification and for a clear reason.

But above all things, a prince must not touch the property of others, because men more quickly forget the death of their father than the loss of their inheritance. Besides, excuses for taking away men's property are never wanting; for he who has once begun to live by robbery will always find reasons for seizing what belongs to others; but the reasons for taking a life, on the contrary, are more difficult to find and sooner fade.

"Thoughts?" Baker asked.

Justin contemplated what he'd just read, then answered, "So it's better to be feared than loved."

"Right."

"But you've still got to avoid bein' – being – hated."

"And how does one become hated?"

"By messing with another guy's property or his woman."

"And of the two – property and women – which are more likely to get you hated if you mess with them?"

Justin re-read the text. "Well…he says a guy'll get over it sooner if his father dies than if you take his property."

"Right."

"So I guess he's saying that property is more important to people than family."

"It would appear so."

"So if you don't want to be hated then you just need to keep your hands off other people's property."

"Right. Now as it turns out, up there on Mars the only ones who're going to have any property to speak of, at least for the next several years, are you and Megan. That means that you don't need to worry too much about the other colonists hating you, even if you're cruel. They might get angry with you for a while but that won't last indefinitely." Baker smiled. "Isn't that good news?"

Justin shrugged and nodded. "Sure."

"Great. Now let's go see where those cracks in the cave lead."

XXIII

Justin's second descent into the cave was far less stressful than his first.

As he repelled down in, and reached the floor near to where one of the cracks had been located, Baker explained that, "This first crack is the more promising of the two. From the robot's camera shots we can see that the crack leads into a large interior space. What we don't know yet is how big that space actually is."

Justin was equipped with a pickaxe and a hi-tech blow-torch, and Baker instructed him to start hitting the wall around the crack with the pick. If the area didn't give way after a few hits then he should torch it and then hit the area again with the pick.

The crack in the wall was about two inches wide and about three feet tall. Justin knelt down beside it, then flipped on his helmet light to illuminate the space inside. That interior area was deep enough that he could only vaguely see an opposite wall.

"Okay," Baker told him, "have at it."

Justin stood up, grabbed the pick and swung its narrow end into the wall, next to the crack. Some rock bits chipped off but otherwise the wall remained intact. So Justin swung again. And again. He blow-torched the places where the axe had impacted, then swung the pick some more.

After twenty minutes a small portion of the wall next to the crack caved in. Justin used the broad side of the pick to pull the debris out of the way, then he knelt down and leaned forward into the hollow space, his helmet lamp illuminating the inside. What he saw was a narrow space, three feet tall and about two feet wide, running about twenty feet away from the spot where he was crouched.

"What do you see?" Baker asked impatiently, though he could see nearly everything that Justin was seeing via Justin's helmet camera.

"It's just a...space. 'Bout twenty feet long."

"Do you see any cracks in the walls in there – any openings that might lead to another space?"

"Nothing from here. Want me to go inside this thing to see what I can find?"

"Please."

So Justin grabbed the pick and the blow-torch and headed inside, pushing himself along the flat floor of this subterranean, million-year-old crawl space. He looked for other cracks as he moved but found nothing. When he reached the far wall he tapped against it with the end of the pick. It was solid.

He then spent the next hour trying to break through that wall but made very little progress both because he couldn't get any sort of swing angle with the pick and because the wall was not only solid but hard. With little to show for his efforts, he crawled backwards out of the cave, then rode the repelling system up to the surface, where Megan was waiting for him with a replacement oxygen tank. After she switched in the new one he descended back into the cave and set to work again in the crawl space. Another hour and a half passed and almost no headway was made, so he exited the space again, returned to the surface and then Megan drove the two of them back to Bakersville.

The next morning, for the first time since they'd begun their daily study sessions together, Baker informed Justin that rather than reading Machiavelli that day he wanted Justin to spend as much time as possible in the cave, to see if anything could be found by examining the second wall crack. So Megan and Justin loaded up the rover with several backup oxygen tanks, drove out to Jeanne, and then Justin repelled into the cave near to the second crack's location.

"This one looks less promising than the first crack," Baker noted, "and since that first crack hasn't given us much of anything, it's difficult to be optimistic about this one. But we need to try. Frankly we need to try anything we can."

Justin nodded as he walked up to the crack. It was smaller than the first one – only about an inch wide and about two feet tall. When Justin shined his light into it he could see that the space only extended inwards for a few feet.

"It looks small," he confirmed.

"I know, but let's see what we find."

So Justin began swinging his pick against the wall next to the crack. After about a minute a section of the wall gave way, revealing, as

Justin had presumed, a small interior space, which reached only a few feet inwards and was about a foot wide.

Baker sighed deeply on the other end of the line; it was a sigh that travelled millions of miles through space to reach Justin.

"Well," Baker said, after a pause, "let's have you try hitting that area around the opening there with the pick. That wall gave pretty easily. Maybe the walls around there are thin. It's worth a shot, at least for a few minutes."

So Justin swung the pick as instructed, just above the entrance to the newly opened space. After a few hits a square-foot area of the wall came loose and fell in small clumps around Justin's space boots.

"Let's keep going at it there," Baker directed, sounding cautiously encouraged.

Justin swung the pick several more times against the area above the opening until that opening was four feet tall and then five feet tall. Next he worked the sides, broadening out the opening space from one foot to three. He returned to the space above until the opening was six feet tall, then he picked away the sides until the opening was five feet across. This done, he could now begin picking at the back wall, which gave way as easily as the rest of the cave wall in this area. Within an hour the space was roughly five feet long and wide and six feet tall.

Justin returned to the surface, Megan switched his oxygen tanks, then he repelled back down in again. He continued to make rapid progress against the space's back wall, knocking it away a further five feet. This took approximately two hours, towards the end of which he returned to the surface, restocked on oxygen, then went back in yet again. Two hours later the tunnel was approximately fifteen feet in length.

Both the intercom and the video transmission cut off as soon as Justin was inside the tunnel wall, so he was periodically obliged to walk back out into the main cave to tell Baker how far he'd gone.

"Alright, that's good for today," Baker finally told him, his voice now thick with enthusiasm.

Justin nodded. He was exhausted. He dropped the pick next to the tunnel's opening and headed back up to the surface.

That night he fell asleep early, not long after dinner, and he slept soundly. If he had any nightmares, they didn't wake him.

The following morning Baker instructed Justin and Megan to head straight back to the cave, without any studying or gardening beforehand, so that's what they did. As soon as they arrived, Justin set to work. He hit at the tunnel's back wall again with the pick, and the wall gave. He hit it again and it gave some more. Around twenty feet in he found something.

"There's another crack," he told Baker, stepping back out into the main cave area.

"Where?"

"On the right wall. It's 'bout an inch wide and a couple feet long, runnin' at a diagonal."

"Interesting. Why don't you start working on it."

Justin headed back into the tunnel and began hitting at the newly found fissure with the pick. Within minutes a large portion of that right wall – nearly six feet tall and about three feet wide – fell inwards, away from Justin, revealing an entirely new space which was about ten feet by ten feet.

"Bingo!" Justin yelled, elated, running back out into the main cave space. He told Baker what he'd found.

"Excellent!" Baker responded. "Why don't you explore that new area and see what you find!"

Justin hurried back into the tunnel, then stepped gingerly into the newly discovered area, circling his head in all directions in order to cast light on every angle of his surroundings with his helmet lamp.

As he rushed out into the main cave again, he told Baker, "Looks like more a the same, but I see another crack in this new space, over in its far wall."

"How big?"

"Not big. But I'll see what I can do with it."

Returning to the ten by ten space, he swung the pick against its far wall, just above the crack. After a minute the crack and everything within a few feet of it fell inward, away from Justin.

And more importantly, it fell inward and *down.*

"Bingo number two!" He yelled, and ran back out into the main cave.

"The pieces a the wall fell down below the ground where I was standing!" He informed Baker. "It looks like there's some sort a space in there that slopes downward!"

"Excellent! That is fantastic news! If it's a lava flow chute then who knows how far it could lead! Please continue!"

Justin did as directed, stepping into the new space which had just been revealed by the collapsing wall. This space was about three feet long – sloping downwards at roughly a twenty-degree angle – and about four feet wide. Justin began picking. And picking. After half an hour he'd progressed another three feet. At that point he returned to the surface to change out his oxygen tank. As he climbed onto the rim of the cave and stood up on the Martian surface, Megan was waiting for him, not only with the backup tank but with her chef's knife smile stretched widely across her face. She helped him switch tanks, embraced him, then patted his shoulder as he climbed back into the repelling system's leather seat.

Several more hours passed while Justin worked inside the sloping space. The wall progressively gave way, and the space continued sloping downwards at a twenty-degree angle. By the end of the day he'd pushed through nearly fifteen more feet.

When Justin finally stepped back out into the main cave, Baker directed him to carry the two robots into the sloping space so that their sensors would have a chance to send out probing signals for water. The information they gathered could then be relayed back to Nevada once the robots were brought out again into the main cave area.

The next day was very much the same. He repelled into the cave, worked on the far wall of the sloping space, and cut his way through nearly fifteen more feet.

"The more it slopes," Baker kept telling him, "the closer we get to water!"

Periodically Justin picked up a robot and carried it back out into the main cave so that it could transmit its findings to Nevada. Then he'd send the robot into the sloping space again to run more scans.

As he picked and he picked, Justin couldn't help thinking about how much faster this digging would have gone if the other four men were still alive. But of course that never would have worked. If they'd all lived long enough to find out that Megan was on the shuttle, they all would've turned on each other in about five seconds. Still, he couldn't keep an image from returning to his mind, of the five of them working in the cave, picking their way down further and further, and singing as they went.

XXIV

While driving back to Bakersville that afternoon, Justin asked Baker if more digging was in store for the following morning, and Baker said that no, there wasn't, since Justin needed to finish his studies before the new colonists arrived. Besides, there might still be weeks' worth of digging to do in the downward sloping space before they reached water or even got close enough to detect water on the robots' sensors. Rather than exhausting himself, therefore, it was best for Justin to spend these final days preparing himself for the imminent arrival of his subjects.

Chapter eighteen of *The Prince* – which they examined the next morning – was particularly appealing to Baker because it emphasized the importance of not keeping one's word. He asked Justin to read it out loud.

Everyone says how praiseworthy it is for a prince to keep his word, and to live with integrity and not with craft. Yet experience shows that those princes who have done great things have held good faith to be of little account, and have known how to circumvent the intellect of men by craftiness, and in the end have overcome those who have relied solely on their word.

You must recognize, therefore, that there are two ways of contesting: the one by the law and the other by force; the first method is appropriate for men, the second is appropriate for beasts; but because the first is frequently not sufficient, it is sometimes necessary to have recourse to the second. Thus a prince must understand how to make use of the ways of the beast and the ways of man.

This has been figuratively taught to princes by the ancient writers who have described how Achilles and many other princes of old were given to the Centaur Chiron to nurse, and the Centaur then brought them up in his discipline; which means simply that these princes had a teacher who was half beast and half man, because it is necessary for a prince to know how to make use of both natures, and that one without the other is not durable.

A prince, therefore, being compelled to adopt the ways of the beast, ought to choose as his models the fox and the lion; because the lion cannot defend himself against snares, and the fox cannot defend against wolves. Therefore it is necessary to be a fox to discover the snares and a lion to terrify the wolves. Those who rely simply on the lion do not understand what they are about.

Therefore, acting the fox, a wise lord cannot, nor ought to, keep faith when such observance may be turned against him, and when the reasons that caused him to pledge it no longer exist. If men were entirely good, then of course this recommendation would not be valid, but because men are bad and will not keep faith with you, you are not bound to keep faith with them. Nor will a prince ever lack legitimate reasons to excuse his faithlessness. Endless examples could be given in this regard, showing how many treaties and engagements have been made void and of no effect through the faithlessness of princes; thus the prince who has known best how to employ the fox has succeeded best.

But of course, it is necessary to know how to disguise this characteristic, and to be a great pretender and dissembler; and since men are so simple, and are so inclined to focus on present necessities, he who seeks to deceive will always find someone who will allow himself to be deceived.

There is one recent example that I cannot pass over in silence. Alexander VI did nothing but deceive men, nor ever thought of doing otherwise, and he always found victims; for there never was a man who had greater power in asserting, or who with greater oaths would affirm a thing, and who would observe it less; yet his deceits always succeeded according to his wishes, because he well understood this side of man.

Following in the spirit of Alexander VI, therefore, Justin continued for the next few days to train in the art of lying.

He also completed the remainder of *The Prince*. Chapter nineteen revisited the topic of how to avoid being hated. Chapter twenty dwelt on the point that if a prince is not hated then he has no need for a fortress, since if the people support him they will protect him better than a fortress will and if his subjects want to destroy him then no fortress can protect him. Chapter twenty-one spelled out the ways for a prince to gain a grand reputation, chapter twenty-two dealt with how to appoint useful assistants, and chapter twenty-three warned against the charms of flatterers. Chapter twenty-four blamed the Italian nobles, rather than ill fortune, for causing the Italian city-states to become weak, and chapter twenty-five argued that fortune is best seized by force, so that you can make of it what you will.

And then at last the infamous text wound its way to a close with chapter twenty-six, in which Machiavelli exhorted Lorenzo De' Medici – or, as the case might be, some other particularly capable prince – to take up the cause of liberating Italy from foreign powers, to unite her provinces, and to restore the power and grandeur of the ancient Romans.

"Thoughts?" Baker asked, after Justin finished reading the final paragraph of the book.

Justin shrugged. "Many."

Baker smiled his pressed-lips smile. "Good."

Later that evening – the last evening before the arrival of the new colonists – Justin and Megan lay on their bed, facing each other.

"Tomorrow's the big day," she whispered.

"Yeah, it is. Or as Baker would say, "It is indeed.""

They both smiled, but they both knew that they both were nervous. After a while her knife-like smile faded and her lips returned to their normal position as her eyes studied his eyes.

"It's time to be a prince," she said.

He nodded.

She studied him some more. "Are you ready?"

"As ready as I can be."

"Baker's in the background if you need him."

He nodded again.

"But I'm right here with you, all the time." As she said this she took hold of his hand and squeezed it.

"I'm glad."

"Whatever happens next," she told him, "I'm here for you."

He nodded as he smiled at her.

Her facial features tightened. "Whatever happens next, I'm your woman."

PART III

THEM

I

A spaceship landed on Mars on the 5th of September, 2018. It was an *Orion Multi-Purpose Crew Vehicle*, NASA's latest design. Yet not even NASA knew that it had landed there. Very few people back on Earth knew, aside from a select group of scientists and engineers who were all working for one very wealthy man and who were all holed up in a secret location somewhere in the middle of nowhere Nevada.

The butterscotch-reddish spacecraft touched down without incident upon the rugged Martian terrain. If its crew had been awake they would've considered it a smooth landing, but they were asleep and would remain so for the next three days as the ship's tank-like wheels carried them the few mile's distance to Bakersville.

All of this was handled by remote control, with the shuttle's driver sitting in the Nevada facility, facing a wall of computer and TV screens. The driver made sure to park the *Orion* precisely on the spot chosen by the man who was paying him an extremely generous salary. That generous man didn't explain why he wanted the craft parked precisely there, and the driver didn't ask. It was a logical spot, after all, located a few hundred feet from the shuttle and roughly the same distance from the box-shaped garden.

Once the *Orion* was parked, the driver typed a code which caused the spaceship's tank wheels to retract into its frame while the bottom of the craft settled softly onto the planet's rock-and-sand surface. This task complete, the driver was congratulated for his good work and then sent on his way. The paychecks would soon start arriving – via direct deposit into an account which had been set up for him in a bank in Liechtenstein – every month for the next ten years, so long as the Mars project remained a secret. If the public ever found out about the project prior to the end of that ten year timeframe, however, then no one who worked on the project would ever get paid another dime, and all those people would also be told who the rat was, provided that the rat was ever found. And of course William Baker knew people who knew how to find rats.

Onboard the *Orion* the incubator beds – which were arranged in a cluster in the middle of the spacecraft's only room – deactivated, causing their metal covers to retract. Shortly thereafter the eyes of each of the beds' occupants blinked open, one pair after another, until all ten of them were awake, although exceedingly groggy.

Cynthia Wu was the first one to attain full consciousness as well as unimpaired vision, and after she sat up, with her hands gripping the bed's metallic sides, she glanced around and smiled at her still-reclining companions.

Wu was the daughter of Taiwanese immigrants – they'd moved to the U.S. when she was five – and her parents had always had very high and very specific expectations for their only child. She was to get a top-flight education at an Ivy League school; she was to become a first-rate computer programmer; and she was to return to Taiwan one day to assist the Taiwanese government – via her computing skills – in preparing to defend Taiwan against any invasion attempt by China.

None of these goals panned out. She got into decent universities, but they weren't Ivy League; she became a computer programmer, but not one of exceptional skill; she was never hired by the Taiwanese government since Taiwan is full of superb computer programmers; and, as she arrived at the twilight years of her professional career, the Chinese invasion had yet to materialize. But then a second chance did come along for her, and it was something extraordinary. So now here she was, and she was going to do something that would make her parents proud, in the end, after all.

Georges Morel sat up next, blinking. As soon as he saw Wu sitting there and smiling at him, he smiled in return.

"We're there?" He asked.

"I guess so."

He nodded. "Bon."

Morel's motivation for joining this mission was simple: geology, for the most part, had ceased to interest to him. But he was trapped in that career so what could he do? Thus he'd stuck with it, and that proverbial French boredom had settled in with him something fierce and grown ever deeper over the decades. Only one aspect of geology retained any interest for Morel: the non-Earth variety. But he was hardly prominent enough to get himself a ticket on a space mission. Still, he dreamed. He'd read the adventures of Tintin as a boy, and that vision of Tintin and his friends heading off on a journey to the moon had always stuck with him, as it did for so many Tintin-reading kids. And then of course there was also *Le Petite Prince*.

Robert Olambayo sat up next. When he saw the other two sitting there, smiling at him, he glanced around, took a deep breath, and said quietly, "Thank God."

Olambayo had grown up on the tough streets of Lagos but by a series of minor miracles – a scholarship here, a charitable priest there – he received enough education to get himself admitted to a U.S. university. That university, however, was expensive, and he was periodically obliged to take time off to get full-time jobs, notwithstanding his student loans. Thus he finished his schooling late, and all the educational interruptions also impacted his GPA. The end result was that after graduation he got stuck needing to take unenjoyable but relatively well-paying jobs at non-prestigious pharmaceutical companies. Under different circumstances, of course, his life might have turned out differently. But then of course that's a tautology.

Maria Manfredi sat up next, to the right of Olambayo. The way she rose up to a sitting position – with her back remaining nearly straight as she did so – had a certain vampire-rising-from-a-coffin quality about it. She blinked multiple times after reaching an upright posture, then nodded without looking directly at the others.

"How long?" She asked, still not yet making eye contact with the other three. "How long have we been here?"

"I was the first one to wake up," Wu told her, "and that was just a minute ago."

Manfredi nodded some more.

She was a very serious person, which sometimes made her less than wonderful to work with. This may have been at least part of the reason why her career had been less than exemplary. She, however, blamed her career fizzle on the pervasive sexism of the male scientists with whom she worked. Chances are that that was part of the reason as well. That and the fact that she simply wasn't *that* good at her job. She'd managed to get a research grant from the University of Bologna at one point, but that was the highlight of her professional trajectory. The rest of her career was spent at smaller and progressively less prestigious institutions. Thus when Baker's people approached her with the proposition for the Mars mission, they barely had time to finish explaining to her why they were there before she accepted their offer.

Oscar Suarez sat up next and said, "Ohhh." He was feeling dizzy and gripping the metal sides of his bed. After a few seconds he managed to glance around, and when he saw the others he smiled widely, but then he quickly raised a hand in front of his face as if he might throw up.

Suarez – unlike Morel – remained an enthusiastic geologist. He loved the subject and was thoroughly nerdy when it came to discussing rocks. Unfortunately the university where he taught was in the Mexican state of Sinaloa, home to powerful drug cartels which were in the habit of kidnapping and ransoming university personnel, including Suarez, twice. These two interruptions to his research, combined with the extended leave time necessary to emotionally recuperate, put a real dent in his academic career. Further complicating matters was the fact that he was high-strung by nature. After the second kidnapping he became prone to severe anxiety attacks, and any unanticipated changes in his surroundings were cause for serious alarm. Thus the prospect of spending the rest of his life in a highly controlled environment, surrounded by fascinating and un-analyzed rocks, and located far, far away from any drug cartels, proved irresistible.

Olga Malenkov was the next to rise. She blinked twice, smiled, then raised her arms in the air and extended two fingers on each hand to form the "v" for victory sign.

"We made it!" She declared. "We are on Mars! This is it!"

Malenkov was an energetic, charming, smart, witty person whose tempered career had nothing to do with her abilities and everything to do with the geopolitical situation which she found herself in during the post-Cold War years in Russia. In many respects Russia had collapsed in the early 1990s, and thus her career path in biology – which would have been highly regimented and hence highly predictable during the Soviet era – became unclear. She took a prestigious teaching position at a university but that institution quickly ran out of money. She took another prestigious position with a bio-research firm which ceased to exist after its oligarch CEO was gunned down in a restaurant in St. Petersburg. She then returned to academia as an assistant administrator at a university's biology lab, until one day the lab was purchased by a mysterious bank, and when it became clear that her facility was about to get turned into a center for processing illegal narcotics, she quit. A prestigious job at the Moscow branch of a major German pharmaceutical company came next, but when Russian relations with the West soured early in the second decade of the century, the Germans shut down their Moscow office. And so it went. By the time Baker's people approached her, Malenkov was ready to try another planet.

Mukesh Mishra sat up next, glanced at the others, and said, "You all look beautiful!"

Mishra was brilliant. Brilliant to the point that it got in the way of a normal life. He recited rocket science equations whenever he made love to his wife. She left him. He sang – loudly – in the halls of the universities where he worked whenever an interesting idea occurred to him. They fired him. When scientific journals didn't publish his findings, he'd show up at the homes of the editors to complain. Sometimes the police would be called, and sometimes they'd arrest him. In any event, now he was on Mars.

Adiba Al-Arabi was the next one to sit up, cautiously. An Arab woman from a traditional Egyptian family, she'd been allowed to attend a university only after she threatened to drown herself in the Nile if her parents didn't let her. While enrolled, she fell in love with the scientific aspects of gardening and ultimately wound up doing her doctoral research in the U.K., analyzing gardens in the English countryside. Those were her paradisiacal years. But eventually she needed to find a job, which proved challenging. The academic offerings were limited and it was also almost impossible to land positions overseeing famous gardens.

Of course all this simply confirmed her parents' suspicions that she never should have gone off to a university in the first place. So her life had been quite hard, and disappointing, and frustrating, when all she'd ever wanted was to treat her intellect to the joys of science and her eyes to the views of beautiful hedges and flowers. As such, it wasn't too difficult to persuade herself that if she couldn't run a scientifically sophisticated garden on Earth then she should run the very first one on Mars.

As for Edgar Allen, he had a drinking problem. He'd wondered, when they closed the bed's metal covering over him and he drifted off into a seven months-plus sleep, if he'd be cured of this affliction when he arrived on Mars. Perhaps during all the time spent unconscious his craving for the next shot would have drained away. And of course if it hadn't it didn't matter anyway since there wouldn't be any alcohol in space. This was important to him, since his hankering for the bottle had ruined his life: his marriage, his relationship with his children, his career as a biologist.

He'd tried all sorts of ways to break the addiction, to no avail. But now – now he was certain he'd found a failsafe method. Where the twelve-step programs had failed him, this one-step program – namely, fly on a ship to Mars – was sure to do the trick.

As he sat up, blinked, and glanced around, he thought to himself, 'I could really use a drink.'

Suzanne Ritter was the last one to rise; a fact she no doubt found annoying. She was highly competitive. She was also still vaguely attractive, even into her sixties. In her earlier years she'd been truly stunning. And that characteristic had mixed with her strong ambition and her marked intelligence to produce a volatile existential cocktail. She wound up in problematic relationships with powerful men; she had children with men to whom she wasn't married while she was married; she was obliged to "raise" those children on her own sometimes; these and other financial obligations generated a great deal of "pressure"; that pressure, combined with her ambition, pushed her into computing-related jobs which weren't entirely legal, which she engaged in with brilliant tech entrepreneurs who couldn't resist her; legal proceedings eventually ensued; ultimately her children became criminals as well. It was a mess.

As she blinked and glanced around, Ritter couldn't help assessing the others in the group, just as she had back on Earth, to determine which of the men were the most eligible and which of the women were her closest competitors. Seeing that she was the last one to revive, she frowned, then smiled and said, "Looks like I'm the last one to the party."

II

The *Orion's* door slid silently open.

All ten scientists were now dressed in their spacesuits. It'd taken about an hour for them to get their bearings and suit-up.

There was a small window in the *Orion's* door but it only allowed for a narrow view of the outside world, and thus it was truly now, as they stood there and the door slid open in front of them, revealing the breadth of the horizon, that they collectively "encountered" their new reality, and they gasped.

In front of them stretched the vast nothingness of Mars....

In the foreground was the shuttle. To its right was the rectangular box-shaped garden. And in the middle of the triangle formed by the two ships and the garden stood two people: the ones that these new colonists had been told would be waiting for them; a man and a woman; a husband and wife; the first humans on Mars; heroes.

Justin spoke the words that Baker had advised him to speak at this point:

"Welcome, everyone," he said, loudly. "Welcome to Mars!" As he spoke both he and Megan waved and the others waved back excitedly.

"Thank you, hello, thank you!" They all replied at once.

A retractable ladder had automatically extended from the *Orion* as the door slid open, and now the new arrivals made their way down it, with Malenkov in the lead. She wobbled as she adjusted to the gravitational change, then she walked unsteadily across the twenty feet to where Megan and Justin were standing. Justin extended his hand in order to shake hers but she leaned in and gave him a hug instead, wrapping her arms around him vigorously, while also being careful not to bang his helmet with her own.

"It is so, so very good to meet you!" She exclaimed, hugging him. Then she released him and turned to Megan. "And you!" And she hugged Megan, who laughed.

"Welcome!" Megan said.

"Thank you!" Malenkov exclaimed. "Thank you for everything you have done!"

Mishra followed quickly behind her. "This is so exciting!" He practically yelled. He also ignored Justin's proffered hand and embraced him. Then he embraced Megan. After he released her, he told them, "You two are the most amazing people I have ever met. It is such an honor to be here with you!"

Justin and Megan both smiled without blushing. Baker had told them to be prepared for this sort of effusive admiration and to accept it calmly as a matter of course.

Manfredi wobbled up to them next. She shook Justin's hand, then Megan's, and then she told them, "This is the greatest moment of my life." And it was.

Wu followed close behind her, half-bowing as she took hold of Justin's hand with both of her own. "Very good to meet you!"

"Good to meet you," Justin replied, smiling calmly.

Wu turned to Megan. "And very good to meet you!"

"Welcome," Megan said. "Welcome to your new home."

Allen was the next to wobble up, feeling like he was a little drunk. "Edgar Allen," he said, smiling and shaking Justin's hand. "Pleasure to meet you." He said the same thing to Megan as they shook hands as well.

Ritter followed after him, making a good show of trying to walk normally while she strode up and shook Justin's hand. As she did so, she gave him a knowing look, then wrapped her arms around his hips and gently but meaningfully embraced him. "It's good to be here," she said, quietly, significantly, as if she was telling him a secret. Then she turned to Megan, hugged her briefly, and said, "Hello."

Olambayo was the next to step forward, cautiously, and he shook both their hands warmly yet with a certain reserve. "Thank you," he said to both of them, several times. "Thank you."

Al-Arabi was speechless. The fact of being on Mars, of being so far from her home planet – a planet filled with so many flowers and so much cruelty – overwhelmed her with feelings of joy and sadness. That, combined with the presence of this loving couple – two wonderful people who'd not only found each other back on Earth but who'd paved the way for the colonization of a new planet – put a massive lump in her throat. She'd never found her life partner just as she'd never landed her dream job, and now, as she shook their hands and tried to speak, tears welled up in her eyes and she didn't manage to say anything.

Morel, by contrast, was beaming; the first real smile he'd smiled in a long time. Images of Tintin's *Explorers on the Moon* and of *Le Petite Prince* were running through his mind and merging with his awareness of himself. "Bonjour!" He said loudly as he approached the heroic couple. "Hello! "I'm Georges!"

Suarez was the last one off the ship and he had the most difficulty steadying himself as he adjusted to Martian gravity; so much so that he fell to his knees after taking a few steps. As he landed in the Martian sand he wondered if he was about to vomit inside his helmet. But this thought was immediately replaced by the awareness that he was surrounded by an endless sea of new rocks! He gasped with happiness and began picking up the ones nearest to him and holding them close to his helmet. This went on for several seconds, until the other astronauts began laughing.

Hearing the laughter, Suarez remembered that he wasn't alone. "Oh, sorry," he said, sheepishly, rising to his feet and wobbling over to the heroic couple. "Thank you!" He embraced them both with genuine joy. "Thank you so much!"

III

The tour of the shuttle took about half an hour. Megan and Justin showed the new arrivals the round room and the adjoining bedrooms, then the container spaces, the cockpit, and finally the lower level, but without walking them into either the couple's bedroom or Justin's office. Then they all made their way back up to the round room, where Justin addressed the new arrivals – some sitting, some standing – in the manner that Baker had advised.

"There aren't any words," he said, "to express how any of us are feeling. No language that was made on Earth can express what it's like to start a new society on a totally different planet. And as a soldier, not a politician, I'm certainly not going to try to give a speech that could match this moment."

Baker and Justin had rehearsed this statement many times during the previous days. Its premise provided a convenient way to get around what would otherwise have been a real difficulty: namely, Justin pulling off an extended, stirring and eloquent peroration, much less one which wouldn't feel starchily rehearsed.

The others all nodded and smiled as he spoke, impressed by his ability to say something moving by saying that he wasn't going to try to say something moving.

Several of the scientists thought to themselves, 'What a man!'

"I'm used to dealing with facts," Justin continued, in the manner which Baker had advised, "and plans of attack. I'm all 'bout completing the mission. And the mission that we're here to complete is to make sure this colony can survive and grow."

He paused, while the others nodded, basking in the confidence which he was conveying.

"If this colony survives, that means the human race has a second chance. It also means we'll have a chance to find what we all came here hoping to find, and 'course I'm talking 'bout finding life forms."

A collective, quiet gasp of hope escaped the others' lips.

"And you all know it all comes down to being able to grow our own food. And I've got news for you 'bout that. We've got plants growing in all the planter boxes except the ones with Martian soil. So that means we can deal with the gravity issues and the radiation issues. It also means we're gonna need to focus on generating as much compost as possible."

The others all nodded, encouraged and somewhat chastened by this news.

"And I know you're all wondering 'bout the water situation. The fact is that we haven't found any yet but we have found something that's giving us a lot a hope. You've all been told 'bout the caves, and 'bout the most important cave, named Jeanne. Well we've been explorin' Jeanne a lot, and what we've found is some sort a lava-formed tunnel system. It's been filled in by some pretty soft rock and sand. And we've dug away at it and what we've found is that the lava tunnel's heading downwards."

The scientists took a collective breath and nodded their heads, fully appreciating the significance of this information.

"How far down so far?" Mishra asked.

"'Bout six feet down in a tunnel that so far's 'bout thirty feet long. And 'course that's at the bottom a Jeanne, which is 'bout six hundred feet deep."

"That's deeper than anyone anticipated," Malenkov noted.

"Yeah, the thing is huge. And I want us to get to work on it right away tomorrow. I can take three with me on the rover at a time, so I need three volunteers for that first run."

Everyone raised their hands. Not everyone was equally enthused about participating in the cave mission but they felt compelled to show good spirit. Justin selected the ones who were closest to him: Malenkov, Suarez and Olambayo.

"The rest a you are spending tomorrow getting up to speed on the garden, and you'll also be moving some supplies from the *Orion* into this ship's container spaces. But for the time bein'," and now Justin grinned gamely, "you all haven't eaten for more than seven months, so it's time for our official welcomin' feast!"

The scientists laughed and clapped and hugged each other, then everyone began foraging for appetizing options among the selection of food items which were still stored onboard the ship.

"I hope it doesn't feel like the rest of us are intruding on the two of you," Al-Arabi said, as everyone sat either around or near the circular table, "after you've been up here together all alone."

"No, of course not," Megan assured her.

Justin conducted a quick review in his mind of all the steps that had been taken to ensure that no traces remained of the other four original astronauts. This had included, among other things, burying the deceased astronauts' backup spacesuits next to the three graves so that those suits were now likewise ensconced below the *Orion*.

"It must have been so romantic though," Ritter said, "just the two of you up here together all that time with no distractions."

Megan shrugged and smiled. "We've had a lot of work to do."

"I can't wait to get to work," Suarez said.

The others nodded.

"Did you read the adventures of Tintin when you were young?" Morel asked Justin.

Justin shook his head. "…Uh, no."

"How about *Le Petite Prince*?"

"Uh, no."

"Every French and Belgian boy reads them. They made me dream of flying into space ever since I was young."

"Tell me," Al-Arabi said to Megan, "have any of the plants begun to show leaves and buds?"

"Yes, they have," Megan confirmed. "In the planter boxes that have actually produced something, all the plants now have leaves and are budding."

Al-Arabi beamed. "I can't wait to see them!"

"I can't wait to see everything!" Malenkov said. Then she asked, "Did anyone else dream on the way up here? I dreamed that I was already here and that we had a garden with thousands of plants. And even better, that there were no criminals, and no politics!"

"Hear, hear!" Allen endorsed this sentiment.

"No more cartels!" Suarez added.

"Or oligarchs!" Malenkov said.

Allen raised his glass of grape juice as if making a toast. "No more Tories and no more Lib Dems!"

Olambayo shrugged. "Still I'd take British politics over Nigerian politics any day."

"And I'll take Nigerian politics over Taiwanese politics," Wu added, surprising herself. This was the boldest political statement she'd ever made. Evidently the elation of the moment, combined with the sense of finally being free of the social and political expectations of her family, was irresistible.

"Really?" Olambayo was intrigued.

Wu nodded. "It gets *really* old; constantly obsessing about whether Taiwan is getting politically too close to China or if it's not close enough; wondering when the invasion will come...."

"But we don't need to worry about any of that anymore," Ritter noted. "We're done with politics. Now we can just engage in science and live naturally. It's funny but I think that up here, on this alien planet, we have the chance to live like humans were always meant to live, without unnecessary rules and constraints." She smiled suggestively.

Manfredi tried to smile but it worked itself out as a frown. "So then you're a supporter of anarchism?"

Ritter shook her head. "I'm not a supporter of any ism. What I am is a woman who conducts science and lives like she wants to live."

"How's the food?" Justin asked, to everyone in general.

The scientists all nodded enthusiastically, except for Morel, who shrugged and said, "It's not Michelin quality but it's not bad."

"How often do you check in with the people in Nevada?" Mishra wanted to know.

"Not all that much," Justin lied, as Baker had instructed him to do. "They want us to get used to being up here, and not thinking too much 'bout things happening back on Earth."

The others nodded. Some of them looked melancholic as they let this thought sink in.

"I never met the man who arranged all of this," Olambayo said. Did any of you meet him? William Baker?"

The others shook their heads, then turned to Justin.

Justin shrugged. "I've talked to him a couple times."

"He must be a great man," Mishra concluded, "to make all of this possible."

Justin smiled a little, then nodded, searching for the rights words. Not necessarily the accurate words, but the right words.

"He's remarkable," Megan said. "A truly remarkable man."

"When the history books are written," Suarez opined, "they will say that he was the greatest humanitarian because he gave our species a real second chance. Landing on the moon was nothing compared to this."

"I wish I could have met him," Wu mused.

"Edwards – the guy who managed all our affairs back in Nevada – he told me that Baker didn't want to get too closely involved," Allen said, with a definite tone of approval. "He told me that Baker thought it should be left up to the scientists and engineers to work out the important details."

Malenkov raised her class of apple juice for a toast: "To William Baker!"

The others colonists all heartily joined her, clinking their glasses together. "To William Baker!"

"And to our lovely heroic couple, Justin and Megan," Ritter said, raising her glass for a second toast and staring particularly at Justin.

"To Justin and Megan!" Everybody replied, clinking the glasses again.

"And to all of you," Justin said, raising his glass for a third toast.

"Yes," Megan concurred, smiling at them with her chef's knife smile, "to all of you – to our new friends!"

IV

"So...what do you think of them?" Megan asked as they lay in bed later that evening.

The door that connected the shuttle's two main levels was now closed, and five members of the crew – Suarez, Olambayo, Ritter, Wu, and Morel – were sleeping or at least lying in the beds upstairs, while the other five, having lost the sleeping options coin toss, had settled back into the beds on the *Orion*.

Justin shrugged. "Not sure yet."

"You're thinking lots of thoughts – I can tell."

Justin shrugged again. "Baker wants me to pick one, to be like my second in command. I'm gonna have to figure out who that's gonna be."

They shared this thought in silence, considering the candidates.

Then Megan told him, "I thought you did a great job with them. That little speech you gave at the beginning and everything. Baker would be proud. In fact I'm sure he is because I'm sure he was watching. And I'm proud, too."

Justin smiled at her. "I think you're better at all this than I am. Better at interacting with these people."

She shrugged. "I'm not supposed to be in charge, so it's easier for me. I can be more natural. Your job is harder than mine."

"For now. But I'm not the one who's gonna be having a baby on Mars."

She smiled. Then she asked him, "Did you notice how Ritter was flirting with you?"

"Yeah – you don't need to worry 'bout that."

"I'm not worried. I thought it was funny."

"When she gets that I'm not interested, which a those other guys you think she's gonna go for?"

Megan pondered this question. "It's too soon to tell for sure. But if I had to guess right now I'd say Suarez."

"Seriously? Why Suarez?"

"Just a hunch. Who do you think?"

"I was thinking Allen."

"Why?"

"Not sure. Plus I'm a guy, so what do I know? You've got that whole intuition thing going."

"Shall we make a bet?"

"Sure, but what're we betting? We don't have money."

"Whoever loses has to cook dinner for a week."

Justin frowned. "I don't like that bet. If I lose that means I gotta cook it *and* I gotta eat it. Your cooking tastes ten times better than mine."

She ran her hand through his hair. "Not to me."

Eventually they both drifted off to sleep.

It was sometime in the middle of the night when Justin woke up, sweating from another nightmare. But he hadn't woken up Megan in the process, so he simply lay there for a while, in the silence, thinking about which scientist he might choose to be the d'Orco, if in fact he was going to choose one of them at all.

V

The four-person team set out from Bakersville at 10:00 the next morning, heading for Jeanne. Two extra seats had been attached to the rover to allow them all – Justin, Suarez, Malenkov and Olambayo – to ride at the same time. And each of the newcomers had been supplied with their own pickaxe and backup oxygen tanks.

Malenkov, sitting up-front next to Justin, kept exclaiming about this and about that, enthralled by the size of Arsia Mons, by the vastness of the Martian landscape, by the "glorious" reddish hues of the horizon. Meanwhile Suarez kept encouraging Olambayo to admire various rocks, and Olambayo, though clearly not as interested, kept replying to all of this with polite comments.

Justin couldn't help smiling; these people really were scientists, and they were enjoyable too. And besides, it was just nice to have more humans around.

When they reached the cave the new arrivals went crazy.

"Look at that!" Malenkov declared. "Look at that!"

"It's enormous!" Olambayo agreed.

"Think of all the rocks!" Suarez swooned.

"There're plenty down there," Justin assured him, as he parked the rover a hundred feet back from the spot which had now become the regular point of descent into the cave.

As they all climbed off the rover Justin informed them that, "The ground's firm near the cave's edge but you still wanna be careful as you get up close to it."

The scientists didn't need him to tell them about being cautious. Ten feet from the mouth of the cave the three newcomers got down on their hands and knees and crawled forward until they could peer straight into the massive hole.

"Wow…." Malenkov said, on behalf of all three of them.

"We're going all the way down there?" Suarez asked, the fear evident in his voice.

"Yes sir," Justin confirmed. Then he spent a minute explaining how to use the repelling mechanism.

This done, he asked them, "Who's going first?"

"I'll go!" Malenkov declared bravely.

So Justin got her settled into the leather seat and sent her on her way, with one of her hands holding the repelling rope and the other hand gripping her pickaxe, which was lying on her lap.

"Woo-hoo!" She yelled as she repelled down into the vast empty space.

After she arrived on the cave floor, the seat was brought back up and Olambayo settled into the leather strap, holding his pick, then down he went, quietly, without making any enthusiastic gesticulations.

When it came time for Suarez to go, Justin wondered if the guy was going to make it. He looked petrified.

"You said…there are lots of interesting rocks down there?"

"Lots," Justin assured him.

Suarez nodded. "Okay. Okay." Then down he went, willing his panic reflex into quiescence, clutching the repelling rope in one hand and his pick in the other.

Justin soon joined them at the bottom of the cave and walked them over to the tunnel he'd made, pointing out along the way one of the robots which was trolling nearby. When they reached the tunnel he grabbed the pick which he'd left near the entrance and led the three newcomers twenty feet in, then turned right, heading into the ten by ten space, and from there into the downward sloping tunnel which was now nearly thirty feet long.

"You did all of this?" Olambayo asked Justin.

"Yeah. The rock here is pretty easy, like I mentioned."

Olambayo shrugged. "Still…."

Suarez ran his gloved fingers along the walls, mesmerized by the rock structures. Malenkov just kept smiling.

"And here we are," Justin announced as they reached the end of the downward sloping portion. "This is where we start picking. You're still getting used to this environment, and the gravity and all, so don't push it. We don't need to make a whole lot a progress today. The main thing is just to get you used to doing it. So let's go two at a time, a couple minutes each, and then we'll trade off."

Which they did for the next hour and twenty minutes. Then Justin walked them back out of the tunnel, over to where the repelling system was hanging against the wall, and they made their ways up to the surface and helped each other switch out their old oxygen tanks for new ones. This done, they descended again and spent an hour picking at the tunnel's far wall. By the time they stopped they'd pushed the tunnel another seven feet forward, bringing them nearly a foot-and-a-half further down.

Upon returning to Bakersville they were informed that Megan had given the other seven scientists a basic introduction to the garden, and now the newcomers were taking turns running scans on the boxes, registering data in the cockpit, etc. Everyone was in good spirits and appeared to be making a rapid adjustment to their new surroundings, thanks to the work and the camaraderie.

Later that evening, around dinnertime, Justin informed the other colonists that he and Megan would henceforth be preparing and eating their dinners down in their private suite while the others all ate their meals in the round room. The scientists nodded, slightly surprised but not overly so. Little did they realize that this was, as Baker explained to Justin when they'd been preparing for the arrival of the ten, the first in a series of many "adjustments." The point of the adjustments was to progressively convey to the new colonists that they were not on an equal footing with the original two and that, fundamentally, Justin and only Justin was in charge.

The next day Justin took Ritter, Wu and Mishra out to the cave, leading them through the same routine as he had with the first three. By the end of their shift they'd pushed through another six feet and gone more than a foot further down. Meanwhile Malenkov, Olambayo and Suarez were trained up with regard to the garden and the shuttle's onboard instruments. Eight more planter boxes were also unloaded and placed – four each – in the garden's gravity-testing and radiation-testing rooms.

That evening Justin and Megan once again ate alone.

The following morning Justin headed out to the cave with Allen, Manfredi, and Morel. The day after that he took Al-Arabi, Olambayo and Malenkov.

In the meantime Suarez and Morel began conducting analyses of rocks in the vicinity of Bakersville as well as of rocks that they'd collected down in the tunnel. Ritter and Wu began running various tech tests via the computers they'd brought with them on the *Orion*. Malenkov, Olambayo and Allen began studying the plant tissues from the garden. Manfredi and

Mishra set up telescopic equipment which they'd brought with them. And Al-Arabi took charge of the hour-by-hour running of the garden, although there wasn't a great deal to do in this regard.

The second "adjustment" arrived in the form of an order. Justin told them, "The sloping tunnel's almost sixty feet long now and almost twelve feet down and when the robots go in there they're still not picking up any water readings. That means we're gonna need to move faster. So starting tomorrow I'm only taking the best diggers to the cave, every day, 'til we find what we need to find. That means Allen, Olambayo, Suarez, and Malenkov. The rest a you are gonna stay here and work in the garden and do other things."

They all nodded. The seriousness of the situation made it easy for them to agree.

So the next morning the five-person team headed out, with four of them sitting in seats and Allen sitting on the rover's roof, holding onto the back of the front two seats to keep his balance. Upon arriving at Jeanne they repelled down in and then walked to the end of the sloping tunnel, at which point Justin explained that they'd be going at it in shifts of two like before but that he'd be one of the two members of every other shift.

He and Olambayo started in. After a while they switched out for Suarez and Allen, and eventually those two switched out for Justin and Malenkov, who then switched out for Allen and Olambayo and so on. By the end of the day they were fifteen feet further in and another few feet down. The following day they returned and made similar progress. In the midst of this work Suarez recommended that they fasten one rope to all their packs so that if the cave started to collapse in on them and any of them got buried then the rest of the crew could potentially pull out those who got stuck. This seemed like a good idea and so that's what they did.

By the end of its second consecutive working day the five-person team had pushed the sloping tunnel forward to the point where it was now roughly ninety feet long and nearly twenty feet down. Yet the robots still weren't picking up any signs of water. The mood, as such, was somber as they all rode back to Bakersville that afternoon.

When Justin entered his private residence he found that Megan was waiting for him, with a question. But she didn't ask it, because she didn't need to.

"Nothing," he said, after the panel door closed at the top of the stairs above his head. "Nothing yet."

He collapsed onto the couch, feeling exhausted both physically and emotionally. As he lay there, he exhaled deeply.

Megan came over and sat down beside him. "If we don't find water soon, what are you going to do?"

Justin stared into her eyes. "You know what Baker said, how if we don't find water I'm gonna have to start makin' some tough decisions."

She nodded. "How will you do it? Just order one of them to walk away from Bakersville?"

Justin shook his head. "I dunno. I dunno if that would work."

There was silence, then he added, "The easiest thing would be to just leave one or more of them down in the cave, overnight or something." As he spoke these words the taste of bile arrived on his tongue. He knew that Baker might be listening so he said nothing more out loud, but what he was thinking was, 'Did I just say that?'

VI

They ate a dinner of salmon and onions. Then Justin went up to the shuttle's top level to see how the others were doing, and in particular to check on their morale. He could only imagine that they might be talking among themselves about the fact that no water had yet been detected, and he didn't want that to cause panic.

"Hey everybody," he said loudly as he ascended the staircase into the hallway.

They greeted him cordially. Everyone was there, lounging inside the empty areas of the container spaces. They didn't seem all that worried about anything, or at least they were putting on a good show in that regard.

Ritter was lounging next to Suarez. Evidently Megan had been right about who the German would zero-in on. How did she guess that? Now Justin would have to cook for a whole week!

Allen was lounging ten feet away from Ritter and Suarez, casting furtive, unhappy glances at the two them. He'd seemed on edge for the last couple days and Justin noticed that he'd been drinking lots of water. His conspicuous consumption could become a problem if a water source wasn't located soon.

Wu and Al-Arabi had become fast friends and were sitting across the hall, inside another container space. Near them were Olambayo and Morel, while further over, somewhat off on her own, was Manfredi, who also kept casting glances across the hallway at Ritter and Suarez, unable or unwilling to hide her displeasure. Meanwhile Mishra – who was walking inside the round room, doing laps around the countertop, with one hand pressed against his chin and his other hand gesticulating in the air – was apparently lost in abstract contemplations. As for Malenkov, she was in the hallway, leaning against the wall, smiling and eating mint chocolate-chip ice-cream out of an ice-cream bucket.

"Want some?" She extended the bucket towards Justin.

He smiled and shook his head. "Thanks, I'm good."

Then he looked past her into the round room, at Mishra. "What's he doing?"

Malenkov smiled and shrugged. "No idea."

"I'm curious about that myself," Suarez said, rising to his feet and stepping into the hall. "I'll go ask him." He walked into the round room and began conversing with Mishra.

'Interesting,' Justin thought. Suarez seemed eager to get away from Ritter. So if Ritter chose Suarez but Suarez didn't respond in kind did that mean that he, Justin, wouldn't get stuck doing a week's worth of cooking?

Ritter looked playfully annoyed while she watched Suarez stand up and walk into the other room. As she turned to watch him go, she made eye contact with Allen, who smiled and raised his eyebrows. Ritter rolled her eyes, then looked over at Justin.

"I smelled something tasty when that door opened in the floor," she said. "It smelled like Megan made you something nice."

Justin nodded. "She's a great cook."

"You're a lucky man."

"Yes I am."

"How'd you two meet?"

Manfredi folded her arms across her chest. "You know we're not supposed to ask them anything about their past."

"But it's harmless," Ritter retorted. "And besides, it's romantic." She smiled at Justin.

"And it's classified," he replied, smiling good naturedly.

Ritter smile-frowned, then pretended to pout.

"It was fish, yes?" Morel asked. "I'm sure that's what I smelled coming up through the door. Was it salmon?"

Justin nodded, impressed. "Good guess."

Morel shrugged. "It wasn't a guess. I'm French."

"That brings back memories," Olambayo said, "of growing up in Lagos. Along the wharfs every afternoon there'd be vendors lined up next to the water with their outdoor ovens, selling every kind of cooked fish you can imagine. I used to walk by there all the time just to smell it all. It was delicious."

"Tell me more about your childhood," Ritter said. "I think it's fascinating. I've never been to Lagos."

Allen frowned, then took another drink from the bottle of water he was holding.

Manfredi, not missing any of this, rolled her eyes.

Olambayo shrugged. "I don't have very much to tell. I was poor. The city was big and dangerous. All I wanted to do was read books but I couldn't afford any and neither could my parents."

"At least they'd let you read books if you could get them," Al-Arabi said. "My parents were always trying to get me to stop reading."

"Really?" Wu was surprised. "My parents never stopped telling me to keep reading." She mimicked them: "Keep studying! Keep studying! Why aren't you studying?"

The others laughed.

"What about in Russia?" Allen asked Malenkov after taking yet another swig of water. "Was it hard for a woman to get a good education?"

"No, not at all," she said, swallowing some ice-cream. "In Russia the women do everything."

"Why are you drinking so much water?" Manfredi asked Allen, out of the blue.

Allen blushed. "I'm dehydrated. I've been out pickaxing Martian lava for the last two days straight. Trust me, it takes a toll."

Justin thought about letting Allen take a day off from cave duty, but decided against it; they needed the best diggers working in the tunnels. Besides, he suspected that there was more wearing on Allen than just the digging.

An awkward silence ensued, as everyone contemplated the same questions: Would they find water? If so, when? And if not, what then?

Malenkov broke the silence by declaring, "Speaking of digging in the tunnel, I have a very strong sense of intuition, I always have had it, and my intuition tells me that we are going to find water very soon. I felt that when we were down there in the cave today."

"So are you a mystic?" Ritter asked, playfully but sarcastically.

Malenkov nodded as she gulped down another spoonful of ice-cream. "In a way, yes. A bit of a Russian mystic."

"A scientist mystic?" Manfredi queried.

Malenkov shrugged. "Yes, why not?"

"Isn't that a contradiction in terms?"

"Why should it be? According to science, according to quantum physics, the electrons at the tips of our fingers should never be able to interact with the electrons at the tip of something else. Which means that we should never be able to actually touch anything. And yet we touch things all the time. If that's not mystical, what is?"

"So…are you part of an organized religion?" Al-Arabi asked.

"No, no, don't worry about that," Malenkov assured her. "I am completely unorganized in that regard."

"You remind me of something," Allen said, "talking like that about mysticism. Back when I was at Cambridge I knew a professor of Russian Literature and he once told me a quote by Tolstoy. It goes something like this: a Frenchman is confident because he thinks he's irresistible, and an Englishman is confident because he believes he lives in the world's most well organized society – of course this was back in the 1800s – and the German is confident because he can use math and charts and graphs and so forth to explain the way the world works, and the Russian is confident – and of course Tolstoy was saying this as a Russian – because he realizes, unlike the German, that he has no idea how the world works and he's also certain that no one knows how the world works and he's completely fine with that."

Malenkov nodded and smiled and tipped the bucket of ice-cream in Allen's direction. "Russian mysticism for you. Exactly."

"That's from *War and Peace*," Morel confirmed.

"You've read it?" Malenkov was impressed. "I didn't think anyone read *War and Peace* except professors of Russian Literature."

Morel nodded. "Mais oui. Of course. It's a classic. My favorite part is how there are these characters who are experiencing existential crises, and then they sit down to a big meal, and Tolstoy explains that after eating that meal they all have a sense of well-being that no amount of philosophy could possibly give them."

Everyone laughed, and as they were doing so Suarez and Mishra walked out of the round room and into the hallway.

"What is the joke?" Mishra asked, standing in the hallway next to Malenkov while Suarez returned to his previous spot on the floor, although now he sat a few inches further away from Ritter than before.

"We're talking 'bout what makes different people feel confident, like what makes them happy," Justin explained.

"Ahh, I see," Mishra replied. "Yes, happiness. Well, I can tell you what makes me happy – being on this shuttle with all of you good people. I am the happiest I have ever been. If I start singing you will just have to ignore me."

Wu studied Mishra for a few seconds, as if puzzled by him. Then she asked the group a question which had been on several of their minds for the last few days but which no one had yet chosen to raise. "So, I have a question for the group."

They all turned and looked at her.

"Why do you think that we were the ones who were chosen for this mission? I understand why Justin and Megan were chosen – they have high level training in survival skills. But what about the rest of us?"

"They told me they wanted a biologist from Africa who'd been educated in the States and who'd worked at a pharmaceutical company." As Olambayo said this he shrugged, and added, "That was pretty much it."

"They told me," Allen boasted, "that they were searching for the handsomest biologist they could find, and I was it." He raised his bottle of water in a toast to himself, and smiled.

"They told me something like what they told Robert," Al-Arabi said, nodding at Olambayo. "They wanted a horticulturist from the Arab world, a woman, someone educated in the West."

"Similar for me," Manfredi added. "They wanted a woman, from a Mediterranean country."

"They told me they were looking for a male geologist from a Latin American country," Suarez said.

"Well," Ritter joined in the sharing, "they told me they needed a brilliant German woman who was ready for anything."

The others assumed that that might in fact have been the case.

"Justin," Morel asked, "do you know? Do you know why they chose us?"

Justin shrugged. "They told me you were all good scientists. That you were dedicated. Ready to take on this mission. That was pretty much it. And so far, I agree with them." He pulled off this statement with just the right vocal staging, making it sound like he was a tough but supportive commander; in fact he impressed himself by how well he nailed the line, especially since he still felt uncomfortable every time he lied to them. He couldn't help wondering when that feeling would pass, and if he wanted it to.

The others nodded, as a pensive silence settled in the air.

Justin assumed that this was a good moment to give the pep talk.

"Look," he said, "I just want you to know that I know you're all probably wondering what we're gonna do 'bout the water situation. But we all know that there are reports by NASA saying that there's water not far below the surface a this planet. Thanks to our tunnel in the cave, at this point we're down more than six hundred and twenty feet. Which means we've gotta be close. I'm not a mystic like Malenkov," and he smiled at her; she smiled in return, "but I'm as sure as I can be that we're gonna find it soon."

"And if we don't?" Manfredi couldn't resist asking. Her words were like fingernails getting dragged down a chalkboard.

"We will," he assured her. Then he added, "In the army, you never give up. I'm not givin' up. And none a you are allowed to give up either. That's an order."

VII

The digging team left Bakersville at 10:00 the next morning and drove in silence to Jeanne. They dug all day, or so it seemed. By the end of the afternoon the sloping tunnel was another fifteen feet long and three feet down, such that it was now a total of one hundred and five feet long and twenty-three feet down.

The following day they knocked their way through another ten feet. Their pickaxing took on a moderately frantic quality until they hit a soft portion of the wall which caved inwards and revealed a space which was about four feet wide and another ten feet long. They all cheered and felt elated but when they began picking at the wall at the far end of this space they found that it didn't collapse inward like the other wall but had to be slowly chipped away. And thus their work resumed....

They headed back to Bakersville that afternoon without anyone uttering a word. But after they'd parked next to the shuttle and everyone climbed off the rover, Malenkov indicated to Justin that she wanted to talk to him in private. So the two of them walked over to the garden, checked to see if anyone was inside, and, finding it empty, stepped into the chamber where the gravity-impact testing was done and took off their helmets.

"What's up?" Justin asked her.

Malenkov took a deep breath, as her facial features shifted into a serious expression; the most serious expression Justin had yet seen on her. "I know what happens," she told him, "if we don't find water."

Justin's stomach instantly knotted up, and he didn't say anything. Did she know that he was supposed to start killing people if water wasn't found soon?

"I know that our current water supplies won't last much longer," she said. "They can't. Not with the supply capacity that we have on the two ships."

Justin stared at her, waiting for the next statement, but what she said wasn't what he was expecting.

"I know how it is in the army," she continued. "My father was in the army. Self-sacrifice, all of that. But this group can't afford to lose you. We need your leadership. And Megan needs you to help her raise the baby that the two of you will have."

He was utterly uncertain how to reply to this.

"What I'm saying," she went on, "is if we need to start sacrificing people…I'm ready. I knew when I signed on for this mission that I was taking my life in my hands, that a million things could go wrong. I made my peace with that back on Earth before I went to sleep in my incubator bed."

He was stunned, speechless.

"I know it's not my place to request this," she continued, "but if I could, I would ask you to promise me that you'll give me up before you stop looking after yourself, and your wife."

"I'm not going to give up anybody," he managed to reply, trying to maintain his composure. "I'm not going to sacrifice myself. And I'm not going to sacrifice you, either."

She looked deeply worried. "If we don't find water soon then some very difficult decisions are going to have to be made."

It couldn't have been more ironic, the way she sounded so much like Baker, motivated by the same logic but the exact opposite sentiment.

"I know it," he assured her. "Course I do. And if the time comes to make those decisions, I'll make them. And I'll do it by thinking 'bout what's best for this colony. For this colony in the long run."

He stared straight into her eyes, and after a moment she nodded, seemingly convinced.

"Okay," she said. "Thank you."

He nodded in turn, then they fastened their helmets back on and walked out of the garden.

Later that evening, after dinner, while they were lying together on the couch in their private residence, Justin told Megan what Malenkov had relayed to him.

"That's amazing," Megan said. "What a brave woman."

"She's really something else. Truth is, if I had to choose any a them to sacrifice, she'd be the last one."

Megan thought about this for few moments. Then she asked him, "Has Ritter selected which man to target yet?"

Justin smiled and nodded. "Yeah. And you were right – she went straight for Suarez."

Megan flashed her knife of a smile in victory, but Justin quickly added, "Suarez wasn't interested. So now I think she might be zeroing in on Olambayo. Which means...."

"Which means you still have to cook for a week!"

"I do? Why? Nothing happened 'tween them! Suarez doesn't like her. But you know who does like her – Allen. Remember I called Allen."

"Does she like him?"

"No," Justin had to admit.

"Then that doesn't count for anything."

"How 'bout we base this on who she finally ends up with?"

"Totally not fair."

"I...." Justin began to retort, but he was cut short by the sound of a familiar voice which echoed out from the overhead intercom.

"Sorry to interrupt...." Baker said.

The couple on the couch jolted out of their playful repartee.

"Oh...hey, Baker," Justin replied.

"Hello," Megan added.

"Greetings, you two. How are things?"

"They're going," Justin said.

"As you can imagine, I've been watching."

Justin nodded, and exchanged a glance with his wife.

"I must say, I've been impressed. Excellent role playing, both of you."

"Thanks," Megan and Justin replied simultaneously.

"But of course we do still have that one little issue of the water supply rapidly running out."

Justin inhaled. Megan glanced at him sympathetically.

"And in that regard I have some ideas that I'd like to talk to you about, Justin," Baker said.

"...Okay."

"Shall we meet in your study?"

Justin and Megan both raised their eyebrows.

"...Sure," Justin said.

"Great."

When the study's door was closed and Justin had taken his seat at the antique table, the TV screen flicked on and Baker's image appeared.

"Now then," Baker launched right in, "I couldn't help overhearing that Malenkov has volunteered to kill herself."

Justin immediately shook his head. "She's too valuable. I can't let her do it."

"It certainly would simplify matters if members of the crew were to take themselves out of the game without causing any fuss. But of course that would then deny you the opportunity to exercise supreme executive authority and thereby terrify everybody else."

Justin inhaled and said nothing.

"And as you know," Baker added, "that's something that you *are* going to have to do eventually, in any case."

Justin remained sitting in silence.

"On that note," Baker continued, "have you selected your d'Orco yet?"

Justin nodded. "I'm thinking Allen."

"Good choice."

"Glad you like it."

"Tell me your reasoning. I'm curious how it compares to mine."

Justin shrugged. "He seems unstable. I'm thinking maybe he has – or had – a drinking problem."

"He did and therefore he does. He simply doesn't happen to have access to any alcohol up there. But that doesn't mean that he doesn't still have a problem."

"And he and Ritter already have some tension 'tween them. He's into her but she's not into him. So that sets the two a them against each other, and it sets him against anyone else she's into. At least potentially."

"Very nice. Go on."

"And I think Manfredi doesn't like him either."

"Agreed."

"And of the other four guys, Olambayo's the strongest but he's a sweetheart. So is Suarez, plus I think any violence would completely mess with him. And I don't think I could get Mishra to focus on any plan a domination long enough for him to get anybody angry at him. And then there's Morel's, but he's just too…French. I think he'd think that being a henchman wasn't all that interesting."

"Completely agree."

"So that leaves Allen."

"Yes it does."

"But I guess none a that matters if we don't find water here soon. There's no point having a d'Orco if everybody's dead."

"True."

Justin sighed.

Baker studied him, then said, "…Yes?"

Justin shook his head. "I…I still can't believe I'm in the middle a all this. That I'm up here leading a team a scientists searching for water on Mars."

"Would you prefer to have met your maker in an Ohio prison?"

"No, course not. I'm just sayin'…I mean, saying…."

Baker smiled. "I've been admiring your i-n-g words lately. The speed of your improvement in that regard is truly impressive."

Justin nodded, as his thoughts wandered off….

"Now what are you thinking about?" Baker asked, bringing him back to the moment. "Or would you prefer that I guess?"

Justin smiled resignedly. "You mentioning prison….It reminded me of a song they used to play back when I was locked up. They'd play it over the loudspeaker."

"Which song was that?"

"'Folsom Prison Blues,' by Johnny Cash. Ever heard it?"

"Of course."

Justin shrugged. "I think they used to play it just to mess with all the inmates…." His thoughts drifted off again.

Baker let Justin's words hang in the air for a few moments. Then he said, "You need to find the water, Justin. You need to find it or you'll need to start letting people die. But whatever you do don't let anything happen to Allen. If he's going to be the d'Orco then you need to keep him alive until the time is right to get rid of him."

VIII

Grim considerations accompanied the prince of Mars as he and the digging team drove to Jeanne the next morning. If they didn't find water in the next few days then it wasn't only going to be Baker who'd be urging Justin to start offing people. Everyone would understand what needed to be done. And the rest of the crew probably wasn't going to be as self-sacrificing as Malenkov.

But who would he choose? He couldn't select anyone from the digging team; they'd have to be given priority. And since he wasn't ready to consider killing any of the women, that left two first candidates: Morel and Mishra. But how would he decide which of them should die, or die first? Maybe he'd just have to take them both out at once.

He shook his head inside his helmet as the rover rolled over some more sand dunes and then rounded another rocky clump, heading towards the cave.

"Today we find water!" Malenkov declared as they parked near the cave's rim and dismounted.

Suarez gave her a thumbs-up, then they all made their way down into the massive hole, headed over to the tunnel, followed it down into the sloping portion, walked up to the far wall and then set to work right away, picking at it hard.

Their digging momentum was faster than their previous pace and it got even faster as the time ticked by. At a certain point Justin realized that his pick-swinging was becoming frantic; that he was hitting the wall twice for every time it was hit by whoever was standing next to him, and that this was happening despite the fact that all the others were swinging frantically as well. But he didn't let up. Even if it made the others panicky he was going to go at it hard.

At a certain point he and Olambayo both switched out in order to allow Malenkov and Suarez their turn. Dragging his pick and sweating inside his spacesuit, Justin went and leaned against one of the cave's walls. He wanted to wipe his drenched brow but of course he couldn't. So he closed his eyes and leaned his head back against the wall, trying to ready himself to swing even harder during the next round, while also trying to will the target wall to finally cave in and open up a more vertical chute. When he re-opened his eyes he saw that Allen had walked over and was leaning against the wall beside him.

"I had a great uncle who was a coal miner," Allen told him. "He always used to tell me stories about it. I keep thinking about that while we're down here."

"Oh yeah?"

Allen nodded, frowning forcefully. "He made it sound quite bad. Very ugly work."

Allen glanced around for a moment, then added, "Of course coal would be worse to dig through than this. This stuff isn't going to give us black lung. The trouble with this is, we don't know where we're going or if we're going to find anything when we get there." There was anger in his eyes as he spoke. Things had gone badly for him back on Earth, and now things were going badly for him up on Mars as well.

"I do know where we're going," Justin told him, playing his part. "We're going down. And we're gonna keep going down 'til we get where we need to get."

Allen nodded, trying to appear reassured, but he looked even more discouraged than before.

Eventually Malenkov and Suarez switched out, so Justin stepped up to the target wall and Allen took his place beside him. They exchanged glances of determination, then began swinging their picks.

They swung. And they swung. And they swung. The wall gave up itself piece by piece, submitting to the impacts of their violence, but no matter how much the wall surrendered it still stood there, right in front of them.

They grunted and yelled, gathering strength from their sounds. And the wall gave of itself, and the wall was still there. And they swung. And they grunted. And the wall crumbled yet stood straight. They went on like this for longer than what had become the typical length of a turn. Allen's weakness increased more rapidly, until he couldn't raise his arms to swing the pickaxe one more time. At which point he sank to his knees and sat down on top of his space boots, the torso portion of his spacesuit heaving as his lungs gasped and then gasped some more.

Justin kept going, frenetically. Eventually the others exchanged worried glances but they knew not to interfere. They had to let this play itself out.

And then Justin likewise dropped his pick, collapsed to his knees and sat down on top of his space boots, his strained chest heaving.

The others weren't sure what to do. The obvious thing would be for two of them to rotate in and keep with the picking, but Justin and Allen were sitting in the way and the others didn't want to ask them to move.

Malenkov sighed as she pressed her side against one of the cave walls, and Olambayo leaned heavily on his pick. Suarez, meanwhile, was standing behind the two sitting astronauts and studying rock formations which had just been revealed in the newest layer of the target wall. He followed a line of sediment which ran nearly straight up and down from the floor to the ceiling. And then he realized something.

"Wait a minute…."

The excitement in Suarez's voice caught the attention of Malenkov and Olambayo, but Justin and Allen were too exhausted to really notice; they barely budged or turned to look as Suarez stepped gingerly past them and placed the front of his helmet up close to the target wall.

"This is a crack!" He announced, then turned back to look at the others. "This is a crack in the wall here!"

Justin and Allen both raised their gazes; Olambayo and Malenkov stepped forward to get a better look.

"It runs from the top to the bottom!" Suarez ran his gloved finger up and down in front of the crack. "We should be able to knock through this!"

Justin took a deep breath, nodded, and, rising awkwardly to his knees and then up to his feet, ambled stiffly out of the way. Allen – even more slowly – did the same. Then Olambayo stepped forward, taking his position next to Suarez, and the two of them began picking aggressively at the wall. Within thirty seconds the whole thing caved in, revealing… another small open space, barely two feet wide by seven feet long.

A collective sigh-gasp of despair issued from the group as soon as their helmet lights lit this new area. Malenkov dropped her pick on the ground, as did Olambayo, who leaned his large frame against a side wall, while Suarez leaned against the opposite wall and, still holding his pick, let himself slide down until he was sitting on the ground, utterly spent.

"Aaaiiirrgghh!" Allen yelled, holding the pick up in front of him and running into the narrow space which had just been revealed.

Justin caught a glimpse of Allen's eyes as Allen rushed past him, and what he saw in those eyes was rage.

"Aaaiiirrgghh!" Allen screamed as the sharp side of his pick's head hit against the narrow space's far wall. His arms were too weak to swing the pick so all he could do was push his weapon into the beast's side.

And the beast…gave. Gave fully. The wall went. And not simply onto the ground but down, below, and out of sight, taking Allen with it.

"Wooaaiiaaah!" Allen shrieked as he disappeared.

Malenkov screamed.

Within a few seconds, however, she and the others realized that wherever Allen had just fallen he couldn't have fallen far since the rope which connected them had not gone taught between him and Suarez, who was the next person after Allen on the rope line.

"Allen!" Justin yelled, running into the narrow space. The others ran in behind him.

"Allen!" Justin yelled again as his helmet's light beam poured into the area that Allen had just discovered, the light mingling with light which was already being generated by Allen's own helmet beam.

And then Justin stopped, and gasped. This new space was vast. At least forty feet stretched between him and the opposite wall. Looking up he saw that the distance to the ceiling was roughly the same.

His eyes swiveled down and he saw that this new space's floor – which was about four feet below the hole that Allen had created – sloped downward from right to left at a forty-five degree angle. He followed the slope with his light beam, turning left to see how far the beam extended, and as he did so the light faded into the darkness without landing on a wall.

"What…just happened?" This was Allen's voice.

Justin stepped closer to the edge of the opening and saw – a few feet below – Allen lying on his back on the sloping ground.

"Hey there!" Justin jumped down beside him. "You hurt?"

Before Allen could reply, Malenkov – who had stepped up to the edge of the opening – exclaimed in delight, "Look at this!"

She sat down on the ledge of the new opening and then dropped down beside Justin. Suarez and Olambayo – equally ecstatic – followed in turn.

"Good work!" Malenkov said, kneeling down beside Allen. "Did you break anything?"

"...I don't think so."

She grabbed one of his arms, Justin grabbed the other, then they pulled Allen to his feet. Once he was steadied, Allen glanced around and took in the area he'd just discovered.

"Well...it's about time," he said, circling his head, awestruck like the others. He turned in the direction towards which this wide floor was sloping downwards, to see how far it ran, but the beam from his helmet light dissolved into the darkness, like Justin's. "This goes quite a ways."

"Thank God!" Olambayo exclaimed.

Justin laughed out loud with relief. All the tension that had been mounting inside him for the last many days instantly drained.

The others joined him, laughing in shock and joy.

Then Justin remembered that he was supposed to act like a military officer, so he gathered his composure and said, "Let's see where this thing goes."

The others nodded, and the group began walking slowly – testing the solidity of the ground with each step – down the wide incline, while the beams from their helmet lights faded into the murky darkness in front of them. With every step they grew more excited by how far – and how far down – this new tunnel stretched, and with every step they also grew quieter in order to allow for greater alertness to any sounds or sights they might encounter.

They continued in this way for about three minutes while the air around them grew progressively colder. Eventually the beams from their helmet lights began bouncing against a facing wall.

"This is it," Justin announced, "we've reached the end."

"Wait," Suarez insisted. "Look!"

His light beam was picking up a depression in the ground directly in front of this facing wall, and as he turned his head rightwards his beam revealed that the depression dropped precipitously, veering into a two foot-wide cavern which stretched away and down from the inclined ground on which they all were standing.

"Ha!" Malenkov exclaimed. "More down!"

Everyone stepped up closer to the narrow cavern.

"Careful," Justin said.

As their light beams poured into the cavern they could see that the space stretched steeply downward at roughly a seventy degree angle and descended beyond the point which their beams could reach.

"It's steep," Olambayo noted.

"We need to go change out our oxygen tanks before we go much further," Allen said.

"Yeah, you're right," Justin agreed. "And we can come back with more equipment, to handle this slope. Plus we should get the robots in here to see what they pick up with their sensors."

"We can change our oxygen tanks and bring down the robots now and then return tomorrow with more equipment," Malenkov suggested.

Justin nodded. "Okay, let's do that."

So they headed up to the surface and switched out all their oxygen tanks, then returned to the narrow cavern with the robots in tow, placing the mini-rover-like creatures near the cavern's edge. While the two robots roamed for an hour, the five humans relaxed, sitting on the large expanse of inclined ground, chatting happily. Then they took the robots back out into the main part of Jeanne to transmit any findings to Nevada.

About a minute after this transmission began, the small screens on the backs of the robots lit up, with each screen displaying the same word in capital letters, followed by an exclamation mark:

WATER!

IX

Justin experienced something unfamiliar while driving back to Bakersville that day; it was a feeling he'd never felt before. He felt like a hero. Which is what he was. He'd led a team of people on a challenging and potentially doomed mission to find a life source so that they could all survive and their colony could grow and thrive. It was the most important thing he'd ever done. It was the best thing he'd ever done. In a way it was the only real thing he'd ever done. All the other things he'd accomplished in his life had – to varying degrees – just been about going through the motions.

This would've been the proudest moment of his life if everything else that he was saying and doing hadn't been a lie, much less a lie which was blended with the potential for profound brutality.

'Who am I?' He wondered as the rover bounced along and his companions chatted ecstatically around him.

Ever since the ten scientists showed up on Mars, Justin had been feeling like he was losing his grip on his identity. Once he began acting out the lie, it was as if something inside of him became unmoored. A fissure was opening up, psychologically, between who he thought he was and who he seemed to be. It wasn't a good feeling. It made him want to close the gap between perception and reality. And now there seemed to be a way to do that: he could become the hero that he was pretending – but not entirely pretending – to be. He could turn the lie into something real. Or relatively real.

Of course if he began believing his own lies then wasn't there a fairly good chance that he'd wind up losing his mind?

As the digging team rolled back into Bakersville, Justin's thoughts found a new focus. He was struck by the fact that there was something profoundly primitive about what they were experiencing at that moment. They were like prehistoric hunters returning to their village after finding a useful cave, a cave which contained something as basic and fundamental as water. As if they'd travelled millions of miles through space just to start the process of human civilization all over again.

A few of the crew members were standing near the shuttle, waiting for the digging team to return, anxious to hear hopeful news. Before the rover even rolled to a halt, Malenkov shouted to them, "We found it!"

At which point everyone started dancing and laughing and shortly thereafter the entire crew gathered in the shuttle's round room, practically beside themselves with relief and joy.

Justin figured that he ought to make a little speech. "This is a truly historic day," he said, trying to sound official. "Today we found water, and that means that from now on this colony isn't just an experiment. This is something real we're doing up here. We're gonna survive. Bakersville is gonna survive. And now the human race has a second chance."

The others beamed like lightbulbs. Wu, Suarez and Al-Arabi all got tears in their eyes.

"It also means another thing," Justin continued. "Because where there's water there can be life. When we go down there tomorrow, who knows what we're gonna find. Maybe it'll be water and nothing else, or maybe it'll be water and everything else we've ever wanted." As he spoke he surprised himself with his own quasi-eloquence.

The rest of the crew became hysterical and began dancing around the circular counter like a tribe dancing around a bonfire. Each member of the group stopped to hug Justin as they danced by, and he hugged them in turn, absorbing their joy yet trying not to lose his composure, while also reflexively holding back from accepting a reality that he knew to not be entirely true.

It felt particularly strange when Mishra and Morel hugged him; earlier that morning he'd been contemplating their deaths and now they were embracing him like he was their savior.

Periodically he caught Megan's glance as she participated in the celebration, and the look she gave him – of pride, and joy, and a hint of concern – reinforced the feelings which were mixing together inside him. Eventually he became nauseous, so he stealthily exited the scene, walked down into his private residence, closed the door above his head and then sat down on the gray leather couch, awash in a kaleidoscope of emotions.

"Hello Justin," Baker said, his relaxed voice transmitting through the intercom system.

"...Hey, Baker."

There was a long pause, then Baker said, "Good work today."

"Thanks. Thought you'd be happy."

"I'm the happiest I've been in a very long time."

"Really? You sound so…calm."

"When I'm this happy I get very calm."

"You always been that way or is that just part a your *Mona Lisa* mask routine?"

There was a pause, as Baker evidently contemplated the question. "Hard to say," he replied. "I don't remember at this point which came first."

Justin raised his eyebrows, appreciating the significance of that statement.

Then Baker suggested, "Why don't we talk in your study. I want to tell you what you're likely to find down in the cave tomorrow."

Justin took a deep breath, then nodded and rose from the couch, stepped into the study, and shut the door.

"Now," Baker said, after his face appeared on the screen, "allow me to elaborate upon the message you received earlier today via the robots. There is, indeed, water down in that cave. It's located about two hundred feet below wherever you placed the robots. Presumably you can get closer to it by heading down into that cavern which you told the rest of the group about. Indications are that it's buried under some more ground so you're going to need to take a drill down there with you."

"Do we have a drill?"

"You do, in a box that you haven't unpacked yet. Another thing you haven't unpacked is a machine that emits microwaves, which is going to be important because any water you find down in the cave is likely to be frozen. The microwaves will turn the water into gas and when the gas rises you can collect it in another machine which is in another box that you haven't unpacked."

"And then we'll take that water back here to Bakersville on the rover?"

"That's right. You'll be able use the water in the same ways that you typically would, to drink or to do washing or whatever, or you can use it as a means to create oxygen via electrolysis."

"How?"

"There's a machine in the round room that's built into the wall. All you need to do is pour the water into that small hole in the wall near the refrigerator. The water then goes through a tube that's connected to the machine in question, and that machine takes care of the rest – water storage or electrolysis – depending on which program you enter into the onboard computer."

Justin nodded, as his facial features stiffened. He wasn't frowning, exactly, but he didn't look happy either.

"Like I said," Baker noted, "the happier I get the calmer I get. As for you, that isn't the face you make when you're happy. And it's not your *Mona Lisa* mask."

Justin shook his head and exhaled. "No, it's not."

Baker nodded. "Speaking of *Mona Lisa* masks, I must say, your lying technique is getting better by the day. That little speech you just gave upstairs, about possibly finding alien life in the water – very nice indeed."

Justin shrugged. "Maybe that part's not a lie."

"The sensors on the robots didn't detect any indications of life in the water. Most likely you're not going to find anything."

Justin shrugged again.

"It doesn't matter, of course," Baker noted. "All you need to do is to keep reminding them of the possibility."

"And then lying 'bout everything else."

"Well by the looks of it that shouldn't be a problem for you."

"It still feels strange when I do it. I don't seem to be getting used to it no matter how many lies I tell."

"But it doesn't matter what you feel. All that matters is what the others believe."

"Yeah, I guess." At which point Justin didn't exactly sigh but he gave the impression of doing so.

"Do you want to talk about what you're feeling at the moment?" Baker asked.

Justin shook his head. "No, not really."

"Good. Naturally I assume that I can already guess what you're thinking and by extension that I can tell what you're feeling. So there's no reason for me to hear you say it out loud. And it's good for you to get used to not talking about how you're feeling, in any case. Such is the life of a prince."

Justin smiled sadly.

After Baker bid him goodnight and the screen switched to black,

Justin stood up, unlocked the safe and took out *The Prince*. He opened it to the dedication, where Machiavelli addresses Lorenzo De' Medici, and he read that part again. Then he read it for a third time.

X

The narrow cavern was cold as they descended down into it the following day. Justin went first, followed by Malenkov, then Olambayo, Suarez and Allen. They'd left the new tools which they'd brought with them – the drill, the microwave machine, and the container for capturing the gasified water – back up in the large sloping tunnel which Allen had discovered the day before.

The cylindrical-shaped drill was roughly a foot in circumference and three feet long. The microwave machine and the water container were both rectangular – each was about the size of a filing cabinet – and came with rollers. It'd been challenging enough to strap these machines to the repelling device and then lower them into the main cave. Thus the team decided that, until they knew what they were dealing with in terms of the slope and slipperiness of the sharply descending cavern, it was best to stay unencumbered by any extra weight and supplies. All they brought with them for this initial descent were their picks, not only for digging but also to help them cut into the walls or floor of the cavern in the event that one or more of them lost their balance and started to slide.

"Slowly," Justin kept saying. "Just take it slowly."

The cold air inside the cavern kept getting colder the farther down they went, which heightened their collective tension. And Suarez slipped twice, which didn't help either. But they arrived safely at the cavern's base – which turned out to be roughly a hundred and eighty feet down – within ten minutes and discovered that the cavern emptied into another "room" which was about twenty feet by twenty feet, with a relatively flat floor and a low – roughly five foot tall – ceiling.

Crawling around on their hands and knees in this low-ceilinged room, the five of them tested places in the floor and walls with their picks to see if any of these surface areas cracked easily. But the floor and walls of this room were solid and hard.

"This's gotta be it then," Justin decided, pointing at the ground. "Below our feet here. Everything we came here for is right under here."

So Olambayo, Allen and Justin hurried back up to the large sloping tunnel. Allen grabbed the drill and the other two grabbed the microwave machine, then the three men carefully re-descended into the cavern and returned to the low-ceilinged room.

The drill had a keypad at the top, and clamps which could extend out in four directions, allowing it to be anchored to the ground. Allen set up the drill and then pushed a button on the keypad to start the thing up. It was surprisingly quiet, and while the drill's bit dug into the low room's floor the little screen on the drill's keypad listed out the depths that were achieved. It had a maximum range of twenty feet and when that depth was reached the keypad's screen turned yellow. At which point Allen pushed a button which caused the drill bit to retract up into the cylinder.

Next they dragged the microwave machine – which had a metal grill at the bottom through which the microwaves were transmitted – over the hole that the drill had made. Olambayo turned a knob on the machine to activate the microwaves, then they let the machine run for half an hour. Eventually they pulled the machine away from the hole.

Everyone just sat there. Staring at the hole. Shining their helmet lights on it. Waiting to see if steam would, in fact, rise out of it.

And…steam rose.

It condensed upon the low ceiling.

Then it dripped.

It was beautiful. It was the most beautiful thing that any of them had ever seen. Every drop seemed to contain within itself the potential to support another human life in the colony.

For a long time no one spoke. It was as if they were witnessing something holy; as if, by uttering the slightest sound, they might scare the steam away.

Eventually Justin indicated to Allen via hand gestures that the two of them should head back up to the large tunnel and get the water storage container. So they quietly exited the low room and made their way back up the incline of the cavern. When they reached the top, and after Allen had had time to catch his breath, Justin stepped up close to him and, in a low voice, said,

"I wanna talk to you 'bout something. Just the two of us."

"…Yes? Alright. What's on your mind?" Allen's tone had a tinge of anxiety, as if he wondered whether he was in trouble for something.

"Now that we've found water and we know this colony is gonna make it, things are gonna get a little more serious. What I mean is that we gotta start concentrating on making sure that things really run right, that people stay in line, follow the rules, all that sort a thing."

Allen's eyes tightened up; evidently his fears of being in trouble were justified. All his life he'd been making mistakes and then finding out afterwards that he'd made them. Apparently things weren't going to be any different on Mars.

"What I'm saying," Justin continued, "is that I need a right-hand man, someone to be my second pair a eyes and ears, to help me make sure everybody does what they're supposed to do. You get what I mean?"

Allen nodded, but he was not yet "getting" it, insofar as it hadn't occurred to him that he might be the right-hand man in question.

"My choice is you," Justin told him. "I want you to be that right-hand guy."

"…What?" Allen flinched as if he'd just been hit in the face with something.

"I'm choosing you."

"…Me?"

"Yeah."

"You want…me, to be your right-hand man?"

"Yeah, like I said."

Allen's eyebrows rose up his forehead and he took a deep breath, trying to comprehend this information. "Is it…is it because I found this big tunnel?"

Justin nodded. "That's part of it. And I just think you're the right guy for the job."

This was the nicest thing that Allen had ever heard anyone say to him in his entire adult life. "Wow…." He said after several seconds. "Um, yes….Sure. I'm happy to help, in any way I can…."

"I knew you would be. And here's the thing: it's best if we keep this 'tween ourselves for now. If any a the others find out I've chosen you like this they might get jealous. It'll get clear to them as time goes by that you're my guy, but let's ease into it, okay? Let's not make it too obvious at first. The main thing is just for you to start reporting back to me 'bout anything you hear or see that you think I should know. Got it?"

Allen smiled, deeply touched. "Got it." Then he gave a mock –

and not so mock – military salute.

"Great. Now look, there's no way we can carry this water storage thing up and down the cavern, especially not when it's filled with water. So I'm gonna go down there and tell the others that we need to head back to Bakersville to get more equipment."

"Makes sense."

"Okay then." And Justin put out his hand.

Allen shook it.

Then the two men exchanged meaningful nods.

XI

Everybody in Bakersville wanted to hear about the water. They wanted to know what it looked like, how it behaved, how much of it there was. Since no one knew the answer to this last question, and since they couldn't risk causing too much water to evaporate too soon by digging too many holes in the low-ceilinged room, they agreed to restrain themselves from starting the exploration for lifeforms until they had a better sense of what they were dealing with in terms of water supply.

Given that, for the time being, there wasn't going to be any more man-powered digging in the tunnels, other members of the crew could now head out to Jeanne again, in addition to the core digging team. Thus the next day a group of them drove to the cave without Justin. Allen was put in charge of the rover, and Wu, Al-Arabi, Mishra and Ritter rode along. There was an extension hose – which Baker had informed Justin was in one of the remaining unpacked boxes – which this group now hooked up to the water container at one end, then they ran the hose down the cavern into the low-ceilinged room and dropped the free end of the hose into the drilled hole. The water container had a suction capacity which allowed it to pull steam up through the hose; once the steam was inside the container it then condensed into water.

The Allen-led group returned to Bakersville later that afternoon with the water container completely full. They loaded the container onto the shuttle's external lift, brought it onboard and then placed it in the long hallway. The whole crew gathered around as Allen opened the container's top, revealing the water inside.

Everybody stared at the water as if they were staring at a chest of diamonds. And in a way, they were.

"How beautiful!" Mishra exclaimed.

Malenkov smiled at him and gave him a hug.

The water container performed a scan and determined that there were a variety of sediments in the liquid, but nothing particularly toxic, and there was a water purifying system onboard the shuttle in any case.

Everyone was eager to drink this life elixir, so they ran the water through the purifying system, then gathered together in the round room, poured the cleansed water into glasses and held the glasses in the air.

"To Mars!" Justin said, not sure what else to say.

"To Mars!" The others repeated, clinking their glasses together.

"To the future!" Allen added.

"To the future!"

"And to Justin and Megan's future children," Ritter said with a grin, "whenever they come along!"

"To the children!"

Justin and Megan blushed.

And now suddenly everyone was drunk with anticipation.

"I'm looking forward to being a surrogate grandmother," Ritter said.

"Me too!" Al-Arabi seconded that emotion.

"Those babies will certainly have the run of the place," Olambayo pointed out, "with so many extra grandparents around." He smiled broadly, likewise pleased by the prospect of having children onboard.

"I'm going to tell them all about *Le Petite Prince*," Morel added. "And I'm going to teach them to speak French."

The others laughed.

"I am definitely not going to teach those poor kids Chinese," Wu said.

"I'm going to teach them all about rocks!" Suarez joined in.

The others laughed again.

"Hopefully they like rocks," Ritter replied, "or they're not going to care for this place."

"But they won't know any other place," Malenkov said, "so this will be their home. They'll like it for that reason alone."

A thought occurred to Al-Arabi. "Are you going to teach them about trees?"

Megan shrugged. "Yes, of course. They'll need to know all about Earth. We can't hide that from them. They'll need to know where we've all come from."

"But..." Manfredi asked, "don't you think that if they see pictures of Earth and hear all about it then they'll want to go there, and that they'll think this planet isn't so great by comparison?"

There was an awkward silence, then Megan replied, "They won't be able to go there, so whether they like Earth better or not won't really matter. And besides, we'll tell this child – we'll tell all our children – that this planet is better because it's up to us to turn it into whatever we want it to be. We'll tell them that we chose this planet as a replacement for Earth. And we'll tell them how fortunate we are to be here, that we're the hope of the human race, and that they are especially."

The others all nodded solemnly, not only satisfied by her answer but further fortified regarding the significance of their mission.

Later that evening, while Justin and Megan lay on the gray leather couch in their private residence, they both smiled and laughed, although they also grew serious as they discussed the other's comments regarding their eventual children.

"These are going to be the most completely spoiled children ever," Megan predicted. "With all those grandparents and no other children to compete with for attention."

Justin nodded and shrugged. "At least starting out. Until the next group a colonists arrives and there are more people up here having babies."

"But still...." She smiled.

"Besides," he added, "it's probably good for the future prince or princess a Mars to think a themselves as being pretty important."

"Hmm, maybe. Le Petite Prince. The Little Prince."

Justin smiled. "Right."

There was a pause, then Justin added, "I wonder if you're pregnant already?"

She shrugged. "Chances are."

"Maybe we should start considering names."

Megan shook her head. "No, not yet. Not until we know for sure that it's for real."

He conceded her point automatically, naturally submitting to her will when it came to any topic relating to children. He might be the prince of Mars but she was the queen of this household. He didn't need William Baker to explain to him how that power dynamic was going to play out.

"Okay, sure," he replied.

XII

Another week came and went on the red planet and then Megan gave herself a pregnancy test.

Justin was out with a crew at the cave, and when he returned that afternoon he found Megan doing preliminary prepping for the evening's meal. She asked him to help her, so he did, but after he joined her at the sink counter she set down the tongs she was using and went and stretched out on the couch.

"Oh I see how it is," he said good-naturedly.

"You have to take special care of me now," she told him.

Justin froze, and stared at the wall in front of him. "Special care of you...*now*? Now as in, like, now being different than before?"

"Mmhm," she nodded, smiling, watching him, waiting for him to turn around. While she waited her smile expanded.

"You're pregnant?" He asked, turning to her.

She nodded again, as the edges of her smile neared her earlobes.

"Ha!" He exclaimed, rushing to her side. "Ha ha ha!"

They embraced, and held each other in silence for a few minutes. Eventually the silence was interrupted....

"Allow me to be the first one to congratulate you," Baker said, his voice echoing out over the intercom.

The hugging pair released their embraces.

"Uh...hey, Baker," Justin replied.

"What a wonderful development."

"Thank you," Megan said, trying not to allow any annoyance to register in her voice.

"First we find water and now there's this," Baker said. "Our little endeavor is certainly on an upswing."

Neither Justin nor Megan replied, so he kept talking.

"And water is merely a primary need, whereas children embody our whole purpose for being up there." He let this point dangle in the air for several seconds before continuing. "Which means, of course, that the rearing and education of these children will be not only a personal project but a political one."

This statement made Justin acutely uncomfortable. He registered the tension in his wife as well, even without looking at her and even though her facial expression didn't change in the slightest.

"Now I know we don't want to get ahead of ourselves," Baker said, "but if I may simply note that we will need to start considering the child's name here pretty soon. The name of a prince or a princess, after all, isn't just a name; it's a propaganda statement. For instance, you Justin happen to have an ideal name for a founding prince. The name "Justin," after all, is etymologically derived from the Latin name "Justinus," which is derived from "Justus," which ties into the word "justice." And of course justice is what politics is all about, isn't it?"

"…Is it?"

"Of course it is. So then, in that same spirit we ought to be very careful about how we choose the name of this first child of yours."

Justin wondered what his wife would think about "we" choosing the name for the child she'd be bearing. He sensed her tension increasing. But she said nothing.

"Naturally this decision is ultimately up to the two of you," Baker quickly added. "And to the mother in particular. But if I may offer a few suggestions which you can of course accept or ignore at your pleasure…."

'Typical Baker,' Justin thought.

"Staying with the Roman theme," Baker continued, "which we've picked up thanks to the name of Mars and Arsia Mons and Olympus Mons and all the rest of it, and considering that our goal is to set up a strong state which will eventually become a very large state, I'm in favor of selecting from the names of the Roman emperors. And in that regard, naturally, the ideal is Julius Caesar. So my vote would be for the name "Julius" if your child's a boy and "Julia" if she's a girl."

"Julius Jones," Justin said. "That does have a certain ring."

Megan didn't say anything.

"At any rate, give it some thought," Baker suggested.

And then he didn't say anything further.

Eventually Megan and Justin concluded that the conversation with him was over, and they lay together in silence for a while longer.

After dinner they walked up to the top level of the shuttle and announced to everyone that Megan was pregnant. All the middle-aged scientists were thrilled, and from that moment forward Megan was treated differently by the crew. They all became solicitous of her well-being; they made her things to eat, checked in on her, refused to allow her to over-exert herself. Like a band of frontier folk, they began circling the wagons around the prospect of an impending human life.

A few days later Baker asked Justin to meet him in the study, and when the door was shut and Justin seated at the antique table, the screen switched on and Baker's face appeared.

"How are things going?" Baker asked.

"Don't you know? Or have you stopped watching all the time?"

Baker shrugged. "Even if I watch and listen that doesn't mean I see everything or hear everything."

"Is there something particular you're wondering 'bout?"

Baker smiled. "Naturally. In this case I'm wondering about your wife. How's she doing?"

"Fine."

"She seems to be handling the pregnancy well so far."

"Yeah, she's good with it."

"And have you talked any further about the child's name?"

"A little."

"And...?"

Justin shrugged. "I mean ultimately it's really up to her, isn't it?"

"Is it?"

"Pretty sure."

"But you can encourage her in certain directions, can't you?"

Justin smiled. He inhaled. He exhaled. Then he said, "Baker, you know how I chose Allen to be the d'Orco? I chose a guy to be my right-hand man and now you want me to kill him."

"Eventually, yes."

"Okay, so that's one kind a power. Political power. With my wife, that's something else. And I'm not gonna play games with her the way you want me to play with everybody else up here."

Baker nodded. "I see. I'm not surprised by this. Women are very powerful. And now, to a certain degree, she has you under her spell. It's understandable. In fact it's necessary, for the survival of the species. And I'm not going to fight against the forces of nature. After all, I didn't stay married for forty years by ignoring the basic dynamics of male-female relations."

Justin felt relieved.

"But that being said," Baker added, "once your child is born, you – we – are going to need to play a prominent role in his or her education. And you're going to need to help Megan understand that."

"What – you're gonna teach my kids just like we've been doing, here in this room, with you on the screen?"

"That's the idea, yes."

Justin considered this, and felt disturbed. It was one thing for him to follow the Machiavellian lead. It was another thing for his children to do so.

"After all," Baker added, "it's working out nicely thus far, don't you think? Look how well you're doing with the crew. You've got them eating out of your hand. At least for the moment."

Justin nodded.

"But of course, as we've discussed, that's not going to last. Before long they'll start pushing back; they'll begin questioning your judgement. You're a mere mortal, after all. Which is why it's going to be important to remind them of their own mortality when the time is right. And that time is coming."

"What if they don't push back?"

"They will, now that the fundamentals are taken care of. You've found them water and you've impregnated the queen of the hive. In their minds your relevance is already beginning to recede."

Justin shook his head. "I'm not seeing that."

"Oh I am. And you will too, before long, no doubt."

XIII

Ritter's interest in Olambayo had increased over time. In part this was due to a simple process of elimination. Allen was annoying, Mishra was eccentric, and Suarez continued to dodge her flirtations; she couldn't tell if he was gay or just obsessed with rocks. As for Morel, he was French, and she was German, so that was the end of that. Besides, Olambayo was a kind man and a strong man, both of which qualities appealed to her in varying degrees. Olambayo, in turn, was flattered by the attention. He'd never been a ladies' man, or had much luck at all with the opposite sex. In his entire life he'd never taken a really attractive woman out on a date. Granted, Ritter was no longer particularly attractive but she once had been and that fact counted for quite a lot in his mind.

They lounged beside one another in the evenings, in one of the container spaces; unbeknownst to them, in precisely the spot where Troy and Tristan had been inclined to hang out. She asked him questions about Nigeria and he asked her questions about Germany. When these subjects were exhausted he asked her about computer programming and she asked him about biology. This latter topic was inherently erotic and thus led to discussions about their previous dating and marriage experiences. He had very little to share in this regard; she had much to share. Just hearing her talk about her past made Olambayo excited, and slightly uncomfortable.

Allen, meanwhile, typically spent the evenings sitting in the round room, conversing with Morel – and anyone else who wished to join – while casting glances into the hallway, trying to steal glimpses of the courting couple while simultaneously attempting to bury his frustration at the sight.

The Allen-Morel repartees inevitably devolved into debates about World War II. A typical exchange would run as follows:

"De Gaulle just didn't understand war fighting. Fundamentally, he didn't understand it." This from Allen.

"Of course he understood it," Morel would retort. "He'd been an officer in World War I. He fought in the Battle of Verdun! In the trenches! And what had Churchill done? He'd fought where – in Sudan? That hardly even counts!"

"Yes it counts! Besides, the key isn't only battlefield experience. It's a question of commanding whole armies and planning grand strategies. Churchill spent his life doing that. He'd been the head of the navy!"

At which point Morel would throw his hands in the air and shake his head as if this was the most ridiculous thing he'd ever heard. "If he was so great, why did the British people kick him out of office as soon as the war was over?"

"Because Britain is a real democracy!"

"France is not a real democracy?"

"It's not. In the soul of every Frenchman is a longing to submit to an all-powerful king. The Capetian dynasty didn't last as long as it did for nothing!"

"It lasted so long because it was truly superb!"

"You make my point! Even here on Mars you're pining to have a king in Paris that you can bow down to!"

"Non!"

And so it would go, with Allen's voice occasionally rising a few decibels, not so much to win the argument as to ensure that Ritter heard him and was impressed by his flourishes of historical argumentation. But of course she wasn't impressed. She wasn't much interested in anybody's history, other than her own, which she continued to divulge to Olambayo in generous spoonfuls.

Wu and Al-Arabi, meanwhile, tried as best they could to shut out the other conversations and discuss subjects which they found interesting. Eventually they ran out of subject matter, however, so they switched to chess. Manfredi would frequently join them, playing the winner, although neither of the other two really wanted to play her since she was tediously slow and excessively serious. While she waited her turn, Manfredi would pretend to not be listening to the Ritter-Olambayo exchanges even though she was keenly intrigued by whatever they were discussing. The more she heard, the more she disliked Ritter, and of course Ritter could sense this, and she drew satisfaction from Manfredi's jealous vibe.

The only woman in the colony who made Ritter feel uneasy was Malenkov, since Malenkov was well-liked by everyone else. The Russian could join in the Allen-Morel debates with ease. She could play chess with Al-Arabi and Wu and was welcome to do so. When she walked past

Olambayo and Ritter, Olambayo would stop his conversation with Ritter and give Malenkov a polite nod. It also annoyed Ritter that Malenkov had grown quite close to Suarez, having assumed a supportive sister/mother role towards him. And as for Mishra, he thought Malenkov was beautiful.

Allen reported back to Justin regarding all these dynamics, or at least all the ones that his less subtle, male brain could pick up on. He and Justin would snatch a few minutes here and there – while working in the cave, or doing instrument checks in the shuttle's cockpit – to conduct their intel relays.

"Nobody likes Manfredi," Allen informed Justin during one such session, about two weeks after Megan found out that she was pregnant.

Justin nodded. "I can tell."

"And of course you know about Ritter and Olambayo…." Allen tried to mask his frustration behind a wry conspiratorial smile.

"Is anybody saying things 'bout not being happy, like with how the colony's run?"

Allen shook his head. "No, but I can tell you the one to watch out for is Malenkov."

Justin was surprised. "Seriously? You think she might be plotting something?"

"Her – plotting? No. But I could see other people plotting on her behalf. If anyone gets it into their head that they don't want you in charge anymore, Malenkov is going to be the alternative they turn to."

Justin nodded. "I get it."

He didn't bother to inform Allen about Malenkov's earlier offer to sacrifice herself so that he – Justin – wouldn't do so. Based upon that prior offer, he assumed it was highly unlikely that she'd accept a role in overthrowing him. So he took Allen's report to be benign. All of Allen's reports, in fact. And as the days passed by and no major push-back against his rule arose, Justin found satisfaction and relief in the fact that Baker had apparently been wrong about the likelihood of revolt.

And then it came time to install the "real" garden….

One evening, in the study, Baker explained to Justin that he wanted him to launch the next phase of the agricultural plan. The conclusions to be drawn from the experiments conducted thus far in the small garden were now conclusive: 1) both filtered and unfiltered radiation from the sun were suitable for growing crops on Mars, 2) the gravitational difference between

Earth and Mars could be compensated for, and 3) Martian soil was useless. It was also clear by this point that the water source they'd tapped into in the cave was extensive.

In light of these four conclusions, the logical method of proceeding was to lay out an extensive, compost-based garden beneath a translucent, filtering canopy.

"A canopy? You mean like a tent?"

"Precisely. One of those large, tunnel-shaped gardening tents."

"Do we have one up here?"

"Of course."

Baker explained that the bottom, third level of the shuttle housed not only a small nuclear generator – located towards the back of the ship in a sealed compartment – but also a wide and deep storage area which was roughly four feet tall. By entering a code into one of the computers in the cockpit Justin could open a panel on the shuttle's exterior and gain access to this lower container space.

Inside this space was all the equipment required for a state-of-the-art "high tunnel," passive solar, thirty by one-hundred-and-twenty foot "hoop house." This included the truss kit, brace kit, brace purlin, brace bands, cross connectors, aluminum channels, snap clamps, shade cloths, specialized butterscotch-reddish greenhouse plastic, foundational oxygen seals, folding benches, layered benches, parts for assembling raised beds, specialized air-filters, mulch, and lots and lots of seeds. It was all in there along with ten microphones and two miniature video cameras which were disguised as indestructible bolts and which were already fitted into place along the truss, such that there would be no reason to tamper with them.

In preparation for this next gardening phase, Baker walked Justin through a training video, several times. He also explained how to activate an onboard system for transferring all the human waste and biodegradable garbage to the garden. But before activating that system the crew would need to lay a pipe – which was stored in the lower-level container space – so that it ran underground and connected the garden to the shuttle.

The first garden, meanwhile, would be dismantled once the new garden was in place and after all the existing plants were transferred to the new facility. The only part of the original garden that would remain intact would be the airlock compartment, which also housed the oxygen and water tanks. This compartment would be placed in front of the hoop house and serve the same function as it had in the first garden.

"Make sense?" Baker asked him.

"Sure."

It was all so simple in the abstract. But as is often the case, reality was more complicated. Because with reality comes politics.

The problem originated with the gardener.

As noted, Al-Arabi had spent her entire adult life unsuccessfully attempting to land a top position at a prestigious garden. Thus as soon as she found out that they had the wherewithal to erect a large greenhouse – rather than merely building incremental additions to the existing garden – her long pent-up need to direct a gardening team was unleashed.

Not all at once, of course. Decorum required that any passion be released in progressively escalating stages. But over the next many days, unleashed it was. Justin tried to maintain command over the operation based upon the instruction video he'd watched but his education in this regard was nothing compared to Al-Arabi's expertise. She was here, she was there. She was explaining when to anchor the cross-poles and showing how to layer the plastic. She directed the crew where to run the aluminum channels and how to manage to snap clamps. She determined the layout of the raised beds and where best to set the benches. She took over.

After the big greenhouse was in place she extended the breadth of her command. This included, among other things, issuing instructions to the biologists – Allen, Olambayo and Malenkov – about which plants to study and for what purposes.

Justin tried to regain control of the situation but Al-Arabi politely informed him that she had the project in-hand. When he kept attempting to exert his will she responded by ignoring him. Eventually she informed him that he needed to stop bothering her.

So he decided to put his foot down.

One afternoon, while everyone was working in the garden as per Al-Arabi's instructions, Justin told the crew that he wanted to head to the cave and try digging out some of the walls in the water-extraction room, and that he wanted the top digging team – which included the biologists, along with Suarez – to go with him.

"The biologists can't go," Al-Arabi retorted. "We need them here. You should take some others."

Her tone was brusque, more so than previously, and the rest of the crew looked up from the planting they were doing and stared at her and Justin.

"Adiba," Justin replied firmly, "I'm in charge here and if I say I need them to come with me then they're coming with me."

"In charge?" Al-Arabi shot back. "In charge?" The thought of someone interrupting her grand gardening scheme made her blood boil. "You founded this colony, and we're grateful. You helped us find water, and we're grateful. But now you need to let the rest of us do our work. We've trained all our lives for this!"

"Your work takes place when and where I say it takes place!"

"But…I can't believe this!" Al-Arabi threw up her arms as if she'd just been dealt the greatest possible injustice.

Megan, who was standing nearby, sensed the significance of this moment, and she threw her authority – as the bearer of the colony's future – into the fray. "Adiba," she said, "Justin has been put in command for a reason. He's running the colony for all our sakes. We have to accept his decisions."

This was just too much for Wu. She'd spent her life kowtowing to her domineering parents and now here was the best friend she'd ever had – Al-Arabi – getting pushed around by the "parental figures" of the colony. The fact that these "parents" were younger than anyone else on the planet made the indignity seem all the worse. Something inside of her snapped.

"Adiba is right!" Wu declared, rising to her feet. "She knows the most about gardening. And the garden is now the most important thing. We have plenty of water. What we need now is food!"

"Anyone can grow a plant!" Justin countered. "Not everyone is a good digger. And nobody knows how long the steam's gonna keep rising in that hole. We need to find backup supplies. No water, no plants. Allen, Olambayo, Malenkov, Suarez – come with me!"

Allen immediately rose to his feet and walked over to Justin and Megan. Suarez, looking extremely ill at ease, followed suit, eager as he was to leave this tense situation as quickly as possible. After a pause, Olambayo and Malenkov did the same.

Justin cast a stern gaze at Al-Arabi, who returned a harsh stare of her own, while water began rimming the edges of her eyeballs. Then the digging team marched out and spent the rest of the afternoon at Jeanne, picking into the walls of the low-ceilinged cave, although without much effect.

Later that evening Justin sat down in the antique chair in front of the antique table in his study and waited for the screen to switch on. He knew he wouldn't be waiting long and in fact he'd only been sitting there for a few seconds before Baker's image appeared, wearing a sardonic grin.

"Hello Justin."

"Hey there."

"How are you?"

"Great. You?"

"I'm doing well, thank you."

They shared a pause, then Baker continued, "At this moment I'm thinking two thoughts."

"Oh yeah?"

"Indeed. First I'm thinking that the Romans may have had more in mind than I'd previously realized when they made Mars a god of both war *and* agriculture."

Justin nodded and chuckled silently. "I'm thinking maybe yeah."

"The other thing I'm thinking is that now you may be starting to truly appreciate all our Machiavelli sessions together."

"I thought you might be thinking that."

"And so I am."

Justin shrugged. "Al-Arabi and Wu…they're something."

Baker nodded. "When wars occur and armies are raised the former clerks and ditch diggers tend to be the most domineering commanders."

He let this point linger for a few moments, then he said, "People want power, Justin. Machiavelli tells us that. Some people want to rule a state; others want to be left alone to rule their household or their cubicle or their ditch. They just want to run their little kingdoms. Which is why Machiavelli advises us not to touch other people's property. Leave them to lord it over their private castles, and if you do that then most of them will let you run the state as you wish. Of course there'll still be the ones who contest with you for political power, which is why you need to cut those peoples' heads off, all at once and early on."

He paused again before continuing. "The situation you're facing is that, up there, the private is the public because there are so few of you and you're all thrown in so closely together. That dynamic is accentuated all the more by the fact that no one else has any property. On the one hand that's an advantage for you; on the other hand it means that all of them are directly engaged in the public activity of making sure that the colony survives. Which, in turn, makes every one of them a potential challenger to you. And that's precisely what's happening now, just like I've always said it would. You're being challenged. So the question is: what are you going to do?"

Justin had been anticipating this question and he had his answer ready. "I'm gonna wait, and see where it all goes."

Baker nodded. "That's prudent, since clearly the situation is only going to get worse. Besides, the impact of decisive action will be all the greater once the collective temperature up there rises closer to the boiling point."

XIV

Allen's intel now became much more valuable. Justin told Allen as much when they had a moment alone in the cave on that same day as the initial showdown with Al-Arabi and Wu.

"You saw what happened?"

"Yes I did," Allen replied. "That Al-Arabi is a pushy little thing, isn't she. And Wu – who knew she had it in her?"

Justin nodded. "From now on I need you to keep a close eye on those two."

"Will do."

A few days later Justin and Allen took a moment when they were alone in the cockpit to conduct another surveillance report.

"I heard them – Al-Arabi and Wu – talking last night while they were playing chess," Allen said.

"Yeah?"

"The entire conversation was about you."

"…Yeah?"

"They think you're quite the tyrant. Both of them kept saying, "Who does he think he is?" I think they must have said that, between the two of them, maybe fifty times."

"Could anyone else hear them talking like that?"

"I'm not sure. Olambayo and Ritter spent a few hours together in Olambayo's room." Allen could barely conceal his anger about this fact. "Manfredi played chess with the two angry ladies for a while but that was only after they'd been talking about you. And the others were with me in the round room, in and out, coming and going the whole evening, and I don't know if they made any effort to eavesdrop on the chess players."

Justin nodded and was about to ask further questions when the conversation was cut short by the appearance of Mishra, who walked up to the cockpit, smiling widely, without a care in the world.

"Hello to you two. Am I interrupting something? I am very sorry if I am."

"No, don't worry 'bout it," Justin assured him. "What's up?"

Mishra's bright eyes twinkled. "I have been having an idea. Ever since we dismantled the first garden, it's been something which has been buzzing around inside my mind."

"What's that?"

"The panels you used for constructing the first garden – they fit together so that they become air-tight. And now we don't need them any longer for gardening purposes."

He paused and smiled widely. The other two men waited for him to continue.

"We can put them all to use in the cave," he explained. "We can place them at the openings we've made between the different tunnels, and use them to seal certain areas, then pump oxygen into those sealed areas. After we do that we'll be able to walk around inside the sealed sections without needing to wear our helmets. We'll have all kinds of room down there just to walk around in!"

The other two men contemplated this idea for a few seconds, then Allen said, "Why on Earth didn't I think of that?"

"Because we're not on Earth anymore," Mishra replied.

Several others had the same reaction as Allen when they were told about the idea, so the next day Justin headed out to Jeanne with Mishra, Morel, Manfredi, and several boxes which were filled with panels from the first garden. Allen stayed behind to keep an eye on Al-Arabi and Wu.

When the team arrived in the tunnels Mishra was given the lead in deciding where to set up the walls since the whole thing was his idea, so he ran about, tossing out suggestions and making a variety of bizarre predictions.

"We can place the first air barrier here," he said, pointing at the opening between the first tunnel which Justin had dug – heading straight into the side of Jeanne – and the ten by ten room to its right. "And then we can put the second barrier here," he suggested, indicating the opening between that room and the long sloping tunnel. "Then after that we can turn this entire sloping tunnel into a livable space. It can be a beautiful processional ramp, bringing people into our subterranean kingdom. We can carve flower boxes into the walls and decorate the whole thing with pieces of equipment we no longer use. Like when ancient hunters used to decorate their caves with pictures of the animals they hunted, to teach their children about their culture. All the children who are born up here will have special initiation rituals in this cave, and there will be music we can make with drums, and there'll be singing. It'll be wonderful!"

"Is there any way we can pull oxygen out a the water right here in the cave without taking it back to the electrolysis machine on the shuttle first?" Justin asked.

"There must be," Mishra assured him.

"Do you think you could figure out a way to do that?"

"Definitely not."

Following Mishra's basic plan, they began by turning the ten by ten room into a sealable space. They set up the panel walls, bolted them securely into the ground and into the tunnel wall, then arranged for the central panels of each panel wall to function as five foot by three foot doors, by linking up the panel sides marked S1 and S2, in the same manner as was done for the entry door to the garden's airlock. This task completed, they headed back to Bakersville.

The next day Justin returned to the cave with Mishra, Olambayo and Ritter, plus more panels for the walls which would be built inside the long sloping tunnel. They also brought several extra tanks of oxygen as well as the water transporter.

The four of them gathered water from the low-ceilinged cave and transported it back up to the ten by ten room. Then they mixed the water with dirt in that room to create mud, which was packed into the thin spaces between the man-made walls and the cave walls' rims. It wasn't a perfect solution for trapping air inside the room but, once it all dried, they then taped and bolted pieces of packing foam – taken from inside the boxes which had been unloaded on the shuttle – along all the panel walls' mud-caked edges. When this was done they drove back to Bakersville, leaving behind some of the unused oxygen tanks.

The following day Justin again drove to the cave, this time with Mishra, Morel, Suarez, and several more oxygen tanks. The two geologists – Morel and Suarez – were particularly excited by the prospect of spending extended periods of time sitting in the cave and examining rocks without wearing a restricting helmet on their heads.

After checking to make sure that all the newly constructed walls remained securely in place, the team opened up ten of the oxygen tanks and allowed the tanks' contents to pour into the room. Mishra had brought an atmospheric gauge with him and after twenty-two minutes it told him that the oxygen concentration in the room was sufficient to allow for healthy human breathing.

"It is time," he declared with a brave smile. "Now, may I claim the privilege of being the first human to breath freely in a Martian cave?"

The others were impressed by the dignity of his request and they were also pleased to not have to be the guinea pigs themselves so they nodded solemnly and then waited to see what happened to him.

Mishra inhaled and, with his eyes closed, he lifted off his helmet. Then he exhaled. As soon as the exhalation was complete his eyes popped open and he shot nervous glances at his companions. Then he inhaled.

As his chest expanded Mishra's eyebrows simultaneously rose up his forehead, then he exhaled once more, and waited.

"I'm fine!" He declared, excitedly.

The other three breathed with relief.

"I'm fine!" He said again. "I'm fine! Ha ha!" Then he set down his helmet and began singing.

"No, no!" Morel stopped him. "You're going to create too much carbon monoxide too quickly. We need to conserve the air in here."

Mishra stuck out his lower lip to pout and set his hands on his hips but after a moment he nodded and said, "Yes, you are right. Okay fine."

The other men's helmets were promptly removed and all of them began savoring the gulps of oxygen.

"Ahhhhh," Suarez said. "That's the sweetest air I think I've ever breathed.

Morel nodded, inhaling deeply and smiling. "It reminds me of the air in Annecy. That's a town on a lake in Eastern France, on the way to the Alps, where the air always smells like flowers. This smells even better."

"Man, it's just nice to be able to take that helmet off down here," Justin said.

"Man oh man," Mishra added, gleaming.

They all sat down on the room's floor and breathed as gently as possible to conserve oxygen, speaking only a little, feeling nearly drunk on the air. While they sat there Morel and Suarez casually began inspecting the rocks which lay around them, smiling unconsciously. As they did so Justin studied their faces, noting that these two appeared content with the way things were going and were thus natural allies for him against Al-Arabi and Wu.

In the days that followed, all the other crew members aside from Al-Arabi – who only wanted to tend the garden and who was annoyed at having her workforce repeatedly thinned out – and Wu – who wanted to support Al-Arabi – were taken to the cave to enjoy an underground oxygen bath.

More panels were brought to the cave during each of these trips in order to create walls at various intervals within the thin sloping tunnel, and doors were set within each of these walls. More oxygen tanks were likewise carted to the cave and the original tanks were refilled back on the shuttle and then brought out again so that in total there were twenty tanks in the cave at any given time. With all these tanks in use the colonists were able to supply sufficient oxygen to three separate fifteen foot-long rooms inside the thin sloping tunnel for approximately twelve hours.

Morel and Suarez were naturally eager to engage in even longer stays at Jeanne in order to conduct rock examinations, and Justin wanted to indulge them, so he checked in with Baker and asked if it was possible to disconnect the electrolysis machine from the shuttle and periodically transport the machine out to the cave.

"Are you sure you really want to do that?" Baker asked.

"I am. Having people out in the cave is the best way to keep Al-Arabi from claiming center stage in what we're doing up here."

"The best way to keep her from claiming center stage is to have Allen bully her and everybody else and then for you to get rid of Allen."

"We're not there yet."

"But you could get things there very quickly if you wanted."

"It's too soon. Trust me – I'm up here, I can gauge the mood."

Baker nodded. "Alright. But if you're going to have two groups, in two different places, they'll be harder to control, especially since you haven't established real dominance yet."

Justin shrugged. "The geologists just want to sit around and look at rocks."

"Perhaps, but now others may want to spend extended stretches in the cave as well, and obviously I can't monitor the ones who are down in the tunnels so I won't be able to assist you in that way."

Justin nodded. "I think it's worth the risk."

Baker studied him for a few seconds, then said, "Alright. I'll ask my people about it."

The following day Baker informed Justin that it was possible to extract the electrolysis machine from the round room's wall and take it to the cave. But it would be ill-advised to do so before sufficient water was on reserve in the shuttle's water tanks.

The next few days were thus spent conducting multiple water runs between Bakersville and the cave in order to load-up the shuttle's system with both water and oxygen. Then Ritter deprogrammed the electrolysis machine's connections to the shuttle's computer system, after which the machine was removed from its embedded place within the wall.

This done, the machine – which was a metal rectangle and about the size of a one-drawer filing cabinet, like the microwave machine and the water storage receptacle – was loaded onto the rover along with extension hoses and driven to the cave. Manfredi, Ritter and Olambayo joined Justin for the drive.

When they arrived at the cave they placed the machine inside the ten by ten room, hooked it up to an extension hose, then hooked that hose to another and then that one to another and so on until they could connect the entire hose line to the hose they'd previously stuck down in the water hole. Within minutes a fresh supply of oxygen was pouring into the ten by ten room.

XV

Al-Arabi was irate. She didn't appreciate having members of her gardening crew siphoned off for work in the cave; she particularly didn't like the idea of them spending multiple days away from the garden, and she hated the fact that the Bakersville water supply – her garden's water supply – was potentially about to be interrupted. Wu, in the role of Al-Arabi's champion and defender, was irate as well.

They glowered together in the garden the next day, while the rover rolled away, transporting Justin and the geologists to the cave so that the latter two could engage in extended rock-observational bliss. The rover had been loaded up with extra food supplies to last Suarez and Morel for a forty-eight hour cycle.

It required a force of will for Justin to suppress the pleasure he was feeling as he drove back into Bakersville that afternoon. He'd cut into Al-Arabi's sense of authority by depriving her – at least temporarily – of some of her workers, and he'd done it without killing anybody. His happiness was then amplified when he saw Malenkov – his second favorite colonist after Megan – waiting to greet him as he parked the rover near the shuttle.

"O Captain! My Captain!" She said when he stepped off the rover. He had no idea that she was quoting from Walt Whitman – the only bit of American poetry she knew – but it sounded good to him.

"Hey there," he replied, smiling.

"So they're all set up out at the cave?"

"Yep. Snug as two bugs."

"…What?"

"They're all set up out there."

"Oh, good. Yes, in fact I wanted to talk to you about the cave."

"Oh yeah? What's on your mind?"

She shrugged. "Robert and I have been talking, and we mentioned it to Edgar too, that now that it looks like the water supply is extensive, we would really like – to be honest with you, we are sort of dying – to get a chance to explore down in the ice and see what we can find in the form of organic matter."

Justin nodded. "I'll bet. And it looks like we've tapped into a big water source. So yeah, I'm for it."

Malenkov clapped her hands and embraced him. Then she clapped some more.

Justin was happy to make her happy and he was also pleased to have another reason to rotate colonists out to the cave for extended stays so as to further prevent Al-Arabi from consolidating control. But he knew it didn't make sense to have half the crew away from the garden at any one time. The ten scientists were all sixty years old and over, after all, and putting in half a day in the garden – about five hours – per person, with a crew of seven or eight, was ideal for maximizing the gardening workload. In addition to which Justin had registered Baker's warning about having too many people out at the cave on their own for too long without him. All this implied, therefore, that he'd have to rotate people out to the cave in groups of no more than three at a time.

The next day he broke the news to Al-Arabi. "Adiba," he told her, "tomorrow I'm gonna take the biologists to the cave to see what they can find in the ice. I'm gonna let them stay out there for forty-eight hours, like Suarez and Morel, but I'll be bringing Suarez and Morel back here with me after I drop off the others."

"What? You're taking more people out there? But we can't spare them!"

"We're rotating them. They're not all gonna be there at the same time."

"But this is crazy! First you send out two, now you're sending out three? We're all going to die if we don't get this garden going!"

"Are you trying to kill us?" Wu added for good measure.

"You'll still have seven workers plus some a my time too. It'll be fine."

Al-Arabi set her hands on her hips and shook her head. Wu did likewise.

Justin nodded curtly, then he turned and walked away, wearing a small smile on his face which they couldn't see.

The following day Justin headed out to Jeanne accompanied by Allen, Olambayo and Malenkov, along with extra food supplies. When he got there he picked up Suarez and Morel, who were reluctant to return to

Bakersville.

"It was so nice to have some peace and quiet," Morel told him as the three of them rode away from the cave.

"So nice," Suarez added.

"We'll get you back there soon," Justin assured them.

But it wouldn't be soon enough as far as they were concerned.

The following morning, while Justin was taking a stroll around the Bakersville perimeter, Suarez approached him, looking vexed.

"I can't take it!" He said, breathless, without further explanation.

"Whad' ya mean?"

"Adiba – she's a garden Nazi! She can't stop ordering me and everyone else around. It's driving me crazy!"

"Yeah, but we all gotta do it. The garden's important."

"So is geology! And besides, she doesn't have to act like that!"

"I've talked to her. I'll talk to her again."

Suarez wasn't fully satisfied with that answer but he nodded, took a deep breath and walked back towards the big tent.

Later that day Morel approached Justin when they both happened to be foraging for food in the shuttle's top floor container spaces.

"Monsieur mon capitaine," Morel said in a pleasant, conspiratorial tone, sidling up beside him.

"Georges – what's up?"

"Alors, tell me…do you believe in true love?"

"What?"

"Love. True love. Do you believe in it?"

"Uh…sure. Why?"

"So if you believe in something that is pure and absolute then you must also believe in its opposite, yes?"

"Uh…."

"If there is true love then there must also be true hate, yes?"

"Uh…."

"And in that regard I have to say that I've made a very important discovery. I have realized, today, after all these years, that there must be such a thing as true love because I find myself experiencing something that can only be described as true hate."

"You…?"

"I've never found pleasure in gardening. I've been married twice.

The first marriage ended because the woman was insane and the second marriage ended because I refused to work in the garden. I don't know that I hated the work, but I didn't like it. And now I find myself here on Mars, and I have to be honest with you, I genuinely do not care for Madame Al-Arabi. She's simply too much. And my feelings about her have fused with my feelings about gardening. When you take all those feelings together, you arrive at hate. True hate. And as I say, that means that there must also be true love. So in a way it's a beautiful revelation. But the point is – I hate her."

Justin nodded. "Okay...."

"All I want from life is a little peace and quiet so that I can look at Martian rocks. And I'd also like to eat a few more good meals."

"Sure...."

"Which leads me, mon capitaine, to make a simple request: from now on I wish to be permanently excused from gardening duty."

Justin smiled at him sympathetically. "I already talked 'bout that with Suarez. As much as I'd like to leave you guys out of it, we all gotta do some time in the garden."

Morel shook his head. "I am French, so I protest."

Justin smiled some more. "You're protesting? How?"

Morel crossed his arms, hunched his shoulders and pushed out his lower lip to sulk. "Like this."

"Ha!"

"You think I'm joking?"

"No, I don't think you're joking."

And he wasn't. The sulking lasted for the entire next day.

Even when Justin drove the two geologists back to Jeanne on the morning thereafter, he sensed their annoyance at having been compelled to spend so much time in the garden. They barely spoke to him when they offloaded their supplies and then repelled down into Jeanne.

Allen picked up on this vibe when he and the other two biologists greeted Suarez and Morel at the bottom of the cave.

"What was eating those other two?" Allen asked after he reached the surface and then climbed onto the rover with Malenkov and Olambayo.

"Gardening," Justin answered.

"Ahh, I see."

"We didn't find any life forms in the water," Malenkov admitted, sounding disappointed but not defeated.

Justin nodded. "I figured you'd a told me and been jumping up and down."

"What we did find though," Olambayo added, "was a lot more ice. We drilled more holes, all of them bigger than the first one, and everywhere we dug we hit thick ice."

"Good news!"

"And where there's water there's life!" Malenkov declared.

"Right!"

The ride back to Bakersville was pleasant enough, but while they rode along Justin couldn't help wondering if things might not get worse with the geologists. There was no real way to placate them since it was necessary for everyone to do their shift in the garden. And there was no way to placate Al-Arabi and Wu either since they'd only be satisfied if everyone was working in the garden full-time.

Or in other words the group dynamics were developing as Baker had warned him they would. And this was something that he – Justin – had already known might occur even without Baker mentioning it. These were the same dynamics which had arisen with the first group of five men. Without a strong point of command, you get factions, and factions lead to fights. The difference now, as opposed to with the first group, was that he didn't have the option of joining a faction and since certain factions were growing progressively less pleased with his leadership he might wind up with at least half the crew turning against him.

The following afternoon Justin and Allen found an opportunity to hold another covert conversation.

"Manfredi is now fully with the garden witches," Allen told him.

"Is that right?"

"Quite. They spent all last evening complaining about you. Those other two don't particularly care for Manfredi but they do enjoy having someone to complain with, and Manfredi is good at complaining."

Justin shook his head. "I never did anything to her."

Allen shrugged. "That's not really the point."

"Guess not. And what about the others?"

"I think Malenkov and Olambayo will be fine as long as they can keep studying ice. Ritter clearly doesn't like Manfredi and she isn't crazy about Al-Arabi or Wu, so you don't need to worry about her, I don't think.

And Mishra is Mishra; whenever Al-Arabi comes near him he just smiles and heads off to some other part of the garden."

Justin contemplated this intel. Then later that evening he checked in with Baker and mentioned the geologists' escalating annoyance.

"I seem to recall saying that I thought the whole living-in-a-cave idea wasn't the best," Baker reminded him.

"The cave isn't the problem. It's the people you sent up here."

"Oh I beg to differ. It's not those people I sent up there at all. It's the fact they are, simply, people. If I'd sent you ten golden retrievers then your situation would certainly have been much simpler."

"If Al-Arabi wasn't so crazy I think this would've been more manageable."

"But she's not crazy. Neither is Wu. Neither is Manfredi. Nor are any of the rest of them. That's the point. Sooner or later you were going to reach this stage. It just so happens that the situation is compounded by the fact that some people have begun treating themselves to extended cave vacations."

"Being in the cave makes some of them really happy."

"But my dear Justin, Bakersville isn't supposed to be the capital city of a subterranean civilization. You're human beings. You're meant to live above ground. When the next spaceships land up there they'll each be carrying added cargo-chambers which NASA is designing for the *Orion* models. Those chambers will be packed with equipment and materials for erecting a network of enclosed walkways and recreational spaces which'll be made out of material like what we're using for the garden's canopy. It's going to be wonderful for all of you. You'll have plenty of space to move around in, above ground. That's the vision we want for you. Not for you to live like Martian cavemen or to burrow underground like some colony of Martian moles."

"But what 'bout the symbolism a the cave? You said it was Plato, right, who wrote 'bout most people living inside the cave? And you said Machiavelli wanted us to accept that fact and deal with it."

"Yes, well, you see the thing about Plato's allegory of the cave is that it happens to be an allegory. The cave of political reality that I want you to inhabit is very much above ground."

Justin considered this point. "Speaking a political reality, I think it's time…to put Allen in charge, officially, as my second-in-command.

And to announce it to everybody."

"My thoughts precisely."

"But so how do I do that without it seeming like I'm giving up my authority? How did Cesare Borgia do it? I'm thinking the only way to do it is for me to be sort a out a the picture somehow."

"Agreed. So why don't you inform the rest of the crew that you've received orders from down here directing you to go explore Arsia Mons? That will give you an excuse to be away from Bakersville as much as seems useful."

"That's actually exactly what I was thinking."

"Excellent. I'll type up an order, make it look official, then send it up there to the screen in the round room so they all can read it."

"That'll work."

XVI

Justin woke up around 3:00 the next morning with a gasp and in a sweat. He woke up Megan in the process.

She pressed the back of her hand against his sweaty brow. "Same type of dream as before?"

"Not entirely. There were more people in it this time."

"Who?"

"The crew."

"Was I in it?"

"No, and I'm glad."

They shared some moments in silence, then Justin told her, "The time's come when I've gotta make some pretty hard decisions...."

She nodded, as her lips tightened.

"Some a the crew are starting to get out a control."

She nodded some more. "I can see it."

"And it'll only get worse unless I do something 'bout it."

"Like what?"

"I'm gonna put Allen in charge as my second-in-command and let him absorb some a their anger. Then after he's done that I'll step back in again."

She thought about this. "Do you think he's up for it?"

"Baker and I've been talkin' 'bout it. Allen's the right guy for the job."

"And you think you definitely have to do this now?"

He nodded. "Wu, Al-Arabi and Manfredi are against me. Suarez and Morel are only gonna get unhappier the longer they've gotta work in the garden. I know I can count on Allen to be on my side, and same with Malenkov, and probably Mishra too. And I think Ritter is with me 'cause she still tries to flirt with me."

Megan rolled her eyes.

"It's only 'cause I'm the head a the colony."

"And because you're a younger man."

"I think that's secondary."

"It's a fact."

"Yeah, but still, the point is if she's with me then Olambayo will probably go along with her. But all a that might be temporary. And if one more person turns against me I'll have a serious problem. We all will."

"So you're just going to turn things over to Allen for a while?"

Justin explained the plan that he and Baker came up with, about pretending to do research on the mountain.

Megan nodded again.

Then they lay awake for a long while, not saying anything.

Around 9:00 that same morning Justin and Allen held another of their covert conversations, which turned out to be *the* conversation; the one that had been in the cards for a long time coming.

"Look," Justin told him, "later today I'm gonna let the whole crew know that I've been given orders from the people in Nevada to go explore Arsia Mons."

"No kidding?"

"Yeah. They want me to go check it out. Which means I'm gonna be spending most a each day out there."

"Do you…do you really think that this is the opportune time to start doing that, to be away from the crew so much? I'm getting the feeling that things could begin to get out of hand without you around."

Justin nodded. "I agree. That's what I told Nevada. But they say science is the first priority. And they need me to go check things out. So that's where you come in."

"Me?"

"Yeah. It's time to give you a promotion. You're not just my spy any more. Now you're gonna be my second-in-command, officially."

"Second-in-command…officially?"

"Yeah."

"I…."

"I need you to step up and do what's right for the colony. To make sure everyone stays in line while I'm not here."

"I, um.…"

"I know you can do it. You're the right man for the job."

"Well, sure.…"

"You've got my blessing to do whatever it takes to make sure that things don't get out a control."

"I….Whatever it takes?"

"Whatever it takes."

Allen nodded. He looked worried. The more he thought about it, however, the more he also looked pleased. Then he took a deep breath and said, "Yes, yes, okay, sure. I can do that. I'd be proud to do it. Of course."

"Great. I knew I could count on you."

"Sure," Allen said again.

"So the first thing I want you to do is let the other biologists know that I won't be taking any a you out to the cave today when I go pick up Suarez and Morel. Then when I get back I'll explain to the whole crew 'bout the orders I received from Nevada and how I'm putting you in as second-in-command."

Allen nodded. "Okay. I can do that." He was still processing the responsibility that he was about to be given.

Justin didn't want to shake Allen's hand, because that would make the lie taste all the more bitter in his mouth, but he knew that a handshake was what would be expected at such a moment so he shook the man's hand and then gave him a congratulatory nod.

Later that day Justin drove out to the cave and collected Morel and Suarez.

"Where are the biologists?" Suarez asked. "You're not dropping them off?"

"No, not today."

"So we could've stayed here longer?" Morel asked as he climbed onto the rover.

"No, we're gonna have a crew meeting and everybody needs to be there. Then tomorrow I'm gonna drive the biologists out here."

"A crew meeting…about what?" Suarez asked, a little nervously, exchanging a glance with Morel.

"I've got new orders from the people in Nevada. I'm gonna brief everybody 'bout it."

"Does it have to do with the garden?"

"No, it has to do with that mountain," Justin replied as he pointed towards Arsia Mons, off in the distance.

"Oh," Suarez said, relieved.

"Speaking of the garden," Morel added, as the rover rolled away from the cave, "Oscar and I have been discussing that situation."

"Oh yeah?"

"Yes. And we've made a decision."

Despite the fact that they were bouncing along on the rover, and even though Morel was sitting behind him, Justin could sense an increase in tension between the three of them. He got the feeling that Morel was seizing an opportunity to say something that he – Justin – wasn't going to like; an opportunity which allowed for there to be two against one.

"What's that?" Justin asked.

"We've decided," Morel stated, matter-of-factly, "that we're not going to work in the garden anymore."

"But I've already told you both that we need you to do it. We can rotate you but we can't cut you out of it completely."

"Non," Morel replied. "We've decided. We're not going to do it. The plants will grow without us. That's it."

Justin shot a look to his right, at Suarez, who was staring straight ahead, assiduously avoiding eye contact.

"I get that you don't wanna do it," Justin said, "but it's not up to the two a you – it's up to me. And I'm making the call."

"By what authority?" Morel demanded, his voice suddenly shrill.

"The authority I was given by those people down in Nevada. You know that. You all got the briefing 'fore they sent you up here."

Morel shook his head. "You have authority to oversee the general security of the camp, not to make specific decisions about other things, not without giving the rest of us a vote."

"What're you talking 'bout? That wasn't part a the briefing."

"It's a basic principle of democratic government!"

"Since when was this a democracy?"

Morel was aghast. "You're saying it's not?"

"Course it's not! Have you been paying attention? I give orders and the rest a you follow them. That's how it's been since you got here!"

"Non! You've been giving us directions, introducing us to the way things work up here. Directions are different than orders. If I'd known you were giving orders and not directions I never would have accepted it!"

"What are you talking 'bout? Nevada's plan for how things should run up here couldn't a been clearer. I'm in charge! And now you're just making stuff up!"

"Non!"

Suarez said nothing.

Eventually they arrived back in Bakersville and when they did the three men dismounted the rover without saying a word. Morel stomped dramatically to the ground to register his disgust, then he grabbed Suarez by the arm and led him away, presumably so that the two of them could go commiserate together.

"Meeting in half an hour in the round room," Justin reminded the two of them as they hurried off. They didn't reply.

Justin watched them walk away, then remained standing next to the rover for a minute, collecting his thoughts. As he did so, Allen emerged from the garden and walked over to him.

"Hello there," Allen said in a buoyant mood, still drinking in the realization that he was about to become second-in-command.

"Hey. Look, I need you to tell everyone that we're gonna hold that meeting in the round room in half an hour. Everybody needs to be there."

"Can do. By the way, we had a little drama while you were away. Manfredi tried to enforce the writ of Al-Arabi with Ritter and Ritter told Manfredi a bunch of things in German that I didn't understand but didn't need to, if you know what I mean. I stepped in between them so that they couldn't get physical, but I thought I should let you know."

Justin rolled his eyes. "Thanks."

Half an hour later the full group – the ten scientists plus Megan and Justin – assembled in the round room, standing in front of the TV screen. On the screen was the following statement:

Greetings to our brave astronauts from your friends in the Nevada facility. We send you our praise! We want to let you know how excited we are that the garden is progressing so quickly and that you are exploring for life in the ice. What could possibly be more important? You are all heroes and we salute you!

In light of all the rapid progress that is being made thanks to your excellent teamwork, we have decided to initiate the next phase of our colonization plan.

This involves the surveying of Arsia Mons. We want to get an on-the-ground understanding of the mountain's contours and general characteristics. In order to do that we need Mr. Jones to conduct a series of reconnaissance missions on the mountain. We therefore want him to make daily trips out there for the next few weeks.

Please support him in this effort by staying on track with all your tasks. And in general, keep up the great work!

"So there it is," Justin said. "Tomorrow I'll start in on that."

Various members of the crew exchanged various sorts of glances with various other members of the crew. Wu, Al-Arabi, Manfredi, Suarez and Morel were all pleased by the prospect of Justin spending time away from both Bakersville and Jeanne. Ritter was also pleased, insofar as she planned to start defying the Al-Arabi team more openly – even though she still intended to work in the garden – and she could do that more easily without Justin around. Olambayo and Malenkov, however, worried about what might transpire while Justin was away now that tensions among the crew were starting to build. Mishra, meanwhile, thought it was wonderful that Justin was going to explore that beautiful mountain. As for Allen, he stood waiting, nervously and excitedly, for the next announcement.

"And when I'm not here," Justin continued, "Edgar is gonna be in charge."

Allen took a deep breath, smiled stiffly to the rest of the group and gave a curt nod.

"What?" Manfredi said, shocked.

"When I'm not here, he's in command," Justin reiterated.

"Why him?" Morel asked.

"Because I chose him."

"But," Wu protested, "you can't just choose other people to be in charge."

"Excuse me? Why can't I?"

Wu wasn't sure what to say in response to this, so she frowned.

"Justin," Malenkov asked, "could I go with you to the mountain? I'd love to see what it's like up there?"

"No." And he shook his head but hated to lie to her. "I need to go alone. I'll be riding around a lot a rough terrain and we can't risk having another person on the rover. It's a safety precaution. And the less I need to worry 'bout someone else the freer I'll be to react to any situation that might come up."

Malenkov nodded, disappointed but also instantly resigned to his decision.

Ritter, meanwhile, was smiling ironically. "So then," she said to Allen with a suggestive role of her words, "now you're going to be the big captain."

"I serve at the pleasure of the real one," Allen replied deftly, but he was clearly pleased by her sudden attention, which he'd tried in vain to obtain since they'd first arrived on Mars.

Olambayo tried not to frown.

"Before I head out a here tomorrow morning," Justin continued, "I just wanna say that I know some a you are having different ideas 'bout working in the garden and 'bout how the garden should be run. And how much time to spend in the cave and who gets to do that. I know some a you've got issues. What I want to say is that we all need to remember why we're here. We're here to make sure the human race has a second chance. And we're here to try and find alien life. Those things are really, really important. So we need to set our priorities and focus on the big picture. Whatever issues come up 'tween us, we need to solve them peacefully. We need to be reasonable with each other. And when I'm away that means you need to follow Edgar's lead. You do that, and everything's gonna be fine. Okay?"

He said this last word forcefully in order to elicit nods, and a few of them gave him the nods he was looking for, but he was fairly certain that the crew as a whole wasn't going to follow his advice and that things were not, in fact, going to be fine.

XVII

Arsia Mons absorbed the entire horizon as Justin drove towards it. At long last he was going to get acquainted with this mountain which had loomed off in the distance all this time like a massive metaphorical question mark about the future – something to be explored, understood, and if possible, conquered.

He'd already dropped off Malenkov and Olambayo at the cave so they could conduct another forty-eight hour research stint, then he'd turned the rover south and headed towards the mountain.

The rover began climbing Arsia Mons' gently sloping base with ease while Justin dodged the larger rocks and skirted ditches and cratered spaces. The physical experience of ascending the massive slope triggered a psychological response inside him: a feeling that he was rising above all the petty turmoil which was beginning to boil back at Bakersville. And as this sense of liberation took hold he felt tempted to just keep driving higher and higher and not stop until he reached the mountain's peak.

Baker had shown him an image of the mountaintop. It consisted of a vast, partially sunken central space – called a caldera – surrounded by a higher rim of land: a hard place to get to, an easy place to defend, and with the central portion protected from all the winds that rolled up the mountain's sides. Perhaps someday they'd set up their second town there, and call it Jonesville. Or perhaps, if things got truly crazy with the other colonists back in Bakersville, he'd take Megan and their child and relocate with them permanently to that place.

But not yet. For the moment his primary objective was to find a comfortable place to sit and wait.

He located an ideal spot a few hundred feet up the mountainside; it was a smooth-surfaced rock which jutted out from the mountain's slope, paralleling the flatland of the plain below. He parked the rover so that its wheels angled horizontally to the slope and then he dismounted, grabbed a backpack off the rover and went and sat down on the rock.

"Hello there," Baker said, after Justin switched on his helmet's mic, which he'd kept turned off until that point so that he could enjoy the silence and the solitude.

"Hey Baker."

"Enjoying the view?"

"Yeah. It's nice up here."

"Makes you feel like you're above it all?"

"Exactly."

"I know that feeling. I have a house in Colorado on the side of a mountain. That's precisely how I feel whenever I'm up there."

"So…how many houses do you have?"

"A few."

"In different countries?"

"Yes."

"Which ones? Which countries?"

"Does it matter? They're countries you're never going to see. You might as well forget they exist."

Justin nodded, and smiled sadly. "Yeah, maybe so.…"

"By the way, on another topic, I want to compliment you on your lying technique. You really are getting quite expert in that regard. The way you pulled off that lie to Malenkov about not being able to take anyone else up there with you for, what did you say, safety reasons? Honestly, you said it so naturally I almost believed it myself."

Justin smiled a bit wider while his eyes looked all the more sad. "I've had a good teacher."

"Yes you have."

A long silence ensued, as soft Martian breezes rolled slowly up the mountainside. Eventually Justin asked Baker, "How long do you think it's gonna take for things to get going down there?"

"You mean for Allen to get violent?"

"Yeah."

"Not long. I've hired many middle managers in my time and I'm certain that Allen is going to be a total disaster. He's what I call a 'category three.' A category one is someone who can be put in command and then exerts their authority effectively to keep everyone in line. A category two is someone who can't exert their will and then gives up. A category three is someone who fails to exert their will and gets angry and then instead of giving up gets desperate."

"Which is what you want, right?"

"It's what *we* want, yes."

"Right."

This thought hung in the air for a few moments, then Baker said, "Now then, shall we begin to observe?"

"Sure."

Justin unzipped his backpack and took out a small tablet computer which Baker had instructed him to bring along. When he pressed the power button the screen flicked on and showed eight video camera views. One view provided a live feed of the shuttle's round room, another camera was focused on the shuttle's hallway and cockpit, two cameras were angled to the container spaces along that hallway, another had a panorama shot of the outside area in between the ships and the garden, one was set up inside the *Orion's* main room, and there were two shots inside the garden.

It felt creepy to suddenly see Bakersville from the same vantage points which Baker had been enjoying for these last few months. Creepy and empowering.

Justin was relieved to see that his living quarters weren't on any of the screens. He'd advised Megan to stay inside those quarters as much as possible while he was away on the mountain, in case things started to get out of control in Bakersville. And it looked like she'd followed his advice. She wasn't on any of the screens.

As for the others: Wu was walking out of the garden and heading towards the shuttle; Suarez and Morel were sitting at the round room's counter; Al-Arabi, Manfredi, Mishra, Ritter and Allen were all working in the garden.

'So,' Justin thought, 'this is what it's like to sit up on the mountain and look down on the people, like Machiavelli talked 'bout.'

He found it hard to resist the feeling of pride which accompanied this perspective. Although of course he wasn't yet sitting all the way up on the mountaintop. That spot was still reserved for Baker.

"You've really got this whole thing wired," Justin said.

"I try."

"You do more than that. This is really something, frankly."

"Thank you."

"The more this whole project goes along, the more I can see how you've thought everything out."

"I appreciate that." Baker sounded genuinely flattered. "It's taken a lot of doing. I'm glad my protégé is able to recognize that."

"The more I recognize it, honestly, the more honored I feel to be your protégé."

There was silence, and then Baker said, "Thank you, Justin. That means a lot to me. You're like a son to me. I'm pleased we've arrived at a point where we're both on the exact same page."

"It's pretty much the only page to be on. I can see that now."

"It *is* the only page. Everything we're doing is simply the outcome of rational analysis. That colony is necessary. A prince is necessary. And now, what's about to happen next – that's necessary too."

"I'm kind a curious to watch it happen."

"Good."

And happen it did, there in front them on the screens, while they were talking.

Wu had boarded the shuttle, then taken off her helmet and walked indignantly into the round room to confront Suarez and Morel.

"What are you two doing?" She demanded to know.

"We are sitting and talking," Morel replied. "I would have thought that that was obvious."

"Why aren't you working in the garden?"

"Because we don't want to work in the garden."

Suarez tensed up as the other two spoke; this was evident even on the video screen.

"You have to!" Wu retorted.

"No we don't. We are free, autonomous beings. We are that way by nature," Morel explained.

"What are you talking about?"

"Have you ever read Rousseau?"

"What?" Wu's voice rose a few decibels.

The more animated she became the calmer Morel seemed to get, obviously enjoying the experience of making her angry. "Jean-Jacques Rousseau," he replied.

Wu shook her head, disgusted. "You two need to get out to that garden now!"

"Non," Morel said, with insulting calm.

Wu stared at the two geologists for a few seconds, then stormed out of the round room, spent several awkward moments fastening on her helmet, then exited the shuttle and charged across the open ground to the garden.

"They're just sitting in there!" She told Al-Arabi as she entered the garden and pulled off her helmet.

"Why aren't they out here working?"

"They say they don't want to!"

"But they have to!"

"That's what I told them!"

"Allen," Al-Arabi half-yelled, turning to the second-in-command, who was kneeling in the lettuce patch, "you're supposed to be in charge! You need to go in there and tell Suarez and Morel that they have to come out here!"

"Don't you yell at me!" Allen shot back at her.

"But Justin said you have to handle things!" Wu interjected, not quite yelling at him but with her voice loud and pinched nonetheless.

"Listen you two," Allen declared, rising to his feet, "I'm not taking any rubbish from you! If you have a problem then you can tell me about it calmly and politely and I'll listen to what you have to say. If you have a complaint – fine, tell me about it. But we're all going to stay civilized about this. No one gets to give orders around here other than Justin, and when he's not here, it's me. Understand?"

"You can't talk to us like that!" Wu countered.

"You heard what Justin said – I have the authority! That's final!"

"We need workers in this garden!" Al-Arabi protested. "If some people don't do their fair share then we're all going to die up here!"

"Fine! I'll go talk to Suarez and Morel. If you're asking me to do that, I'm happy to talk to them. But if you're trying to order me around, forget it!"

Wu pressed her hands together and bent forward slightly. "Dear Mr. Edgar Allen," she said with mock solicitousness, "would you please be so kind as to ask Suarez and Morel to come out here and do their work so that the rest of us don't die? Thank you very much, kind sir."

"Fine," Allen replied unpleasantly, then he grabbed his helmet and strode to the garden's airlock. A few moments later he exited through the airlock's external door and headed across the open ground to the shuttle.

"This should be interesting," Baker observed.

"He's even worse than Justin," Wu said to Al-Arabi.

"They're the same," Al-Arabi replied. "They want to control things they can't control. If they wanted to run a garden so badly they should have studied how to do it."

"That Adiba is a menace," Justin said to Baker.

"But she' acting logically," Baker noted. "After all, she does know best how to run that garden. And so she wants the authority to run it. The fact that she's convinced herself that she's acting in the best interest of the colony simply reinforces her perspective."

Justin shook his head and exhaled.

Allen, meanwhile, had entered the shuttle and was walking into the round room.

"Greetings gents," he said to Morel and Suarez in a conciliatory tone, obviously trying to win them over by conveying his sympathy for their situation.

Neither of them said anything in reply.

"I hear you're not all that inclined to take part in the gardening."

Again, neither of the other two spoke.

"I can't say I blame you."

"If you're here to try to persuade us to do it nonetheless," Morel told him, "the answer is non. We refuse."

Allen nodded and sat down at the counter, trying to seem relaxed. "I understand."

"So then we don't have to do it?" Suarez asked, sounding nervous but also relieved.

"No, mate, I'm afraid you do. There isn't any choice."

"There is always a choice," Morel shot back, as his decibel level inched up a few notches.

"We all need to do our part," Allen said. "Fair's fair."

Morel shook his head. "Have you read Jean-Paul Sarte?"

"No....Why?"

"He has a play, *No Exit*, in which some people are stuck in a room together forever after they die, and one of the characters concludes – and certainly this was Sartre's view – that "hell is other people." Alors, I'm beginning to think he was right!"

"Georges, we're not in hell, we're on Mars – there *is* a difference. And all I'm asking you to do is a little gardening."

"Then fire that Cleopatra! Gardening is unpleasant enough without being ordered around by an Egyptian dictator!"

"We can't fire her – she's the one trained to run a garden."

"If she stays there then we stay here!"

"Georges, Oscar, look," Allen said, raising his voice while rising from his chair and pointing towards the shuttle's airlock, "you need to get out there!"

"Non!"

Baker chuckled.

"You're right," Justin said, "he's a category three."

"Indeed."

When Allen returned to the garden he informed Al-Arabi and Wu that, "They're not coming out."

"A lot of use you are!" Wu snapped.

"Don't you talk to me like that!" Allen snapped back.

A few minutes later Ritter walked up to Allen and began working beside him. "Tell me," she said, "why do you think Justin chose you to be the second-in-command?"

Allen shrugged. "How should I know? He just told me that that's what he wanted."

"But don't you think Robert would be a more suitable candidate? After all, he's stronger than you are."

"Robert wouldn't hurt a fly!" Allen spat out the words, wounded by her statement.

"So that's why you were chosen then – because you hurt flies?"

"That's not what I meant."

"Or maybe you think you're the *Lord of the Flies*."

"That's not what I meant either."

"Well clearly our captain sees something in you. You must have something going for you."

"You say that as if the thought never occurred to you."

"Maybe I haven't been giving it enough thought."

Justin laughed silently. "Now she's flirting with Allen."

"Naturally," Baker said. "She's attracted to power. You weren't available to her but he is and now he's there and Robert's away."

"Suzanne," Manfredi said to Ritter as she walked past Ritter and Allen, "you must be missing Robert, with him out at the cave while you're

here." The sarcasm in her voice dripped through the intercom system.

"Of course I am," Ritter hissed.

And Baker chuckled some more.

Justin remained up on the mountainside for the remainder of the day. Eventually a pink evening began settling over the Martian landscape so he climbed onto the rover and headed home.

When he arrived back at Bakersville he parked next to the shuttle and then walked quickly to his living quarters to avoid interacting with the others. In this he succeeded. Some crew members were gathered around the counter in the round room but they didn't seem to notice him. Only Mishra waved at him and smiled. And Allen was fixing himself a salad and didn't see Justin come in.

"Hey there," Justin greeted his wife as he descended the staircase into their private quarters and then pushed the remote to close the ceiling door above him.

"Hey there," she replied, stirring something in a pot.

"Here," he said, walking up behind her, "let me do that for you."

She smiled at him, although not too widely. As she set down her ladle and turned to face him he wrapped his arms gently around her waist and pressed his stomach against hers.

"Hello pregnant lady."

She smiled a bit wider, but then frowned. "I've been stuck down here all day."

"I know. I'm sorry. It'll only be for a little longer. The natives are getting restless. Pretty soon they'll have a better idea why they need your husband here."

She flashed her chef's knife smile at him. "I know why *I* need my husband here." Then she kissed him.

"Oh yeah?" He asked, as their lips separated. "Why's that?"

"You want me to explain it to you?"

"I do. But explain it slowly, 'cause I'm a slow learner."

She smiled again. "Slow is good."

Then they went and sat down on the couch and forgot about what they were cooking.

The following morning Justin set out again for Arsia Mons, this time driving twice as far up the mountain's rise. When he found another suitable rock outcropping he parked the rover, took the computer tablet out of his backpack and then settled in for another session of spying on his fellow colonists. Baker joined him for this activity, and they talked intermittently until lunchtime, at which point things took a dramatic turn back in Bakersville.

Morel and Suarez were eating at the round room's counter, having been the first to fix themselves lunch since they still refused to work in the garden and thus they'd already been sitting inside.

Then Allen walked into the round room and, without speaking to them, began making himself a salad, chopping up vegetables with one of the chef's knives.

Ritter came in next and grabbed a sandwich out of a refrigerator, then she took a seat at the counter, across from Suarez and Morel, and was soon joined there by Mishra, who settled in for a light meal of fruits and nuts.

Manfredi was the next to board the shuttle. Instead of taking a seat in the round room, however, she grabbed some spaghetti and meatballs out of a refrigerator and then went and sat down in one of the container spaces, in the spot where Al-Arabi and Wu liked to sit.

Those latter two soon arrived, and, as a protest against Suarez and Morel's own sit-in protest, they joined Manfredi in the container space, without bothering to walk into the round room to collect something to eat. Instead they searched through the remaining unpacked boxes and found some trail mix and beef jerky.

Meanwhile in the round room Allen finished chopping vegetables for his salad, then he tilted the chopping board and, using the chef's knife, slid the chopped pieces onto a plate and set the plate on the round counter. Before taking a seat, however, he looked sternly at Morel and Suarez and, still holding the knife, told them, "Listen, I think it's high time you two stopped fooling around. Justin's put me in charge, and I want both of you to go out to that garden and start working after you're through with lunch here."

Dead silence ensued. The three ladies out in the container space overheard Allen's statement and now they ceased talking as well in order to hear whatever happened next.

Morel glanced down at the knife that Allen was holding, then he glanced back up at Allen's face. "Edgar, are you…threatening us?"

"I'm simply telling you how it has to be."

"…While you're holding a rather large knife."

Allen paused before replying. Then he said, "You two need to get back out there."

"Mr. Edgar," Mishra asked, "what are you doing? What is going on?"

"I'm just trying to explain a very simple point to two very stubborn people."

"There are two chef's knives, Edgar," Morel observed. "Perhaps I should get the other one and then we can continue this conversation."

"Don't even think about it."

"But I already have thought about it. If I hadn't thought about it then I couldn't have stated the point I just made. That's a basic premise of cognitive theory."

"Stay where you are, Georges."

"That's been my plan all along, thank you. I'll see you back here at dinnertime."

"Stay where you are until you finish eating then go outside to the garden! You have to do it!" Allen's tone grew louder as he spoke. "Those are Justin's instructions and we have to follow his lead! I, for one, don't intend to let him down and we can't let down the people back in Nevada either! So after you two finish eating then you get back out there! Am I making myself perfectly clear?"

Morel shrugged. "Perhaps we will. Perhaps we won't."

Allen pointed the knife at Morel, "You think I'm fooling around?"

"No, I think you're acting like an imbecile!"

Allen's eyes flashed with rage and he gripped the knife's handle harder as his knuckles turned white.

"Stop this!" Suarez yelled, panicky. "This is too much!" He rose to his feet and threw his hands in the air, then hurried off into his room, pushing the button to slide the door shut behind him.

"There, are you happy?" Morel asked Allen, with an ironic smile-frown. "You've upset Suarez."

Allen just stared at Morel, his chest heaving. "You'd better start gardening!" He said this harshly, though almost in a whisper.

Morel folded his arms across his chest and shook his head.

"Start gardening or else!" Allen yelled.

"Non!"

The two men's gazes locked, and as they did so Baker said, very quietly, "The moment of truth."

Then Allen threw the knife against the wall, stormed out of the round room, put on his helmet and exited the shuttle. Morel, meanwhile, shrugged and, after waiting for the airlock door to slide shut, leaned over, pulled Allen's salad towards him and proceeded to eat it.

"That was dramatic," Baker said amusedly.

"If Allen really is a category three," Justin noted, "then he's not gonna give up yet."

"No, no, he's not giving up. Next comes desperation."

"That wasn't desperation right there?"

"No, that was merely assertion. Desperation is what happens when he decides not to throw down the knife."

Justin nodded and wondered how much longer he should stay up on the mountain that day.

While he sat there mulling that question Al-Arabi and her allies were pondering a question of their own: namely, whom to dislike more: Allen – and by extension, Justin – or Suarez and Morel. They ultimately decided that Allen was worse since he demanded that they treat him like he was in charge even though he didn't have any gardening expertise and even though he couldn't get the geologists to work in the garden.

Eventually everyone – except the geologists – returned to their gardening chores and for the rest of the day there was little conversation amongst them, other than a brief comment from Ritter to Allen when she told him, "After the way you pointed that knife at Morel, I'm beginning to think maybe you're a dangerous man." She said it like a compliment, and he certainly took it that way.

Justin returned home earlier that evening than he had the previous day, figuring that it was advisable to be there before dinnertime in case any knife-related violence ensued. But the fact of his presence seemed to dampen down Allen's assertive tendencies, and nothing serious occurred. When Allen couldn't locate the salad which he'd left behind at lunch, he didn't ask questions, and instead went and ate some cold pizza, choosing to sit alone in one of the container spaces. As for the Al-Arabi team, they ate dinner in the round room with the other crew members while casting cold glances at Suarez and Morel.

Around 21:00 there was a knock on the door of the royal couple's quarters. Justin asked Megan to step into their bedroom and lock the door, just in case, then he climbed the stairs and opened the door above his head. Allen was standing there.

"Can I speak with you?" Allen asked.

Justin nodded. "Sure."

Allen began to step onto the spiral staircase but Justin motioned for him to step back. Then Justin walked to the top of the stairs and pushed the remote so that the door slid shut beside his feet.

"Let's go talk in the cockpit."

Allen glanced down the hallway towards the round room where the others were still seated. Then he took a deep breath and nodded. "Yes, alright."

As soon as they were inside the cockpit, Allen whispered, "These people are maddening!"

Justin smiled sympathetically.

"Morel and Suarez simply refuse to work in the garden. I basically threatened them today, physically, and they still won't do it. And Al-Arabi, Wu and Manfredi are getting worse – more demanding, more annoying."

"What 'bout Ritter?" Justin asked, likewise in a whisper.

"She seems to be getting more sense. I'm thinking she's an ally."

"And Mishra?"

"He's fine. Still relatively happy. I'm beginning to think he's the only sane one of the lot."

They both smiled.

"Are they all there in that room?" Justin asked.

"Yes."

"Okay. I'm gonna go talk to them." Then he exited the cockpit and strode down the hallway. Allen followed close behind.

"Hey there everybody," Justin said, stepping into the round room.

"Captain Justin," Mishra replied, pleased to see him, "how is the mountain?"

"It's still there. It seemed even bigger today than it did yesterday. And I'm gonna be heading back there a lot more, so Allen's still gonna be in charge. But I hear there've been some problems and I wanna talk 'bout things for a minute."

He paused for effect, then continued.

"Allen tells me that you and you" – and he looked at Suarez and

Morel – "still refuse to work in the garden, and he also tells me that you" – and he looked at Al-Arabi – "still keep trying to order everybody around. I think it'd be great if we could all just act like adults, but since things keep going on like this I guess I've gotta start coming up with punishments. So what that means is that tomorrow, when I drive out to Jeanne to pick up Malenkov and Olambayo, I won't be taking you or you" – and he looked at the two geologists – "with me."

"What?" Morel and Suarez said simultaneously.

"You're staying here for a couple days. If you won't work in the garden then you don't get to work in the cave."

"You can't do that!" Morel protested.

"'Course I can. And as for you" – he looked at Al-Arabi – "you're gonna come with me tomorrow on the rover, out to the cave and back."

"What? Why?"

"So you can't work in the garden for at least part a the day."

"But...why?"

"Weren't you listening? This is punishment."

"You can't make me go on the rover!"

"Actually I can and it'd be easy, but I don't wanna have to force you physically so I'm ordering you to do it instead."

"But this isn't right!" Wu protested.

Justin ignored her. "So that's that. Now let's see if we can all start acting like astronauts." And he strode out of the round room and returned to his private quarters.

The following morning, exactly at 10:00, he approached the *Orion* and knocked on its metal door. The door slid open, then he stepped inside. Everyone had their spacesuits on and they were all standing except for Al-Arabi, who was sitting on her bed.

"Let's go," he told her.

He sincerely hoped that she'd do as he commanded; the last thing he wanted was to grab hold of her and carry her to the rover. And to his relief – which he made sure not to show – she stood up, exited the craft, walked with him to the rover and then climbed onto it and took a seat.

Neither of them said a word on the ride to the cave.

He felt happier when they got there since at least now he'd have other people to talk to. But Malenkov and Olambayo weren't scheduled to come out of the tunnels until 11:30, so Justin sat near the edge of the cave and waited, while Al-Arabi remained where she was, sitting on the rover a hundred yards back.

"Greetings!" Malenkov yelled to him, waving, when the repelling mechanism eventually lifted her up to the cave's rim and she saw Justin waiting for her.

"Hey there!" He called back. "Good to see you. How're things?"

"Still no signs of life," she reported, not sounding too discouraged. Justin offered her a hand as she climbed out of the repelling mechanism and she accepted his help even though she didn't need it. "But the process of exploration is exhilarating!"

As she rose to her feet Malenkov noticed that Al-Arabi was sitting on the rover. "Oh," she said, surprised that Al-Arabi had come along and confused by the fact that Al-Arabi hadn't walked over to the cave's edge. "Did she want to go for a ride?"

"No, I ordered her to come out here with me. It's punishment."

"For what?"

"Acting like a dictator. And Morel and Suarez refuse to garden so their punishment is that they got left back in Bakersville."

Malenkov frowned and then smiled ironically. "You have to be the school teacher for the children?"

"Seems that way."

Olambayo arrived at the surface soon thereafter, and Justin told him what he'd told Malenkov, then they all went and took their seats on the rover and headed back to town. Very little was said during the drive, which was awkward, and Justin knew that further tensions awaited him in Bakersville, yet as they approached the settlement he was struck by how peaceful it all looked, at least from a distance.

Allen walked out of the garden as the rover rolled into camp. He greeted the four of them and then, after the other three walked away – Al-Arabi headed straight for the garden, followed by Olambayo who wanted to see Ritter, while Malenkov boarded the shuttle to take a shower – Allen gave Justin a status report. There was a worried tinge to his words.

"Morel and Suarez still refuse to work, Manfredi and Wu just glare at me when I'm in the garden, and Mishra has figured out that things aren't going entirely well. He looks worried and he's stopped humming."

Justin nodded. "And Ritter?"

"Oh she's fine," Allen replied, a little too enthusiastically.

Justin nodded. "Okay, let's give it a couple more days and see if people start changing their tunes."

But the tunes didn't change.

At dinnertime all the scientists sat in the round room, more as a show of defiance towards the people they didn't like than out of any sense of solidarity. Morel glared at Allen, then at Al-Arabi and Wu, then back at Allen. Al-Arabi and Wu glared at Allen, Morel, and Suarez. Manfredi glared at Allen, Suarez, Morel, and Ritter. Suarez occasionally glanced up – his face wearing an uncomfortable expression – and then he quickly looked back down at his food. Mishra kept glancing around at everyone, not saying a word, but clearly he was worried. Malenkov likewise studied the other people at the table and quickly realized just how angry they were with each other. She was tempted to break the tension by asking the group, right up front, why they were all so upset, then she'd try to help them talk it out. But she decided not to pursue that option until she'd gathered more information about what had transpired while she was away at the cave.

Allen, meanwhile, tried not to but couldn't quite keep from staring at Olambayo and Ritter, who appeared to be the only happy people at the table, their chairs set so close that their sides pressed up against each other as they chatted and laughed. Between the fact of having people glaring at him and the site of Ritter and Olambayo being so affectionate in front of him, Allen's nerves began to fray, and after a little while he stood up and went into the bathroom to get his wits together.

While he was away Manfredi leaned over and spat in his chicken stew. Wu, Al-Arabi and Morel chuckled. Malenkov gasped. Suarez didn't see what happened because he'd been looking down. Ritter and Olambayo didn't see either, distracted as they were by each other. As for Mishra, his mouth hung open; he couldn't believe what he'd just observed.

"What? What is it?" Ritter asked playfully, assuming that all the chuckles were in response to her flirtations with Olambayo.

"Maria!" Malenkov exclaimed in a remonstrative whisper. "How could you do that?"

"What did she do?" Ritter asked.

"She spat in the tyrant's stew!" Morel answered approvingly.

"Allen is a tyrant?" Malenkov asked.

"He's awful!" Wu confirmed.

"He threatened me and Georges with a knife!" Suarez whispered.

"What?"

"It's true," Manfredi confirmed. "He did."

"When did that happen?"

"Yesterday afternoon."

"Were you in any danger?" Olambayo asked Ritter.

She shook her head. "I don't think so."

Eventually Allen exited the bathroom and reclaimed his place at the counter.

Quiet chuckles accompanied him while he lifted the spoon from his stew and began to put it in his mouth.

He glanced around, suspiciously.

"Edgar," Malenkov said, looking pained, "don't eat that."

"...Why not?"

More chuckles bubbled up from around the table.

"Just...don't," she said.

Allen hesitated for a few moments, then he set the spoon back in the bowl and glared at the people who appeared to be experiencing glee.

"What's going on?" He demanded. "What did someone do to my stew?"

"Edgar, really," Ritter said, in a warm soothing voice, making eye contact with him and giving him a consoling look, "just let it go."

Allen stared at her, angry at her for flirting unabashedly in front of him with Olambayo, yet he was also ready to grasp at any straws which indicated he might still earn her affection. When he saw that look in her eyes, he nodded, then frowned and huffed.

"Fine!" He stood up angrily and stomped out of the room.

Olambayo noted the tone in Ritter's voice and the look in her eyes when she spoke to Allen, and a tight feeling of concern knotted up inside him. He studied her as she smiled and pressed against him. Eventually he tried to shake off his worry and make a good show of smiling and seeming happy, but he didn't quite succeed.

Manfredi, who'd observed Ritter's prior flirtations with Allen, her current flirting with Olambayo, and her momentary flirtation with Allen yet again, was disgusted. She stared at Ritter and frowned, then she stood up and left the room.

The others soon followed suite, aside from Ritter and Olambayo, who remained at the table a while longer.

Malenkov, having concluded that real trouble was afoot, went and knocked on the door of the private living quarters. When the door in the floor slid open and Justin greeted her she asked if she could speak with him in private. He nodded.

The two of them walked to the cockpit and proceeded to converse in whispers.

"Something very bad is going on here," she told him.

Justin didn't react, so after a pause she continued to explain.

"Did you know that Edgar threatened Georges and Oscar with a knife?"

Justin feigned surprise. "When did that happen?"

"I don't know. They were just talking about it at dinner. I guess it happened when I was in the cave and you were on the mountain."

Justin nodded, as if giving this some thought.

"And everyone is angry with everybody else," she said. "During dinner they were all staring at each other like they wanted to do something hostile."

"Everybody was like that?"

"Nearly everyone. Mukesh just looked worried. And Suzanne and Robert just kept flirting the whole time. Which was making Edgar angry. And everyone is angry at Edgar. Maria even spat in his stew when he went to the bathroom."

Justin's eyebrows rose up his forehead.

Malenkov ran her fingers through her hair. "Suddenly everybody is angry and suspicious and they're threatening each other and there's all this intrigue....It's like being back on Earth!"

"We're going through an adjustment phase," Justin said, trying to reassure her, "and people are still figuring out how things are gonna be up here. And that means Al-Arabi's gotta learn that she can't run this colony. It also means Allen's my second-in-command so people have gotta learn to follow his lead, even if they don't like it."

"But why him, of all people? I'm sorry, I don't want to seem like I'm questioning your judgement, but Allen is...unstable."

Justin looked straight at her and he told her, as if he believed it, "Allen's the best person for the job."

She stared at him, then exhaled, and in that moment he knew he'd lost her. Not that she was going to turn against him, but clearly she could no longer trust his judgement. She could see he wasn't going to appoint a more suitable second-in-command, and that he wasn't going to do anything more to halt the group dynamic which was heading towards a blow-up. So she nodded, sadly, and walked out of the cockpit.

The following morning, after Justin had driven off towards Arsia Mons, Malenkov tried to talk to Allen about the situation and to suggest to him some better ways of relating to the other crew members.

"Edgar," she said, kneeling down next to him while he worked in a planter box of radishes, "I know it must be difficult to be the second-in-command...."

"It's not difficult at all. It's just fine." His voice had an edge. His nerves were evidently getting raw and he looked haggard, as if he'd been awake all night stewing.

"I want to help you," she said, in the gentlest tone that she could muster.

"Why would I need help?"

"Well, obviously, things aren't going...."

"I don't need your help!" He cut in before she could finish. "Now go and work somewhere else if you don't mind!" His voice rose rapidly as he spoke.

"Edgar, please!"

"That's an order! Go away! Leave me alone! I'm perfectly fine!"

Mishra, who was kneeling nearby amidst the carrots, refused to tolerate this behavior any longer. It was bad enough for Allen to threaten the geologists with a knife, but to act so disrespectfully to a lady!

"Mr. Allen," he said, rising heroically from his knees, "you can't simply push us all around like this. Perhaps you haven't been informed but the British Empire has been over for some time now. In my country it was defeated by a half-naked little mystic."

Ritter, who was working nearby, laughed.

Allen's eyes instantly blazed; he'd never expected to be chastised by Mishra of all people, and Ritter's laugh made it even worse. "Oh yes? I'll give you a taste of the British Empire!" He rose to his feet and shook his fist as his tone escalated correspondingly.

"Edgar, please! Stop this!" Malenkov pleaded, standing up beside him. "You don't know what you're doing!"

Allen's eyes blazed even brighter. "*I* don't know what I'm doing?

I don't know what I'm doing? Oh that's very nice, coming from a Russki! Remember what Tolstoy, your own countryman, said about all you Vodka snorters – you don't have the first clue!"

"Edgar!" Malenkov protested.

But it was hopeless. There was no point trying to reason with him. So she shook her head and walked away.

"Come work with us," Al-Arabi said as Malenkov passed her and Wu on the way to the garden's airlock.

"No, thank you," Malenkov replied, shaking her head, "I want to be alone for a few minutes."

She hurried out of the garden then proceeded to walk a few fast laps around the Bakersville perimeter.

"See that?" Baker asked, as he and Justin watched her leave the garden.

"Yeah, I see," Justin confirmed.

He'd driven farther up the mountainside than he had on previous visits, and since he couldn't locate any useful outcroppings he was leaning back against the slope, above the rover, using one of the rover's wheels as a footstool, with his legs bent in front of him and the computer resting on his thighs.

"It won't be long now," Baker predicted.

"It looks like Suarez and Morel are having a debate in the round room."

"Let's see." Baker increased the volume for that intercom feed and decreased the other sources of noise.

"I just want to get back to the rocks!" Suarez was saying.

"Oscar," Morel retorted, "you can't submit to arbitrary authority!"

"But this is making me crazy!"

"Hold it together, mon vieux! This is the time when we should be reinforcing the barricades, not giving in!"

"But if we work in the garden then we can go to the cave!"

"No garden, no cave!"

"But Georges!"

"Non!"

Baker smiled. "That seems to be going well."

Eventually Malenkov stopped doing laps around Bakersville and returned to the shuttle.

"And what do we have here?" Baker asked, intrigued, as Malenkov knocked on the door that led to the private quarters.

A few seconds later the door slid open and Megan appeared.

Justin tensed, instantly worried for his wife's safety and feeling extremely uncomfortable about the fact that he and Baker were spying on her together.

"Megan, can I please speak with you?" Malenkov asked.

Megan hesitated, remembering Justin's recommendation that she remain inside their private quarters while he was away. But she could see that Malenkov was upset, and since she and Justin made it a firm policy not to allow anyone into their living quarters, she nodded and stepped up onto the top floor, closed the door behind her and walked with Malenkov to the cockpit.

Justin took a deep breath.

"Megan," Malenkov whispered intensely once they were seated in the cockpit chairs, "this colony is in serious trouble."

"What do you mean?"

"Everybody is going crazy!"

"Crazy – how?"

"I think an explosion is coming! I think someone is going to do something violent!"

"Who?"

"Maybe Allen, or one of the others. I don't know for certain but I can feel it coming!"

"Olga," Megan said, trying to sound reassuring, "it's going to be okay. Justin has everything under control."

"I'm sorry to say this," Malenkov replied, her eyes growing wet, "I really am, but I don't know if that's true any longer. I don't know if he sees what's going on!"

"That's ironic," Baker commented.

"Olga, trust me," Megan told her, "he knows what he's doing. You have to believe me."

This was followed by a long pause as Malenkov took a slow, deep breath. Then she dabbed her eyes, shook her head, pressed Megan's hands – which were folded in front of her – with her own hands, and stood up and walked out of the room.

Justin felt genuinely bad for her. But he didn't voice that feeling.

Instead he sat there on the mountainside waiting for the storm to break.

Lunchtime came and went at Bakersville without any incidents. Morel and Suarez ate in the round room, along with Malenkov and Mishra. Ritter and Olambayo retreated to their favorite spot in the container space. Al-Arabi, Wu and Manfredi did the same. Allen, meanwhile, ate alone in another container space across the hall from the three ladies. He was well on his way to feeling miserable and desperate for a drink.

Cold fear was welling up inside him: fear of disappointing Justin, of not living up to the trust which the colony's captain had placed in him. At the same time he was filled with anger towards the other scientists, and it wasn't entirely clear which of those two emotions – fear or anger – was hitting him harder.

The only solace he found in that lonely moment was the fact that he noticed something which he hadn't previously picked up on: Wu was getting to the point where she simply couldn't stand Manfredi any longer. It'd been obvious from the start that Al-Arabi and Wu were just tolerating Manfredi's presence, but Wu's ability to sustain that charade was evidently wearing thin. No doubt she didn't like Manfredi crowding in on her prized friendship with Al-Arabi, and there was also the fact that Manfredi was just basically annoying.

Allen contemplated this for a few moments, then took a bite of his salami sandwich, trying to draw as much satisfaction as he could from the taste of the meat and from the simultaneous experience of schadenfreude regarding Manfredi. Notwithstanding this effort, he knew he was heading towards a dark place – a place he'd visited many times before when he was stressed.

And the embers of anger crackled in his eyes....

After lunch everyone – except Suarez and Morel – returned to the garden and resumed their work in total silence without anyone talking to anyone else for the next few hours.

Eventually Justin set down the computer tablet and folded his arms behind his helmet, then leaned back and rested against the rocky surface of the slope, staring at the sky. As he did so he realized something: he was beginning to forget what a blue sky looked like. If he tried he could force an image of one into his mind, but that was getting harder to do. Before long it'd be impossible to conjure up a genuinely accurate picture, just like it was hard to remember someone's face if he hadn't seen them in a while.

And if he couldn't remember what a blue sky looked like then he was truly becoming a Martian. The butterscotch horizon was now his new normal, the red rocks and sand were his milieu. And it would be like that entirely for his child....

Given the way things went during lunch back at Bakersville, he figured there wasn't any pressing need to hurry home. So he just enjoyed the feeling of lounging alone up on the mountainside, waiting until the sun began to fade. Then he mounted the rover and drove it slowly down to the flatland, then took his time as he traversed the empty Martian landscape.

He was about ten minutes from Bakersville when Baker's voice came on the intercom.

"Justin," Baker said, "things are getting heated back at the shuttle. You're going to want to see this."

Without stopping the rover, Justin pulled the computer tablet out of his backpack, then braced it against the steering wheel and pushed the computer's power button. What he saw, a few seconds later, was that the entire crew had assembled in the round room and, as Baker said, things were getting "heated."

After gardening, everyone had wound up in the round room all at once, foraging in the refrigerators for food and tossing each other dirty looks.

Allen decided to make a salad and began chopping up vegetables on the wooden chopping board, using one of the chef's knives. He spent a few minutes at this, then he turned to Ritter and said, "Suzanne, why don't you help me with this and then we can both have a nice salad?"

As anyone – other than Allen, apparently – could have predicted, Olambayo didn't like this at all. He immediately stepped in between Allen and Ritter and said, "Why don't you make your own food, Edgar Allen, and leave Suzanne and me to ours."

Allen's eyes, already etched with anger, instantly blazed. "I give the orders around here, Robert! Now get out of my way. I'm trying to have a conversation with Suzanne and it doesn't concern you!"

Olambayo didn't move. "Edgar," he said, "the British Empire is over. I know what your people did to my country and I'm not going to let you do it to me!"

"I said, get out of my way!" Allen spat out the words and grabbed Olambayo by the shoulder, trying to push him aside.

As anyone – other than Allen, apparently – could have predicted, this had absolutely no effect. Olambayo simply remained where he was. For a moment. Then he grabbed Allen's hand, turned it until Allen's grip broke and then he kept turning it until Allen's arm twisted and Allen was forced to face away from Olambayo and grunt with pain. Then Olambayo shoved Allen forward against the countertop.

Seizing the wooden chopping board, Allen spun back around like a boomerang and smacked the board across Olambayo's head with a loud CRACK! Ritter, Malenkov, Wu and Al-Arabi all screamed.

But Olambayo remained standing exactly where he was, with the same expression on his face.

Horror now flashed inside Allen's eyes, as he concluded that he'd just hit Olambayo with his best shot and made no impact. A few seconds elapsed, and the two men remained standing there, staring at each other. Then Olambayo's knees buckled beneath him and he collapsed to the floor, unconscious.

At which point several things transpired concurrently.

Malenkov rushed to Olambayo's side, knelt beside him and asked him, "Robert, are you alright?"

Ritter rushed to Olambayo's side as well, grabbed Malenkov and shoved her, yelling, "Get away from him!"

Suarez, instantly gripped by extreme anxiety, jumped onto Allen's back, wrapped one arm around Allen's throat and another around Allen's head and screamed, "You've gone completely insane!"

Manfredi grabbed Ritter by the hair and yanked her away from Malenkov, yelling, "How dare you do that to her!"

Wu backed Al-Arabi against the round wall and stretched her arms out in either direction, shielding her friend from the melee.

Allen dropped the chopping board and stumbled backwards with Suarez on his back, banged Suarez against the wall, then bent forward and threw Suarez onto the floor with a loud THUD!

Malenkov grabbed Manfredi's hand – which was clasping a clump of Ritter's hair – and then she grabbed Ritter's hand – which was clasping a clump of Manfredi's hair – and sought to de-clasp each of them. For her efforts she received kicks from both Manfredi and Ritter, who turned in unison to assault her, then they returned to attacking each other.

Allen was now kneeling over Suarez and throttling him.

Mishra had pulled off a shoe and was slapping it against Allen's back. Allen barely noticed that Mishra was doing this.

Morel rushed over to Malenkov after the dual kicks which she'd received had sent her spiraling backwards until she banged face-first into the wall. He put his hand on her shoulder.

Malenkov assumed that the hand on her shoulder belonged to one of the ladies who'd just kicked her and that now one or both of them were following up for a further assault so she spun around with her bent elbow leading the way. The elbow made direct contact with Morel's nose before she had a chance to see that it was him.

Ritter and Manfredi continued gripping each other's hair as they staggered around the room, both screaming in pain and anger.

Allen's eyes blazed with frenzied rage as his fingers progressively tightened around Suarez's throat like a vice. All his anger had zeroed in on this one single target and he wasn't about to let go.

Morel stumbled backwards until he banged into the round counter. His hands were pressed to his nose and blood was already spilling between his fingers.

Mishra continued to slap Allen's back with a shoe.

Suarez's eyes bulged with a full-throttled panic and saliva began gathering at the edges of his lips as he tried hopelessly to push at Allen's arms.

Justin, watching all this on the computer screen, hit the gas on the rover and tore across the landscape, racing back towards the shuttle while the faint remains of the Martian sunset spread out in front of him and as dust clouds billowed up beside his wheels.

Ritter and Manfredi, gripping each other's hair, staggered in front of Wu, who was still standing in front of Al-Arabi. Wu, unable to resist the impulse any longer, lunged forward, grabbing Manfredi around the waist and tackling her to the ground. Ritter was pulled along with them and fell on top of Wu.

Malenkov, horrified by what she'd done, ran to Morel's side and knelt next to him as he slumped to the floor and then leaned back against one of the counter's chairs.

Ritter rolled off of Wu, rushed over to Olambayo and proceeded to cradle Olambayo's head in her hands.

Wu straddled Manfredi, holding the Italian's flaying arms to the sides.

"I'm so sorry!" Malenkov swore to Morel as she reached up to the counter and grabbed some napkins and then gave them to him to press against his bleeding nose.

Seeing Ritter cradling Olambayo's head, Allen became even more incensed and gripped Suarez's throat all the tighter.

Al-Arabi, still standing with her back against the wall, remained where she was, with her hands pressed against her temples and her mouth hanging open in horror.

Suarez passed out from the panic, as his hands let go of Allen's forearms, his own arms went limp and fell to his sides, and his eyes closed shut.

Mishra, who was standing behind Allen – still hitting him with a shoe – couldn't see that Suarez's chest was still heaving, and he yelled out, "You've killed him!"

Everyone else instantly stopped what they were doing and looked first at Mishra, then at Allen, then at Suarez.

Allen, having been startled out of his frenzy, released his grip on Suarez's throat and leaned back on his heels. His chest kept heaving but his eyes quickly began losing their blaze. He could see that Suarez wasn't dead but he also realized that he might have killed the Mexican geologist if Mishra hadn't yelled out like.

All the others could now likewise see that Suarez was still alive, although unconscious. And they could observe the fading look of madness on Allen's face.

Justin raced through the shuttle's airlock and into the round room and found both Olambayo and Suarez lying unconscious on the floor, Wu straddling Manfredi, Morel sitting at the base of the counter with bloody napkins pressed against his face, Malenkov kneeling beside him, Ritter holding Olambayo's head, Allen sitting on his heels and facing away from Justin, Mishra standing next to Allen, holding his shoe, and Al-Arabi still pressed against the wall, seemingly frozen there.

Everyone – except for Allen – looked at Justin as he entered the room. Noting this, Allen turned on his heels and looked up at Justin as well; an expression of sad, desperate, angry, resigned, hopeless, righteous shame was etched across his face.

Then Mishra hit Allen one more time with his shoe.

After which, things quickly quieted down.

Even though Justin already knew what had transpired he acted as if he didn't. When he demanded to know what had happened, those who were still conscious pointed their fingers at Allen. So Justin ordered Allen to go sit in the *Orion* while the others remained in the round room. None of them were allowed to leave until Justin said so.

The first order of business was to revive Olambayo and Suarez. After that was done and ice was applied to Olambayo's head, Justin asked Malenkov to tell him what had occurred. She relayed what Allen had said to Ritter, and Olambayo's response, and then how Allen had hit Olambayo with the chopping board, etc. Then Justin asked each of the other people in the room to give their version. There were variations in the details but everyone's rendition ultimately added up to the same, central point: Allen knocked out Olambayo and then proceeded to throttle Suarez.

Once that was established, Justin ordered them all to remain in the shuttle for the night. Those whose beds were in the *Orion* would just have to sleep on the floor of the container spaces. Although in all likelihood none of them were going to sleep very much that night. Justin also told Ritter, Manfredi and Wu to stay well away from each other. Meanwhile Malenkov tended to Morel and also tried to keep Suarez calm. And of course Ritter huddled with Olambayo, off in their corner, as Olambayo pressed the ice against his head and Ritter told him how brave and strong he was.

Eventually Justin exited the shuttle, walked over to the *Orion* and knocked on its door. It slid open almost instantly. Allen was standing there in his spacesuit, seemingly resigned to his fate.

"I...think I got carried away," he said after Justin stepped into the *Orion* and the door slid shut.

Justin nodded. "Sounds that way."

"...So what happens now?"

"I'm gonna think on that. I'll come back here tomorrow at 9:00 and tell you what I've decided."

Allen nodded. "Alright."

There was silence between them, and Justin turned to go, but then Allen said, "I'm sorry I let you down. You put your trust in me. You gave me the responsibility for this colony while you were away. And I failed. It's not the first time for me, I can tell you that."

There was a pause, and Allen continued, "I thought...to be honest I thought that if I left Earth behind and came to this new place, with new people and with none of the old temptations and...entanglements, that I'd be able to start over. That I could be a new man, maybe even a good man. And then when you chose me to be second-in-command, I thought all my hopes had been confirmed. But in fact...coming here has only made all the bad things in my life – and all the bad things in me – get even worse. I'm...I'm sorry. I'm not telling you this to try to influence your decision about what you decide to do with me. I'm just telling you to...to tell you, I guess....To say thank you, for believing in me. No one else ever did."

Justin took a deep breath and nodded, then walked back outside, entered the shuttle and followed the staircase down to his private quarters.

"What's going on out there?" Megan asked, relieved to see him, especially in the wake of her conversation with Malenkov that morning.

"There was a fight."

"A fight? Between who?"

"Everybody."

"Everybody? Who won?"

"Nobody."

"So...who started it?"

"Allen."

"How?"

"He hit Olambayo in the head with the chopping board, knocked him out."

Megan raised her hand near her mouth. "Is Olambayo alright?"

"He'll be fine. But Allen also tried to strangle Suarez."

Megan clasped her hand tightly to her mouth. "And...?" She asked as she pulled her hand away.

"He's alright. He's just freaked out."

"And everybody else is okay?"

Justin shrugged. "Morel's got a bloody nose. It looks like the rest a them are basically alright."

Megan stared into his eyes, concerned. "Earlier today Malenkov came to me. She said she felt something like this was going to happen."

"Well she was right."

"It's what you thought would happen?"

Justin sighed. "Yeah, pretty much."

He stared back at her, deep into her eyes. Then he said, "Come here," and motioned for the two of them to sit down on the couch.

"Look," he said, "you remember you told me, before they all got here, that no matter what happens, you're my woman?"

She nodded. "Of course I remember."

"Yeah, well, looks like I'm gonna need to collect on that promise now."

She took a deep breath, then nodded some more.

"I'm gonna need you to stand by me now, 'cause things are gonna change. There might be some tough times coming at us."

She touched his cheek with the palm of her hand. "I'm right here with you," she whispered. "Just like I told you."

"Thank you," he whispered back, gently taking hold of her hand and kissing the palm.

They shared a few moments of silence....

Then the voice of William Baker reverberated through the room. "Now then, Justin," he said, "shall we talk in the study?"

Justin sighed. "Let's talk in the morning, Baker."

"...Don't you think that *now* is a particularly appropriate time to chat?"

Justin shook his head. "I'm not doing anything with Allen 'til the morning. So let's talk then, before I go see him at 9:00. I'll check in with you at 8:30."

There was a long pause, then Baker said, "Alright. Let's do that. And I agree that it makes sense to wait until the morning to handle Allen. It'll give the rest of them the impression that you're taking some time to decide what's best."

"That's what I was thinking."

"Alright then," Baker replied. And he left the two of them in peace for the remainder of the evening.

Justin actually managed to fall asleep that night, but only for a few minutes.

When 8:20 finally rolled around he slid gently out of bed, so as not to wake Megan, then he put on some clothes, walked into the study and shut the door behind him.

The TV screen flicked on at precisely 8:30.

"Hello Justin," Baker said.

"Hey Baker."

"Did you get a good night's sleep?"

"Yeah. You?"

"I never sleep that much. I just nap occasionally. It's one of the reasons I'm as rich as I am."

Justin thought about this for a second. "Isn't that like a shark? Don't they say that sharks never sleep?"

"That's true of Great White sharks, yes. And it's true of princes, by the way."

"So now I'm not gonna be getting much sleep, either?"

"You're not going to be getting too much sleep in any case once your child is born."

Justin nodded. "I guess that's true."

"Of course it is. But now then, on to more pressing topics – what are you going to do about Allen?"

Justin took a deep breath. "I know what you want me to do."

"Well I certainly hope so. After all, you selected him. He's the d'Orco. And the d'Orco has to die."

The two men stared at each other.

"Do I sense some lingering reluctance?" Baker asked.

Justin said nothing.

Baker frowned. "After all this time and you're still not ready?"

Justin said nothing.

Now it was Baker's turn to take a deep breath. Following a long exhalation, he said, "My dear Justin, in so many ways, and on so many occasions, I've sought to impress upon you the importance of what we're doing. Of the stakes involved. Allow me to give it one more go. Tell me, have you ever heard of a man named Nicolaus Copernicus?"

Justin shook his head. "…No."

"He was a Polish astronomer who lived in the 14 and 1500s. His lifetime matches up quiet closely with Machiavelli's in fact. And there's a similarity in their work. As you know, Machiavelli wanted to explain the way things really are, to provide a roadmap for action to people who're trying to survive in this world which doesn't appear to have any ultimate order. Copernicus, for his part, sought to scientifically explain the way the universe really works, and he was the one who made the analysis of the planets which led to the conclusion that Earth isn't at the center of the solar system. His model of the solar system was then picked up by Galileo and, as they say, the rest is history.

"But it's also the future. You see by removing our planet from the center of the solar system Copernicus shattered all the cozy assumptions that men had about themselves standing at the center of the universe; a universe which seemed to make sense precisely because they were at the center of it. As soon as that assurance was taken away, as soon as the universe wasn't so obviously well-ordered and men couldn't be certain of their place within it, then all hell broke loose philosophically speaking. Or to put it in more academic terms, it gave birth to what is known as the Copernican Revolution. Do you follow my point?"

"...Uh...."

"Now guess what caused Copernicus to make his discovery, or at least played a major part in his discovery."

"...What?"

"His examination of Mars. He would climb up into his tower and spend his nights examining the heavens. And Mars in particular. He was the first person to identify it as being a planet. And his recognition of that point, and of the way in which Mars' orbit relates to Earth's orbit, helped him to understand that Earth is not at the center of the solar system. Which is to say that it was the study of Mars that led to the displacement of Earth as man's primary focus.

"Now isn't that exciting to consider! From that moment forward, we, as a species, were destined to eventually leave old Earth behind; to go out there into space and conquer it! And the most important step in that journey was always going to be the colonization of Mars. Mars, Justin! Mars is man's true destiny! His rightful home! Earth is just an accident. Mars is our choice – a planet we can mold to all our needs and inclinations. Mars, Justin! Don't you see? What we're doing, you and I, is nothing less than completing the Copernican Revolution!"

Baker paused for a moment, then he added, "Now then, you need to go out there and you need to kill Edgar Allen!"

Justin couldn't believe the speech he'd just heard. And yet, in a way, he could. After all, this was William Baker.

"You want me to kill him...for Copernicus?"

"For Copernicus and so much more! For all of us and everyone!"

Justin didn't reply; he simply remained sitting in the antique chair, with his hands folded on the antique desk.

"Alright fine," Baker frowned, losing patience, "I'll give you one more reason. It's something much closer to home. You remember how I told you that I wanted you to be the one who survived, of the original five we sent up there? Well it's true. You were the first one I selected; the rest of them were window dressing. But I never told you exactly *why* I wanted it to be you.

"The reason is very simple. You see, with the other four men we could trace the trajectories that led them to commit all the murders they committed. Tristan, as previously noted, was the byproduct of the violent circumstances into which he was born. As for Byron, he'd developed an inclination towards mayhem in his youth and habits formed early on like that can sometimes be hard to break. As for Calvin, he'd clearly made a decision at some point in his life that he wasn't going to allow his small size to serve as a reason for him to get pushed around. And as for Troy, I think it's fair to say that the man was permanently petrified. I wouldn't be surprised if he was clinically paranoid.

"But you – there aren't any of those reasons for you. Aside from some minor incidents in your youth, you had a clean record prior to that bar fight. You didn't demonstrate violent tendencies and cultivate bad habits. You worked relatively hard. You kept your nose clean. You had a decent job, by many people's standards. But then one funny evening you met some woman in a bar; a woman you'd never seen before and would never see again. You hadn't even been talking to her for more than a few minutes. Yet when some barfly tried to intrude upon your conversation with her you decided to drive over him with your car. Now, I happen to know why you did that. Do *you* know why you did that?"

The two men stared at each other. When Justin said nothing in reply, Baker said, "Alright, I'll tell you why. The answer is very simple because it's the only possible answer." Then Baker leaned in closer to the screen. "And the answer is this: at the core of your being you are, quite simply, a murderer."

He paused for effect, then continued.

"That is why I chose you. That is why I wanted you to survive. Because that's what I need up there. So accept your fate, accept yourself, and" – and as Baker enunciated the following phrase, he paused for a split second after each word, "get out there and do what needs to be done!"

As he spoke, Baker's *Mona Lisa* mask fell away. For the very first time Justin saw directly into Baker's eyes, saw through them, and what he saw there was something truly, deeply, darkly black. And he gasped.

Then a song came into his head: "Sympathy for the Devil" by The Rolling Stones. Justin had never been a big Stones fan, but Darrell – his supervisor at the factory where he'd worked – had loved them and played them every day in the accounting office. After a while Justin knew all their songs by heart. And so now, as that song began playing in his head, Justin nodded to Baker, then he rose to his feet and walked silently out of the study.

Baker nodded as well, until Justin had stepped out of view, then he leaned back away from the screen and – ever so slightly – he smiled.

Megan was still asleep so Justin put on his spacesuit quietly. Then he grabbed his gloves and helmet and turned off the helmet's video and audio feeds. This done, he walked up the spiral staircase and clicked the remote to open the door, then he clicked it again to close the door behind him.

Everyone else was wide awake. Ritter and Olambayo were sitting in their usual place; Wu was with Al-Arabi in their typical spot; Manfredi was in another container space, sitting by herself; Malenkov was alone as well, in yet another area; Suarez, Morel and Mishra were seated at the circular counter in the round room.

Justin didn't make eye contact with any of them; he didn't even glance in their general directions. Instead he walked down the hallway, entered the round room, placed his helmet and his gloves on the kitchen countertop, opened the center drawer in the counter, pulled out one of the chef's knives and then pushed the knife, very carefully, up inside the forearm area of his spacesuit's sleeve. This done, he put on his helmet, pulled on his gloves, walked out into the hallway, entered the airlock, exited it, followed the external stairs down to the ground and headed for the *Orion*.

The smaller ship's door slid open as Justin approached. Allen was already standing there, fully suited, waiting for him.

Justin stopped and looked up at the British biologist for a moment. Then he motioned for Allen to follow him, and Allen did so, descending the steps as the *Orion's* door slid shut behind him.

Neither of them said a word. They just walked over to the rover and then both climbed aboard.

As Justin started the engine, he turned and stared at the man who was sitting next to him. But that man didn't turn to look at him. Instead Allen just kept gazing straight ahead, very focused, as if trying to discern his fate, out there, somewhere in the distance. So Justin nodded, grabbed the steering wheel and then drove them away from Bakersville, heading towards the cave.

It was always quiet out there, on the ride to Jeanne, but somehow, in that morning hour, in that silence that they shared, it all seemed even quieter still. The occasional sand-laden Martian breeze only reinforced the effect.

XVIII

Megan was sitting on the gray leather couch. She wanted to pace but somehow that seemed too cliché. She was the prince's wife, after all, the princess, the mother of the future Martian monarch, and there would no doubt be many more moments like this. She might as well get used to them; get used to not letting it seem like they were eating her alive.

The wall clock read 13:15 when the door at the top of the spiral staircase slid open. Justin descended, then he closed the door behind him. His helmet and gloves were off and he appeared calm but not relaxed. As he stepped off the staircase and onto the floor he looked at her, and the two of them held each other's gazes for a few moments. Then he tossed his helmet and gloves onto a chair and walked into the study.

After the door slid shut behind him and he'd taken his seat, the screen flicked on.

"Hello Justin," Baker said.

Justin said nothing for several seconds; he just stared at – and through – the man on the screen. Then he spoke.

"I did it," he said. "I killed him. His body's in the cave."

Baker displayed no reaction, at first. But after a few moments he began studying Justin, as if he was watching a wild animal in a cage, trying to predict its next move. He cocked his head to one side, then cocked it to the other. And then at last, he smiled. A wide, lips-pressed smile.

Justin exhaled, shaking his head in quiet disgust. "You're happy because a man is dead?"

"No," Baker replied. "I'm not happy because a man is dead. I'm happy because I don't know if he's dead or not. I'm happy because it's no longer clear to me when you're lying and when you're telling the truth; not even when you're telling me about murder. And if I, of all people, can't tell whether you're lying about that, of all subjects – well then, my dear Justin, now, truly, you are ready to be a prince."

THE END

(OF THE BEGINNING)

ABOUT THE AUTHOR

James Thompson is a professor of political science at Hiram College, where he teaches courses on international relations, political theory, public leadership, and the relationship between politics and architecture. He is also the director of Hiram's James A. Garfield Center for Public Leadership and the co-coordinator of the World Government Research Network. In addition to *The Prince of Mars* he is the author of *Making North America: Trade, Security, and Integration.*

Made in the USA
Middletown, DE
30 January 2017